Of Love and Slaughter

ANGELA HUTH

LARGE PRINT
Oxford

First published in Great Britain 2002
by Little, Brown

Published in Large Print 2005 by ISIS Publishing Ltd.,
7 Centremead, Osney Mead, Oxford OX2 0ES
by arrangement with
Time Warner Book Group UK

British Library Cataloguing in Publication Data
Huth, Angela, 1938–
    Of love and slaughter. – Large print ed.
    1. Farm life – England – Fiction
    2. England – Social life and customs – Fiction
    3. Large type books
    I. Title
    823.9'14 [F]

ISBN 0–7531–7427–8 (hb)
ISBN 0–7531–7428–6 (pb)

Printed and bound in Great Britain by
T. J. International Ltd., Padstow, Cornwall

MAFF	Ministry of Agriculture, Fisheries and Food
DEFRA	Department of Environment, Food and Rural affairs
CAP	Common Agricultural Policy
IACS	Integrated Administration and Control System
NFU	National Farmers' Union

For Robin and Lindy Head, with my gratitude and thanks for all their help and advice, and for showing me the practicalities of life on their West Country farm. My thanks too, to many other farmers who spared time to tell me their stories. This book comes with my sympathy for all those who have suffered in the farming world, and my hope that a better future will be resolved.

"Ill fares the land, to hast'ning ills a prey . . ."

"The Deserted Village", *Oliver Goldsmith*

George

I can't ever remember exactly how we came to be sitting on a bank of the river, some miles from Oxford, on an April day shortly after the end of term. With finals not far off, I was staying in college for a week of the vacation, concentrated study being so much easier there than at home. I suppose Lily had the same plan in mind, though I didn't ask her.

Sometimes I try hard to recall details, but they elude me. Perhaps because, at the time, they were of no importance. I hardly knew Lily. She was at the Ruskin, I was at Trinity. Our paths rarely crossed. I'd occasionally see her at a party. We'd exchange a few words, nod, smile. She always seemed to be at the centre of some vivacious swirl of friends of which I was no part. Had I been drawn to her perhaps I should have made some bold effort, jostled my way through the crowd to spend more than two minutes at her side. But I wasn't drawn to her. I never thought about her. The placid Serena was my girlfriend: undemanding, accommodating, good-humoured. We had the sort of arrangement that's convenient at university: doesn't tie you down, no thoughts of permanency, but nice to fall back on. I was quite happy with Serena.

1

I do know that on this particular day it was in the Broad Lily and I met. She was ruffled by a breeze, carrying two plastic bags of food from the market. She wore that expression, somewhere between pain and outrage, common to women who have to transport heavy shopping. Naturally I offered to help. I had no definite plans for the rest of the morning.

It seemed Lily knew I was the owner of a car. (How did she know that? In our brief exchanges, mentioning that I had an old Ford Escort was simply not the sort of thing that would have occurred to me. Very puzzling, but I didn't think much about it.) "In that case," she said, "you could give me a lift to somewhere on the river. *I want to think*," she said, "and there are no convenient buses."

I concurred with neither pleasure nor irritation — rather, with the simple acceptance of a man being given an order. In the car I must have followed her directions, asking no questions. We ended up somewhere near Bablock Hithe. "Arnold's stripling Thames," she said. I think I smiled and nodded, not knowing the reference, though I looked it up years later.

We sat on the grass in a foursome with the plastic bags. I can't remember what kind of sky there was — bright, I think — but the grass was dry. An almost transparent sensation of early green was flung across the landscape, of the kind that precedes the brightness of May. I do remember suggesting I should leave so that Lily could think in peace, but she seemed to have changed her mind about her desire for solitude. She pointed out that if I left she would have no way of getting back, so I'd better stay.

We ate a few things from the bags — fruit, biscuits — and shared a bottle of very sweet apple juice. Lily talked almost without cease. I only half listened, as one does to birdsong — perhaps the reason I remember so little of what she said. I learnt that she was in some confusion over her future: should she be an art historian, a teacher, an art critic? Her aim in life was to teach people to *look*, to *see*. Here she became very emphatic, fiercely screwing up a small paper bag in her hand. She had learnt from her father that most people don't use their eyes, thus missing so much of what the world, and art, had to offer. I think I had become rather drowsy at that point, though was returned to full alertness by a piercing shriek. "*Look!*" she suddenly shouted, clutching at me. She fanned her arm across sky, trees, meadows, river. I was unsure which of these things she was intent on my looking at most, so nodded in a general, affable way. She then accused me of plainly not being a man interested in *really looking*, and how disappointing that was. But then most men were disappointing, she added.

Soon after that we returned to the car and I drove her back to Oxford. Despite the disappointment I had caused her she didn't seem affronted. We sat in easy silence and I dropped her off — where? That's one of the things that has puzzled me for years. I have no picture in my mind of her getting out of the car, though I imagine she must have thanked me. I'm sure we made none of those silly, meaningless plans to meet again. I

3

don't remember seeing her walk away, or even what she was wearing, though a flash of blue comes to mind. A scarf, perhaps.

Our last term at Oxford I saw her in the distance at a Commem. Ball. She looked with more interest at Serena that she did at me and we did not speak. Then I became submerged in the next part of life: my training as a lawyer. Lily was an insignificant detail in a time that was past, and I did not think about her again.

Lily

I remember precisely. Desmond had been more irritating than usual that morning, trying to pin me down to promises for the future. Trying to hem me in, as always. I'd spend the night with him in his grand rooms in New College: always a mistake, because the next morning he judged he'd gained on me. Scored another notch of my affection. He put great faith in the seductive qualities of his rooms: huge windows looking on to the chapel, the sound of the choir practising — that'll get her, he seemed to think. Of course it didn't. I couldn't be moved by Desmond in the most beautiful place on earth, and was annoyed by myself when I gave in to him. But it wasn't always easy to find the energy to fight him, make excuses. Guilt forced me to be not too unkind when I looked at his stricken face. Desmond was an unwise fixture. I'd become involved with him by mistake, flattered by his attentions but knowing he absolutely wasn't the right man for me. I'd had much more fun when I was a freelance, flirting with lots of people, accountable to no one. Still, there was only one more term, then he'd be off to Harvard Business School. It would come to a natural end. I'd resolved to try to be my nicest for the few remaining weeks, but it was hard.

That particular morning I had stomped out, not saying where I was going. I had a cup of coffee in the market, to calm myself down, and thought I'd like to go down to the river, the place of childhood picnics, to think in peace. Hopeless idea, I knew, as there was no way of getting there. Downcast, I set off for my rooms in Jericho, determined to unplug the telephone.

My luck changed when I ran into George Elkin in the Broad. He was ambling along, his usual vague expression indicating he was preoccupied by thoughts far from the present. I didn't know him well. We were what's called nodding acquaintances, but he always seemed agreeable, harmless. Not the sort of man you'd want to make a particular effort to befriend, but I was happy enough to exchange the time of day. He was known to have a rather dull girlfriend, Serena. You could have guessed her name from a mile off.

I knew George had a car. Desmond had once seen him stalling at some traffic lights. *Pathetic*, Desmond had reported. He himself, in his MG, regarded a quick getaway at a green light as something to be proud of. It was one of the things I disliked about him.

Anyway, I interrupted George's daydream with a suggestion of a spontaneous picnic by the river. He looked a little startled, but agreed at once. I guided him patiently — it was true, he was a pretty hopeless driver, hesitant. I guessed at once he was probably hesitant in life in general. Serena must have been very patient.

6

We chose a place — at least, I chose a place — on the river bank where the grass was short and dry. It was an overcast day, solid cloud reflected brownly in the river. There was a swan nearby, pinned to the still water like a brooch. George made no comment about the bird. People usually make some mundane observation on seeing a swan. I rather warmed to him for that. I thought it said much about him.

I warmed to him even further when I passed him the bottle of apple juice, having drunk myself, and he put it to his mouth without hesitation. Desmond would have gone through all the palaver of wiping it with his ironed handkerchief, even though we were lovers.

George was very quiet, hardly spoke. I babbled on about my future, the sort of thing that bored Desmond, who scorned those who did not have a detailed life-plan. George didn't come up with any helpful suggestions, but he looked sympathetic. I forgot to ask what his plans were when he came down. I suppose I wasn't that interested. Then somehow I got on to my favourite subject of people not looking at things, and how my passion in life was to encourage real, conscious observation all the time. Here, George indicated slight bewilderment but gave a small laugh of, I think, agreement. I was suddenly very anxious to push him further, try him out. So I shouted to him to *look* — at everything, I meant. Tell me what he could see. But here I lost him. He was completely bemused. And again I found myself approving his reaction to my demand, not immediately obeying me and then coming up with silly questions. I wanted to tell him that if he *really* looked he would see that the little piece of earth before us could be a significant piece of the jigsaw of our memories. When we were old, and had forgotten each other's names, we would still remember the unique moment when sky, river, meadow and swan made a kind of harmony in the soul. But I decided not to. I didn't think he'd understand, and I couldn't be bothered to explain.

On the way back in the car we talked about avocado pears (the difficulty of finding the perfect one) and our sadness at the ugly development of Oxford. We agreed it was lucky we were leaving before things became much worse.

He dropped me outside my lodgings in Jericho. I wished him well in his finals (mention of them caused him to look a little nervous) and kissed him on the cheek by way of thanks. Our parting was completely unmemorable. He drove off with a small wave in his stuttery old car and I hoisted the bags — lighter, now — through the front door. I remember thinking how much easier he was to be with than Desmond. Uncritical. Desmond had criticised me for something or other at our first meeting, though later he declared he had been teasing. Also, there was no denying George's profile was in every way superior to Desmond's: a fine Roman nose, he had, and prematurely old but appealing lines crowded his eyes when he smiled. But I felt no desire to seek George out in our last term, or see him again. He'd been a kind chauffeur, that's all. I didn't think about him again for some years.

8

Part One

CHAPTER
ONE

When George was nine years old, not long after his mother had died, he was taken to see his father's office. "By way of a treat, old son," David Elkin said.

George was driven from the farm to the city by Silvia Dust, a local girl employed to look after him. Out of his father's hearing George called her Dusty: in his father's presence he remembered to call her Silvia, for his father hated nicknames, abbreviations of any kind. Dusty, like her charge, was in some doubt as to how much fun this visit to the office would be. But at least tea was promised afterwards in a place near the cathedral known for its home-made ice cream.

George found the wooden stairs leading to the first floor of the old building were even steeper than the stairs at the farm. He imagined they would cause his father to puff and splutter and pause for breath, just as he did at home, and felt sorry for him. If the right moment came, during the conversation in the office, he would suggest a lift might be a good idea.

At the top of the first flight they came to the door of Elkin, Anderson and Pease, Solicitors. The names were engraved in old-fashioned writing on a brass plaque. George thought it was rather funny, seeing his name on a door. But not funny enough to smile. "Chin up," said Dusty, and rang the bell.

The door was opened by a woman George supposed was Rosemary Hollow, his father's secretary. He had heard a lot about her. His father was always saying what a treasure she was, though occasionally he hinted that he found her just a little annoying. Apparently she was always mislaying things. Sometimes she even sent the wrong letter to the wrong client, and her spelling wasn't tip-top. But there was no question of ever changing her for a more efficient model. The office wouldn't be the same without her, David Elkin said.

Hollow (as her boss called her in the office) gave George and Dusty a smile that looked as if it wasn't often called upon. George's eyes moved down to her chest. The very complicated Fair Isle pattern of her jersey, in raw bright colours, made him dizzy. He felt for Dusty's hand.

In the waiting room, where Miss Hollow urged them to make themselves at home for a few moments, George could see why she mislaid things so often. Papers and files were piled up on the floor, squashed into shelves, even balanced on the seats of upright chairs. Of course it wouldn't be easy to find anything in this muddle. George felt sorry for Miss Hollow. He could hear her, or someone, tapping away at a typewriter in another room — a soft, sad, spongy noise in the silence. George swung his legs. He hadn't expected his father's office to be a bit like this. He hadn't expected the strong smell of tea and smoke, which reminded him of the station waiting room. And it was very peculiar, considering his father made such a fuss about being on time, that they were now kept waiting.

When at last they were shown into Mr Elkin's office there was another surprise: George saw that his father appeared oddly small. Perhaps it was because of the huge size of the desk, or because he was huddled, shoulders hunched, into a curved armchair that swung from side to side. He didn't look at all like the tall man George was used to seeing raking up straw, or driving the tractor. Also, he was wearing a dark suit and a dull tie — clothes George scarcely saw in the early morning when Mr Elkin, in an old army overcoat, drove him to school. Altogether, he looked older, strange. George held on to the wooden arms of the chair his father had told him to sit in, on the opposite side of the desk. And what a piece of furniture that was. Black wood, unshining. There was a leather blotter with pink blotting paper unmarked by any splodge of blue, an ivory paper cutter, a fountain pen and a bottle of Stephen's ink. Not a paper or file. The telephone, placed well out of Mr Elkin's reach, sat in a nest of muddled brown cord. Such a waste of space, George thought. He would have liked to have something this size for his trains.

"Well, my son, what do you think?"

George swung his legs again. He didn't think anything much except that he didn't like the strong smell of cigar. Sometimes, when his mother was alive, people used to come to dinner. When he passed the open dining-room door next morning, the same smell jumped out at him. But when he came home after lunch it was gone. His mother was a great one for opening windows. Here, perhaps the one window, behind his father, was never opened.

"Welcome to Elkin, Anderson and Pease," Mr Elkin added. "Your future, if you've any sense."

George wished Dusty was at his side. He wanted to hold her hand, but she had been ordered by Miss Hollow to take a seat at the back of the room. He raised his head and looked his father in the eye as he was so often bidden to do. No immediate response to the welcome, and threat, came to mind. Through the window he could see the sky was a brownish colour with no clouds. The spire of the cathedral and the bare branches of a single tree were the only things to pattern the brown. He hoped very much there would be no time, when the visit was over, to see something of interest in the cathedral. He had been once to a very long and boring service which his father had declared was magnificent. He hadn't liked to disagree but didn't want to go again.

Something came to him.

"Where do Mr Anderson and Mr Pease work?" he asked.

His father chuckled. "Bill Anderson's office is down the corridor, looks over the back. Nice enough. But obviously, as the senior partner, I get the biggest room."

George took this in.

"And Mr Pease?"

"Henry Pease died years ago. He had the top floor. Low ceilings but the best view. Marvellous legal mind but always had a weak chest, poor Henry. We keep his name for balance. Rhythm. You appreciate my meaning, George? Elkin, Anderson and Pease has a certain *gravitas*, you must agree, that plain Elkin and Anderson would lack."

George nodded. It was always best to agree with the many hard-to-understand things that his father said, mostly to do with rhythm. His father was always on about that. "This desk would be a good place to play with my trains," he added, aware it was his turn to speak again.

"So it would." Mr Elkin gave one of his quick smiles, like the ones he gave the farm manager when there was good news about milk yields or the market price of sheep. "It's called a partners' desk. In the old days two partners of the firm would sit one at each side."

"That wouldn't be so lonely."

"No." Mr Elkin flashed his son a pensive look. "But we like our own offices, a desk to ourselves these days. Well, I've got to get back to work. Hollow and Silvia will take you out to tea. Any questions before you go?"

George wondered what his father would do at the empty desk once Dusty and he had gone, but decided it was best not to ask. He shook his head, slipped off his chair. When his father, too, stood up he looked more ordinary again. He came round to where George stood, by now next to Dusty, hand in hers, and ruffled his hand through his son's hair.

"Been meaning to get you here for ages. You must come again, whenever you want. Get to know the place. Now, go and enjoy yourself."

"Thanks, Papa."

A few moments later he sat between Miss Hollow and Dusty in a tea shop, faced with pale, disappointing ice cream. It didn't taste at all of strawberry. He wished there had been a van somewhere near selling those very white ice creams speared with a chocolate dagger. But the scones with cream and strawberry jam looked good. For some reason he could not understand he was allowed to eat these *after* the ice cream, which added to the strangeness of the afternoon.

"Well," said Miss Hollow, "did you enjoy yourself, young Master Elkin?"

George nodded. His eyes avoided her dizzy-making chest.

"And are you looking forward to taking it all over, running the firm, chairman?"

George weighed up his answer as he ate three more spoonfuls of the pink ice.

"Not much," he said at last. "I'd rather stay on the farm, look after the animals."

"It's all some way ahead, isn't it?" Dusty said to Miss Hollow. "He's got plenty of time to make up his mind."

"By which time, of course, I'll be long gone." Miss Hollow made her solemn prediction at the same time as biting into a scone top-heavy with jam and cream, so her words came smeary from a full mouth. But her intention was plain, and George felt no need to say he was sorry about that, because it would not have been the truth.

CHAPTER
TWO

When George returned to Elkin, Anderson and Pease twenty years later, Miss Hollow was still there. She greeted him with the same rusty smile, quickly followed by a look of hostile annoyance. She made it clear he would be not only an interruption in the normal course of her day, but also an unwanted addition to the firm, where things had been done the same way for as long as she could remember.

George was to spend the morning in conference with his father and Bill Anderson. The old remaining partner was well past retiring age. Years of sorting out others' problems had made him careless of his own: for too long he had ignored the ill health which now attacked him with force. He was to leave that afternoon after a farewell lunch with his lifelong friend David Elkin, and begin his retirement.

George sat, as he had twenty years ago, in a chair opposite his father, who was now further shrunk into his own chair. It still swung a little from side to side, creaking like an old boat fretting at its moorings. Bill Anderson was beside George, knees apart, trouser legs hitched up to reveal odd socks spiralling round legs of mulberry flesh. His waistcoat was encrusted with dried egg, dandruff powdered the shoulders of his jacket. When he turned to George there was a blast of halitosis. He ran a hand over the hairless freckles of his head. Jesus, thought George: in forty or fifty years' time, that could be me. My retirement day: the handing over of the firm — to whom?

Miss Hollow brought in a tray of coffee, horribly weak in porcelain cups decorated with dragons. Mr Elkin, whose idea this meeting had been, plainly had no idea how to conduct it. He and Bill fell into conversation about some client who was disputing a will. Miss Hollow was asked to bring in a file, whose rotting covers scarcely managed to contain the disorganised papers within. It lay on the desk, still as bare as George remembered it. The telephone had not been updated, the blotter was still pristine. But the edges of the room had avoided any efforts of organisation on Miss Hollow's part. Stacks of papers and decaying files had thickened like spring hedges, reducing the area of carpet and furniture. There would have to be a good many changes, George reflected. Considerable investment. But today was not the time for suggestions. Outside the sky was knobbled with cloud, the cathedral in sharp outline. The smell of cigar smoke still thickened the air. It was no wonder Mr Elkin gasped and coughed every few minutes. George longed to be outside, at work on the farm.

Two hours passed in inconsequential talk in which George was not included. He took the odd note to show that he was taking in the sort of thing he himself would shortly have to deal with, but in truth he learnt

19

nothing. The firm's finances were not mentioned, nor his salary, which his father had said would be discussed that morning. From what he could gather, those clients who had remained loyal to E, A & P for many years had been coming for advice on matters of a minor nature. George wondered, not for the first time, what the future held for the firm. He had his misgivings, though perhaps if he managed to modernise the whole place, bring it into line with contemporary life, replace Miss Hollow . . . it could stand a chance of surviving.

At midday Miss Hollow, by some pre-arrangement, appeared with four small glasses and a bottle of sherry. They all sipped at the oversweet stuff, constrained by the sadness of the occasion, but uncertain as to the procedure of a farewell ceremony. Mr Elkin raised his glass in Bill Anderson's direction: George did the same. Miss Hollow, who had knocked back her sherry as if it were vodka, was left with an empty glass for the silent toast. Embarrassed, two scarlet spots high on her powdery cheeks, she left the room. David Elkin leant forward in his chair.

"Emotional," he whispered.

"Not sure I'm not feeling a bit the same myself." Bill Anderson pulled a dirty handkerchief from his top pocket and rubbed his eyes. "Can't really believe it, not after so long. Going, I mean."

"Afraid I've slipped up concerning gold watches," David replied, striving for lightness. "Hope you understand." The two old boys laughed thinly at each other. "But there's one thing young George and I must settle with you before you go." He made his fingers into a spire, moved them from side to side. "A final important matter, Bill. Our name . . ."

"Your name?" A single pink tear was running down Bill Anderson's cheek. The handkerchief had been put away, but was brought out again to check its progress.

"I mean, it's jolly good your boy going into politics and all that. Could be Prime Minister one day. Just a bit . . . well, disappointing, I suppose you could call it, not to be taking over from you. And with no Anderson here, by rights we should give up your name. I've been envisaging that, and worrying about the rhythm. It would be quite spoiled, as you can understand, if Elkin and Pease were deprived of the Anderson. Don't you agree?"

George could tell from his father's grinding fingers the effort it was costing him to ease his way into this delicate matter. There was a long pause while Bill Anderson marshalled his agreement. He was both confused by the reference to rhythm — his dear partner had been showing signs of decay of late — and pleased at the thought that his name was required to live on in the firm. In fact, it had never occurred to him that on his leaving Anderson would go too. Of course: he would do the same as Henry Pease, leave his name where it had always been, between his friends.

"No question, old boy," he said at last. "I should be most upset had you suggested erasing Anderson. It's yours for as long as you want it."

This called for second glasses of celebratory sherry, and two further tears to hesitate down Bill's cheeks. David Elkin remained dry-eyed with relief.

"That's very good of you: thought it might be the answer. Can't tell you how pleased George and I are, aren't we, George? There'll still be the rhythm. Applies to a firm of solicitors as well as to anything else."

"Quite."

"Now time for some lunch."

The two old men stood up. They had known each other since they were children, worked together for forty years. They leant across the vast desk and shook hands. George looked away, not wanting to witness the weight of their professional parting. As his father did not return in the afternoon he began to go through papers and files, at some loss as to how to acquaint himself with the general disorder. Disinclined to take the swinging chair until the appropriate time, he sat in the muddle of Bill Anderson's old office wondering what on earth he should do in the general scheme of things. A profound sense of gloom slowed his hands as they sifted through the papers.

It became apparent very quickly, during the next six weeks that George worked alongside his father, that there was little work to be dealt with at Elkin, Anderson and Pease. The telephone rarely rang with clients requesting advice. There were few letters to be dictated to Miss Hollow, who took them down in slow shorthand in a notebook that must have been in use for several years. George's sense of misgiving daily increased.

"Of course, the arrival of these new people doesn't help," pointed out his father one morning as the two of them sat either side of the barren desk, having dealt with the exiguous amount of post Miss Hollow had delivered. He glanced out of the window to avoid his son's eye. "Just round the corner. Opened a few months ago. Slasher, Reed and Hedley — not what I call a serious name, but a lot of white marble and black glass frontage, as if it were New York. Can't imagine how they got planning permission. But people are seduced by such fancy stuff. Give it a go, rather than come to a reliable old firm — I suppose you could say a touch Dickensian — like ours."

"I think," said George, after an interval in which he contemplated how best to make the suggestion he had been toying with since the day he had arrived, "we could probably could do with a little updating. Get a new telephone, for a start." His father's mouth tightened. "A fax machine. Email. No office these days —"

"We have a faxing machine somewhere, though I believe Hollow has some trouble working it. She says it's not necessary."

". . . a computer . . ."

"A computer?" The old solicitor looked suddenly close to tears. George saw in his face a gathering of elegantly phrased reasons as to why there was no need whatever for a computer. Then he saw the familiar raising of the white eyebrows, always a sign of willingness to oblige, to be thought reasonable. Action rarely followed.

"Perhaps you're right, boy. But machinery means investment."

"We could invest, couldn't we?"

"Daresay we could, a little. But there would still be the problem of poor Hollow. She'd never find her way round one of those things, any more than I would. They're for your generation. They're for the young."

A long silence between them was brushed by the old man's wheezing. Both knew what George was going to venture next, and both feared it.

"Perhaps the time has come for Miss Hollow herself to move on . . ."

"Move on?" David Elkin's eyes, dull brown beads in whites of sluggish yellow, jerked round all that was familiar in the room.

"Go," said George.

"I'd never have thought of that. I must say it would never have occurred to me, Hollow going."

George remembered that, on rare occasions, his father considered loyalty more important than the truth.

"It's only that she's . . . getting on, isn't she? Excellent in many ways, loyal, knows the business inside out. But perhaps someone younger, trained in the technical skills essential these days —"

"I understand you." Mr Elkin folded his hands, as if in prayer, on the virgin blotter. "But don't ask me to do it, George. I couldn't do that. Perhaps when I'm gone, that would be the time. It's up to you what happens then. You can be the one to fire her, poor Hollow." His mouth twitched very slightly, prelude to a smile that died still-born. "Many years ago your mother and I came across a rather good antique clock. With one

24

accord we agreed it would be perfect for Hollow on the occasion of her retirement. I'll see if I can find it. All I ask is that you give no indication that things might eventually be different."

"Of course not."

"So she'll have a while left innocent of what's to befall her. I'm glad of that."

The old man had envisaged a couple more years working for the firm he loved, but in the event it was just two months after his partner retired that he himself left E, A & P for ever. Signs of general decline after the departure of Bill Anderson were followed by a bad attack of asthma and a week in hospital. He returned home to be looked after by Dusty, whose job, now she was married and had children of her own, had turned into that of a daily house-keeper. But the fight seemed to have gone out of him. Years of asthma had hastened his elderly appearance. On his return from hospital, shrunken and feeble, the determination to keep going that had been his stay for so long had all but disappeared.

"It's all yours, prematurely," he said to George his first evening home. "I'm sorry. So you must go ahead, boy, do what you think fit."

As George looked upon his father, wrapped in rugs by the study fire, he reflected on the nature of swift change. One moment normality is on the march, the discipline of years practised every day. The next, the stuff of anticipation is snatched away so fast that those concerned are left ill equipped to deal with the new emptiness of life.

David Elkin, who had married in his mid-forties, had always been a father older than most. But it wasn't until very recently that George had become aware of his real age — the struggle it now was for him, in his new slowness, to leave the house at eight in the morning: the look of exhaustion that shrivelled his face when he returned in the evening. Frailty descends so gently on those we love that it's not until it has cast its entire web that the spectre of mortality becomes clear. George admired his father and had always loved him, but feared it was too late now to express that love. He cursed himself for not having shown — indeed, felt — more appreciation years ago. He felt ashamed when he remembered the embarrassment he had sometimes experienced in his youth when his father had entertained his schoolfriends, addressed them in his quaint, formal way, unable to contain small frowns of disapproval at shaven heads or ringed ears. Now, there was neither the time nor the opportunity to repair such things. Nor was there any means of dispelling the late regret.

The old man indicated he wanted more whisky. George refilled his glass although the doctor had advised against alcohol. He stoked up the fire. The house had never been well served by the ancient heating system — north winds blasted through the old window frames. Some said it was the cold that had caused Mrs Elkin's pneumonia, thereby implying her husband's lack of care. But George knew it was the cancer that had beaten her. Three weeks, only, between its detection and her dying. He remembered that time as the most terrible of his life — not, at six, completely understanding, but knowing his mother must be prayed for through clenched fingers. This new anticipation of an ending, therefore, though less mysterious, was not unfamiliar.

George did not have to wait long. His father died in his sleep a few days after his return home. Ever thoughtful of others, David Elkin had always declared that he would not want to be responsible, when the time came, for the damage to the funeral limousines (he had hesitated over the undertakers' word, then endowed it with the trace of a sneer) attempting to drive up the narrow lane and the rutted track to the farm. In the middle drawer of his office desk George found his will: he had left instructions that his coffin should be transported to the church in a farm cart, drawn by the tractor, just as his wife's had been. David Elkin had arranged her journey with great care: straw bales were placed so that she should not be rocked. George did the same for his father.

He was buried on a day of white frost and startling cold. His many friends, mostly farmers he had known all his life, came with black ties under their weatherproof jackets, distant-eyed. Bill Anderson, wearing a coat so thin it was as if he was bent on hurrying his own demise, wept throughout the service. Miss Hollow, who thought it best to appear cheerful at funerals, came in a red scarf and fragile shoes that made awkward her journey across the frost-clenched sods of earth to the graveside. Prodge and Nell, the Elkins' nearest neighbours and George's childhood friends, stood each side of him. It was the first time he had ever seen either of them dressed in black and it was almost his undoing — Nell's solemn eyes and pale curls shining from the depths of an elderly shawl, Prodge's boyish face hardened by the effort to withhold tears. George himself kept his hands clasped in front of him. He wore no gloves. The intense cold numbed his hands and he was glad not to be able to feel his fingers, to feel anything.

When the burial was over the mourners gathered in the local pub for mulled wine and sausage rolls. George was conscious of the strange, pleasant sense of his body thawing. After several glasses of the highly spiced wine he felt himself smiling. With a cheerfulness he never imagined he could have assumed, he answered questions about his future.

"What now, George? You'd never sell up." They meant the farm.

"Of course not. Never."

"Your father wouldn't have wanted that. Elkins farmed their land for a good many generations." No one mentioned Elkin, Anderson and Pease. That side of George's life was of little interest to them.

George paused for a moment beside Bill Anderson, patted him on the shoulder. His father's old partner seemed to have been fortified by the drink. His cheeks blazed but his eyes were dry.

"What a turn-up for the books," he said. "Never thought your father would pop his clogs before me. The Almighty has some rum tricks in store for us, doesn't he? If there's anything I can do, any help or advice needed at the office, don't hesitate to call me."

George thanked him and left. By the time he drove up the hill it was beginning to snow in slow motion. He tried to calculate the distance between each flake: more than a yard, he reckoned. He could drive between two flakes without touching them. Their descent was so slow you could follow each one from sky to earth, each one significant for a few seconds, then gone. Some metaphor for life, there, George pondered, knowing he should not be driving after half a dozen glasses of mulled wine. Foolish snow-thoughts switched to a picture of himself: unmarried man in possession of a thriving farm, chairman of the family firm of solicitors. Whither now? Empty house ahead, no enthusiasm for the business he had been left to run. Was there anything in the fridge for supper? Would Hollow be in the office next morning, or would she be taking a few days off to grieve for her old boss? George knew he was in no mood to ring her and find out.

The house was freezing. A tangible cold prowled after him, brushing against him like an animal. In the hall the grandfather clock tapped against the silence, impervious to change. Mocking, thought George, who was having difficulty in pulling off his great-coat. Bloody clock. He had always hated it. It might have to go.

He went to the study and shut the door behind him to regain absolute silence. The fire which had warmed his father's last few days was a pile of ash and cinders. The rug that had warmed his father's knees was a whirlpool of cold tartan in the armchair. George picked it up, sat down and laid it over his own lap. He wept, but only for a few moments. Then his father's voice rose from the ashes: *You do as you think best, boy.* George knew he was drunk, but the voice was louder than an illusion. Well, he would do as he thought best. Then, through darkness, cold, ash, silence and an emptiness that made him giddy, an idea came to him. He shut his eyes.

Three days later the new chairman of Elkin, Anderson and Pease sat in his father's old chair behind the empty desk. Miss Hollow came in, shaggy-eyed, tight-mouthed.

"I came in yesterday," she said, "but you weren't here."

"No," said George. "I was sorting out a problem about a late delivery of feed at home. I should have rung you. I'm sorry."

"I didn't like to disturb you. I thought, there being nothing important, nothing pressing, I wouldn't phone."

"That was very kind. I needed a day or two."

Their relationship, George appreciated, seemed to have taken a less hostile turn. There was something to be said for the unification of grief. But it lasted only a moment. Hollow slammed a single handwritten envelope down before him.

"I've dealt with the usual stuff. Nothing important. This seems to be for *you*."

The fact that a letter had arrived for George, so newly in his role as chairman, she saw as betrayal, an affront. George picked up the envelope: loopy, fountain-pen writing in black ink, postmarked Cornwall. Another letter of sympathy, he supposed.

"Thank you, Hollow — I'm sorry, Miss Hollow."

"The old partners always addressed me as Hollow, but it's up to you."

George acknowledged this concession with a kindly smile.

"I've a few things to go through, then we could have a talk about pending cases."

"Not many pending, Mr Elkin, as you're no doubt aware."

"Please call me George. I'm a different generation . . ."

Hollow sniffed.

When she had gone, George glanced at the view of the room that his father must have studied for the past forty years. Brown wallpaper peered through chinks in the bookshelves which rose like cliff-faces of leatherbound and gold-tooled legal tomes. There were four watercolours of the local hunt by Lionel Edwards, an artist David Elkin had greatly admired and fiercely supported against critics of his mode of unfashionable, skilled draughtsmanship. He would never sell those, thought George. They would come to the farm. There was a small looking glass that held a clouded reflection of the window behind the desk and the spectral outline of the cathedral. Piled on the floor were dozens of files tied with pink tape. George tried to imagine what it must have been like for his father, who loved the open air, being cooped up in this claustrophobic room for so many years. He failed. He knew only that he was not going to do the same.

George slit the envelope and drew out a postcard, a picture of St Ives. The loopy black writing was randomly flung across the back.

George! he read. *Tracked you down at last. I hope. I saw an obituary of your father and Oxford glimpses of you (so like him, judging by the handsome photograph) came back to me. Then by chance I ran into Toby Talbot — remember him, Christ Church? — and he said he hadn't seen you for ages but knew you'd joined the family firm and somehow knew its name. I pondered, as you can imagine, so long after Bablock Hithe, before deciding on an impertinent question — could we meet for a drink? Am in St Ives writing about the current painters, lovely job, fantastic fish, about to set off slowly through the West Country back to London and am planning a night at the Bridge Hotel on Wednesday, have to see the collection of some old woman near Exeter. My hotel can't be far from your office, would a short meeting be in order? Is there a wife to meet? Children? I'd love to catch up with what's been happening to you since those ginger biscuits by the river. I ran into Serena the other day, plus pushchair and twins. Give me a call if you think meeting is a good idea. I'm still Crichton.*
    Love, Lily.

Serena! George thought about her. Eager, friendly, good. Pretty apricot hair, shy about sex, nothing to enchant a man's heart. He was glad she had twins. She would be a good mother. Serena was a long time ago. So was Lily, of course, and he could remember even less about her. Lily the Accoster in the Broad, Lily the emphatic one: that was it. Picnic by the river: she'd accused him of being unobservant, hadn't she? Odd girl. Hadn't given her a thought. Wasn't very keen on the idea of a reunion now: bad timing, the sadness still heavy. Reunions with people you've shared little with in the first place are usually misguided. But it would be churlish not to respond to her signal. Later in the morning, when he had written a few thank-you letters about his father and gone through the scant business with Hollow, he would ring the Bridge Hotel. He had no idea in mind what he would suggest. He did not fancy the thought of a long lunch with Lily. A meeting, just because she happened to be in the same area, was no guarantee of reward on either side. It could be a waste of time.

Hollow returned, sullen.

"Mrs Williams rang about her will. I made an appointment for her, two o'clock, seeing as the diary's clear."

"Fine." So lunch with Lily would have to be short. George took in Hollow's disgruntled face. He felt sympathy. Her world, as much as his own, had been turned upside down. "Hollow," he said, "surely you weren't always the only secretary?"

"Office manager."

"Office manager. Of course. Sorry. I remember my father speaking of others."

"There was a time when there were two under me. Jennie and Magda. We had more work than we could manage, then. When Mr Pease retired it began to tail off." She folded her arms, making a shelf for her undulating breasts, indeterminate beneath the sloppy red wool of her jersey. "You could say the firm's been . . . going downhill ever since then," she said.

"You could indeed." George sighed. Hollow stared at him, challenging. He knew she could read his mind, but now was not the time. He needed to think further about how, and when.

"Anything I can do for you?"

George managed a smile. "I'd be grateful if you could organise a new telephone." Hollow's face began to close. "I mean, it's not that I've anything against this one. But it's quite a weight." He lifted the receiver, attempted to untwist the gnarled brown cord with his free hand. "Cord always in a muddle. So slow to dial . . . don't you think? We'd be better off with a . . . wouldn't we?"

Hollow did not appreciate his lightness of tone.

"Very well," she said, and left the room.

An hour later George, defeated for the time being, rang the Bridge Hotel. Miss Crichton was expected but had not yet arrived. He left a message. At lunchtime he left the office, telling Hollow he would be back in an hour.

"Mr Elkin used to go to the Bridge most days for a ploughman's," she said.

"I'm off to do the same." It occurred to him that this might cheer her, the knowledge that the new chairman was instinctively following the ways of the old one. But her eyes did not leave the high bank of her Royal typewriter — God knows what there was to type — and she offered no word of encouragement.

He went into the hotel bar, crowded as always with murmurous locals. The ceiling was low, black-beamed. The open fire always smoked, so a scent of apple wood mixed with the smell of beer and thick country clothes rank from years of farm life. It was the kind of room in which a sense of outdoor life — the life most of its inhabitants came from — mingled with the safe fug of indoor life, and George liked that. It was reassuring, though not by design. Several of the drinkers had been at the funeral. They nodded at George, decided no words were preferable to clumsy sentiment.

George ordered himself a pint of lager. While he waited he contemplated the massed chorus of bottles beautifully organised against the mirrored wall behind the bar, the wine glasses hanging from their stems, the least popular bottles of aperitifs and liqueurs marshalled together in the highest row. Here was a barman who knew his job, thought George. He admired those who maintained order in their work, and thought sadly of the hopeless muddle into which the firm — *his* firm — had descended. He tried to bring Lily's face clearly to mind.

It came to him in fragments of reflection through the glass behind the bar. For a moment he watched its jigsaw pieces approach him, memory and reality confused. Then he turned and the unbroken face looked at him, enquiring. George remembered. She seemed ruffled as she had that day by the river: just the same.

George had always harboured a — perhaps foolish, private — thought that meetings of any kind would be eased if each party knew, without explanation, what the other one had come from. If that were the case, Lily would know at this moment that George's less-than-welcoming expression was nothing to do with her, but because his father had recently died and the heaviness was still upon him. In return, he would know what caused her eyes to dance so merrily. Both would approach the other accordingly. But hampered by the obfuscation that impedes all human contact before the process of discovery has begun, they could only employ the simple tools of politeness, enquiry, surprise.

"It's you!"

"Lily!"

"You didn't mind?"

"Course I didn't mind. What would you like to drink?"

"Goodness. It's been quite some time. Fizzy mineral water, please."

"You've driven up from Cornwall?"

"I've driven up from Cornwall."

"Look: why don't you go and grab that table by the fire. I'll bring the drinks and something to eat. You must be hungry."

Lily nodded and moved away. She bent her way through the crowd. Several farmers glanced at her passing. George joined her with plates of bread and tomatoes and cheese. Lily smiled. She had taken off her coat and, like Hollow, but to different effect, folded her arms under her breasts. She seemed grateful for the warmth from the fire.

There was no awkwardness at that short reunion, but nor was there the flaring of instantaneous ease that signals a harmony of souls. They exchanged news, Lily first. She had tried many things since leaving Oxford. At present she was the art critic for a quarterly magazine with a small but knowledgeable readership. This had led to her being called upon to give her expert view on a collection of nineteenth-century English watercolours — hence the journey to the West Country. She had on occasions lectured to sixth-formers studying history of art, but she felt unsettled, unstretched. Her wish now was for a regular job teaching children — "Still the old desire to make *looking* into a habit," she smiled. "But it's hard to find a school that's remotely interested in children studying pictures." George gave a much briefer account of his own life since university, not imagining it could be of any real interest to her. He ended with the death of his father.

"I'm sorry to have barged in so soon after that," Lily said.

"You haven't barged in. It's good to see you again."

"So: what now?"

"That's what I'm wondering."

"The alternatives?"

"I either imitate my father — come into the office every day, help out a little on the farm at weekends. Try my hand at being a solicitor, make use of my training. Or I give all that up, sell the business and become a full-time farmer."

"Which do you want to do?"

"I was never a natural lawyer. I only agreed, not knowing what else I wanted to do, because my father expected me to take over the firm. It's been in the family for generations, though it's currently on its last legs. I'm not sure there's any point in trying to re-establish things if my heart's not in it."

"Course not." Lily paused. "Have you made up your mind?"

"I think I have."

"Good. That's good. What about the farm? Thriving?"

"Sheep, mostly. Small herd of cows. We do pretty well."

"And the house?"

"It's where I was brought up. I love it, though it's been rather neglected since my mother died. It could do with a lick of paint. My father never noticed cold, draughts, peeling walls, that sort of thing. I was away for a few years, law school and bumming round the world a bit: when I came back I was shocked by the general decay. My father was astonished when I told him a whole side of guttering had collapsed. He was past noticing. The plan was for me to live there for a while — goodness knows how that would have worked out. Probably not too well. But he was in poor health, had been alone for too long, and I didn't fancy a small flat in the city when I could be living on the farm. So the dutiful son moved in with the aged father, and in the event we only had a few months together."

"I'm sorry."

"I'm glad I was there. Now I've got to brace myself for the whole business of selling up the firm, forcing the poor old secretary, who's been there for ever, to retire early." He looked at his watch. "Speaking of whom, I must go now or I'll be late for our only client of the day. I'll be chided — my father was never late." He paid for lunch, was anxious to be off. "Before you go, if you've a moment, come and see the farm," he said. "I'd like to know what you think."

"I'll be through by five tomorrow." Lily's answer was so swift that the idea of a visit might already have been lodged in her mind. "I'll ring you at the office and see if it's a good time to come when you finish work. Perhaps you could lead me there. We could drive in convoy."

"We could do that," said George. "Bring your boots, or I'll have to carry you across the yard."

"That would be a first."

"For me, too." They smiled at each other, their parting lifted into a mutual amiability which had been hovering at lunch, but had not fully taken off. Now, through a trivial exchange which conjured in both their minds an unlikely picture, it was established. George left quickly. Had he been in less of a hurry he might have noticed the hint of firm intent in Lily's suggestion of a visit. As it was, this did not occur to him till he was on his way home that evening. Then, in his long fight with the boiler, determined that the emptiness of the house should at least be made more bearable by a modicum of warmth, Lily Crichton faded from his mind.

The next morning George rose at six and walked up the hill behind the house. It was less cold than it had been for a week. The frost had begun to lose its grip: grass, hedges, bare trees now silently jangled with a billion quivering drops of water, each one holding a particle of sky more intense in its sparkle than the actual sky. George could not understand this trick of light but it had some effect on his spirits. A curious feeling of buoyancy began to spread upwards from his feet — he stamped each foot in turn on the earth, his earth — and he sensed the sludge of grief that had muddied his head for a week beginning to evaporate as keenly as the frost.

He looked down the valley. Long yarns of mist, as if wound from each end by invisible hands, were thinning, rising. Beneath them George could see a glint of the river where he and Prodge, and sometimes Nell, had raced small plastic boats when they were children. He could see a huddle of sheep in the corner of one of the fields, so closely jammed together that from this distance they looked like a solid wool rug. Soon it would be lambing time. George looked forward to that: he hadn't helped with the excitement of each birth since he was a boy. This year he would be there, up all night when necessary, dealing with his sheep.

If any doubts had remained in his mind about his plan when he ascended the hill, they had vanished completely by the time he came down. He was further elated on finding Dusty in the kitchen frying eggs and bacon. He had not expected her. In all the flurry of the last week he had given little thought, he realised with some shame, to her future.

"You could do with some breakfast," she said.

She sat beside him as he ate, just as she used to every morning when he was a boy before he left for school. For George she had made a pot of strong coffee and toast. She herself sipped dark tea. The boiler had responded to George's urgings, so the room was warm again and a winter sun, strong through silted windows, relighted the place, igniting even further George's spirits. He loved the solid presence of Dusty, the safety of her. Her unexpected arrival this morning (though not so unexpected if he had thought about it) confirmed the whole feeling of a casting-off into a new life.

"This is wonderful," he said. "There's no one like you when it comes to breakfast."

"I was wondering if you might be needing me, still, now things have changed? Of course I'd understand if you felt —"

"Dusty: my apologies. I should have said something before. Of course I need you. The job's always here. How on earth could I manage without you?"

"I could come in every morning. Keep things in order, leave something for your supper."

"Perfect." Strange how things fall into place, even in times of sadness. "Can't imagine anything better. I shall be the most spoiled man for miles."

"Out at work all day, a man can't be expected to run a house."

"I tell you what, though, Dusty. I shan't be out at the office any longer. I'll be out on the farm. I've decided to . . ."

"I thought as much," said Dusty. She had always had an uncanny habit of guessing his thoughts.

"I think my father would have understood."

"I think he would."

"He said to do as I thought best. After much reflection, I think farmer rather than solicitor is best for me."

"It's a grand idea. You've always loved being outdoors. A hands-on farmer. Mr Elkin would have liked that. He missed so much, letting others do most of the work for him."

"Quite." Dusty's approval of his plan was yet another positive piece in the exhilarating pattern of the morning. In the warmth of her approbation he suddenly remembered that Lily Crichton might drop in this evening. The thought of her visit, encompassed in his general feeling of well-being, did not disturb him. But he had nothing to offer her. "Dusty," he said, "the cupboards are all bare as you've probably noticed, and there's someone coming to supper. Would it be possible —?"

"I'll leave a pie and carrots ready. You used to like my rice pudding . . . I'll put one in the bottom oven."

With Dusty behind him, relieving him of domestic arrangements, it was all going to be much easier, much better than he could have imagined. George had no fear of living alone so long as it was in the place he knew and loved. Should he be in need of company, Prodge and Nell were just a mile up the road: they could visit each other, as they always used to before George went to Oxford, most evenings. By day, he would be wholly occupied, making the most of his physical strength on the land. Thanks to his father's skills and the dedication of the helpers employed, the farm was a small but profitable business. He would like to expand it, of course: buy more land, more animals, do up the farm buildings. He could imagine a good life ahead. He was eager to get on with it.

At the office later that morning he made an effort to maintain an impassive expression, but there must have been some light in his eyes that he could not hide from Hollow. When she brought his cup of coffee at eleven, he asked her to sit down. For the first time in her career she took the visitor's chair. As she lowered herself, her distaste encompassed a certain dignity. She sat with a very straight back, like one who has been through the rigours of deportment lessons at school. Surely her jersey, thought George, was the same one that had dizzied him as a child. His eyes skidded along the uncomfortable reds and blues of her chest. He watched her clasp her ringless red fingers, steady herself. Concentrating on the fineness of her behaviour, George remained silent. He was then appalled to hear her speak before some apt opening to this unhappy meeting had occurred to him.

"It's all right, don't worry." Hollow gave something between a gasp and a sigh. "I know what you're going to tell me," she said. "I've seen it coming."

CHAPTER
THREE

George drove slowly home that evening, Lily's headlights just behind him. He was annoyed with himself: whatever had caused him to agree to this? He should have realised that, having broken the news to Hollow, he would need more time alone to deliberate, work out the absolute certainty of his plan. Should he change his mind, it was not too late to withdraw, carry on as his father intended. But now the evening would be crowded with small talk to Lily. No time to think further. The opportunity to agonise finally over his decision would be swept away by his polite, foolish invitation to a girl he scarcely knew. Idiot, he said to himself.

Despite all his efforts the previous evening, George had failed to get much response from the boiler. Lily had come in thick jerseys and made no mention of the cold in the house, but George, senses heightened by the presence of a visitor, was suddenly aware of a dark smell of damp in the study. The fire had not been lighted there since his father's death. They moved to the kitchen. Lily gave a slight shiver, but still she said nothing against the temperature. George liked her for that. He put a match to the fire and opened a bottle of wine.

They sat each side of the fire. George remained more preoccupied with his own thoughts (what sort of evening is Hollow spending? he wondered) than with entertaining Lily. She was looking round, blatantly curious. He watched her taking in the chaotic gathering of things in the room, the muddle of objects crowded on to shelves, the piles of farming correspondence on the dresser. He found himself looking where she looked, and saw cracked walls, paint lacerated by years of steam, cobwebs slung between high corners — all revealing that a critical eye had long ceased to concern itself with such familiar signs of decay. Deterioration is only realised, George thought, when a stranger arrives to swoop over the imperfections. And it's then that your protective instinct, the instinct to defend your own territory, comes into play.

"Nothing's been changed since my mother died," he said. He intended to say *I'm afraid*, but those two words, indicating apology, or shame, did not appear. Lily nodded. "My father and I got so used to it all I suppose we didn't notice things in the house have been . . . slipping a bit. I'll have to make an effort to sort it all out. Maybe get in a painter."

Lily smiled. "I like rooms," she said, "where signs of the past are gathered. Where you can look about and be reminded by objects about certain events, certain years. That old bottle of dried-up ink, for instance." She nodded towards the top shelf of the dresser where a scarcely visible bottle of Quink stood between a skein of untreated wool and a cracker decorated with imitation holly. "That bottle of ink: can you remember the day you bought it? What you were thinking that day? What was happening in your life?"

"Haven't a clue. No memory of buying it."

Lily gave a sigh, almost impatient. "My flat's full of junk, most of it small memorials to some time past. But then I like to keep the whole thing, the time thing, going all at once: past, present and future. I don't like to abandon any one of them. You don't feel like that?"

"No," said George. This time he added, "I'm afraid I don't." He remembered thinking, that day by the river, that Lily was slightly eccentric. The feeling was still there.

"It probably means a cluttered mind, cobwebs that ought to be swept away. But I can't quite manage it. I can't ever shake off what's gone before, eager though I am for today and tomorrow."

Silence fell between them. George was aware he was not fully concentrating on what she was saying and had little desire to do so. Although she had won his approval for not complaining about the cold, she still felt like an intruder on this difficult evening. He looked at the clock — daresay she'd observed its cracked glass face — and saw there were several hours of politeness to go. Perhaps he was being unfair, not trying. Perhaps she saw his hostility, was making an effort to win him over with her slightly potty talk about time and her liking for shambolic rooms. But having invited her in the first place, George knew he should do the decent thing: put aside his regret, make an effort.

They sat down to the cottage pie and carrots at the kitchen table. Dusty had swept piles of farming magazines and old newspapers to one end, leaving a clear space to eat. George lighted the stub of candle in the blackened pewter candlestick, fearing it would not last the evening. At the table, he floundered in the next silence. It was all much harder going with Lily here than it had been in the bar of the Bridge Hotel. He could not think how to unlock the awkwardness he felt — though it was apparent that this was something Lily did not share. She was eating hungrily. When she looked up at him she smiled. If his present mood had not been so heavy upon him, he might have found her beguiling. What the hell should he say?

"You seem very happy," he ventured. "I mean, for one who hasn't found her exact path. Most people fret so, unsure of what they want to do."

"I positively like the not quite knowing. I'm sure of the direction, the area. But waiting for a signpost to the precise road to appear — and I'm sure it will, just out of the blue — is exciting. I don't fret at all. You're right: I'm very happy."

"Were you happy at Oxford?"

"Oh yes. In all sorts of different ways. I was lucky enough not to have any disastrous love affairs. I always knew exactly when to leave someone, before he had a chance to leave me. Then, I loved my subject. I loved working hard." She paused. "I suppose I've been very lucky in that nothing terrible has happened to me so far: nothing to shatter my world. Secure childhood, parents still alive, home still there when I want to return. My brother Mark had a drug problem, but he got through it, he's fine. I realise this all sounds very smug, but it's true. I'll pay for it, I daresay. Something terrible will happen to blast the fragile structure. But for the time being I feel so charged with various joys that all I want to do is reinvest them in others . . . I'm not really sure how. I know teaching people how to see is one way, but does that really work?" She paused again. "If you asked me what I'd most like to be, my answer would be someone who had the ability to inspire joy in work, joy in life. But of course that's the one thing one can't ever *become*. To be inspirational is a gift from God, and you're either born in a cloud of gold dust that touches others, or you're not."

Lily lowered her head as she took a sip of wine. Then she looked up, met George's eyes. Light from the candle gilded her serious face. For a moment he saw an illusion of the gold dust she had just mentioned.

"I've gone on too much, haven't I?" she said. She smiled, easing away the seriousness. "But I'll tell you one other thing. My father — he's a judge — says I've never outgrown my childlike sense of wonder. I'm not sure if that's good or bad — whether, as a grown-up, one should employ more scepticism, cynicism. Be more realistic. But I think he's right. I'm full of wonder every day. I'm a leaf, really, blown about, hither and thither, by sensation. It doesn't have to be caused by people, which is a help, I suppose — nature and art have a profound effect. But it's the hardest thing in the world, isn't it, to describe one's own kind of happiness — the lightness of being that transforms every day, every hour.

But for heaven's sake, stop me. Your wine is going to my head." She put a hand on George's arm. He filled her glass.

"I'm enjoying it," he said, automatically. Lily looked at him with doubtful enquiry.

"You're teasing me. You think I'm too . . . hectic."

"No. I'm not teasing. I've never met a leaf before, but I do know what you mean. Really. I rather envy your ability to be gusted about. Much more exciting than being of the firmly-planted-in-my-ways school, like me." He smiled to himself. "I confess I do sometimes aspire to spontaneity, but I can never get the timing right. I'm always too late. By the time the idea and the urge have come, the event — where I *could* have shown how spontaneous I can be — is over. I'm left with regret."

"Then you must alter your timing," said Lily. "That's what you must do, or you'll miss a lot of fun."

George thought about that in the silence that followed, and reflected that his reaction to her confession of happiness was true: he had enjoyed it. To try to describe happiness, and he guessed his own experience of the sensation was of a very different order from Lily's, was something he would never have contemplated. Her attempt was a little overblown (he was glad to have been the single member of her audience), but she had managed to convey her meaning in a way that touched his own less explicit heart. Her two little speeches of conviction, of energy, pleasantly unsettled his solid base. He suddenly felt as he sometimes did at the top of a hill, looking across

50

wooded valleys to exuberant skies. "I think there's some cheese," he said.

Later they returned to the fire and Lily confessed her love of dancing.

"Second best," she said. "If I hadn't wanted to do something with pictures, I'd have liked to have trained as a dancer, though I'm sure I wouldn't have been any good."

"Oh, I don't know." George's eyes went to her leg, crossed over one knee, swinging in time to music in her head. The small pointed foot moved in and out of a flickering fan of light from the flames.

"I'd like to dance round your kitchen table, swirling scarves, Isadora Duncan . . ."

George scratched his head. The awkwardness that had clouded the beginning of the evening returned. He dreaded her rising from her chair, seizing a dishcloth and flinging herself round the table. Her element of dottiness both appealed to him and unnerved him. This solid old room had never before entertained a woman like her. George's thoughts went to his father: what would he have made of her? Would he have been enchanted or repelled? George wasn't sure what he felt, which made him wary. He kept his eyes on her foot, twirling faster, and the impatient swing of her leg. To his relief she did not get up and entertain him with her Isadora act round the table.

At ten o'clock Lily said she must go back to the hotel. George offered to lead her to the main road, but she said she would be fine. There was a full moon, she said.

Oddly, now that she was about to go, George was assaulted by a desire for her to stay. He looked down at her feet.

"You didn't bring any boots, I see," he said. "Look at your shoes."

Lily glanced at the tidemarks of mud on blue suede. The brightness of the moon lighted the wet mess of the yard. "Too late," she said as she walked to the front door. "They're ruined. It doesn't matter."

"Far from ruined, and they can be saved from getting worse." George picked up Lily with a dramatic swoosh, balancing her across his arms. He registered the lightness of her.

"Spontaneity!" she cried. "Perfect timing." One of her hands gripped the back of his neck. "Or did you plan this?"

"Course I didn't plan it. Your shoes were the trigger. Right: we're on our way." George stepped out of the door. "I feel like one of those firemen who are always there to rescue old women from floods." He began to make his cautious way across the yard. To have slipped would have ruined the whole delicacy of his gallant gesture. "Have you ever noticed, they carry women in a polite cradle, like this. Men they just sling over their shoulders."

They reached the car. George put Lily down. She was laughing.

"I can be quite gallant, if called upon," said George.

"You certainly can."

Was she grateful? Surprised? Amused? Hard to tell, George thought.

"Can't count the times I've had to lift a ewe out of a ditch. You can't weigh much more than a lamb . . ." He trailed off, aware his stalling tactics were petering out.

"Really?" She put a hand lightly, briefly, on his arm. Again, he felt their parting was endowed with the sort of merriment he had not felt for a long time, though he judged it best to keep this thought to himself. He wondered if she would suggest, with a tilt of her head, a social kiss of farewell, as she had when he had driven back after the picnic. But she got quickly into the car, pulling on her gloves. George wiped a glitter of frost from the windscreen.

"Thanks. Thanks for supper, too."

"If ever you're this way again," George heard himself saying, "well — you know where I am."

"I do."

When the lights of her car had disappeared round the corner, George, cold, returned to the kitchen. Her absence was acute, in the way that the overnight disappearance of snow that has lain for a short time, transforming all about it, takes some getting used to. George felt physically exhausted, but disinclined to go to bed. He would go up to Prodge and Nell for a nightcap, he decided. He hadn't seen them since the funeral. He needed them, his oldest friends, to restore his equilibrium.

A hundred yards from their house George came upon a car parked in the narrow lane. Lily's, he saw. He stopped, got out, puzzled. She appeared from the front of the car, where she must have been bending down. In the light from the unclouded moon George could see she carried the hectic remnants of a dead pheasant. She did not hold it at arm's length, but close to her body.

"Not me," she said, as George approached. "Must have been someone just before I got here. It was fluttering in the middle of the road, poor thing. So I wrung its neck. I was just wondering what to do with it."

"Here. I'll take it."

Lily handed him the bird. It was still warm, its body a bloody pulp that spewed from still-brilliant feathers. Its head flopped from the broken band of white round its neck. Its eyes were cynically half closed, as if it had always expected death on a midnight lane. George tossed it on to the sack that covered the back seat of his car. He returned to Lily.

"Blood on your coat," he said.

"No matter."

"That was a kind thing to do. I don't know many girls who'd —"

"I'm a country girl, remember." Lily smiled. "Brought up in Norfolk. I used to beat for my father when I was a child."

"Did you really? I used to do that, too. Five bob a day." The moonlit creature before him turned into a girl of eleven or twelve bashing at the bushes at the edge of a field of purple cabbages that clacked against her boots. He saw the pleased look on her face when a pheasant rose from the undergrowth and clattered up into the Norfolk sky.

"I must go," she said, "or I'll be locked out." She hurried back into the car: was gone.

As George drove into the Prodgers' yard, he saw Nell coming towards him carrying a dead chicken. I come upon two girls carrying dead birds within the hour, he thought. What's up? He could see Nell's was headless, a messy bunch of feathers darkened by blood. George got out of the car.

"About time," said Nell. "We haven't seen you for a week. Bloody fox." She swung the bird. "This one escaped being shut up. Go on in and I'll be with you in a moment." She moved away.

In the kitchen, a hundred times more chaotic than the one he had just come from, George found Prodge sitting in front of the stove, his legs propped up on its top. He wore the thick bristly socks that went under his boots, and tapped the stem of a pipe against his teeth. He was the only young man George knew who smoked a pipe, but the habit had gone on for so long that George was weary of teasing him. Prodge was instantly pleased to see him. He got up and poured a glass of whisky from a bottle embedded in the muddle of things on the table.

"Sorry I haven't been over this last week. We've been a bit rushed off our feet, both Nell's horses lame, vets coming and going. And anyhow we thought you'd be pretty busy sorting things out, knew you'd ring if you wanted us."

"There's been a certain amount to see to. Pretty grim, all the post-death stuff." George took the chair beside Prodge. From its split leather back a foam of discoloured stuffing threatened to irritate any head so foolish as to lean against it. Once lowered between its battered arms, he regarded the familiar facade of the Rayburn cooker, its enamel the colour of aged teeth, scratched and muddied. But in its old age there was no lessening of the warmth it produced. "The worst thing was giving Hollow her notice."

"Hollow? Going? You mean you're going to modernise things a bit, bring the old firm more in line with the twenty-first century?"

"Not exactly."

Nell came in holding out bloodied hands. She went straight to the sink, held them under a tap. The sound of the gush of water making its metallic landing in the old sink, mixed with the smell of pipe smoke and clothes touched with night-ice, was a combination so familiar to George, in this house, that it fed his senses with a comfort beyond compare. He sipped his whisky, a second warmth, keeping his eyes on the glass.

"I'm giving up the firm. Closing it down."

Nell turned off the tap. She came to kneel on the rag rug that covered the stone flags in front of the stove.

"That's good," she said after a while.

"That's right," agreed her brother. "I never reckoned your heart would be in any kind of office business. You're always happiest out in the open."

George was not surprised by their approval. For years they had always understood each other's plans and would not presume to question them. But he went on to explain a little of his reasoning, the fact that the firm had scant potential in the hands of one whose real ambition was to work on the land.

"But there's one problem," he ended. "I've a lot left to learn about farming, as you know. I only ever did a bit of casual labour — weekends, holidays. Helping my father. There was nothing he didn't know about it all. I never learnt about the science."

"No need to worry about that," said Prodge. "Science of farming? What do Nell and I know about that? Long as you watch carefully, think ahead, use your common sense, you learn as you go along. Besides, you've got Saul and Ben up there. Two exceptionally good men. There's little they don't know."

"I'm lucky there." George paused. "I'd like to buy a bit more land, couple of hundred more sheep."

"Good idea," said Nell. "Investment."

"I'll be coming to you for advice. You'll have to make sure I don't decide on some damn fool thing."

"You come to us often as you want," said Prodge. "Your father would expect our generation to work together, just as he did with our old man."

The three of them sat in silence for a while, envisaging George's future as a new, lone farmer.

"Of course," Prodge went on after a while, "owning your own place, you've got that difference going for you. Not that we don't love this place, slave our guts out to make it work. But there's always the thought in your mind: in the end it belongs to someone else. If things went wrong for us, we'd have nothing to sell, nothing to fall back on. We do quite nicely, but we're a long way off being able to buy something of our own.

We couldn't cope with a mortgage on top of all the other commitments, could we, Nell? Fact is, I reckon we'll always be tenant farmers."

This difference between his own status — the security of owned property — and that of his friends had always troubled George. He felt an irrational guilt, but knew there was nothing he could do to erase it. The fact was that his father, a lawyer by profession, was a richer man than Prodge's father, who had begun life as a farm labourer and become a tenant farmer at the same time as David Elkin had bought his farm. The properties, a mile apart, were very different. His was a large distinguished farmhouse (before it fell into decay) with three hundred acres and handsome outbuildings. This house, which old Mr Prodger had been so delighted to find, was small, unkempt, north-facing on a bitter hillside. There were a hundred acres and, initially, a scrawny flock of sheep. Gradually, some of the buildings were renovated and the flock increased: Will Prodger won many prizes for his sheep. He worked exhausting hours with help only from his wife. When her father, who had won a few thousand on the football pools in his youth, left her enough to buy a flat on the Costa Brava, the Prodgers' decision to leave was instant. They were worn out, longed for a few years of carefree life before they were too old to enjoy it. So the tenancy of the farm was passed to their son Prodge (as George, aged five, had nicknamed John) when he was twenty-five. Prodge, who had assumed that the chance to run the place himself would not come for many years, was invigorated by the challenge. Nell, who had

had youthful ideas of training young horses, abandoned the plan in favour of staying to help her brother.

They had lived on the farm all their lives, seen it develop with their help, had no desire to move. George, so close, was their constant companion. His years away at boarding school, then university, meant long partings. But reunions between the three, both as children and then as grown-ups, were never hard. They did not go in for the exchange of news: simply carried on wherever they had left off. As children it was the race to the top of a tree (George usually won). As grown-ups it was looking at progress on each other's farms: a new milking machine for the Prodgers' few cows, a new roof on the Elkins' barn.

"So how are you going to manage, alone in the house?" asked Prodge eventually.

"I'll be fine. Dusty's going to stay on, keep it in order for me. See to it I don't starve. She wants to keep on with a small job. I don't think she could contemplate leaving after so long, luckily for me."

Prodge grunted. A crooked smile began to crack his serious expression.

"Probably," he said, "what you could do with is a wife."

It was impossible for George not to notice that Nell, head down examining the weary old rug, blushed vividly. She laughed. But she always disliked it when Prodge made one of his teasing references to a future in which she and George married one day: good solution all round, in Prodge's opinion. They knew each other well enough. They'd make the perfect couple. Nell allowed a pause just long enough to convey how stupid she thought her brother was being, then she tipped up her ruby cheeks, looked George squarely in the eye.

"That's just what you need," she agreed. "You better start looking. Though where you're going to find one, these parts, God only knows." Her voice, straining for merriness, held a fine hairline crack. George smiled back at her, nodding.

"See what I can do," he said.

George was aware that Nell had had a profound attachment to him all her life. As young children, she had always stuck up for him in any argument against Prodge, and was always willing to carry out some task she thought would please him. Mostly, she did little to show her affection for fear of Prodge's teasing, but there were occasions when it seemed clear to George that he was one of the most important people in her life. Once, he briefly kissed her in East Coppice, when she was twelve, and he was fourteen. They had stopped to shelter from rain under the dense branches of an oak tree. Nell was holding a collie puppy, which squirmed and whimpered between their closely pressed bodies. Then Nell dropped the puppy and they drew quickly apart, horrified to think it might have been hurt. They were so busy checking that it was all right, comforting the small yapping creature, that neither noticed the other's cheeks rubbed to sore red, and the shakiness of their hands. Four years later, at a Young Farmers' Dance, George had kissed her again. This time, after no more than five seconds of blissful engagement, in which George tasted strawberries on her mouth and lodged

60

one hand on her collarbone, one on her waist, she resisted. She had removed his (amazingly controlled) hands and turned her head away with a small moan. Then she had resolutely walked away from him, a fan of material at the back of her skirt swishing from side to side, melancholy as a goldfish's tail. George had felt confused, sad, guilty. He hoped his crass gesture would spoil nothing between them, and evidently it did not. The next day he helped her load up the sheep for market. Nell behaved as if the crude attempt, and her rebuff, had never taken place. After that, George did not try again. He appreciated Nell was a friend as devoted to him as she was to her own brother, and in the same way. Sibling love, it was, and therefore not threatening. George also realised — with some relief — when they were teenagers, that Nell knew his own love for her was not the kind that would ever change from affectionate friendship to the scarier realm of lover. He imagined her ease with him came from sharing that relief.

The three of them sat round the stove talking, as they so often did, of sheep, market prices, hunting. When these topics were exhausted, they shifted to their store of mutual childhood reminiscences. These always caused them laughter and the astonishment that events of the past, however innocent, can bring in recollection. How foolish they had been, on occasions: how thoughtless, how wild, how happy. The thing that most intrigued him, said Prodge, was that their very different education had done nothing to sever their friendship. He and Nell had been to the local school, frustrated by the lack of available subjects on offer, and the large classes barely contained by too few overworked teachers. George had been to public school and university, and had thrived in the scholarly atmosphere. But these differences made no division between them. George made new friends and sometimes brought them home. But no one could replace Prodge and Nell in his affections. They in turn looked upon his new friends from a different world with interest, eager to like them, and safe in the knowledge that their position in George's life was unlikely to be usurped.

As children, only occasionally did they show any curiosity about his school life. Sometimes, sitting high up in their favourite tree, they would ask him for stories of ancient Greece or Rome. He was good at telling stories, they claimed, and listened to him for many hours. This pastime was only abandoned when, as teenagers, the appeal of visits to the pub took over. When George went up to Oxford, Nell looked wistful. In another world, she would like to have studied history there, she said. Keenly she questioned George, each vacation, about parties and tutorials: the wistful look returned with each description. Prodge showed no interest in George's university life, and turned down an invitation to spend a weekend there. By then he was working full-time on his father's farm, and his preoccupations were very far from those of his old friend. When George returned home he was anxious to talk about matters of the land, which he loved, to Prodge, while Prodge had no inclination to discuss things intellectual with George. This arrangement worked with a natural ease that gave no reason for discussion.

It was midnight when George arose to go. Nell came out into the yard with him.

"So you'll be home from now on?" she asked.

"Not entirely, for a few weeks. There's quite a lot of boring stuff to be done, selling up, closing down, writing to the few remaining clients. But I'll be home tomorrow afternoon for a meeting with the lads, get their views on what should be done. Then I'm going to creosote a fence." He glanced up at the moon. "I think I shall rather enjoy that."

"I can't hunt tomorrow," said Nell. "Both horses out of action. I could come over and help if you like."

"Why not? I'd like to know what you think about the barn, too. Whether it's beyond repair . . ."

"I'll be there." Nell nodded. George kissed her on the cheek.

"You run in," he said. "You'll freeze out here."

It occurred to him, driving home, just how much help Nell had been on the Elkin farm over the years. However relentless and exhausting the labour needed by her and Prodge on their own land, she always found time to come over to assist — frequently with the endlessly dull paperwork. David Elkin once observed that she came so often he scarcely noticed her. George guiltily recollected that he sometimes took her for granted, too. He would look into the office, see her at the desk, give her no more than a friendly nod. At harvest time she always lent a hand for no reward and, skilled as she was with birthing ewes, her help with lambing went way beyond the call of friendship. This was all wrong, George reflected. Very wrong. In future, as part of the general change, her help — and God knows how she made time considering all the work on the Prodgers' farm — must be put on some sort of formalised footing. He would speak to her about it. She would resist. He would insist.

Home, tired, he stoked the almost cold ashes in the grate. The flames of what now seemed a long, long time ago had died down to the odd firefly sparkle in the grey powder that had been such handsome logs. The picture came to George of Lily twirling her flame-lit foot, talking, talking: and of Nell, quiet on the rag rug, her pale countenance briefly disturbed by the deep blush. They were pictures with no thoughts behind them. He went up to bed.

George was both touched and impressed by the efficiency with which Hollow worked to close down the firm and put the premises on the market. He knew what heartbreak this last job must be causing her, and did his best to maintain a measure of sympathy just deep enough to provide comfort, but not so great that it would mean a fight against tears. He felt there was little he could do to help, unacquainted as he was with the years of records, filing and general paraphernalia, so he gratefully left it mostly to Hollow, who worked away throwing things out, packing in boxes only papers she thought might be of interest to George, to be kept in the farm attics. George himself worked hard on the composition of a letter to the remaining clients, suggesting they might like to move to Slasher, Reed and Hedley — a very different sort of firm, he was bound to point out, but doubtless able to provide an up-to-date service.

The premises of E, A & P were fought over by several businesses who judged that the view of the cathedral meant it was a valuable site. There was a secret bid. George thought how astonished his father would have been at the sum the building went for: in 1927 he had bought it for two thousand pounds. He was indeed surprised himself, pleased to think he could now buy more land and improve his buildings without a mortgage, and also put a comforting amount in the bank.

Just five weeks after breaking the difficult news to Hollow, he arrived to find her sweeping the floors of empty rooms. Walls and shelves were bare. The stalagmites of files had disappeared. The partners' desk had been moved to the office at the farm. The place now looked bigger — and pathetic, now that its shabbiness was fully exposed. George gave Hollow the antique clock, explaining its provenance. Hollow said she would prefer to unwrap it at home. Then George took her for a proper lunch, with sherry and red wine, in the dining room of the Bridge Hotel. She recalled for him several memorable occasions during her career working for the firm, and allowed herself two helpings of jam roll. When they parted, George gave her an envelope containing a cheque which would easily cover the refurbishing of her bungalow. He had learnt that this was her keenest ambition for her retirement. They shook hands, made no attempt at appropriate words of farewell. Hollow tipped back her head and in the last look she gave him, thought George, she was seeing not him but his father as the young man who had employed her forty years before.

CHAPTER
FOUR

The sky was a forest of dark clouds swayed by a slow wind. There was a smell of rain, warning of the downpour to come. In the poor light the view from the farmhouse was indistinct. Hills, valley and fans of leafless trees were affected by this twilight gloom, so strange in early morning.

George came out of the house in his father's leather jacket, some forty years old, infallible protection against the most bitter weather. It was to be his first day working full-time on the farm with Saul, who had been employed by David Elkin for the past twenty years. Saul's wife Betty inherited the village post office from her parents, and used to run it with a flair that brought customers from miles away. She died when their son, Ben, was four years old. Saul looked after the child with no help, while his sister-in-law, Jenny, took on the post office, which thrived just as well as it did in Betty's day. The child Ben spent every moment when not at school helping on the Elkin farm, and loved it. He could never be persuaded to go elsewhere for a holiday.

Ben grew up with ambitions to buy his own farm. As soon as he left school he was employed by Mr Elkin, and worked four days a week with Saul. A single free day enabled him to join a course in agriculture at a local college. While Ben admired his father's experience and wisdom when it came to animals and crops, he himself was determined to acquire some formal knowledge of the science of modern farming. Saul had never had the opportunity to go to an agricultural college, and privately thought common sense and experience was all most good farming people needed. But when Mr Elkin offered to pay Ben's fees, Saul wished his son well, and the theories Ben came home with made for lively arguments in the evenings.

Father and son were a good team: reliable, hard-working, of few words. George, like his father, trusted Saul's judgement, had faith in his advice. Under his guidance the farm had grown and thrived. The eighties were good years for British farming. Subsidies were high, farmers were comparatively rich. When profits were made, David Elkin would always give a bonus to Saul above his salary, and George had every intention of continuing this practice. Also like his father before him, George would be responsible for the paperwork, for Saul was a man by nature uncomfortable sitting at a desk struggling with figures that confused him. To be on the seat of a tractor, or with his stick behind a flock of sheep, whistling to his dogs — that was the point of farming to Saul. In his opinion, to fret over rule books written in incomprehensible language was a waste of precious time.

On the dark morning that George walked towards the lambing shed where last year's lambs were to be vaccinated and three lame rams were to have their hooves trimmed, he sensed the kind of pleasure — the kind of importance — that he knew would never have greeted him in a solicitor's office. Even on his short journey to the shed he saw there was much to be done. The yard was cluttered with obsolete rusting machinery and piles of plastic sheeting discarded from stacks of big-bale silage — for which, as yet, there was no organised method of recycling. Over flagstones, wood, bolts and bricks a veil of green algae had run rampant. The yard needed scraping, scouring. He would do it himself, this afternoon, George thought. For a long time he had known there was too much work for Saul and Ben, but his father had resisted a third helper. Now, his contribution would make all the difference. He delighted in the idea of the improvements that would be made.

In the shed — a vast building with corrugated roof and support beams cut from local trees — Saul was already in the aisle among forty young sheep he had brought in from their pasture. The chorus of bleating, in which individual voices were audible, increased as George came in. The sheep sounded like a bad afternoon in the House of Commons, he thought, smiling to himself. There was no return smile from Saul. Buffeted by animals, he held the vaccinating needle high, ready to plunge into the first sheep to hand.

"You're here, then," he shouted. Tersely, thought George. With a glance at his watch he understood why. He had promised to be here at ten o'clock. He was five minutes late.

"Sorry."

"You take the spray."

George picked up the aerosol can of blue spray and pushed his way in among the clumps of shifting wool of Exmoor Horns and Poll Dorsets. He had often done this job before, but not for a good many years. He wanted to watch closely, observe exactly how Saul, with the swiftness and skill of experience, went about it.

Saul grabbed a ewe, which bucked backwards in protest. He jammed it up against the rails of the pen. In a movement so fast it was almost invisible, he parted a clump of the animal's wool: the dirty white outer wool gave way to the pure cream of the wool near the skin. For a second there was the flash of a small pink star of flesh: Saul's needle shot in and out of this minuscule target. George sprayed a gash of blue on the ewe's spine. She was released. She kicked, moved away. The sympathetic bleats from the rest of the flock increased: or was it indignation, or anticipation of their own jab? George could not be sure. He supposed it would take a long time for anyone working with animals to understand their language. Saul moved on to the next sheep.

Grab, inject, spray, release: here was the rhythm old Mr Elkin so often said dominated life. George felt himself become part of a surreal dream. His legs were warmed by fat wool bodies, his hands were freezing cold. He was trapped in a whirl of outraged faces and oyster-coloured eyes — the Poll Dorsets had a particular look of indignation, like strangers on a bus. The Exmoor Horns, "stroppy buggers", according to

70

Saul, bred to withstand hard conditions on the moor, were more appealing with their close-set eyes and low, frizzy fringes. The faces of the two different breeds churned around George — their eyes, cautious, sideways-looking, never met his — they liked to keep their psychological distance. Their bleating became loud music turned up full blast, no light and shade, more of an atonic symphony than an uproarious House of Commons. George was suddenly aware of sweat running down his back. His hands were warm at last. Forty blue-marked spines shuffled: the job was done.

"Rams, now," said Saul.

They climbed into the rams' pen — three large creatures with camel faces of calm enquiry.

"Never so frantic as the women," said Saul. Quickly injected and sprayed, it was time for their feet. Saul, not a large man but with astonishing strength in his bone-hard flesh, flipped one of the rams ignominiously on to its back, supporting it from behind. It did not protest, merely glanced up at the roof with the kind of bored look an opera singer reserves for the highest, cheapest seats.

"You come and hold Hidden, I'll do the clippers," Saul commanded.

"Hidden?"

"Every time I go down to th' pasture, he be hidden."

George had but a brief look at the ram's indignity: front legs waving, stomach slouched like a beer drinker's, scrotum lolling to one side. He admired the way the animal seemed to have risen above any embarrassment, stared at by dozens of ewes it had served. At a look from Saul, and scoffing at himself for all this unbidden anthropomorphising, he quickly moved to support the surprisingly heavy animal.

With a skill that made it look easy, Saul cleaned out each cloven hoof in turn. George was aware of a bitter, sickly smell from the matter that was gouged out. Then Saul applied his clippers to the overgrown hooves: semi-circles of indigo rind dropped on to the ground of flattened straw. The whole business quickly over, the three rams, heads cocked back, eyes flaring, dignity restored, stood patiently waiting to be returned to their field. George wondered if he would ever be able to accomplish such everyday, humdrum farm tasks as efficiently as Saul.

Later in the day, having dealt with a pile of tedious paperwork awaiting him in the farm office, George returned to the shed to help with the ewes' evening feed. On the way there he met Saul returning the flock of ewe lambs that had been vaccinated that morning to their pasture. By now the sky had cleared of clouds: there was a low evening sun. George turned to watch the flock on its short journey. Saul's two dogs, obeying his quiet commands, kept the flock in absolute control — a feat which always filled George with awe. The sheep shunted along in a close crowd, each animals' armour of wool outlined in a halo of light. He was aware that this was a sight familiar to shepherds and farmers for thousands of years, and the thought kept him standing absolutely still until they were out of sight.

72

There was a final moment of private wonder in George's first full day of work on his own farm. In the shed — where the hungry bleating of the pregnant ewes was in full force — he and Saul heaved down bales of straw from the stack, cut their strings and tossed them into the pens. George copied Saul. He pulled the bales apart, scattered armfuls of the bedding on to the floor of the pens. The ewes, eager for a change of their diet of hay and silage, barged and crashed towards each new pile — greedy, selfish, intent only on their own satisfaction. In bending low to spread the straw evenly, George found himself head to head with four or five ewes: fringes, horns, wary eyes, smiling black muzzles, all within inches of him. He could feel the warmth of their breath. He was aware that their interest in eating straw was quickly sated. For a moment he had a sensation of knowing quite positively what it was like to be a sheep. He was one of them.

"No point 'n bending over, you'll do your back." George heard Saul's voice, stood up quickly. He was embarrassed, confused by his ridiculous imaginings. By now all the sheep were feeding. Some, sated, were already lying down chewing the cud, wrinkled eyelids at half-mast. A sudden quiet washed through the great shed as does silence after music. The ewes, soon to give birth, appeared to be relishing their last few days of peace before maternal responsibility overtook them.

"Settled down for th' night, then," said Saul. He was drawing the blinds down over the open sides of the shed. And yes, thought George, that's most probably all they were doing, simply settling down for the night.

Once again he scoffed at his own sentimentality: of course pregnant ewes did not think ahead like women. Perhaps they did not think at all, though looking at the intelligent cut of some of their faces that was hard to believe.

The two men walked back together to the farmyard in silence. They would meet again tomorrow morning, soon after seven, in the shed for the morning feed. The pattern of the days, months, years would carry on till they could work no more. Already George was beginning to understand his father's obsession with rhythm. For a farmer committed to the well-being of his animals, the growing of crops, the tending of the land, there was no escape from it. George was conscious, that morning, that he had finally stepped on to a treadmill that would become his life.

Saul went off to pick up his son who was at work on a job in the cowshed. George lit the kitchen fire, sat beside it. A pie Dusty had left in a chipped enamel dish that had borne pies for as long as George could remember warmed in the oven. Soon, he knew, he would be fit, muscles in trim. But this evening he sensed a frisson of physical fatigue. Beyond the ache in his back — and somehow confused with it — there was a yearning to talk to someone about his first day as a farmer. After he had eaten his supper he drove up to the Prodgers'.

Prodge's car was not there, and the kitchen was empty. George went to the small room leading off it that was known as the office. The chaos there was even greater than in the kitchen. A vast desk was buried beneath files and papers accumulated over many decades. But it was the warmest room in the house, home to the most comfortable, battered sofa George had ever slumped upon. For hours of his childhood he and Prodge had used its corduroy seat as a battleground, plundering each other with a mass of half-dead cushions that in quieter times flopped over its back.

Nell was on an upright chair at her spinning wheel. She looked up, pleased and surprised by George's appearance.

"What are you doing here?"

"End of day one as Farmer Elkin. I'm exhilarated, quite tired, though. I made the right decision. I did, Nell. I did."

"I can see you did."

George lowered himself into his favourite corner of the sofa.

"Where's Prodge?"

"Gone down the pub. Meeting some man who wants to help with the fencing. Want a cup of tea, a drink?"

"No thanks, I've just eaten. Dusty looks after me well."

"That's good. You need to eat properly, farming."

Nell's foot tapped away. She concentrated on a thread of wool the colour of oatmeal, reminding George of the flash of inner wool he had seen on the ewes this morning. He smiled.

"I think you must be the only person for miles — maybe in the whole of England — who in the late twentieth century would rather spend an evening spinning than watching television. There can't be many who even *know* how to spin these days. You make a very quaint picture."

"Tease me all you like. You've been teasing me all my life. Makes no difference."

Nell was wearing a jersey that George recognised was knitted from wool she had spun and dyed. She made her dyes from greater celandine, rhubarb, powdered madder, horsetail hair fern, walnut shells, gorse flowers, lovage and copper sulphate, dyer's broom . . . the names she had been mentioning for years came back to him in the quiet of the room. Once she had explained the technique of home dyeing. He remembered thinking the whole process sounded too complicated to understand, and had not paid much attention. But he did always notice the pale hedgerow colours of the jackets and jerseys she wore — thick, unfashionable country garments that would hold little appeal for the urban folk whose sartorial whims occasionally turned to rural life for inspiration.

"How did it go, your first day?" she asked.

"Odd. Extraordinary. I went through strange sensations. Something to do with the proximity to the animals, perhaps. I kept on feeling . . . I knew what they felt. Ridiculous, I know."

"We all go through that from time to time. But you'll learn to detach yourself. Treat the whole thing as routine. You'll be too busy to do much empathising. Just have to get on with the job, day in day out."

"Quite. That realisation, too, hit me hard. I mean, I've lived on the farm all my life, helped out quite a bit, but only in a dilettante sort of way. It didn't matter if I was there or not: there was always Saul and Ben. And my father making the decisions. But now it's my responsibility. And as for the physical work — well, I'm in poor shape. Office biceps, not that I was there long. Still, I'll toughen up in a month or so, I daresay."

Nell pushed herself away from the spinning wheel and sat with her back to the fire.

"You will." She held George's eyes, encouraging.

"I felt rather foolish," he said, "to have had such childish thoughts all day."

"No need to."

George shifted. With Nell, there had never been any need to be explicit. A few words were always enough for her to understand.

"Did Prodge tell you he'd finished his shed?"

"No," said George. "That's fantastic. I must go up and see it, but I'm very busy tomorrow. I've got to get the slurry on the fields before this cold snap breaks."

"He's the expert there," said Nell. "It's all rather exciting, isn't it?"

"It is. It is. I love the planning. But it's a bit unnerving, too. I mean, there's so much to learn."

"And do you think you'll ever get lonely up there?" The question was so lacking in both earnestness and guile that George was able to smile.

"I doubt it. If you set yourself a discipline, and have got plenty to think about that deflects thoughts from yourself, I doubt you can be lonely."

"Not many would agree with you."

"Daresay not."

"Goes without saying, if ever . . . I mean Prodge and I are always here. We don't like it if more than a few days go by without your coming over."

"As always."

"As always."

Nell rose, went to a cupboard. When she opened the door there was a landslide of old magazines and papers. She left them on the floor, picked up a box and returned to her chair. None of this, George could tell by the languor of her movements, was a hint for him to leave. Had she wanted him to go, she would have said so. She was forthright, Nell: always had been. Much more so than her brother.

She began to sort balls of her wool into matching colours. He watched in silence as she picked up each fuzzy globe and chose a place for it in the box. Her hands were small but blemished: farmwork had battered them. But Nell was the least vain woman George knew. It would never occur to her to spend time polishing her nails or pampering her face. Years of West Country wind and rain had burnished her cheeks to an eternal russet. Even on the rare occasions she was ill, or tired, it was hard to tell. This evening, contemplating her at her modest task, George felt a keen anxiety for her future. What would happen to Nell? Where, in her hard-working life spent mostly in this remote area, would she find a husband? He could think of no suitable, available farmer. Nell had often laughed about the shortage of men, but said she didn't care. Continuation of her present life was all she wanted, she claimed: she could think of nothing better. Though of

78

course, should some perfect man come along then she might consider a change. She had often declared all this to George, looking him straight in the eye. He would nod in agreement, thinking it inappropriate to challenge her further.

"Found anyone you fancy, Nell?" George had not planned this question. It came out lightly, jokily.

"No. Why? Where'd I find anyone?"

"I don't know. Out hunting."

"Well I haven't." She looked up from her wool. "Why are you bothered?"

"I'm not bothered, exactly. But from time to time I do wonder what'll happen to us, to you."

"I don't spend much time wondering. I'm just happy with things as they are. You know that. I've often said." She shuffled the wool again, rearranging balls she had just arranged with great care. Only the agitation in her hands gave the smallest clue to her feelings. "Prodge, though. There's some girl down in Tiverton with an eye for him." She smiled. "He's met up with her several times, market days. Bought her a few drinks. He says she's a good-looker. But I think she's leading him on."

"What makes you think that?"

Nell shrugged. "I get that impression, from what he says — and you know Prodge, he doesn't say much. Anyhow, I said to him, if you're thinking of bringing some girl here as a wife, upsetting all our arrangements, she'd better be a good 'un or I'm off."

They both laughed.

"Don't suppose it'll come to that," said George. "Prodge has never been the fastest man to make decisions. Any woman he chose for his wife would have to be unusually reliable. He'd have to believe in her potential as a farmer's wife before he made any move."

"I suppose so. But you know his moods. Sometimes he gets fixated on things. You remember how much he wanted to start a second herd, Jerseys? And how down he became when it didn't work out? Just hope he doesn't get obsessed with this Janine. Not that I've ever met her." She bit her lip. "And can't say I'm that keen to do so."

Nell put her box of wools on the floor — George could see how subtly they were regimented — and turned on him with sudden liveliness.

"And what about *you*? All these cheeky questions to me . . ."

George shrugged, laughed. "I've got a long way to go being a farmer. I'm not going to have much time for anything else, drinks on market days with girls." He got up. "Better get going. Early mornings every day, from now on. Tell Prodge I was sorry to miss him. I'll be back in a day or two, or you come over."

"I'll ride over soon as I have a moment," said Nell. "Take my chance before lambing starts." She led him to the back door, stood with folded arms as he kissed her lightly on the forehead. Then he strode into the moonless dark of the yard. "Bitter night," she said.

George drove the mile home slowly. He rounded the corner that would bring the view of the house and the one light in the kitchen which he had left on. But there was more than one light: several windows were amber bricks suspended in the intense darkness. George accelerated into the yard not knowing what to expect, alarmed. A small car was parked: he did not recognise it. He hurried into the house. Had he turned on more lights, misremembered? What had happened? George charged into the kitchen, heart quickening.

Lily sat at the table, a mug of coffee beside her, reading an old copy of *Farmers Weekly*. Beside her on the floor was a large suitcase. She looked up, smiled.

"George! Do you always leave the door open?"

Relief and anger clashed within George. He stared at her, unable to find words to express his annoyance. Gone, now, was the plan for instant bed, sleep. This intrusion would have to be explained. He could see he'd have to spend time listening.

"What on earth are you doing here?"

"I would have thought leaving the house unlocked, even in some remote place like this, was quite a risk."

"What do you want?"

"Oh, George. Don't be cross. I'm sorry. I should have warned you." Lily rose, holding the mug in both hands. "It was probably a silly idea. My car's full of watercolours I've got to deliver back to the old woman near Exeter. I was having a bowl of soup in a pub somewhere, thinking I'd better stay the night there, when it came to me: why not go back to George?" She shrugged, gave a slight giggle. "I rang you, but there was no answer. Perhaps it was foolish, such *spontaneity?*"

"No," said George. As he stood eye to eye with her, he could feel the ache in his back, drifts of sleepiness, fading anger and other, stranger sensations he could not put a name to. At their previous meetings he had vaguely sensed, though not positively registered, that she was beautiful. Now he saw that was definitely so, but the fact did not reduce his irritation.

"I'm sorry," she said again. "I can't make excuses. The fact is, the truth is, I was . . . drawn to this place. I thought about it a lot." She released her eyes from George's, looked round the room. George nodded. "I mean, of course I'll go now, straight away, if that's what you want."

"No, no," George said again, without enthusiasm.

"You don't sound overjoyed, but I'll only stay a short while. Be off at any time you tell me."

George sighed. "I'll show you the spare room and we can talk about your stay tomorrow. Tomorrow evening, that is. Be busy all day."

"Fine." Lily lowered her head, sending a shoal of hair across her face full of pale sparks from the table light. George picked up her suitcase.

"You don't travel lightly," he said.

"But I cover a lot of ground." If she was trying to sound enigmatic, George thought, she failed.

They went up the staircase whose failing joints groaned with various notes of discomfort as their feet weighed upon them. They moved along a dark passage whose wooden floors dipped like a shallow boat. Their footsteps were quietened here by strips of carpet, its ribs breaking through its pile, that George's mother had laid many years ago. He opened a door into a large room with a small window. There was a smell of mothballs, a suggestion of damp.

"This is it," he said. "Not very grand. Hasn't been used much since my mother died."

"It's fine." Lily's eyes journeyed over the dark furniture, the wallpaper of dun stripes, the sad little curtains, the bed plainly unmade beneath its cover.

"I'll get you some sheets."

George went to the cupboard in his bathroom. It housed a cladded hot water tank and shelves piled with linen. Its thick smell of warm linen was a flash of remembered childhood. George had often hidden in this cupboard, squeezed behind the tank, in games of hide and seek. He had crouched uncomfortably for ages, waiting for his friends to find him — which of course they never did, even when they opened the door for a moment, allowing him a small blast of bathroom cold air and a moment of light. He had thought it would be a good place to die, the linen cupboard. Now, standing helplessly in front of the banks of sheets, he realised it was the first time in his life he had ever had to choose a pair. Dealing with bed linen was a part of domestic life from which he had always been protected by able women — his mother, a scout at Oxford, Dusty. Jesus, I've been spoilt, he thought, and tugged at two sheets he hoped would be the right size.

In the spare room, holding them flat on his spread hands like a tray, he presented them to Lily. She had already hung a number of things in the oak cupboard.

"Shall I help you make the bed?"

"Course not."

"You'll be all right?" Even as he asked, George was aware that he did not care very much. The well-being of

83

an uninvited guest, in his fatigued state, lacked importance.

"I will."

"Tomorrow, help yourself to whatever . . . Dusty'll be here if you want anything. Take a look round the farm, perhaps."

"Don't you worry about me." Lily dropped the unfolded sheets on to the bed and came over to George. "I won't be a nuisance, I promise. I'll deliver the pictures then come back and go for a long walk. Then you can give me my marching orders tomorrow evening if you want. I won't take offence, I promise." She smiled, a little wearily. "But it's lovely to be back . . . Just *look*, George." Her arm swept across the vista of the room with a small jangle of bracelets. "Imagine how all this could be."

George, who could not imagine the room any different from its present cheerlessness, nodded. Lily's way of insisting on *looking* at things returned to him clearly, irritatingly. She would be not only an uninvited but also an exhausting guest. He would permit just a few days, then she would have to be off. George was about to put his hand on her shoulder, tell her this, when she moved away to draw the curtains. He said goodnight and left without further exchange.

In bed, the sheep-thoughts turned into thoughts of Nell: how to explain to her about Lily? Did he need to explain? And why should it bother him? No answers came before he fell asleep.

84

CHAPTER
FIVE

John Prodger woke with a feeling of uncommon well-being. Last night he had hammered the final nail into the vast edifice that was to house his sheep. By any standards it was a magnificent farm building, and a sense of quiet pride burned through him. With a roof of soaring corrugated steel supported by pillars of oak and other local woods, it was almost as large as the Elkins' sheep shed, put up the previous year. The difference was that whereas David Elkin had contracted a firm of specialist builders, Prodge had built his shed almost entirely single-handed. It had taken him over a year, working every spare hour when not attending to animals or land. And it had cost him most of the money he had been saving since he started work on the farm after leaving school, and the profits he had made since his parents had "buggered off to Spain", fed up with the relentless hard work, three years ago. These were the days of generous government grants. A large percentage of his building was supplied from tax-payers' money, but he still had to contribute more than he could afford to finish the work.

But it was worth it, thought Prodge. In the past the ewes had either lambed on the hillside — a risky business in bitter weather — or in a rickety old shelter, little more than a roof on stilts, which would now be pulled down. Prodge had designed every detail of the interior of his new shed: the aisles, the layout of pens and troughs, the ingenious way in which the barriers could be switched about to make compartments of different sizes.

Unbelievably, all was finished now, bales of straw and hay already stored to the roof at one end. Soon he would bring in the sheep to lamb. He had been aiming for this deadline, the end of February, and had just made it. Unbelievable, he said to himself again. He'd ask Nell to send his parents a postcard saying *shed finished*. He could just picture them on their blazing patio somewhere above Marbella (he and Nell had never been there and had no intention of going), sipping at their sangria, or whatever expats drank in Spain, and saying *unbelievable*, too. Pity they'd never see it.

There had been several days of drizzle and ill-tempered winds, but this was a fine pale morning, sky dragged with streaks of anaemic primrose. Prodge and Nell, as always, got through the early morning milking with a speed and efficiency that only come from years of working in harmony and wordless understanding. To Prodge the milking parlour (next on his list to be improved) was a place of the music he most loved: the bass clank of chain, the rhythmic swish of milk drawn from full udders. He clumped up and down the concrete gutters between the rows of stalls, wiping down his cows' udders, giving each one a single pat when he had finished. Since his father had left he had taken great care to build up a fine herd of Friesians: by now they were known to be the best in the district, many of them prize winners. In his heart, though he would admit it to no one, not even George, Prodge was proud of them, too.

At breakfast, he glanced at the local paper while eating the large plate of bacon, sausages and eggs that Nell had cooked for him. Normally they ate this meal in silence. Today, with one of her sly smiles, she ventured a question.

"So how did you get on with Janine? You were back late."

"All right," said Prodge after a while. Had not the thought of the finished shed filled him with such molten happiness, Nell would not have had the benefit of an answer at all. He rather enjoyed leaving her curiosity unsated: damned if he was going to tell her everything about the thin side of his life just because they lived together. But he could see how hard it was for her to resist another question, and admired her restraint. After a while, and several more rashers of bacon, he succumbed to her enquiring look. Fact was, Nell had come up with helpful suggestions concerning wayward girls in the past.

"Not much doing there," he said. "Don't think anything'll come of it. Not all she seemed at first. My mistake." What he kept from his sister was the brief disappointment he had felt last night. Janine of the scarlet lips and provocative cleavage was the kind of girl, in a bar full of country folk, to unground any of the young men for whom almost complete celibacy was part of life. A saucy little temptress, she was, down from Cardiff for a visit — though she did not say to whom — on the lookout for "local talent". She had accepted Prodge's drinks, flickered her eyes, given every sign that he was her chosen "talent". But in his car in the car park — impatiently she had rejected his idea of driving to somewhere more private — she had scoffed at him, called him a "bloody country bumpkin". Then she had stomped off, banging the car door so hard that the solid vehicle shook. Prodge, left in a state of ignominious disarray, recovered with a speed that surprised himself. Within moments of starting the journey home the disappointment was drowned by a tide of well-being at the thought of the finished shed.

"I'm going down to the shed," he said. "Think you ought to come and take a look."

"I saw it last night."

"Not in the daylight you haven't seen it. Finished."

"I've plenty to do, Prodge. It's not that I haven't admired every inch of your progress. There's a stack of papers waiting on the desk."

"Bloody papers. They can wait."

"Just for a moment, then."

In the shed, Nell silently marvelled. It was lit by a positive sun, now: ingenious design and beautiful carpentry uncluttered as they never would be again by animals, bedding and troughs of feed.

"You could've been a carpenter, my reckoning," she said, looking up to the roof. "There were times I thought it'd never be finished."

"There were times."

"You've done well. It's the finest shed for miles round."

"We'll bring the ewes in later."

"I'm taking Whisper out this afternoon, just a gentle hack, make sure she's OK. So after that."

"Fine. I'm off down to George's this morning. Wants to talk about his cows."

"Three, then, thereabouts.

"See what I can do."

On the drive to George, Prodge turned his mind to his friend's plan to increase his own small herd of Friesians: he wanted top-quality cows. Prodge enjoyed the feeling of being able to help. George had the money, was owner of a farmhouse and land and a good flock of sheep, but Prodge had the experience. He had learnt everything he knew the rough way. When his parents had made their premature flight to Spain, Prodge, by his own choice, had taken on sole responsibility: tenant farmer at the age of twenty-five. There were those in the locality who doubted his ability to make a go of it. The surly owner of the farm, who mercifully never interfered, made it clear that Prodge was on trial. He made a few mistakes, and the worries and responsibility of it all flustered him from time to time. But they were rewarding years in British farming — generous government help, good prices at the market. With Nell's constant, wise support and encouragement, Prodge made remarkable progress. Local scepticism died. He became confident, content and, from time to time, as this morning, pleased by his own ability to judge a cow as well as anyone in the West Country. To advise George on the creating of a first-class herd would not be difficult. He looked forward to one of their serious planning sessions in the small, warm study where they had played for so many hours as children. Prodge was always touched by George's eagerness to take up any suggestion, and now George was in charge he knew he would be called upon frequently, while George learned the ropes. The thought was a good one.

He found Dusty in the kitchen at the sink, polishing the taps. She was known for her prowess with taps. Wherever she went, she left shining taps in her wake.

"Hello, Prodge." She did not turn to greet him. Prodge sensed in the tense rise of her shoulders that there was the faintest sign of hostility, or perhaps disapproval. He looked down at his boots. Unusually, they were not muddy. He had not messed up her swept floor. Dusty's mood was puzzling, but Prodge had more important things to think about.

"George at home?"

"Upstairs." Still Dusty did not turn round. "Coming down."

Prodge saw that there was little chance of conversation with her this morning, so made his way into the study. The room was warm — the kind of pervading warmth that comes from years of lighted fires — a warmth always lacking in the Prodger household. There was a faint but unfamiliar smell in the air: Prodge could not place it. Some kind of flower, perhaps. But there were no flowers in the room. Since

George's mother had died the house had lacked flowers. He opened the window.

George came in, straw clinging to his shirt. There was something about him that made him look like a very new farmer, thought Prodge. Soon his shirts would be clogged with wear, his jeans would be threadbare and stained. Prodge was strangely moved by the sight of his friend, so eager to get on with being a farmer, looking so cleanly turned out.

"Sorry," said George. "I was upstairs looking out some books."

"I'm over about the cows."

"Right. Good. Thanks."

Prodge took his usual place in one corner of the ailing sofa. It whimpered as he sat.

"Shed's finished," he said.

"No?" George's smile was full of awe. "Christ, Prodge, you really worked on that . . . I must come up and see it. Bad day today. I'll come tomorrow."

"I'd like your opinion."

George sat in a wing chair, its leather as cracked and tired as old skin, by the fire. He looked through the window to the yard. As he gazed, so strange an expression crossed his face — somewhere between bewilderment and annoyance — that Prodge's own eyes followed George's. He saw an unknown young woman cross the yard, tossing her head, sniffing the air. She wore a longish skirt that blew out behind her, unsuitable for the farmyard. Mysteries suddenly fell into place: the flowery scent in the room, the fact that

George was "looking for books" upstairs of a morning. As George said nothing Prodge asked who she was.

"That's Lily Crichton."

"Who's she?"

George turned to Prodge. He looked faintly apologetic.

"A girl I met briefly at Oxford. She suddenly turned up in Exeter that time I was in the office after Dad died. I took her out to lunch — well, only to be polite. Then she came and had supper here."

"And?"

"Never expected to see her again." George laughed.

"Go on."

"But when I got back from seeing Nell last night I found the lights on. She was sitting here with her suitcase asking if she could come back for a while."

"What d'you make of that?"

"I don't know. I was too knackered to argue. I think she's here for a few days. As long as she doesn't make a nuisance of herself I don't really mind. Seems she's at a loose end."

"Funny, really," said Prodge. "I'm the one who'd like a wife and kids and bugger-all comes along. You don't seem remotely interested in all that kind of thing yet awhile, and some tip-top creature, far as I can see, drops out of the sky into your yard." He was silent for a moment. Then: "How're you going to explain this Lily to Nell?" he asked.

"Explain? There's no more to explain than I've told you. Honestly, Prodge. Come off it. She's no girlfriend. What are you getting at?"

Prodge shrugged. "Just this: you tell Nell carefully. You take care in the explaining."

"Of course I will. Nell's bound to laugh. She always laughed when the occasional girl turned up here."

"That's all I'm saying. You be gentle with Nell. Now, about these Friesians."

Later that morning George sat at the desk determined to deal with some of the paperwork that had accumulated since his father's death. Only once did he wonder where Lily might be, what she was doing. Except to hand her his old copy of *Wolf Solent* in response to her request for a novel — she had brought no books with her — they had had no communication that morning. By one o'clock, when George had had enough of the tedious figures and was hungry, Lily still had not returned. George ate his bread and cheese in the kitchen, the local paper his only companion. He wondered again what had happened to her, but forced himself to concentrate on a report about export regulations. At two he was due to meet Saul at the milking parlour to discuss a new extension.

Ten minutes before the appointment he walked out into the yard, glad to be away from the tedium of the desk. He decided to walk slowly to the parlour, giving himself a few clear moments in which to reflect on the advice Prodge had given him. As he left the house he saw Nell riding into the yard, straight-backed on her grey mare. Despite the chill she wore no jacket but one of her fuzzy home-made jumpers the colour of a celandine. When she pulled up, right by George, he put a hand on the single rein, patted the mare's neck.

When they were children Nell would ride over most days on one of her ponies. They grew larger over the years. More times than he could remember George had stood looking at her in the saddle, one of his hands on the rein as it was now. He had always found it hard to understand why the command and the assurance she displayed in the saddle disappeared once she dismounted. On her feet she was a physically strong figure, but the confidence in her own ability seemed mysteriously to evaporate. Only once, several years ago, had George ventured to talk to her about this. She had laughed it off, saying he was quite right: she was on top of things on a horse. Without the height and life it gave her, she felt diminished.

"Is she better?" asked George. He bent down and ran a hand over the mare's near fetlock.

"Much better, but I'll not trot for a day or two." Nell looked over the rising land behind the farm buildings. "It's nice up there. Sun."

"She's the best you've ever had, isn't she?" George gave the mare a final pat.

"She is. Worth all that saving for." She swung her eyes to the yard gate. Lily was striding towards them. "Who's this?" she asked.

Lily was beside George by now, scatty hair blowing about cheeks almost as highly coloured as Nell's. George introduced them with a slight, formal smile. He explained, first, his lifelong friendship with Nell — loyalty made him emphasise this. Then, smiling up at

94

her, he explained that Lily was someone he had met at Oxford. Nell smiled back, friendly. Lily's look went from one to the other of them.

"Where've you been?" George asked her. He would have given anything for this meeting not to have happened.

"Oh, I don't know. Walking. Up there." She nodded towards the land where Nell had been riding. Then she looked at Nell. "I saw someone on a horse. Must have been you." She moved a step nearer to George so that her arm brushed his.

Nell reissued her same polite smile.

"Are you staying?" she asked.

"Am I staying?" Lily directed her enquiry, with mock seriousness, to George. "I hope I am for a few days, if George will have me. I was just passing by, fancied a few days of country air."

Nell's eyes narrowed so slightly that no one but a friend who was used to her wide-eyed look would have noticed.

"Do you ride?" she asked.

"I used to," said Lily. "I'm a bit out of practice, but I love it."

"It's just that I've another horse that needs exercising. We could go out together one afternoon, if you like. They've both been lame so it would be pretty slow and quiet, but it's a good way to see the place."

George sensed the doubt in Lily's moment of hesitation, but quickly she made up her mind. She thanked Nell for the suggestion, and said she would wait to hear when Nell would like to go. Then she swung away towards the house, walking fast, mud-splattered skirt lashing round her boots.

George's hand returned to the mare's rein. He walked beside horse and rider through the yard gate, on his way to the milking parlour. They kept their silence till Nell had to turn off to return home. Then he looked up at her.

"She wasn't *invited*," he said. "When I got back last night I found her sitting in the kitchen."

"Cheeky bitch." Nell's next smile conveyed no false bravery. George was relieved to see she couldn't care less that some girl from his past had turned up. Nell must have judged very quickly that Lily was not the sort of character to settle in a rough farm-house, far from what she would call civilisation. She waved her whip and went on her way. A few yards from him she began to sing: she often sang out riding. Sometimes, on a still day, George could hear her pretty voice from a long way off.

Prodge reckoned he had half an hour to spare until Nell returned from her ride, when they would put the ewes in the new shed. He took his chance to look over hedges in the two high fields behind the farmhouse, check what needed doing. This was the time of year that hedges and fences had to be made secure, ready to turn out the ewes after lambing. No matter how much they were renovated one year, they were always in need of further repair the next. Prodge sighed. Hedging and fencing were not his favourite jobs.

He strode up the hill feeling a sharpness in the air that often succeeded a morning of winter sun. At the top he turned and looked down on the land he had known since he was a child, cared for since his parents' departure, but did not own. One day, he had always sworn to himself, he would. To date his ambition was still a long way off, but hope never left him: in these days of good subsidies, he and Nell were managing to save. In the next few years, he reckoned, he would be able to go to his landlord with a decent offer.

This overriding desire to acquire the land that he loved was what drove him tirelessly to work twelve hours a day — at times much longer — with no holidays, scarcely a day off. It was what produced constant adrenalin that pumped through his body, so that he could heave pitchforks of sodden bedding as if they were weightless, or carry a dead sheep over his shoulder, unbowed, to bury it. Prodge knew his ambition would mean many more years of the relentless work he had grown used to over the last ten years, but that did not daunt him. He was a patient man, single-minded, determined. One day this will all be yours, John Prodger, he said to himself, as he often did, at the top of the hill.

Today, for some reason he did not try to understand, he was aware of a sense of unease as he stood looking over the valley. From here he could not see the cows, but the sheep looked fine. The job of putting the ewes into the new shed was one he was looking forward to, so what was it that caused a speck of anxiety on the horizon? Prodge was damned if he could put a name to it.

Looking down he saw the distant figure of Nell on her grey mare walking towards the farm. That was it: Nell. That young woman he'd caught sight of at George's place this morning — he couldn't imagine Nell being very pleased about that. Exactly what his sister's feelings were for George he could not be sure. She had always acted like a wise protector, advising him against this girl and that who came down in his Oxford days. He couldn't recall Nell being strictly in favour of any of them — they were a pretty daffy lot, far as Prodge could remember — but Nell never seemed worried because it was quite clear that George had never felt anything serious, to date, about any woman in his life. He once said he was prepared to wait a very long time before settling down, and Nell and Prodge believed him.

Prodge hurried back down the hill cursing himself for the idle thoughts which had kept him from doing his round of the hedges. He did not want to keep Nell waiting. She had said she would be back at three, and she was. Always punctual, Nell. One of the many things he admired in her: always did what she said. He wondered if she had ridden over to George, caught a glimpse of this Lily woman.

His anxiety was soon abandoned. Nell merrily recounted her meeting with Lily — "not the usual sort of thing you see in a farmyard round here." She told him of her riding invitation to George's visitor. Prodge laughed. They'd make a rum pair, he said. But Nell's evident lack of worry about Lily was a relief: she was plainly fine — must even have taken to the girl if she offered her a ride. Thank the Lord for that.

Prodge helped Nell unsaddle the mare and turn her out into the paddock. Then they called the dogs and made their way towards the ewes that were to be herded into the new shed. Light-heartedness rose within him. The wind tugged at the bare trees. It was a good afternoon.

When George and Saul had finished their discussion about the extension to the old shed where the cows were wintered, they brought in the herd of Friesians for the afternoon milk. George had never felt the same fondness for cows as he did for sheep, but knew that a larger herd would be good business. He looked forward to the couple of dozen — or even more — new animals that he would acquire once the extension was complete. Development, expansion, production . . . those were all ideas that excited him. British farmers were some of the best in the world, and he was determined to be among them.

George found himself slow and clumsy at milking: he had much to learn. And Saul, less skilled than his son Ben, whose day off it was, was gruff in his commands. The process took more time than it should have done, after which they had to hurry over to the shed for the sheep's evening feed.

"Reckon Ben'll be down the pub straight after he's back from college," grumbled Saul as he thrust pellets into troughs. Not a man to comment when he was at work — he believed that to concentrate on one thing at a time was the art of life — this sudden outburst caused George to realise that the taciturn Saul was concerned about his son. "Reckon he's got his eye on some fancy girl, saw her there last night just as they were closing. Didn't like to ask what time he got back."

"But he did the cows."

"Oh, he took care of the milking. There'd've been trouble if he hadn't, wouldn't there? He's always up in the morning, I'll grant him that."

"He's a good boy," said George. "Hard to deny him a bit of fun. There's not much in the way of excitement round here for a lad of his age. Must be difficult at times."

"I had no fun his age, believe me," said Saul. Apparently put out by his own unusual confession, he stomped off without saying goodnight.

George himself was curiously reluctant to return to the farmhouse. He stayed a while in the shed, eyes running over the sheep. Hunger sated, most of them were lying down, jaws moving slowly, only the odd bleat cracking the quietness. George could not envisage the evening. How would it be, with the uninvited Lily? Would there have to be a formal discussion concerning the length of her stay? Would he have to give up an evening by the fire with the paper to keep making polite conversation? Would he learn anything of what was going on in her mind?

The kitchen was empty when George got back. Two places were laid at the table. He wondered if this had been Dusty's doing. Then he saw there was a small jug of primroses between them, and knew at once that it had not. Also, the fire had been lighted, and from upstairs came the faint sound of a Schubert quartet on the radio. A now familiar combination of annoyance, surprise and curiosity filled George's being. He poured himself a large whisky and soda and waited to see what would happen.

It was easier than he had supposed. Perhaps Lily had sensed that her presence was not altogether welcome. Perhaps equally she sensed that her natural exuberance, her irrepressible desire to urge George to *look* at everything, should be modified. She was not able totally to suppress her enthusiasm — about her long walks, the moor, the farm, the house — but she edited her keen responses to all these to no more than a few admiring adjectives. With some amusement George observed that she was reining herself in. Perhaps, after his cool response to her gusts of overblown delight the other night, it had occurred to her how dementing she could be.

In fact George did most of the talking. Surprised to find that Lily seemed interested in his plans to buy a new tractor and increase his herd of Friesians, he went on to explain that his ultimate ambition was to devise a strategy that might be of help to both farmers and the environment. What this was, exactly, he could not say, as it was not yet formed in his mind. "I'm waiting for inspiration," he said. "I may have to wait a very long time. But all of us who care about the corrosion of rural life have got to keep thinking, or future generations will never know the meaning of real country life." In the meantime, he added, having inherited his father's passion for hedges, he did his best to maintain those on his land, and to keep his copses in good order. "I don't ever want to be accused of robbing wildlife of its natural habitat," he said. Lily was a good listener.

"It's odd to think of you alone in such a big house," she said, soon after they had eaten and George was giving signs of retiring to bed. "It could easily be divided into two. You could have an entire family living at one end and not notice them."

George nodded. Her observation, it seemed to him, sounded innocent, and yet he could not help wondering if she harboured some devious scheme. Women were always wanting to change houses.

"So I could," he said, without interest, "but I don't think there's any necessity for that." He remembered to ask if she was comfortable in her room. She declared everything was perfect, the bed the most comfortable she had slept in for ages.

"And I won't get in your way tomorrow. I'll take the car to Dulverton, look around there, walk."

George hesitated. The things that had previously annoyed him about her were beginning to ebb. He felt a sense of guilt.

"You're a very good guest," he said. Lily laughed long enough to show her appreciation of his compliment, but not so long as to convey a sense of achievement. She said she would like to sit by the fire a while longer, and would put out the lights when she came up to bed. George left her. Not quite knowing what final gesture to make, he blew a kiss from the door: she did not appear to notice. Entangled in some reverie, her eyes were on the flames.

Lily stayed on quietly for ten days, her programme for the day always the same: off after breakfast, sometimes walking, sometimes driving. On her return she would go to her room, or the kitchen, with a book and her radio. She never went into the study, knowing it was George's place of work. Once, the day after the delivery of six new Friesians, George saw her standing at the field gate looking them over with what could have been judged as an expert eye. George, in conversation with Saul, beckoned to her. He wanted to point out why these particular cows had been chosen, and ask her opinion of his choice. But Lily waved, smiled, and wandered away. On another occasion he saw her riding across one of the high fields with Nell. Lily was on the grey mare, Nell on the friskier bay gelding. They must have made their own arrangements: neither had mentioned their plan to him. George smiled at the sight of them, relieved: it meant that Nell had taken to Lily, was convinced of the truth of the situation — that Lily was no more than an old, not very close friend who had asked herself to stay. What he refrained from adding was that by now he considered her a tactful, self-sufficient and in some respects delightful guest.

"Saw you and Nell riding," said George that evening.

"Did you? We were out for two hours. I loved it. We're going again tomorrow. I like Nell," she added. "She's the sort of woman I'd like to be, grounded in her life, happy with it, not yearning for some unknown

103

alternative. Not always having to curb an itinerant spirit, like me. God knows if I'll ever be able to settle down."

George nodded.

"I must say, I can't imagine you permanently anchored anywhere," he said. "Least of all in some remote place far from friends, fun, intellectual stimulus."

"Probably not. Although I can't imagine living in a city, ever. I'm rarely in my flat, it makes me restless. I need to be near earth, the sky. I've a friend in London whose windows only look on to the backs of other people's houses. I couldn't bear that." She paused. "I have to confess I've consulted a few local estate agents. It occurred to me that a minuscule cottage down here somewhere might be the answer."

George frowned. "Found anything?"

"No. And of course you don't approve of those townspeople who buy rural cottages as playthings, hardly ever visiting them but able to pay prices for them that the locals can't begin to afford —"

"I don't, no."

"Well, don't worry. Apart from anything else, I don't suppose you'd want me as a neighbour. In the district, even."

"Why d'you say that?" George smiled, but she was not to be humoured. "I wouldn't mind."

"It's all a silly dream," she said. "In fact, I've got to work out which of my freelance jobs to keep on, which to give up, and settle down to hard work. At the moment I'm just shifting on various tides. Not very satisfactory."

The evening of Lily's second ride with Nell she made a chocolate mousse for supper — not something in Dusty's repertoire — and called it "a small contribution". When George complimented her and ate three helpings, she blushed and swung her head, making a thousand lights in her shiny hair. George's pleasure evidently charged her with courage. She asked about Nell.

Theirs was a friendship that had lasted since they had been young children, George explained, although he knew Lily was already aware of this. It had survived his absences at school and university, his travels abroad and his working in London for three years, he went on. It had survived his previously very different life.

"Whenever I came back, there they were, Nell and Prodge, just the same, working hard, not wanting any other life. They took on the farm at a very young age, and have made a remarkable go of it. Prodge's judgement is respected for miles around, and everyone loves Nell. She's a magnificent horsewoman — if she wasn't so busy farming, she once told me, she would like to have bred horses. You should see her out hunting. Jumps everything. Absolutely fearless." He paused. "And then she's the kindest soul in the world. She'll make time for everyone, drive twenty miles to spend an hour with a lonely widow. When my mother first died she was round here all the time, just a child, then, but instinctively coming up with things to deflect Dad and me from our gloom. Of course, she's a stubborn old thing. She's no time for social niceties, and lots of people think her eccentric, quaint: her dyeing and spinning and so on . . . her hatred of television, which Prodge insists on, her dislike of many changes in the modern world. She's bound to standards that she believes in, doesn't care a damn what people think of her." He dragged his hand through his hair, aware that he had been running on too long. But Lily's eyes were still enquiring. "She's probably the woman I love most in the world," he added, "but she doesn't know that."

Lily's reply was a silent nod of the head. Then she came over to George, eyes a touch wistful — though he might have been imagining it, for in candlelight melancholy is easy to see — and kissed him on the forehead. Surprised, his actions were slowed. Before he had time to react she had darted away and out of the room.

When George came into the house later than usual the following evening, he found a note on the kitchen table.

Dear George, he read, I think it's time I was off now before I outstay my welcome. In all honesty, not much of a welcome. No enthusiasm for my presence showed through your politeness, and I don't blame you. It became quite apparent in my (lovely) time here that I should never have done anything so untoward as to foist myself on you like that. A grave mistake, and I'm sorry. You're plainly in absolutely no need of a companion. If I

106

had thought about it more deeply I would have realised that was hardly surprising — father not long dead, the major decision of selling the firm and turning yourself to the all-consuming occupation of farming. What a rotten time for me to arrive out of the blue. Please forgive me. Enthusiasm has so often been my downfall. I get blown away with the excitement of some idea, then act foolishly without thinking. I won't bother you again.

I'm off now to Norwich. Have to review an exhibition of Rosie Cotman's watercolours. Then I might move on up the coast to a place I love as much as your part of the country. Good luck with the Friesians, lambing, the making of an even more rewarding farm. I envy your certainty. I admire it. I love the idea of your life. Please give my love to Nell, I left without saying goodbye as I couldn't find her or Prodge. And love to you, L.

George sat down. He read the note several times, appalled.

The thought of his uncharitable behaviour, blasted at him by Lily's note, was what most disturbed him. How could he, a man so sensitive, he had always thought, to others' feelings, have been so churlish? So unkind? Lily, after all, had offered to leave the evening she had arrived. When he'd agreed (yes, reluctantly) that she could stay, she had responded very quickly to his irritation by quelling her natural ebullience and becoming a perfect guest — never in the way, never intruding. Now he thought about it, she had gone out of her way not to annoy him. In fact he could not think of a single thing Lily Crichton had done wrong while she was here. While she had tried, and changed, he had responded by not trying, and not changing. He could only hope that if she looked back on his churlish behaviour she might remember, too, the few times when there seemed to be some flare of warmth between them, some charge lighted by each other's presence.

George's immediate idea was to get in touch with her and apologise. It was he who should be asking forgiveness. But then he realised that was impossible: he had no idea where she was apart from being somewhere in Norfolk, or even where she lived in London.

He continued to sit at the table, heavy with shame, unable to explain to himself why he was so unaccommodating to women. Nell was the only one who understood his perversity, though she did not condone it. She expected nothing but loyal friendship from him, and it occurred to him now that he often took advantage of that friendship, relying on her to do things that she would never refuse. Yes, the disagreeable truth was that he was often less than thoughtful where Nell was concerned. This was usually due to preoccupation with work, rather than calculated, but the effects were the same. The irony here, George reflected, was that it would be Nell who would benefit from Lily's message of horrible truth. As she was the one still here, she would be the one to gain from George's new ways, since he intended to change. He might never see Lily again, and could live with that. But Nell: the thought of life without her, their roles clearly defined, was inconceivable.

After a while George took a casserole left by Dusty out of the oven. He then noticed that the table had been laid for two, so obviously Lily had said nothing of her departure to anyone. She had just gone, perhaps on the spur of the moment, disappointed that her idea of coming here had not turned out more happily. Presumably she had no desire ever to return, or to see George again.

He shook his head and poured himself a strong whisky, hoping it would dull his guilt and regret. Then he put away the knife, fork and glass that had been intended for Lily, and without relish began his solitary supper.

CHAPTER
SIX

Even as a child George had fought against the innate sense of caution within him. In his grown-up life he fought harder, though often with no success. The wildest thing he had ever done, he reflected in his shaving mirror the morning after Lily's departure, was to sell the family firm and opt to be a full-time farmer. The shadow of caution which naturally clouded so many of George's decisions, had for once not descended. Guilt had been there — the throwing away of all that previous generations had put into the building of A, E & P — but he now regarded the sale of the antiquated firm without sentimentality. Besides, the old man had always advocated that to try to do two jobs at once was not ultimately satisfactory: to maintain solicitors' office hours and run the farm, even with two reliable helpers, was often difficult. David Elkin, as George told himself frequently in the days after the sale, would have been delighted by the thought of further expansion and improvements to the farm.

It was caution in matters of the heart that struck George most forcibly. When he pondered on this he wondered at its cause: he was not a coward, not afraid of being hurt, not against keeping the rules of a temporary arrangement. But he was also not a man naturally inclined to dare in order to know. He inwardly confessed it was not so much the daring that alarmed him as the *knowing*. Simply (shamingly, perhaps), where women were concerned, he did not want to know too much. He found their need to confess what troubled their souls a burden — usually of no profound interest, and nearly always lacking in humour. The reticence he preferred, the delight of gradual discovery, was deeply unfashionable. He knew that such stern prejudices meant he was left with few girls to choose from, but this did not much trouble him. He did not want to be involved in the whole palaver of temporary relationships.

At Oxford he had seen many of his friends begin by professing their desire for and love of independence, then change their minds on a whim. Suddenly they would team up with a like-minded girl and declare that their new-found lusty companionship had put paid to all previous, foolish hopes of remaining happily unattached. Oh, he had witnessed it a dozen times — "the first, fine careless rapture", the enthusiasm, the hope. And then, often because of the restrictions of student life — exciting love and producing essays on time being incompatible — the paling, the waning, the ending. Rarely the relief. George had given what comfort he could to many a broken heart — with a certain smugness in his own, knowing that the caution within him would swoop down at moments of danger so he was safe from such *mess*.

As an undergraduate, therefore, he was considered a cold fish. He was aware of that. He was also aware that such a reputation presented a challenge. Cold fish are to be won over. Several girls tried. George did his duty by them: often he enjoyed their companionship, their friendship. But as soon as the familiar signs appeared — he sensed a girl was suddenly closer to him than he was to her — his self-protection clocked in and he faded away. He had no wish, as he always, fairly, made it plain, for either commitment or regularity. He did not want to be part of a couple. He genuinely treasured his independence, was in need of bouts of solitude (something few girls understood or cared to contemplate). Such an uncongenial attitude disappointed many of those who pursued him — Serena most of all, who had wrongly assumed she was "getting somewhere".

Since leaving Oxford, on his travels and during his working year in France, "there had been girls", as he told Nell when she enquired. But, as she rightly guessed, they had been of no consequence. In fact they were of so little importance in the general scheme of his life that there had been no need to put up barriers, for not one of them was a threat.

The only girl he had ever unquestioningly loved was Nell: and that love was not of the heart-stopping, interfering kind. It was the love of siblings — unshakeable, unbreakable. Nell was strong, singular: not a recognisable type — her moorland upbringing saw to that — but a strange, original creature. He trusted her, relied on her. She played a vital but undemanding part in his life. He believed their understanding of each other formed the kind of cohesion that he would hope to find, in some vague future, in a wife.

With Nell there had never been a need for caution. And with Lily, in the brief time they had spent together, there had been no need for it either. Lily was no more than a friend, not particularly close, often annoying, but it would be foolish to deny that there was something about her which, had she stayed longer ... As it was, she was gone before George was faced with any such decision, and he liked to think he was glad.

Such a plethora of morning thoughts were brought to an end by his need to make early farm-business calls. Today he was not helping with the morning feed for the ewes, and when the telephoning was done he ate his solitary breakfast. He had come to enjoy the ritual — silence while he eked out his coffee, gathering energy for the rest of the day's labours. The agreeable thought that came to him of going up to admire Prodge's finished shed was interrupted by a bang on the window. It was Ben.

"First lamb," he shouted. "Dad says it's a big 'un."

George hurried out, childlike excitement rising. First lamb on *his* farm ... But before he could leave the house the telephone rang. Nell.

"Is Lily there? We had a plan to ride again this afternoon."

"You've missed her. She left last night, I'm afraid."

"*Left?*"

"There was a note. Something about having to go to Norfolk to review an exhibition. Didn't she tell you her plans?"

"Never said a word about leaving." Nell sounded disappointed. "I thought she was enjoying herself, riding and walking. Very strange."

"I don't think she left because she wasn't enjoying herself . . ." George was aware of an edge in his voice which he knew would not be hidden from Nell. "Perhaps it was just a sudden work thing. Though a bit odd, I agree."

"Well, if she gets in touch, tell her to come back. It was nice having someone to ride with."

"I don't know if I'll *urge* her to return," said George, forcing a laugh. "But I'll tell her you were sad to have missed her. Look, I've got to hurry off to see our first lamb. I'll be up later to heap extravagant praise on Prodge's shed."

Outside, there were intimations of spring. George loved this moment every year — those few days when the weather hovered between temperate and vicious: when a haze of green was still far off, but buds were already precisely formed. But for all the delights of a sharply edged morning, in the back of his mind a faintly disturbing question hung like an icicle against the sun: had he offended Lily so deeply he would never be forgiven? And why did the thought of not being forgiven chafe at him so?

No answer came. And here was the first lamb, rocking and twitching on the wet straw as its mother licked away the caul. Its nose was starry with mucus, its black legs aquiver as if four invisible winds of different strengths were assailing the tiny limbs. The afterbirth lay beside the ewe, a glistening jelly beneath a small halo of steam, indicating its recent arrival. There was a mauvish smell of birth above the deeper scent of acrid bedding. From the neighbouring pens came a chorus of approval from the other ewes awaiting their own labour. George's earlier moment of amorphous guilt and anxiety was extinguished by this powerful rite of spring. For a few moments he was lost in the wonder of it, but kept his silence for fear of Saul scoffing at such sentiment. His contemplation was interrupted, in any case, by a red-faced Ben.

"There's another one just starting up over there." He pointed to a far corner. "Dad says it may be a bit of trouble. Chance to learn you how to put your arm up a ewe's backside, he says."

With an extraordinary sense of purpose, and determined to do well, George followed Ben to the single pen where a ewe jerked in discomfort on her bed of newly tossed straw. Saul was kneeling beside her.

"You come right here, George," he grunted. "Put some of this on, then do as I say." He handed over a tube of lubricating gel and George set about obeying instructions. Within a moment or two the hand that had plunged with curiously little distaste through the animal's vulva was defining legs, hooves, a head that twisted when he touched it: a small struggling creature in the warm mush of its mother's womb. He began to pull, to ease, talking gently to the ewe all the while.

"We're getting there," Saul muttered — grudgingly, George thought. "Fact is, you're a natural shepherd." He gave one of his rare smiles. A moment later the lamb emerged from its mother's parted flanks, slopped on to the bedding. George, Saul and Ben looked down on it: a lamb, potentially at risk, saved. The mother tired but fine. The satisfaction of the moment was shared by the three men. But there was no time to linger in triumph: there were others bleating for help.

For the next few weeks lambing occupied the majority of George's waking hours and he learnt the meaning of exhaustion. He, Saul and Ben devised a rota of shifts, two on, one off, to attend to the birthing ewes. Ben was also in sole charge of the cows. George tried to keep pace with the paperwork, and in any spare moment Saul occupied himself with general farm duties that could never be left. After one long night shift George, coming to relieve him, found Saul scraping the yard with the briskness of one who has had a good night's sleep. He was a man of rare strength and energy for his years, but the perpetual long hours of hard work and little rest had ground into his face a series of cavernous lines that added a decade to his real age.

The three men were rarely able to sleep for more than four hours a night. Ben and Saul, used to this yearly routine, increased the economy of the words between them — on occasions they snapped at each other, and once George saw Ben put down two full buckets of beet pellets and stomp out of the shed, leaving his father to fill the troughs. "The boy's wanting

116

a good night's sleep," Saul observed to George, a trace of a sneer in the admission, as if he himself was in no need of any such thing.

To begin with George was convinced that lack of sleep was something that would little affect him, but after three nights of just four restless hours, the deprivation began to tell. The profound longing to stay in bed when the alarm went at two or five o'clock in the morning, or whatever the time for his turn, was familiar from days at university, when after a very late night he needed to get up to concentrate on an overdue essay. He could cope with that. He forced himself to spring out of bed — not allowing himself a moment's thought of luxury denied — and thrust his head under a cold tap. After a cup of very strong coffee he felt energy begin to move within him — but it was a false energy produced by caffeine, far from the profound sense of well-being that came from his normal nights of deep sleep. Later in the day he would feel a heaviness of head, an invisible sheet of steel pressing down on him, confusing. Sometimes, when he drew himself up after bending over, he had the sensation that clappers had lodged in his skull: they swung from side to side, as if in a church steeple, unbalancing him. And then at times his limbs became clumsy, his fingers dithered over cutting or tying or picking up, and rage against his own incompetence flared within him. Once Saul observed his slowness in opening bags of feed. "You may be dog-tired, but you just have to keep going," he muttered without sympathy.

There was no more time for poetic reflections on the birth of sheep, the wonder of new life. Though inwardly his awe at the safe arrival of each new lamb did not diminish, George began to understand Saul's apparent gruffness, his lack of sentiment or emotion. Helping ewes to lamb was just another job, he began to understand, and a bloody hard one. Although no birth was quite the same, there was a repetitiveness to it all: on occasions George felt that if he had to inspect one more bulging vulva, clear up one more deposit of glistening umbilical cord, he would do something foolish.

Sometimes death would jolt the routine. An old Poll Dorset died giving birth to twins. Saul's only comment was that he thanked the Lord it wasn't one of the more agreeable ewes who'd been called to the eternal sheep pen: this one had always been a right bugger. He and Ben dragged the animal out of the shed, apparently impervious to her death. George was left to choose a foster mother from the few ewes whose lambs had been stillborn. He chose one with — he hardly dared admit it to himself — a kindly eye, that he had been with at four o'clock one morning when her own black, lifeless lamb was born. It had slipped from her so fast that George, his eye on another ewe about to give birth, had missed the moment of its exit from the womb. But he saw at once that it was dead. Under the low, shaded light it lay shining like a slug, its head craned back, its eyes never to open under a web of viscous membrane gathered in the womb. George rubbed his hands hard over his face, glad neither Saul nor Ben was there to see

118

his pity. Then he slung the lamb into a sack, took up a spade and carried it off to bury it. It was a cold dawn. A transparent moon was jostled by uneasy cloud and a mist, waist high, rose from the dark ground. On the hillside George thrust the spade into this mist, unable to make out the ground he was digging. He had to wait for an hour until there was enough light to see clearly, and worried that he should be back in the shed. But he could not face leaving the dead lamb unburied in its sack.

After a couple of weeks of this exhausting routine, George was pleased to find he was becoming accustomed to the lack of sleep. He was toughening. His head still spun, or rocked, and from time to time he tried to shake off the weight that pressed down on his skull. But the heavy-limbed, zombie-like feeling disappeared. He was pleased by this progress, and noticed that the occasional scorn in Saul's eyes was replaced by something near to approval. But still, on occasions, he had moments of such dense tiredness that he doubted the nature of his own judgement.

One night, close to midnight, coming home from a long shift in the shed, he walked towards the farmhouse wondering whether he could be bothered to cut himself a slab of pork pie before dropping into bed. He was cold, aching, stumbling.

To his surprise there were lights in several of the windows. When he had gone out, six hours earlier, he had left on only the kitchen light. Or had he? George, confused, went through the door. By now he could not be certain he had not turned them on, though no picture of himself in the act of putting them on came to him. For a moment he was alarmed: then the solution came to him. It was Lily. That was obviously it. Lily had suddenly returned — although her car was not there. With a certain eagerness, despite his weariness, he hurried to the kitchen. It was empty, but tidy. Dusty had left a pork pie and tomatoes on a plate under an old meshed dome. George, no longer hungry, went upstairs to the guest room. The door was shut: the room was empty.

Silly mistake, he thought, still puzzled about the lights. Too tired to dwell on it, he hastened into his cold bed. The last picture in his mind, before sleep overcame him, was of Lily sitting by the fire twirling her ankle. He did not dream of her. The next day, when he rose at five, the lights in the kitchen were turned off, and now he could not remember putting them off. He came to the only possible conclusion — lack of sleep plays tricks on the mind. He would be glad when the lambing season was over and a less harsh routine resumed.

Nell came over one afternoon soon after that. George had fallen asleep on the sofa at the end of a long shift. She woke him with a cup of tea.

"You'll get used to it," she said. "Next year you'll be hardened to little sleep. It won't be nearly so bad."

Hardened as she was herself, Nell, despite the weather-burnish of her cheeks, looked pale. George liked the idea that for all her experience of the tough life of a farmer, her resilience and strength, even she looked in need of sleep at lambing time. It made him feel less feeble. They had had a busy time, she said, and so far only a couple of lambs stillborn.

"And I heard from Lily this morning," she added, after a pause.

"Oh? I've not heard a word."

"Just a postcard. She apologised for going off without saying goodbye. She said she was staying in Norfolk for a while. She said . . . she hoped we'd be able to go riding together again one day. She'd enjoyed that."

"But she didn't say anything about coming back?"

"No."

"She's a bit of a mystery figure, Lily. I don't know what to make of her. To be honest, I don't think I treated her very well. I found myself ignoring her, not at all sure I wanted her to be here."

"You weren't very welcoming, no."

"Did she say anything?"

"No, but it was easy enough to see. I think she felt she'd made a mistake, coming here."

"Oh God. Her timing wasn't good — Dad's death and everything — but that's no excuse. I'm sorry, I'm guilty. But I don't see what I can do." He rubbed both hands over his face, as if washing. "Did she by any chance give you an address?"

"She didn't."

"Then what —?"

Nell stood up, took George's empty cup from him. "You could think of something, I daresay. But there's always the possibility you're the last person she'd want to hear from. I'm off. Prodge insists we don't need any

121

help, lambing on top of seeing to the cows. But I'm not sure I agree with him."

"I could come over, give you a hand later on this evening."

Nell gave the faintest smile. "You've enough to do here. But thanks."

When she had gone George slumped back on the sofa. He could hear a tap running in the sink next door, the chink of china cups laid to dry on the draining board. Good, kind, strong, thoughtful Nell.

He had intended to have a couple of hours' sleep in bed before the six to midnight shift. But it was a fine evening, and the idea of sleep suddenly held no appeal. He wanted air, exercise, head soothed by the clouds.

George climbed the high ground behind the farmhouse and stood looking down on the familiar patchwork of his fields and woods, the blade of river in the valley, the landscape cobwebbed in silvery light from the sky. Down on the farm he could see the miniature figure of Ben urging the cows from the shed to the milking parlour, and wondered how many thousands of times he had gone through this routine in his working life. In winter, most of Ben's day was spent in the shed or the parlour: it was non-stop feeding, scraping, milking, attending to the calves. Ben's only occasional release from this discipline was to spend an hour or so hedging, a job he loved. No wonder that in the winter months his young face grew pale. But he never complained.

George watched his Friesians slowly plodding their way to the parlour, their short daily journey causing them no hurry or surprise. Then he turned to watch two rooks nearby fighting over the small carcass of some animal, their ruffled blue-black feathers parting to expose shocking white skin which reminded him of his first day with the ram. Their shrieks, sharp as metal, jarred the silence. George moved nearer to them. They flew away.

The harshness of their voices set up a nagging question in his own head: could Nell be right? Might Lily, so unfairly treated, want never to see him again? What, if anything, could he do to make amends?

As George strode along the top of the ridge, valleys clearly defined in their winter bareness each side of him, he felt like a man emerging from a chrysalis. The realisation of his unforgivable behaviour, not only to Lily but others, so heavy upon him of late, rolled away. It left in its wake a lightness of being that comes from redemption, the charge of adrenalin that comes from resolution. He turned and looked down on to the distant huddle of slate-roofed buildings that were his part of his farm, and knew he would return to them a different being from the man who had set out to walk not an hour ago.

George began to hurry. Plans jostled within him. He had never felt less tired. The night ahead would be significant because it would be the night before the day on which he would act . . .

The next morning he drove to the city for a meeting with his bank manager to make arrangements for the large cheque that had come from the sale of the firm. He had a quick sandwich in the bar of the Bridge

Hotel. On his way out he stopped at reception to enquire whether one Lily Crichton, who had stayed a couple of nights some weeks ago, had left her address. The receptionist, an old friend of Hollow's, and whom George and his father had known for years, wrote it down for him. Of course, he thought, he could have come up with this solution as soon as Lily had left. But something had kept it from him, holding him back until now, the right time.

George hurried home to send a postcard. *Do come back*, he wrote, *if you can forgive my churlishness*. Pausing for a moment to scour his soul for the absolute truth, he decided to admit it. *I miss you very much*, he added.

He regarded his own message with some surprise. Its honesty struck him blindingly. He did miss her. He had been missing her, though unable precisely to understand this state, ever since she had left. Luminiferous Lily: a bringer of light, a kinsman of beauty. She had brought something into the chill of the old house, and had taken it away with her. He would like her to return, trailing the singular warmth that had so changed the rooms. George drove with his postcard the two miles to the nearest post office. He hoped he was not too late.

It was a mild spring that year. By the beginning of April all the ewes had lambed and those with just one offspring had been returned to pasture. George returned to the luxury of nights without shifts in the shed, and within a few days the fatigue that had gripped him for the past few weeks evaporated. He turned his mind to the business of increasing his herd of Friesians, and the spreading of organic fertiliser. He enjoyed that job: jogging up and down the fields on the tractor, alone in a small world of the bright papery green of early April, trees suddenly fuzzy with new leaf and blue skies, no longer weighed down by winter cloud, that seemed to rise higher in the hemisphere.

Several weeks passed with no word from Lily. George was driven to think his appeal to her was too late. She was not interested in his change of mind: he had had his chance, she had been there for him, and he had spurned her. Or perhaps she had not received his card: that was his last hope. Perhaps she was still in Norfolk, had not returned to London and found it.

As time went by this seemed unlikely, and George was forced to fight against the regret within him. He tried to put her out of his mind. But there is cruelty in the remembrance of things foolishly committed, and this was hard. Moments that had seemed of no significance at the time returned to him, battering like pellets against glass. He remembered the odd, elegant way she had of running up stairs or steps, her back straight, like a dancer's. He remembered the way she would try out on him a shy smile, and once she had seen it was not rejected by his look, how she would allow it to burst into the most dazzling smile he had ever seen. He remembered her knack of imbuing small, domestic acts in an indefinable way of her own that gave to a perfectly ordinary evening a significance that was almost unnerving. And now he missed all those things. In each of the many pictures that came back to him was always, in the background, the sight of himself — glowering, cold, unsympathetic.

One afternoon he finished in the fields earlier than expected, and knowing there was an hour or so to spare before feeding the mothers of twins or triplets still in the shed, he intended to concentrate on some paperwork. There had been little time for this during the lambing season, and piles had accumulated.

George went into the kitchen to make a cup of tea which he would take with him to his study. He found Nell sitting at the table looking at a copy of *Farmers Weekly*.

"Brought you some bantams' eggs," she said, and pushed a six-egg box across the table.

"Fantastic," said George. "Bantams' eggs for breakfast. Thanks very much."

As George returned the box to the table, he saw a scrap of paper with a message written in pencil. Dusty's writing. *Lily rang*, it said. George glanced at Nell. Her eyes were back on the magazine. It was unlikely she had not seen the note, but he could not be sure. Nell looked up.

"I love my bantams," she said.

George went to the stove, put on the kettle. His mind was a confetti of questions. When did she ring? Would she ring again? Where was she? What else did she say? For the first time he could remember George longed to be rid of Nell so that he could telephone Dusty, try to find out more. Though on second thoughts that would

126

probably be unwise, convey an interest he had no wish as yet to confess.

George stood at the stove, one hand on the handle of the ancient kettle, his back to Nell. He listened to the familiar rumble of water, faster and deeper as it came close to boiling. He heard the click of pages as Nell flipped through the magazine. He knew that somehow Nell had guessed at the thrilling anticipation in his heart, and her knowledge felt like an intrusion. Tension between them writhed like an animal trying to escape, almost tangible. He poured mugs of strong tea and fetched a jug of milk from the fridge, taking his time. Nell's hands were laid flat on the table like sleeping dogs. The silence was porous: the thoughts running through it almost visible. George sat down and shoved a mug of tea and the jug towards Nell. Their eyes met.

"Still no news from Lily?" Nell asked.

George swallowed. He could not lie to her, though he was filled with regret at having to reveal the truth at the moment he most wanted to reflect on this turn of events in solitude. What was essential was to convince Nell that he did not suspect she had read the note.

"As a matter of fact there was a message to say she'd rung this morning."

"That's good." Nell's mouth was working. "I haven't heard another word since the postcard, what was it now — two or three weeks ago?"

"She probably won't ring again." George flattened his voice against the beating of his heart.

"Oh, she probably will. I hope she does." Nell gave a smile that came and went. The silence returned.

"What's Prodge up to?" George asked at last.

"He's gone off to buy — guess what? — a black leather jacket." This time, at the thought of her brother, Nell smiled properly. "Thing about Prodge, beneath the serious young farmer who never had any fun, there's a wild youth who just occasionally wants to behave like most others of his generation. He's also talking about a powerful motorbike."

"A motorbike?" George smiled back. They were on course again. "Does he know what a powerful motorbike would cost?"

"He does, and he says soon he'll be able to afford it. I mean the farm's doing well, all due to his hard work. He's managed to put by quite a bit, despite all the money for the shed. He asked what I thought, and I said, You go ahead, Prodge. You get yourself a bike when you can afford it. I mean, he doesn't have many luxuries in his life, and he works harder than anyone I've ever met. He deserves to treat himself to something he really wants, don't you think?"

"I certainly do," said George. "It's a great idea. I shall be very jealous. Hope to get taken for a ride sometime."

"Of course . . ." Nell sipped her tea. "I daresay there's a hidden agenda. I mean, I daresay he imagines some amazing girl riding behind him. I daresay he's calculated the pulling power of some roaring great bike — very rare in these parts. He's dying to get married, as you know."

George nodded, trying to picture his friend as a married man. Then the telephone rang. He went to the window ledge, where it sat on a pile of papers, determined not to look as if he was eager to answer it. He stood with his back to Nell, staring out of the window, knowing her eyes were on him.

"Lily," was all he said at first. He wanted to say a jumble of incoherent things that might have conveyed the turmoil within him. But he was constrained by Nell's presence, could only nod, listening to her. "Fine," he added, at last, nodding. "OK. Great. See you then."

He turned slowly back to Nell, who was standing.

"Where is she?"

"I'm not sure. I mean, she's not sure. Lily's always vague about where she is." He feared his small laugh hid neither his strange guilt, not his excitement.

"Is she coming here? Is she on her way?"

"Uh, I rather think she seems to be."

"I'll go, then."

"Don't be silly, Nell. She won't be here for a while, and there's absolutely no need for you to go. All I've got to do is begin on the correspondence." He waved at a pile of unopened mail on the table, knowing quite well it had no chance of his attention today.

"No: I must go anyway. Got all our post to see to." She made her way to the door. "Tell her to ring me, though. We could ride any afternoon now lambing's over."

"I'll do that. And you tell Prodge to come up here in his new jacket soon as possible." His words were tumbling over themselves. He wanted Nell to go, go, go.

She was taking an age opening the door into the yard, going through it.

"'Bye, George."

For some reason, George kissed her on the cheek. This was not a custom between them: they met so often that such a social nicety, so fashionable among urban folk, would have been absurd.

"See you," he said.

In the few hours between Nell's departure and Lily's arrival innumerable doubts, questions and anxieties tangled in George's mind, further confused by the unquestionable longing he felt as he threw pellets into troughs, and went to inspect a couple of new cows Saul had bought at the market that day. He had no appetite for the cottage pie that Dusty had left for him (in truth, her repertoire of pies was beginning to pall) but opened a bottle of good white wine. He poured himself a glass and asked himself questions: had he really missed Lily? Yes: though he had not allowed himself to think about this much. Could he envisage the future with her? Possibly. Without her? Didn't like to think about it. How did he feel about her? Not entirely sure: damned excitment at seeing her getting in the way. Did he, well, love her? Impossible to answer. Why were his hands shaking, his heart beating audibly? Goodness knows. Any idea how he was going to behave, what he was going to say? No idea at all.

It was almost midnight when the headlights of Lily's car slashed through the kitchen windows. By now George had assumed she had changed her mind, wasn't coming. He had finished the bottle of wine and felt slightly drunk. When the headlights knifed through him, meaning she had actually arrived, he went out to greet her. The familiar scent of her came to him before he could see her: it was a moonless night.

"Here I am," she said.

George, not altogether certain of his steps, went to the boot of her car and picked up two heavy suitcases. These seemed to balance him, steady him. He led the way back into the kitchen, put them down. A moment or two later — it seemed like an eternity — Lily followed. He turned to her, took her in his arms. He could feel the warmth of her, her heart beating in time to his own beneath the slippery silk of her shirt.

"I'm sorry," he said, and pushed her away so that he could look at her questioning smile, which turned into a long, thrilling laugh before they hugged again, and the embrace turned into a kiss. For George, it was unlike kissing any woman he had ever known and he did not want it to stop.

Looking back on the evening of Lily's return, George could only remember sensations. He supposed he put more logs on the fire and they sat by it in their usual seats, drinking more wine. He presumed they talked a little, but had no recollection of what was said. His head spun and flashed: the solid old kitchen had burst into a million shining fragments. It was an evening so vivid in its enchantment that even while it existed in the present it held the luminescence of the past. George was unaccustomed to such an experience — a man ungrounded by inexplicable joy, treading the waters of something that he had never envisaged, fired by the longing to know what would happen next.

The thing he remembered quite clearly was the darkness in the window fading, and the emergence of a dawn the colour of dew that silvered its way through the kitchen. George suggested it was time to go to bed. There was time ahead to talk, he said. Endless time.

Balanced again by the suitcases — their weight giving blissful assurance of the length of time Lily intended to stay — George led the way upstairs to the spare room. Of one thing he was quite clear: this was not the moment to suggest she should share his bed. He loved the idea of luxurious anticipation, the stretching out of time, neither knowing when it would be that they could wait no longer. For the present, they were both exhausted by marvelling at the turn of events, though deep sleep was unlikely. Lily stood looking round her old room.

"I remember," she said.

"I'll be out on the tractor till lunchtime. Help yourself to whatever you want."

"I will."

"And this evening we can work out . . ."

"Probably nothing to work out."

"No: probably not. Sleep well."

George was detained for a further half-minute as he watched her pulling the curtains across the windows that now admitted a bright dawn. He guessed that the smile she had just given him was still there. The lively snap of her hand, distorting the lilies on the cotton stuff, indicated that her happiness matched his own.

But before she could turn back to him to confirm his imaginings, he left the room and closed the door. The buoyancy in his steps made the old floorboards of the passage sing more loudly than usual as he made his way to his room for what was left of the night.

CHAPTER
SEVEN

The face of his mother had vanished very quickly from George's mind after her death. This often worried him, as he confessed to Nell and Prodge but to no one else. He studied photographs of her to induce memory, but a static two-dimensional image is no evoker of flesh, blood and habit. "Your mother used to tip her head back when she laughed," David Elkin once said, "exposing the full length of her pretty neck. I loved that." But George held no such picture. Her voice still lived in his head — slow, husky, trailing. The feel of her thin hand, the skin warm and soft as ageing rose petals, sometimes returned to the gaping fingers of his own empty hand. And never would he forget the smell of her. This was nothing to do with man-made concoctions, which she never wore, but was a natural skin smell, somewhere between primroses and cowslips. When George was very young and still afraid of the dark, she would lie beside him on his bed, reading to him until he fell asleep. The scent of her, the warmth of her, the music of her voice combined to make him feel utterly safe. He was aware of this safety long before events taught him the preciousness of this state of being. Sometimes, in his attempts to visualise her face, he would think back to those sweet evenings and try to remember how, through drowsy eyes, he saw her chin, her downcast eyes, her hair. But that picture seemed to have gone for ever. On the occasions he dreamt of his mother, she was always turned away from him, or in shadow, or moving too fast. So the subconscious was of no use, and he would awake frustrated and sad.

What he remembered — would always remember — were the funny things she said, her singular way of *looking*, the wisdom of her theories, her belief in magic. This had little in common with his own. While he loved the whole idea of goblins, witches, spells — and when they ran out of books his mother would make up her own stories containing these elements — her belief was in the more grown-up kind of magic. This held little appeal for George, although he would listen politely. "To be honest, Mama, I don't really understand what you're talking about," he often said. "You will," was always her reply.

After she died George cursed himself for not having attended to her magic beliefs more carefully. Her theory was that should something outside the norm happen in a familiar place, that familiarity was shattered. "When your father came to take me out for the first time, he came up the stairs and into my tiny flat, and the small sitting room where I was waiting — nervous, thrilled — broke up into a thousand pieces that came showering down on to me so thickly that I was unable to recognise where I was. It was a sort of snowstorm of sensation. It didn't return to normal until the next morning when I was alone again." George had

had no idea what she meant at the time. She had also told a story about some furious row with her brother, here in the farmhouse kitchen, which, for her, distorted the solidity of all familiar things. That was a dark, frightening magic, she explained, that left you momentarily with nothing to hold on to. But good magic, if you were lucky, was the more frequent. You just had to be able to recognise it: the going for a walk in a place you knew well, with someone you realised you loved, for instance, heightened the sense of importance in every tree, flower, distant field, fading view.

His mother's recounted moments of her kind of magic were too numerous to remember — and, to be honest, at the time George had not found them particularly interesting: they were experiences so far from his own. But one or two stuck in his mind, and by the time he went to Oxford he found himself looking, secretly, for a similar experience. He was mostly disappointed. Sometimes, alone among Magdalen's fritillaries or listening to the New College choir at Evensong, he would sense a frisson that seemed to give special significance to the moment, shaking him from his usual sense of detachment. But it was never caused by a girl, a romantic involvement. He began to doubt it ever would be. His mother, he had concluded, had been particularly lucky in her brushes with magic, but her gift had not been passed on to her son.

But the morning after Lily's return the truth of his mother's belief became suddenly clear to him. He went down early to the kitchen. He had not slept more than an hour since going to bed at dawn, and was impatient to be up. Impatient for the day to begin. He made himself a pot of strong coffee and sat down at the table. It was a fine blue day, the clarity of spring in every leaf outside. But it was not a day he recognised. The fact that Lily was asleep upstairs had altered everything. The furniture of the room swayed as if powered by a rocking sea. The stripes of the blue and white butter dish, which had given service for as long as George could remember, seemed to have been charged with new brightness overnight. They dazzled. The solid things of everyday began to dance. This is madness, thought George, but enchanting.

He sat there unmoving, wondering when Lily would come down, and what would happen when she did. He knew he could not wait for her long: the sheep awaited him. But when he had time to return to the farmhouse . . . perhaps she would be down. And then what? How would this visit be? How long would she stay? What could he do to keep her as long as possible? Buoyed as he was with the light of revelation, the first intimations of powerful feelings for Lily, he would not want her to go again.

George's reflections were broken by the sound of hooves. He looked out of the window to see Nell riding into the farmyard. It was unlike her to come so early. George's happy thoughts turned to unreasonable fury, rage: at this moment he did not want to be interrupted by anyone, least of all Nell, to whom there would have to be careful explaining. George automatically fetched milk, a second mug: control was needed.

Nell came striding into the room, a small birch whip in one hand, an egg box in the other. For an infinitesimal moment George was aware of seeing her as strangers, encountering her for the first time, might see her: friendly, raw-boned, uncouth, thoughtless of her appearance. Would they miss, he wondered, a certain careless attraction that emanates from some girls who have never experienced city life?

"You're early," he said.

"Such a lovely morning. Thought I'd ride." She put the box on the table, sat down. "More bantams' eggs."

"Thanks very much." George wanted to throw the box long and far, smash the eggs into a murk of yolk and slime and shell. He prayed Lily would carry on sleeping, not come down just now.

Nell poured herself coffee automatically. She turned to George.

"Prodge definitely wants to get married," she said.

"Prodge? *Married?*" For a moment George's surprise halted the swinging of the room. Lily faded. "Who to? Why's he not said anything to me?"

Nell laughed.

"Oh, there isn't a *girl*. No one particular in mind. Just an idea."

"How did all this come about?"

"Goodness knows. I think it's been creeping up on him. Shed finished, prize cows, farm doing nicely. Now it's time for a wife. Children, I suppose."

"Good heavens."

"Besides which, I think . . ." Nell narrowed her eyes. "I think it wouldn't be stupid to suppose that he'd like

138

to find a wife before you. I told him Lily was coming back."

There was a long silence. Nell could be devious sometimes, George knew of old. But he was relieved by the lightness of her tone.

"Perhaps that's what set him off," she went on. "Anyhow, last night he gave me a whole long spiel about the kind of girl he was looking for, and how he'd take one on even if she only half measured up to his expectations. Trouble is, he fancies something quite glamorous, but he knows the most important thing is that whoever it is doesn't mind living miles from anywhere and will make a good farmer's wife. Anyhow, he seems to think his black leather jacket — he got it, cost a bloody fortune — is some sort of good-luck token. Now he'll seriously begin looking."

George sighed. The whole notion, setting about marriage in this way, seemed preposterous. And yet, of course, normal. His anger at Nell's ill-timed appearance had fled as quickly as it came, and now his concern was for her.

"What about you, Nell?" he said. "What will you do if Prodge finds this perfect wife?"

"Oh, me. Don't worry about me." Nell shrugged. "He wouldn't turn me out. House is big enough for three. I'd just keep on, wouldn't I? Doing my own thing. Not interfering, of course." She stood up. "Daresay I'd come in useful for baby-sitting." She went to the sink, washed her mug as she always did, turned it upside down on the draining board. With her back to George she asked: "Did Lily come, then?"

"She did, yes. Pretty late. She's sleeping."

"Sleeping." Nell turned to him. There was no enquiry in her eyes. "Well, that's good she's back," she said. "You won't be so alone."

"You know I *like* being alone."

"Things can change. Anyhow, tell her to give me a ring and we'll go riding. It'll be nice for me to have her back, too. Not many girls of my age in these parts, as you well know. Give her my love."

George watched Nell's powerful long strides across the yard. She untethered her grey mare and then mounted with a single, elegant spring. Once in the saddle she was, as usual, an impressive figure: straight and sure, absolutely in command. As she jogged out of the yard her blonde curls sprayed against the sky like small foamy waves dashing themselves to pieces on the sand. Despite the happy turmoil caused by Lily, George was not unaware of the familiar pull of his old affection for Nell in his heart.

Lily had brought lunch. When George came in he found cheeses arranged on a pretty old plate taken down from the dresser — a plate his mother had been excited about finding years ago in a market: too good to use, she said. She wouldn't want it to be broken. Its sudden place on the table shocked George for a moment. Then he saw how right Lily was: how foolish it was to keep things for mere ornament.

Wedges of Dolcelatte and Chaumes and Camembert sat at various calculated angles round the hunk of rugged Cheddar that had been Dusty's only offering of cheese for months. George smiled. There was a delicious smell coming from the oven. Bread, or warming rolls, perhaps. No wonder the kitchen continued to dance.

Lily came in carrying four small pots of tufted greenery.

"I brought herbs," she said. "I remembered that last time there were never any herbs. And there wasn't much salad. So I brought . . ." She went to the fridge and took out several different lettuces, sophisticated curly things with ruby leaves. "I hope you don't mind."

"Of course not. We're rather in the outback, here. Not rich in radicchio."

Lily seemed so busy with the salad-making that there was no chance to go and kiss her, which George longed to do. He stood by the dresser, helpless, grounded, watching her, eyes half shut for fear of too sharp a picture unnerving him completely. It was an impressionist picture he saw: the swishing of a pale skirt, scatty hair shredding the sun that alighted on its waves, pretty hands slivers of light among the reds and greens of lettuces, long fingers twinkling as scissors chopped a length of chives. But for all the vitality of her movements, Lily seemed withdrawn — morning shyness, perhaps, after the acknowledged charge between them last night. Or possibly, thought George, he had misread her then. Perhaps he had assumed she felt what he felt, and had been mistaken.

They ate. The kitchen table was transformed into the corner of a French restaurant: gingham napkins (where had she found them?) folded on side plates, wine glasses, a bottle of fizzy water. Had she been shopping

141

this morning, George wondered? Or had she kept all these things hidden in the boot of her car? So many questions George asked himself: but put none of them to Lily.

Their talk was flat, constrained, as if each seemed bent on not putting a foot wrong. It would be better at dinner, George thought: apart from anything else, time would not be against them. He was always in a hurry at midday: not the moment to linger over wine (in fact neither of them touched the bottle he produced to go with the glasses) and try out all the cheeses on the newly baked bread. George looked at his watch.

"I've got to go and check a length of fence up on one of the high fields," he said. "One of our loutish rams had a go at it last night. Like to come?"

In truth, he couldn't imagine Lily at his side, swaying through the uncropped grass, listening to his plans of how best to repair the broken fence. He rather hoped she would not want to come. It was a job he could accomplish quickly on his own. With Lily by his side he would be distracted. He would want her to sit beside him on the grass, look at the views of this corner of England which he loved like nowhere else in the world. Hold her hand. Stroke the back of her neck. Kiss her again.

"Listen, George," she was saying, "you've not to bother one bit about me. If you remember, last time, I was pretty good at entertaining myself, wasn't I? I'll do that again, not get in your way. Though of course when you have a moment I want to see everything: changes, the new lambs, whatever. This afternoon I'll plant out the herbs in that pot by the back door — is that all right? Then I'll unpack my books. I've brought quite a few. I might read a bit, go for a walk."

George smiled. Relief joined his general state of happiness. He could see ahead the whole enchanted state of coming and going — in and out of the house, meeting, parting, parting, meeting . . .

"Nell's thrilled you're back," he said. "She wants you to ring her, arrange to go riding."

"I'll do that this evening. It'll be lovely seeing her again. And riding again. I've brought proper boots this time. I've come altogether more equipped for farm life."

"Good," said George. He wondered if she had any idea of the lightness in his heart — or if she was disappointed, perhaps, in his lack of demonstration. She had responded so keenly last night when he had held her: today, in bright sunlight, there seemed to be no opportunity. But it was imperative not to dash her expectations: this time, he was determined she should be in no doubt of his feelings, even if his words could never match them. He got up, bent to kiss her on the forehead. To his surprise there was a movement fast as a whiplash and her arms were tight round his neck. For some time they remained in an awkward position arched over the table in a dizzying embrace. At last George pulled away, before allowing himself to be further, blissfully detained. He saw that her cheeks held the same highlights as hollyberries, as did her eyes. Quickly he left. Striding up the hill, sun warm on his back, he tried very hard to think about the broken fence.

Prodge, to whom the success of his farm, the excellence of his cattle, were his life, found himself oddly disturbed by the purchase of his new leather jacket, the most expensive thing he had ever bought. A measure of guilt underlined his pleasure, but not so much as to force him to stop thinking about it. Never before, so far as he could remember, had he ever felt the smack of vanity. But now, looking at the jacket on a hanger in the hall, it assailed him. He had a huge, bloody stupid desire to put the thing on, walk about in it, get the feel of it. All he wanted was to take a quick look in the mirror, then, just, well . . . *keep walking about in it*, here and there, nowhere in particular.

Prodge knew what he would see in the mirror. He wasn't bad looking. Bit on the hefty side, but nice eyes, Nell always said. The jacket would do wonders for him, raise his stock for miles around. When he had tried it on in the shop it had seemed at once like an old friend. It was comfortable, challenging. The shiny black leather was like armour, and yet not too stiff. It was the sort of jacket to give a man status. But in the shop mirrors, crowded with reflections of other men in less superior jackets, he had not been able to admire the sight of himself clearly: he had had to trust his instinct. So now, this sunny afternoon, all he wanted was to make quite sure: glance at himself, undistracted by others in the glass, then try the thing out for a bit.

The plan would have been impossible had Nell been around: she would have laughed at him, as she did last night when he brought the jacket home. But she had gone to the village, would be away for a good hour. There was no one to catch him out, and he had a spare half-hour before he had to check the bags of cattle feed.

Prodge rolled down his sleeves, drew on the jacket. He went to the scullery — his mother had always called it the scullery; in fact it was a rickety extension on the back of the house crammed with junk that would never be sorted out. An old mirror hung high at an angle on one wall. Among its freckles all Prodge could see was a smeary version of his own disappointed face, and the collar and shoulders of the jacket. But even in so useless a mirror he was able to confirm the excellence of the leather, shining and glinting so fiercely that its blackness blazed with a sheen of white. Wow, he thought. It's quite something.

His mind raced round the few rooms in the house: no, there wasn't a decent mirror in any of them. He doubted Nell ever gave herself more than a passing glance in the one in the bathroom, and his mother, from whom Nell had inherited her lack of vanity, would have scoffed at the very idea of anyone wasting time appraising their reflection. For the first time in his life — and the thought was so odd and so out of character that Prodge found himself smiling — he was annoyed by the fact that this ruddy, chaotic farmhouse did not have a decent looking glass.

Prodge stomped out of the kitchen, hands weighing down the pockets, enjoying the softness of their lining.

The sun, strangely warm for so early in the year, burned down through the leather. The zip — a great corker of a zip — he had judged best to leave at half-mast: something sexy about a half-undone jacket, he thought, not that sexiness was going to get him anywhere in a field full of nothing but sheep. Prodge moved his arms. The jacket creaked. He felt as if he had been listening to the friendly sound his entire life.

To *get the feel* of the jacket, to test its bending power, Prodge strode quickly over a couple of meadows towards the river. All he needed now was the *bike*. Wow, what could he not do on a bloody great Harley-Davidson. John Prodger: the one with the jacket and the bike. But that was a dream so far off it was beyond a dream: it was a pathetic hope.

When Prodge reached the bank of the river he stopped, sat down, lit a cigarette. This is all very unusual, he said to himself: he could see the humour of the situation. John Prodger, tenant farmer dedicated to nothing but farming, loving every inch of the land, every cow, every sheep, every hour of his working day, suddenly taking a half-hour break, mid-afternoon, lighting up, sitting on a river bank in a new black leather jacket that cost the same as half a dozen good ewes. Madness! What had come over him? Still, not a bad idea occasionally to act so completely out of character that you surprised yourself. Every man was entitled to experiment with change. So long as nobody caught him, there was nothing wrong with this stolen half-hour. Prodge took a long drag on his cigarette, sucked it deep into his lungs, let the smoke slowly out

146

in a spire that wavered against the sky, then disappeared. If a Harley-Davidson had been parked beside him, he would have been completely happy.

Prodge pulled faster on his cigarette. He let his eyes drag along the water with the fast current of the river. They rose again to the bank on his side, some hundred yards further along from where he was sitting. There he saw a creature, a vision, a woman, walking slowly towards him. This, he knew at once, was the wife he was looking for in his black leather jacket. Funny thing was, she'd arrived far quicker than he'd ever expected. And not through a crowd in the pub, as he had imagined, but all alone in Longer Meadow.

The glorious certainty withered within seconds. There was madness everywhere this afternoon, Prodge realised. Maybe it was the cigarette. He hadn't had one for a week or so. Must have been the Marlboro. Gone to his head. Disappointment struck. He thought he recognised the girl: the Lily girl who'd come to stay with George some time back, and Nell said was returning. They'd only met once, briefly. He hadn't thought her right for George, her in a fancy scarf in the country: but then he'd never thought any girl right for George. Not that there was any reason to suppose George was on the lookout. It was he, John Prodger, in his helpful black jacket, who was in search of a wife. He threw the half-smoked cigarette into the river, pulled himself to his feet. Awkward, now, was what he felt.

"Hello," Lily called out. She was only a few yards away.

"Afternoon."

"I'm Lily Crichton. Don't know if you remember — we met briefly last time I was here."

"I remember. I do." She was right by him now, holding out her hand. Pretty daft thing to do on a river bank miles from anywhere, Prodge thought. But he also liked the idea: all rather Captain Livingstone, British. They shook hands. "Nell's gone up the village," he said. "I'll tell her you were looking for her." The one thing he did not want was for Lily to suggest coming up to the farmhouse with him and waiting for Nell to return. Christ, he'd not be able to walk straight.

Lily smiled. Some looker, thought Prodge. Perhaps George had got lucky this time. "What a fantastic jacket," she said.

The mind-blowing event of Lily appearing from nowhere into the landscape, exuding beauty and friendship in equal measure, had blasted Prodge's jacket completely from his mind. Now it came to his rescue, gave him the self-assurance he had always known black leather would give a man.

"You like it?" he said. "I got it only yesterday. I was sort of . . . trying it out." He smiled. "Hadn't reckoned on bumping into anyone. Looks a bit silly, doesn't it? A farmer in this sort of clobber, a Tuesday afternoon. Should be hosing down the yard . . ."

"I think it looks brilliant. Suits you to perfection."

"Really?"

Prodge, still feeling that he was hallucinating, wanted to summon a golden chariot from his childhood story books, put this goddess inside it and drive her across the skies. Or take her to the village shop where they did

148

cream teas out the back in a nice little whitewashed courtyard, or to the pub for wine or beer, or just walk with her into the copse, bluebells not far off now, and lay her down on his jacket in a private dell, moss and new grass their bed.

"Cigarette?" he said.

"I don't smoke, thanks."

If she didn't want one, then he didn't want one either.

"You here long, then?"

Lily turned away from him, eyes bouncing along the water. He could see her profile. God Almighty. "Plans aren't at all firmed up," she said, quietly. "I just thought it was time to come back."

"Right." If ever a girl of even half the beauty of this Lily decided it would be right to return to *him*, thought Prodge — well, it would be a miracle. Not the finest black leather jacket in the world could make that happen. Suddenly, hands roaming in the pockets that had so recently given him pleasure, he saw his new purchase as nothing more than a cheap gimmick. He felt sickened by the thought of the money he had spent. Sickened in general. "I must get back to work," he said.

"Will you tell Nell I'm longing to ride? Soon as she has a moment. I'll ring her tonight."

"I'll do that." She looked on him with such piercing gentleness and understanding that Prodge knew there was nothing about him she did not know. In another world, another time, they could have *melded* (was that the word? Perhaps it was moulded) together as one, like couples in toshy films. He felt close to tears, uncertain, in the brightness of the afternoon, of what was real, what was throbbing fantasy.

Lily gave him a small, waist-high wave: a rather prissy little wave, he thought, but maybe that was all part of his misjudgement. Perhaps it was really a wave that signalled she was aware of some — well, *something*, between them. She turned away, started to walk back towards George's farm. Prodge, dissatisfaction prickling his skin, headed towards home. He tried to make a mental list of the things he had to do, but all he could think of was lying in a grassy bed, ravishing the girl who had returned to his best friend, George.

Prodge's hope of seeing no one in his black jacket was dashed a second time. As he walked through the farmyard gate, George drew up in his car. He wound down the window, smiled widely.

"Christ!" he said.

Caught off his guard, Prodge had no time to decide whether or not to say anything about his meeting with Lily. A little giddied by the approval in George's face, he decided *not*. A man must sometimes have an innocent secret to keep him going.

"Like it?"

"It's terrific." George grinned. His approbation was the undoing of Prodge's resolution.

"Lily thought so too." Lily, for sure, would report back to George. Silly to think the meeting might have been their secret. She would be bound to report it: it meant nothing to her.

"Lily?"

"I just ran into her down by the river. She was on her way over to find Nell. Told her Nell was in the village so she went back to your place."

"Prodge . . ." George paused, decided to enjoy a tease. "What were you doing in that magnificent jacket in the middle of a working afternoon down by the river? Hoping to run into a wife?"

"Something like that." How the hell did George know the reason for the jacket in the first place? He was something of a mind-reader, sometimes. Spooky. "As a matter of fact, I did run into a wife." He now decided to carry on the tease. "Your visitor. Now there's the kind of woman I wouldn't say no to."

"Ah."

"But bugger me, you got there first."

"I haven't got anywhere with Lily, Prodge. She's just a friend. Invited herself to stay."

Invited herself? Why should George be the receiver of such luck?

"Right. Still, she's out of my class. All I can hope for is some sub-Lily comes my way, takes to my jacket."

George laughed. "Nell was saying you're seriously thinking about marriage."

"So it's Nell been telling tales? Serious as I can be about anything beyond the farm, I suppose. I mean, time's come I wouldn't mind a few kids running round the place, a good woman by my side. Take a bit of pressure off Nell."

"Quite."

"How long's she staying?" Prodge cursed himself for this question. He didn't want George to see which way his mind was jumping.

"She hasn't said. A week or two, perhaps. Nell's glad she's back. They like riding together. Talking."

"So Nell said. How's this for a zip?" Prodge pulled the huge zip up and down several times. It made an expensive sizzling sound. "Ever seen one like it?"

George, impressed, smiled. "This is a side of you I've not seen before," he said.

"I done too much growing up too fast these last years." Prodge frowned, suddenly serious. "This is my youth-flash. Probably too late, but I want to have a go. Anyway, I got cows to milk. Can't stand here all day talking to the gentleman farmer." It was an old joke between them: often they called each other by their titles — gentleman farmer, tenant farmer. George laughed again and started the engine. Prodge, hurrying now, late, guilty — you should never keep a cow waiting — decided that the best way to disguise the fantasy that had so unexpectedly hit him this afternoon was to make the whole thing into a joke. *Pretend* he fancied Lily like crazy. Be quite open about it. That way, he would have an opportunity to flirt with her, and because the whole idea of him and Lily was so unlikely, so outrageous, so jokey, George and Nell would never guess the truth.

"I ran into Prodge on my way over to Nell this afternoon," Lily said that evening. "He was wearing this extraordinarily beautiful black leather jacket. Bit bizarre, mid-afternoon down by the river. But he said

152

he was trying it out. I admired it and he seemed pleased. Odd: he doesn't look the sort of man to be struck by vanity."

"He's not usually," said George. "The jacket is just a little experiment, a little whim, a fantasy he's given in to and he's enjoying it no end. I ran into him, too. He said he'd met you. You rather dazzled him, I think. Well, meeting you unexpectedly on a river bank would dazzle anyone."

"Nonsense! Don't be so silly."

She was moving about again, in her fluid way, from table to fridge to dresser: opening cupboards, taking out bowls and jars and returning them — preparing, it seemed, something that would be added to the cottage pie Dusty had left in the low oven. George remembered that on her previous visit Lily had not acted like this: she had been a more passive visitor, making no suggestions about food, not offering to cook, just accepting whatever was put on the table. She had spent a lot of time sitting by the fire, drink in hand, ankle twirling. George hoped she would resume this former stillness once they had eaten. It was all he could do not to interrupt one of her small journeys and demand she forget about cooking while he kissed her. But he remained standing, motionless, watching her, fascinated by the way she could quarry silence with her movements. The kitchen spun again.

"I've made a — well, I hope Dusty won't be offended. Perhaps she won't find out. I've made an aubergine mousse, first course. Hope you don't mind."

153

"Mind?" said George. The evening sun, intent on catching her, singling her out from the shadows, made her into a pyre of light. A halo danced round her head, shoulders, skirt. The dusting of tiny hairs on her arms were sleek with transitory gold. George sipped his drink, wondering if the wine was the begetter of this vision. Then he shut his eyes, unable to believe.

There followed a couple of days of unseasonably high wind and rain. Lily reported a leak in the ceiling of her bedroom. George said he knew there were loose tiles on the roof: he would ring the man who supplied replacement tiles and mend it.

On the second gusty afternoon George returned from the afternoon milking to find a ladder propped up against the front of the house. He looked up to see Lily balanced against the slope of the roof, intent on work at the tiles. Alarmed, George ran to the ladder, called up to her.

"Lily! What on earth —"

She turned to him. "The man didn't turn up. I waited for ages then decided to have a go myself. I found a couple of spare tiles in the barn."

"Don't be . . . ridiculous. You could fall. Come on down."

"I've almost finished. It was nothing serious." The wind made her voice dip and sway like seagulls flying over waves.

"Please, Lily." George knew he sounded exasperated, had a feeling he was being unreasonable. "What do you know about mending roofs?"

154

"We've a tiled roof like this at home. Tiles often blow off, Norfolk winds. I often put them back." She turned away, raised her arm to check the tile she had been securing.

George cautiously mounted the first three rungs of the ladder. It juddered. Lily snapped her head round again, hair a stiff mask over her face. "What are you doing?"

"Please, Lily."

"I've almost finished. Coming down in a minute."

George, helpless, all too aware of his foolish stance two feet from the ground and gripping the ladder, kept his eyes on her every finely balanced movement. Certainly she seemed to know what she was doing. Very odd. But he wished she'd come down *now*. A gust of wind carried a new squall of rain that freckled his upturned face with stinging cold.

"Please," he shouted once again. Lily gave no sign of having heard. Instead, to his horror, he saw her beginning to climb higher. The ladder reached almost to the spine of the roof. When she arrived at the top, Lily swung one leg over so that suddenly she was astride the house. George gave a wordless scream.

Lily now rode the house like a horse, her visible leg kicking at the flank of firm tiles. Her jacket billowed in the wind, her hair was a stiff flag. She looked down at George laughing, shouting something he could not hear. Then she took her hands from the withers of the roof, flung them in the air.

She's mad, thought George. Mad and wonderful. There's only one thing for it.

On his own journey up the ladder the icy wind and rain blew all sense of Lily's danger from him. He began to enjoy himself. As he passed the patch of tiles that Lily had repaired he saw that, amazingly, she had done a good job of it. He was proud of her.

On reaching the top — less adroitly than Lily — George swung his leg over so that he, too, was astride the house. Lily roared with delight, though her actual words, despite her nearness, he could not hear. In her balloon jacket she was an absurd, happy figure: face aglitter with rain, hands reddened with cold. George joined her laughter.

He had no sense of how long they stayed riding the roof that wild afternoon. George had the impression they were trapped in a cloud. Mists roved about them so that there was no wide view of the landscape: only, in the frayed edges of the mist, the ghostly tops of trees.

Lily at last swung herself back on to the ladder and climbed quickly down. She held on to its sides to steady George's descent. On terra firma again, they moved towards each other simultaneously. George's waxed jacket creaked as he opened his arms. They stood hugging each other, shaky and cold and laughing under the vicious rain.

"Finish off a pheasant, mend a roof — anything else you can do?" asked George, as they drew apart.

"You'll see," said Lily, licking the raindrops from her top lip. "Come on: hot baths, dry clothes."

"Did you set out to astonish me, or did —?" But Lily already running to the door, didn't hear, so George got no answer to his question.

Lily's presence so enchanted and jumbled the next few days that, looking back, George was unable to remember precisely how long she had been there when the evening of the pictures came about. He had come in later than usual, having waited a long time for the vet who had been called to see a cow with mastitis. A light rain was shredding the kitchen window, and Lily had lighted two candles — fine church candles that she would not have found in any drawer. She must have been out shopping again. Over supper they had talked about the perils of farming, animal welfare, the rotation of crops (Lily seemed keen to learn as much as she could), Wordsworth, Ted Hughes, Auden, Nell's bantams' eggs, the forthcoming agricultural show where Prodge hoped once again to win several prizes — shifting from one thing to another, but always avoiding the subject of themselves or future plans. Then suddenly Lily put a hand over George's and said, as seriously as she could manage, "You know, there are an awful lot of pictures all over the house. I'd like a proper tour, a proper look. Explanations."

George hesitated. Then he laughed. "I was hoping you weren't going to show an interest in them. The collection was built up with great pride by my father who always had an eye for a bad picture. You couldn't argue with him. He came from the school of 'I like what I like' and nothing could budge him. I didn't have the knowledge and skill to explain the difference between art and rubbish, and my mother didn't try. She simply put all the worst pictures in rooms that weren't much used — spare rooms."

157

"So that's why there's a sort of hard-boiled egg of a podgy naked girl in my room?"

"Exactly. I'm sorry. I'd forgotten about that. You could take it down."

"No, no. I'm getting used to her. Soon I'll be quite fond of her." She jumped up, pushing away her half-finished coffee. "Come on! I want to see them *all*."

George followed her out of the kitchen. They went first to the old dining room, last used long ago, before Mrs Elkin died. The peppery smell of a room that had witnessed hundreds of heavy meals over the years greeted them as George opened the door. In the solemn hush of elaborate oak chairs regimented round a civic-looking table, a bowl of wax fruit, dimmed by dust imitating the bloom of skin, was the only contribution to frivolity. The windows were low and small, admitting a grainy brown wash of light — poor illumination for the many pictures on the dark walls.

"Shall I put on a light?" asked George.

"No, no. It's probably better, not being able to see them too clearly." Lily smiled and moved down the room, eyes passing from the contents of one dull gold frame to another. "He was a chiefly a landscape man, then, your father," she said at last.

"He was."

"Such terrible, terrible landscapes. Can't have done much for a man who loved the country so much."

"But at least they never cost very much. He was always picking things up in junk shops, declaring he'd bought a real investment."

158

"Oh? He was that kind of a collector? He didn't buy paintings for the love of them?"

"I think he loved them too. He was very proud of them. If you think these are bad, wait till we get upstairs. The long passage probably houses the most dire collection of pastoral art in Britain."

Going up the staircase, side by side, George put his arm round Lily's waist. Thus bound they moved slowly down the dim passage, which creaked like a boat beneath them. They paused at each elaborately framed view — bland sunsets, rustic gates, bare elms of the sort that painters of rural scenes for calendars sacrifice their eyesight for in their conscientious attention to each twig. There was even a sub-Constable haywain beside a drear pond. George smiled.

"The funny thing is," he said, "although I can see they're all absolutely dreadful, I can't quite explain *why*. Give me just a few reasons."

Lily sighed. Her head was tilted to one side, just touching George's shoulder.

"For a start," she said, "and I won't bore you with a long lecture, if paint is applied in exactly the same way to sky, earth, trees, water, whatever, the result is a mush of sameness that drains all *life*. Look at that soup of a pond, stagnant water of exactly the same density as that dull blob of hay. The hay would be just as good in the pond, the water on the wagon." George laughed, suddenly seeing. "Take that horse." She pointed to a bloodless-looking animal in the shafts of the haywain. "It's not made of flesh and blood. It's a stuffed toy.

There's no life there. No vitality. All these pictures are not only so badly painted it's laughable, they're *dead*."

"But perhaps the artists enjoyed painting them, felt they were saying something?"

"Perhaps they did. Everyone's entitled to have a go at painting if it gives them pleasure. They world's full of happy amateurs who call themselves artists to give themselves status. What I find puzzling is why most people can't *see* pictures — the good, the bad, what doesn't work, what makes your spine tingle. That's why I want to try to teach children to look, try to encourage people *how* to look — surely one of the most important gifts there is. It's such a waste, missing so much of what's there, isn't it? Such a bonus if you can see . . . or even think you can see."

Oh God: here was the message that she was soon to be on her way back. Back to work. Off again. George took his arm from her waist, a sudden melancholy trawling through him. He sat down on a hump-backed trunk that had stood in the passage for as long as he could remember. Lily sat beside him.

"It's so odd, when you see the solutions of genius," she went on. "You think: he's solved it — why can't others? But of course that's a silly question. Genius can't be copied, can only inspire, show, make it look easy, which is perhaps why so many people want to have a go. And while painters of little talent can of course improve, they can never produce that indefinable thing that's always recognisable as great art." She sighed. George put his arm round her waist again. "Genius," she went on (George didn't care if she

160

never stopped). "What is it? Think. It's Rembrandt's light on a steel helmet: the steel hard, the light intangible. How does he do it? You can look through a magnifying glass at the brush strokes and still not have a clue. Ingres: fat fleshy hands resting on rich material — Ingres is absolutely certain of the difference between silk, satin, velvet, lace, all lightness and sheen, while the flesh they support is heavy, real flesh of a completely different texture. Then think of Vermeer, painter of absolute silence, of weight. The girl pouring milk from a pitcher. You can *feel* the weight of that pitcher. You can hear the silence. How did he manage that? How did he paint the sound of sploshing milk, the strain in the girl's arm, supporting the weight? How did he? Genius. I could go on and on with examples of things people are blind to, but I won't. I don't want to bore you."

"You're not boring me. But don't you think that possibly you see all these things because you have an acuter than average perception?"

"No. Because I don't think I do. It's artists who have the perception. It's up to the viewers to see — to learn to see."

Night had lowered itself through the windows by now. The passage was husky with darkness, the pictures almost invisible: just the dull glow of gold from the haywain's frame. The trunk on which they sat had become uncomfortable. Lily stood up. She took George's hands.

"Come on: your room now. What great art have you hidden there?"

Lily, George could just see, was smiling again. He led her to his room.

"Nothing much to offend here," he said. "Just a few fish. At one time my father became a keen fisherman, went through a phase of fish pictures. Later on he took up shooting, hence the dozens of precisely feathered pheasants you probably noticed in the study." He switched on the bedside light. "I have to admit, I'm rather fond of that old dolphin — the last picture, I think, my father bought. From some student show, I think, in London."

Lily went to the fireplace and looked up at the picture of a plump green dolphin tumbling in a lace of aquamarine water.

"I could grow fond of him too," she said. "He's full of life, and look at that water. The student understands about painting water . . ." She trailed off, turned to glance without interest at the rigid fish framed on other walls. Then she met George's eye. "Time for you to explain the woman in my room," she said.

"Can't say I can be of much help, there."

They stood side by side looking at the naked young girl lying back on rich Victorian cushions, though plainly the painting had been done in the fifties. Lily had put on a single light on the dressing table: the low wattage (one of Mrs Elkin's singular economies, inherited by her son) leant no clarity to the painting.

"Whoever painted her confused skin with enamel," said Lily, at last. "Look at the hardness. That's not flesh. It's painted in exactly the same way as the cushions."

162

"I see what you mean." George thought for a moment. After the long attack on his father's pictures, he decided to make a stab at supporting the naked woman, if only to provoke Lily to more of her fierce reactions. "All the same," he said, "I do rather like the provocative way her leg's bent."

"Terrible cliché," Lily answered. "But why not? Quite entertaining. There has to be something entertaining in so stilted a gathering of brushstrokes." She said this lightly, smilingly.

"You're a very harsh critic," George said.

"Not really."

"I remember the day my father brought her home. 'I've found an Aphrodite', he said. My mother took one look and brought her up here. Could be my father had had their bedroom in mind . . ."

Lily laughed. "Well," she said. "I suppose if there's anything appealing at all about the poor girl, it's that she's quite sexy."

"She is," said George. "And you probably won't believe me, but I'd worked that one out for myself before you pointed it out."

"You're learning." Lily tipped her head towards George, smiling. There was a small silence between them before he kissed her. Then, when he drew back, thinking it was time to return downstairs now, she said, as if from a long way off, "I've been here over a week, now, George. And —"

"Is that the go-ahead. Does that mean —?"

Lily looked at him quizzically. "Bet you've never seen the naked lady with the morning sun on her."

"I haven't, no."

"There's nothing like looking at a picture in early light," she said.

"Oh, shut up about art." He kissed her. "The time's come." Too quickly for her to protest, George picked her up and carried her to the bed.

CHAPTER
EIGHT

George would like to have lingered in bed next morning with Lily, but duty made that impossible. He allowed himself to lie looking at her for a few moments — head on a bent arm, childlike, lashes that made a lengthening shadow on her cheek so it was hard to tell where lash ended and shadow began. Her hair was scattered randomly over the pillow. Despite the dullness of the room behind the thin drawn curtains, its familiar lights flickered a little as she stirred. George marvelled. Then he left her sleeping.

Prodge had suggested to him that a few pigs would add to the variety of the farm: this morning he was off to buy a couple of Gloucester Old Spots, a distinguished, rare old breed of considerable virtue. They fared very nicely without hormones, growth promoters or appetite stimulants, all things George would not abide on his farm, and they were known to be good mothers. There was also no need for tail docking, teeth clipping or castration, cruelties he equally could not contemplate, so in the experiment with pigs the Gloucester Old Spots were the answer. George looked forward to their arrival.

As he ate his breakfast he could not help smiling to himself: in the choice this morning between remaining with Lily and going to fetch a couple of pigs, the farming instinct won. She would understand, he thought. Heaven knew how she would spend her morning, but it was possible she would be looking forward to his return, late morning, as keenly as he was. And maybe her heart would beat as fast as his beat now, remembering their night.

Three hours later George returned to the farm in the Land Rover, two large pigs in the trailer behind him. To his astonishment he saw Lily crossing the yard, a pitchfork of straw trembling above her head, pieces falling on to her hair and shoulders, making for the shed where the pigs were to be lodged. At the sight of George she waved the pitchfork. The straw fell to the ground. She laughed.

George, after a quick glance round to make sure neither Saul nor Ben was about, dashed across the yard. He wanted to kiss her, to touch her, but took the pitchfork from her instead. They stood on a small gold island of straw. The sound of pigs grunting and squealing came from the trailer.

"What on earth are you doing?" George asked.

"I asked Saul if there was anything I could do to help. He looked at me in complete disbelief, couldn't believe I meant it. But when I persuaded him I did, he said, All right, you can bed down the pigsty. So ..." She smiled up at him, pleased with herself.

"You're even dressed like a farmer." For the first time, Lily was wearing old jeans and gumboots.

166

"Thought it might encourage him."

George was almost overwhelmed by a desire to leave the pigs in the trailer and carry the new farm help into the house. He said, "You pick up this straw. I'll back the trailer up to the shed."

She tried hopelessly to scrape up the straw with the pitchfork, then picked it up by hand. Her eagerness, her wild joy in this minor chore, was plain to see. George's own sense of exhilaration made him clumsy. He had to make several attempts to line the trailer with the open door of the shed.

The two pigs moved down the ramp into their new lodgings with great dignity. A fine launching, it was, said Lily: they were as stately as ships. Only the champagne was missing.

"We could have a bottle for lunch," said George. "I mean, it would be a suitable thing to do, wouldn't it? On this rather unusual day."

He and Lily stood side by side looking over the door at the Gloucester Old Spots as they examined their new habitat. They were magnificent animals, their coarse pinkish bulk broken up by a pattern of large black spots. There was something of the china ornament about them, and also something admirable about their interest in their small new world. They took no notice of their audience, but rootled about with satisfied grunts, deciding which corner of the shed would be their sleeping quarters. George and Lily watched them in silence, fascinated by the efficient manner in which they made themselves comfortable. George, glancing at Lily, wondered whether she regarded pigs in the same critical way that she looked at pictures. He wondered whether she saw all sorts of things that evaded his own eyes.

"No AI for *them*," he said. "Out in the field with the boar."

"You're going to breed, then?"

"Of course. An average litter should bring us about nine to twelve piglets. In five months they should reach some sixty-five kilogrammes live weight —"

Lily laughed. "How on earth do you know all this? I thought you'd never kept pigs before."

"I did a certain amount of research before going down this new road. Of course, I know Old Spots' meat isn't that popular — Saul did his best to persuade me I was mad. All that fat, he said. No one wants to eat that, these days. But I liked the idea of them."

"You're a farmer not entirely ruled by your head, then," said Lily.

"For the moment I can afford a non-profitable little whim like this. But there could be bad times round the corner. You can never be sure of anything in farming."

This note of seriousness did nothing to quell their spirits: for the moment anything other than this untroubled happiness was beyond imagining. They walked back to the kitchen arm in arm.

There were new cheeses on the table, and a salad. George loved the way Lily's mysterious mornings produced such lunches. He looked at his watch.

"Twelve-thirty," he said. "I could do half an hour at my desk, or I could open a half-bottle of champagne and we could have it upstairs. What do you think?"

168

Drawing the curtains in Lily's room, George hoped that Saul and Ben were still occupied with sowing and would not come knocking at the kitchen door. Lily was in bed by the time he turned round. She sat in a great flurry of whiteness, breasts resting on the sheet, struggling to open the champagne. George hurried over to help her. But he became deflected — as a farmer might, he said to himself, by such a girl as Lily Crichton in her bed at lunchtime, freckled with dancing shadows, laughing. In the end they did not bother with the drink.

At two o'clock they came downstairs for lunch, both hungry and in a hurry. George had a dentist's appointment nine miles away, Lily was to meet Nell at three to go riding.

George, watching Lily as she ate and floated to the fridge to collect water, feared her obvious deliquescence would be apparent to everyone. Her apparent happiness, her ease, her exuberance shimmied over her, a gold dust so powerful it would surely brush off everywhere she went. Nell, in her instinctive way, would know at once.

"You won't say anything to Nell," he said.

"Of course not."

"It's just that you look so — well, as if you'd been . . . that she's bound to guess."

Lily laughed. "That's entirely your imagination. I may not feel normal, but I'm sure I look it. I'll tell her I've had a hard morning laying straw for the pigs. We mostly talk about horses when we're riding. Or she tells me about the people who live in the farms we pass. I love all that. She never asks me intrusive questions."

"Good. Because Nell will find out one day. I think she's probably expecting it. But in a sisterly way she's quite jealous of my time and my affection beyond her. It'll be a delicate matter, breaking the news."

"What news?"

"I don't mean just that we're lovers, now. I mean . . ."

In too much of a hurry to work out what exactly he did mean, George kissed her on the forehead and hurried out.

A short time later Lily, about to set off to the Prodgers' farm, discovered the battery in her car was dead. She could walk the mile, but would keep Nell — who always stuck vigilantly to her schedule — waiting. She telephoned: explained the problem. Nell, all sympathy, said she'd ask Prodge to come down and either jump-start the batteries or drive her over himself. Lily sat down at the kitchen table to read the paper.

When Nell delivered the message to her brother, his heart battered so fast he feared she would see something was the matter. He turned away from her so she would not see the reddening heat that had swarmed over his face. His shaky hands he hid in his pockets.

Since that afternoon on the river bank Prodge had suffered all the symptoms of a man poised between lustful fantasy and painful reality. He had dreamt of Lily: he had ravished her in his dreams and woken up out of breath. He had taken every chance he could to catch sight of her, visiting George with some petty excuse more often than usual. A few words had been exchanged, but never had they been alone again for a moment. Now, here was his chance. As Prodge drove perilously fast along the lane to the Elkin farm, he knew he must take advantage of it. Say something: what? He didn't know. But *something* to suggest to the goddess Lily what she meant to him. She might be flattered, not believe him. She might laugh, scoff. She might be angry. Whatever: he had to risk her reaction, for no longer could he contain the restlessness that raged through him, night and day, in his heart and body.

Not ten minutes after Lily's call Prodge appeared in George's kitchen, scarlet in the face. The flush reached right up into his hairline. He looked feverish. Before Lily could ask what was the matter, or rise to go with him to the car, he had sat down beside her. His hands, clenched into fists on the table, visibly shook. A crest of sweat appeared on his brow.

"What's your trouble, then?"

"Battery. It's very sweet of you to come over, Prodge. So busy and everything. But George's gone to —"

"That's all right. Soon sort it out." He gave a small gasp, like someone with asthma.

"Is there anything wrong? You look —"

"Nothing wrong, thanks very much. Well, maybe a touch of some bug."

"Shall I get you a glass of water?"

"Don't want to put you to any trouble. But I am a bit overheated, yes." He ran a fist over his forehead, banishing the sweat. "Please."

In the sun-warm silence, Lily rose and fetched a glass, filled it with water from the tap. Prodge took three long gulps.

"That's better. Thanks for that."

Lily was regarding him anxiously. It occurred to Prodge that she must think he'd been struck by some mysterious illness. But very quickly, having drunk the water, his whole body unclenched, his taut face slackened. He was calm again, though a hint of hostility darkened his eyes.

Suddenly, with no warning, he put one of his huge hands over hers.

"Lily Crichton," he said at last, so quietly that she had to strain to hear him. "I have to tell you this. You are the most . . . extraordinary woman I've ever had the chance to meet. There's no one like you round these parts. No one like you for miles. It wouldn't be that strange, I don't suppose, should it happen to a farmer like me — and I'm not one for chances to get into the wider world — should it happen that a man like me were to run into a goddess like you on a river bank . . ." With each convolution of his declaration, Prodge's face turned more deeply scarlet. He paused, pressed his hand harder on to hers. "Well, in the unlikely event of all that happening, I think it would be a case of . . . I can't find the right word, exactly. But he'd be knocked out. Smitten. Wrecked. Troubled. Something like that." He looked at her, hurried from the abstract to the

172

truth. "Because you're exactly the sort of woman I've always had in mind, and you're not available. George got there first. Almost everything, all our lives, except for prize Friesians, George got there first." He gave a tight smile. "But if another one like you came along, daresay I'd make a play for her."

Lily laughed gently, still did not move her hand. "Oh, Prodge," she said, "I'm flattered. I hardly know what to say. I —"

"Well, I know exactly what to say, though I seem to be tying myself in knots a bit." His voice was stronger now. He removed his hand from Lily's, reclenched it. "I been tossing and turning all night, thinking about it. What I been thinking was: best to get it over. Put my cards on the table, tell her what's going on." He banged his chest. "I'm a strong man, physically. I can muck-spread all day and not an ache in my back. I can plough all God's daylight hours and more besides, no trouble. But I've never been hit like this before — just the one sighting, the few words we had, and down I went."

"Prodge," Lily said again. There were tears in her eyes.

"Silly isn't it?" he went on. "But nothing I can do about it. I been on the lookout for a good woman for some time — thought the jacket might help. And by God it did, but in quite the wrong way." This time his smile was wry. "You're light years from any woman I've ever seen or spoken to in all my life. Not surprising, really, you've brought me down."

"I'm sure I haven't brought you down."

"No, in a sense you haven't, of course." A determined energy strengthened his voice. "Outwardly things'll go on as ever. No one will ever guess what's bugging me, and I swear on my life I won't bother you with it all." He paused. "Trouble is, and it's why I'm confessing all this now — and thank God for your car playing up, I didn't know how the hell I was going to get to see you — is that strong as I am, like I say, I couldn't live the rest of my life with this secret. I had to tell just one person. Lighten the burden, that way, if you see what I mean."

"I understand."

"All I ask is that you take a bit of care. Don't make it hard for me — throw your arms round my neck at some Christmas party, something. Don't kiss me in the general kissing on a New Year's Eve, that sort of thing. I couldn't take that: might undo me. And one other thing, please say nothing to Nell or to George. Not a word. That's more important than anything."

"I promise," she said.

"Thanks. Fact is, a man can be struck down, like by bloody lightning, when he's least expecting it. That's something I've learnt. I've never had much time to think about the whole love business: too busy on the farm. The odd girl, the odd night — that's been me up till now. Not very satisfactory. But not much alternative, living here. I always assumed the right sort of girl would come along, share the farm with me, help Nell out, be my wife and mother of my children. Well, that girl will turn up one day. No doubt about that at all. But one thing she'll never know: one April afternoon I fell in love with a girl called Lily, and that love will never change."

"Prodge — I'm sorry. I understand what you're feeling. But these things are so easy to imagine, especially if subconsciously you're half wanting them."

"This is nothing to do with imagination, believe me. This is real."

"I'll do everything you ask, of course. I don't know what else to say, except that I'm sure that —"

"Don't you say anything," Prodge answered. "There's nothing you have to say. There. That's over." He pushed his chair back from the table, stood up. Chains had fallen from him. He was strong with resolve. "Everything said. I'll never mention it again, I promise you that."

Lily, too, stood up.

"Just the once," said Prodge quietly, after a moment's hesitation, "with your permission, I'd like to touch you." His request was delivered with such dignity, such restraint, that Lily, seeing the charge behind it, again felt close to tears. Filled as she was with all the surety of the last twenty-four hours, and a small hope of certainty with George, she knew there was no danger. To allow the wretched Prodge a single moment of contact would be a minimal kindness. She gave the slightest nod, permitting. Prodge cupped a hand under her chin, fingers splayed across her cheek. "Just to remember," he said.

His touch lasted for no more than a second. He swiped away his hand like a man burned. Then his eyes travelled the whole room before resettling on Lily.

"I suppose you're thinking of staying a while?" he said. "Well I'll not bother you, I promise you that. We'll never mention all this again. George's a lucky bugger, always has been." He stood up, stretched. "But thanks for listening." He lifted both arms high above his head as if to grab a bale of straw. "It's a weight off my mind. As a matter of fact, it's more than that." He lowered the invisible bale. "Confessing it to you seems to have brought me to my senses, got rid of it — almost. I can feel the whole daft business floating away, honest. — Now, this battery." They went out to the car.

An hour later, riding up the hill, Lily had no eyes for the April green of the valley below or ears for the insect drone of the distant tractor she knew Prodge was driving. Her mind was overloaded with thoughts of George, the immense change that had taken place in the last twenty-four hours. And of Prodge's strange, sad declaration. Perhaps it was one of the few disadvantages of living so far from others. A man starved of much human contact is prone to a hawk-like imagination inclined to swoop upon the odd rare prey. Prodge's disturbed state, for all his assurance about casting it off, troubled her. She hoped that the impossibility of it all would mean it would soon fade: fantasy, passion, whatever it was, rarely thrives on arid ground. It was something he had to live with until it vanished. For her part, she must grow accustomed to the guilt it had induced in her. Honour would forbid her to tell George what had happened: she could not break Prodge's trust, but only believe the mad illusion that assailed him might pass.

Nell, turning to indicate that they would have a canter, observed that her friend was unusually pale and pensive. She imagined there had been some kind of dispute with George, but it did not occur to her to ask questions.

The change in George and Lily's lives, once they had become lovers, wrought other changes. So gradually that George could never pinpoint exactly when and how they happened, he was aware of differences taking place. He would catch sight of Lily pushing a huge barrow of manure from the yard to the garden. He would see her digging, planting. She would speak of lettuces, cabbages, beans: there would be daffodils and tulips next spring, she said. Indoors there was a shift, too: Lily took it upon herself to cook, thus releasing the grateful Dusty from her least favourite duty: she continued to clean and polish the house, which she enjoyed, and deal with the laundry. Lily would drive twenty miles to a market to find the cheeses George loved, home-made jams and organic meat. Often she helped him with the paperwork, making light of it, going efficiently through it in a way George had never quite managed, for all his legal training.

There was a feeling of unreality about the new arrangement, George sometimes thought: it suddenly occurred to him that it was because they had never discussed money. Occasionally he had given Lily a wodge of notes to pay for the shopping. But she had never asked for it. Eventually, with some guilt, he realised she must have spent far more than he had paid for.

"Lily: there's the serious matter of money," he said one morning at breakfast. "God knows what I owe you. You've been paying for food and plants for weeks."

"Don't be silly. I'm fine till my stash runs out. Besides, I have to make some contribution. I'm staying here. I'm a long-term guest . . ."

She paused. This was an area neither of them had dared to approach, or wanted to. It had arrived unbidden. But having done so, George knew he must face it.

"Perhaps," he said, "we should put things on some sort of regular footing. I should give you a regular amount to buy the food and stuff. It's ridiculous that you should pay for any of that."

"Oh, George, don't let's talk about all that sort of thing. It's so . . . binding." She turned her head from him, leading him into a difficult silence.

Binding! Her word hung in the air, threatening. Was binding the last thing she wanted? But they remained locked in their own visions for only a moment. Lily broke the tension with one of her sudden smiles. She turned to George.

"But if you could afford it," she said, "I would love to make a few . . . improvements to the house." She looked up at the blistered ceiling, the stained walls, a cracked windowpane. "What do you think?"

George, who was not a man who would ever have considered altering anything in the house he was used to and loved, experienced the swiftest change of heart he had ever known.

"Of course I can afford it," he said. "I'm reasonably well off, having sold the firm. That's a good idea. You're quite right: the place could do with a lick of paint. You get so used to somewhere you don't notice . . . All I ask is that you don't want my opinion about curtains and so on. I'm no good at that sort of thing. But I trust you absolutely. You do whatever you like. Just nothing too drastic."

"Of course not! Oh, that's so exciting. That's a wonderful project to get off the ground."

And to keep you here, thought George.

"Prodge has a friend not too far away who's a good builder," he said. "You'd better get on to him."

There was no more talk of money, and in the weeks that followed George, very busy on the farm vaccinating the lambs, then shearing the ewes and rams, spent little time indoors. When he was there he noticed, as if through a mist, that there were things going on which were no business of his: there were two builders, ladders, pots of paint crowding the floors, dust sheets over furniture. For a while he and Lily took their supper on the small table in the study: the kitchen was temporarily uninhabitable while the walls were being painted. On two occasions Lily went to London for twenty-four hours, leaving George to go back to his own, empty bed, and he yearned for her. She returned with her small car full of drums of paint and rolls of material. He asked no questions, but quietly enjoyed her excitement.

By mid-June the builders had left. The house was theirs again — a different house, but not so drastically changed, as Lily had promised, as to unnerve George. After being so long accustomed to its shadows, its murky darkness and crumbling corners, he saw that light, previously spurned, was now welcomed by the colours Lily had chosen: they caught it, bounced it back, played with it. The long passages were now brighter, though the floorboards still creaked and Lily had not replaced the old carpet. Functional curtains, bought in the choiceless era of the post-war years, were replaced by cotton and linen which, again, received the light rather than hindered it.

George was delighted by all Lily had achieved. Proud of her skills, he invited Prodge and Nell to see the finished result. The four of them toured the house. Lily pointed out the changes in each room, lest they should overlook them. They were polite, but showed no enthusiasm. Prodge kept running a finger inside his collar, twisting his head from side to side, awkwardly. This was not the sort of thing that interested him, and, like George, he didn't go for change in certain areas. The house had been fine for years, in his book: why bother to change it? Besides which, all the tarting-up was surely a signal that Lily intended to stay. Although he had fought hard against his secret passion, and had managed to seduce several itinerant girls since his confession in the kitchen, the idea of Lily *staying* troubled him deeply.

"You've not messed up the study, I hope," he said, as the four of them returned downstairs.

"*Prodge*," said Nell, "Lily hasn't messed up anywhere. It's all a . . . great improvement."

"All that's happened there," said Lily, "is a bit of cleaning. The walls have a new coat of limewash, as near to the old colour as I could find. So it's just . . . brighter." They went to the study.

"That's all right, then," said Prodge, having scoured the room with blow-torch eyes. "Wouldn't have wanted you to get rid of that old sofa. I've sat on that sofa all my life."

Despite the relief of his low-key approbation, supper was not easy. Lily had gone to great trouble with the food, candles, a jug of pansies of seething blue. But the lack of ease persisted. It was the first time, George realised, all four of them had sat down together since Lily's arrival. Although she and Nell apparently enjoyed each other's company when they went riding, and on the few occasions she ran into Prodge she went some way towards winning over his natural gruffness, the evening was haunted by past evenings when it was just the *three* of them. It was impossible to ignore the resentment, caused by Lily's presence, that burrowed within the depths of Nell and her brother. They tried to disguise it, but to George it was a tangible thing. His heart cried out to Lily, knowing she must be aware of it too. It wasn't that they disliked her, of course: that would have been impossible. It was the *difference* they resented.

Lily, throughout the evening, was at her most enchanting, and the effort she made touched George profoundly. She exchanged no looks with him, made no shorthand references, kept up the face of a mere visitor. But George knew that no effort on earth would dissuade his old friends from the obvious truth. His own attempts at assuming a certain distance would never convince them. They knew him too well. It would have been very odd if they had failed to see that he loved her.

Prodge spurned George's wine, both red and white, and drank several pints of beer. He grew redder in the face, more taciturn, and sweated in the way Lily remembered he had that afternoon here at the table. When he refused her chocolate mousse, saying no thanks, he never touched chocolate, George noticed a momentary disappointment cross Lily's face. She refilled her glass of wine before George had a chance to do so.

When they had finished eating, Nell announced she was feeling too hot. She pulled off her home-made jersey of Jacob's sheep's wool. Beneath it she wore an old T-shirt the colour of an aged salmon which reflected nastily on to her neck.

"We can't all be glamorous," she said, suddenly turning on Lily. "We haven't all got the time or the reason to bother."

In the silence that followed George realised that Nell, too, had drunk far more than she was used to, and knew not what she said. For the first time he exchanged a look with Lily: don't rise, it said. Then Prodge made a ponderous statement, the words skidding.

"I'm not used to all this, yet," he said. "All this fancy stuff." He looked at the newly painted walls. "All very nice, Lily, but I'm not used to it. These bright walls, fancy flowers — didn't used to be like this. In Mr Elkin's day it was good and plain, none of this table-cloth business."

"But it was all pretty elegant in my mother's day, if you remember," said George, lightly. "It was just that Dad and I couldn't keep up her standards." He could see Prodge was brewing up to one of his occasional rages: deflection was needed, but he couldn't think how. Prodge stood up, held the back of his chair. He swayed a little.

"True," he said at last.

"So it was," said Nell. "You remember, Prodge, she always had silver napkin rings. You said the only rings you knew about went through a bull's nose. You made her laugh." George saw this appeasement was by way of apology for her rudeness to Lily: and hoped Lily saw it that way, too.

"True," he said again, and turned to Lily.

"Look, I'm sorry if I spoke out of turn. I meant no offence. It's just a matter of . . . well, getting used to George's new kitchen and so on."

"Of course," said Lily. "Of course I understand."

"I'll drive you home," said George.

"No you won't. We'll walk, Nell'n me. We'll fetch the car in the morning."

There were curt thanks: it would not have been in the nature of either brother or sister to make any attempt at false appreciation. George saw them to the door.

He returned to find Lily had once again filled her glass. On one who normally drank so little, it had had its effect. Her cheeks were scarlet, her eyes dizzied by candle flames. But she was smiling, giggling.

"Not a success," she said. "A huge, huge failure. Where did we go wrong, George."

"I'm so sorry." George sat down beside her. "Disaster. After all your effort. I don't know what got into them — drink. But the reason was the truthful reason they gave. Change. I suppose although they honestly are glad for me, all this takes a bit of getting used to."

"Oh, don't worry about any of it," said Lily, airily. "It's not important. I like Nell, I like Prodge. I'm the intruder, but I don't think they dislike me. It's just that I'm still new. I upset the old balance. It's all completely understandable."

"You were brilliant this evening," said George. "And they behaved like louts, my old friends. Though of course that doesn't make one jot of difference to my love of them."

"Of course not." Lily pushed her chair away from the table, stood up. She held up her glass, looked down at George a little uncertainly.

"I want to drink a toast to you, George," she said. "I want to make you a little speech. If I was completely sober I could never do this. But I've had more than I'm used to tonight, so it's not so hard."

She paused, giggled. George folded his arms, sat back to watch her, enchanted.

"I want to tell you, George Elkin, that I've never been so happy in all my life. Now happiness is very difficult — impossible — to describe, as you probably know. All you can do is say the word and hope the other person believes you, and can imagine how you feel. So I won't try to be more explicit." She giggled again, paused to let smiles chase smiles. "But I want you to know that it's a lovely jumble of sensations going on all the time, every moment of the day. I wake up with you every morning feeling so excited about being alive — I think that's it — and great gusts of exuberance sweep me about. I don't know how better to describe it, the utter joy of every day with you. I don't know where it comes from, or why it came to me. But I've a funny feeling it's something to do with a kind of love that's quite new to me."

"Could be," said George, smiling.

"What d'you think, George? Am I right? And I tell you another thing, quite certain. I love this place, this house, your animals, this corner of England, your land. I've explored every inch of it — the old ash coppice, the oaks. I've lain among the bluebells and the betony and the meadowsweet and the cow parsley: I've listened to the stonechats and warblers and skylarks — at least I think they were skylarks. I couldn't actually see them. And one day by the river a kingfisher flashed by me — I forgot to tell you. Oh, George, I love it all."

She stopped. Her voice had run almost to nothing. She sat down again, rested her chin in her hands. A seriousness was gathering in her face. George's heart missed a beat. "But you know what? This is all the stuff

185

of dreams. It's not real life, not for me. I'm used to independence, to working, to earning my own living. I hate to admit this, but I'm running out of money. Much though I love it here, much though I've loved doing a bit to the whole place for you, it's time for me to go back to work, earn my way."

George was silent for a minute. "No," he said at last.

"But I must. Be practical."

"Would there not be a solution . . ." George hesitated, at a loss as to how to put the idea that had struck him blindingly. "Would there not be a solution if we could formalise things a little?"

"How do you mean, formalise? That's a civic word I've never heard you use." She laughed.

"I mean . . ." George pulled one of her hands away from her cheek and held it. He needed time, but there was no time. "I mean, you wouldn't have to worry about earning money, working, if you stayed here for ever. I've plenty for the two of us."

"Is that your meaning of *formalise*?"

"It could be, yes." George nodded, smiling. "Is it becoming clear to you, what I'm trying to say? That I don't want you ever to go? I want you to stay here always, as my wife."

He saw that this suggestion had the effect of sobering Lily astonishingly fast. His proposal acted as powerfully as black coffee on the alcohol in her blood. First she cradled her head in her hands, tossing it about so that sparks of candlelight swarmed over her hair. Then she looked up, her eyes shut, with the kind of half smile

186

that suggested that, if she gave it full rein, her total happiness would escape.

"Me? A farmer's wife?"

For a terrible moment George did not know whether this question meant the absolute impossibility of such a state. Quickly he countered, "In a sense. But of course it wouldn't mean your giving up all the reviewing and writing and teaching and *looking*" — they both smiled — "that you wanted. Once you were my wife I could let you go for a few days. It wouldn't be so hard, knowing you were coming back —"

"Oh, George," she interrupted, "don't let's be practical. There's all the time in the world to arrange that sort of thing. Besides, I love work on the farm. I could do more. I only suggested going back to my kind of work because I was worried —"

"But you're not any more?"

"No, no. I daresay I could get used to being supported, at least for a while, so long as I was making some useful contribution to your life."

"So, is that — well, settled?"

"Of course it is. But let's make it soon. No hanging about. Harvest Festival. What about then?"

"Oh God, I love you, Lily Crichton," said George, pulling her towards him.

For two days George and Lily kept the news of their intended marriage to themselves. Telling Nell, George knew, would not be easy. She would be pleased for him, of course, as would Prodge. But it would change things, and they had already seen, that night at supper, that the Prodgers were shaken by change.

Procrastination does not make for ease of mind, and after two days of fretting about what words to employ, George set off on foot for the Prodgers' farm. He calculated that he would arrive at the time Nell normally groomed her horses, and thought that a horse between them might make things easier.

It was a warm summer's morning, though drifts of rain, thin as vapour, billowed through the air and touched his clothes with a light sheen, but did not wet them. George strode fast along the edges of several of his own fields until he crossed a stile on to Prodge's land, every inch of the way so familiar it was burned into his inner eye. He could have walked the whole way in his imagination, never missing a tree, a bush, a length of fencing and its history. This was the short-cut between the farms that he and Prodge and Nell had used as children. This morning, the old feeling of joy, knowing he would see their farm just over the ridge, did not come to him.

In the yard, he found Nell's bay gelding looking over the stable door. The door of the second stable was open and Nell, as he knew she would be, was grooming the grey inside. She was a large, dappled mare with a gentle eye. Nell, back to the door, whistling to herself as she ran the dandy brush over the horse's withers, was unaware of George's presence for a moment. He stood looking at her: the strong weatherbeaten arms beneath the rolled-up sleeves of her shirt, the powerful shoulders, the uncared for blonde curls snapped back from her face in a rubber band. His heart went into overdrive: he dreaded speaking.

"Nell."

She turned her head. Her powerful brush strokes did not stop. "George! What're you doing here so early?"

"I've come with news for you."

At once she stopped her work, turned to face him. "Oh yes? It can only be bad, a voice like that."

"No. It's good." He gave a half-laugh which, when he met her enquiring eye, petered out. "Lily and I are going to be married."

As, wretchedly, he looked at her, the solidity of Nell became transparent: he could see a hundred reactions within her, clouding her, confusing, clashing. But she tossed her head brightly.

"When?" she asked at last.

"Harvest Festival, thereabouts."

"Well, that's very, very good news. Lily's wonderful. You know how much I like her." Her long smile conveyed the real pleasure George's news gave her. Relief, though not pure, surged through him.

"It's vital to me that whoever I marry has your approval." He tried for lightness. "You know how much that means to me."

Nell, with a flash of defiance that George found almost unbearably moving, looked him straight in the eye. "Do you love her absolutely? Are you sure?"

"I'm sure, yes. I've never known anything remotely like this. So I take it to be the real thing."

"I expect it is. You're a good judge. You'd know."

Nell took a few steps forward, plunging through the bed of straw that came up to her knees. She lifted her arms. George clasped her to him: her head just reached his chest. His chin lay on top of it: they always hugged like this. Her hair smelt of oats and horses. He could feel her inwardly quivering.

"I'm so glad," she whispered after their long, entwined silence. "I'm so glad it's turned out like this for you." She pulled away from him. "Would Prodge could be so lucky."

"He'll find someone, in that jacket."

Nell gave the faintest smile, moved back to her grooming. "Have you told him?"

"Not yet."

"He's over on Mawkin's Field."

"I'll go over there now."

"And I'd best be getting on. Lot to do before I meet Lily to ride this afternoon — I mean, do you think she'll still want to?"

"I'm sure she will."

"Good. And at least as your wife she won't suddenly disappear. She'll be here. I'll have a friend to ride with, a permanent friend." She sounded more cheerful.

"Quite," said George. "I'll go and find Prodge."

Nell nodded at him then turned back to the mare. She began her long brush strokes over the dappled shoulder. Although her gestures — calm, strong, rhythmic — were the same as when George had arrived, there was a hint of disorder now. She moved from the horse's withers to its hocks, then back again to its neck. George walked away. From a few yards off he turned and glanced back into the stable again. He saw Nell was still brushing, hard.

George had no time to reflect on their encounter. He found Prodge in the high, narrow pasture that ran from the top of a hill down to the river — Mawkin's Field, so named because Prodge's father had once owned an outstanding sheepdog named Mawkin, much loved by the children. The field was where his talents had been discovered as a young dog. When he died, he was buried there in a ceremony of elaborate solemnity devised by the three of them. George remembered it as he hurried towards Prodge. At the burial Nell had brought a wreath of cowslips while Prodge put a bone on the grave. The headstone was financed by both sets of parents. George's own contribution had been a poem which came to him from nowhere, which he read with unfaltering voice at the end of the service over the small mound of newly dug earth.

Prodge was standing by a tall hedge running from north to south that divided Mawkin's from the adjoining pasture. His father had planted it many years ago to provide a windbreak for ewes and lambs. It was a magnificent hedge, dense and strong, towering above the other three boundaries which were purposely kept short to reduce shadow at haymaking.

"I was just wondering," he said, "when I'll be able to afford another one of these. I'd like to plant one along Ridge Hill. But to lay it like this one, fence it each side and that — well, you could be looking at near a thousand pounds for a hundred metres. How'm I going to find money like that?"

George's mind raced happily from the matter he had come to discuss.

"Maybe," he said, "a good place for another of these would be between Hemp Hill and Lark's Meadow . . ." These two fields were the only ones where George's land, and Prodge's rented land, joined. At the suggestion Prodge tossed back his head, a movement so like his sister's moments ago. He was a proud man. He wanted no help from George nor anyone.

"We could talk about it," he said, forced to acknowledge the sense of the idea. "Come to think of it, it could be of benefit to both of us. Perhaps we'd find some compromise, the money side of things. What are you doing up here so early?"

"I dropped in on Nell. Had some news for her — for you both."

"Oh yes?"

"Lily and I are getting married."

Prodge gave a sharp swing of the small scythe he was holding.

"You and Lily are getting married," he repeated flatly. "Well, what a thing. I suppose not a surprise. That's good, George. That'll be good for you. She's a rare girl."

"I'm bloody lucky," George agreed.

"How did Nell take it?"

"She seemed pleased."

"Daresay that's the case. Daresay she is. Though in her heart . . . Well, you know Nell. All of us brought up together, used to our threesome. Must be a bit of a shock for her. Besides . . . and she's never said a word of this to me, but I've always imagined, and you know I'm not overburdened when it comes to imagination — that she might have had a secret hope . . . I mean, she loves you. She's always loved you."

"And I love her. Always have, too. Always will. Nothing'll change, really. Except she'll have a friend near by — she likes Lily."

"That's right. That's good." Prodge screwed up his eyes against a brightening sun. The rain had stopped. The grass was sparkling. "Wouldn't want anything to change too much."

"It won't. And you like her?"

Prodge looked him full in the eye. "What I've seen of her, she's a good 'un. She won me over that day she caught me out in my jacket down by river. She didn't laugh. Seemed to be all sympathy. Reckon you've got a proper one there, George. Sort of thing I'd like to find myself. Not much chance. My congratulations."

He moved the short distance between himself and George, held out his hand. The two men shook, something they had never done in their lives before. But it seemed appropriate to both of them. It covered the spell of silence, rampant with different imagings of the future, that fell upon them. Then George said it was high time he got back to work, and Prodge agreed.

"Let's think about that hedge," he said.

George turned back towards home, his step lighter than it had been on his outward journey. Despite their years of close friendship, there were some things about

Prodge and Nell's hopes and fears that he had never known, and he judged it best to continue in his innocence.

Prodge stood looking at his friend move quickly into the distance. The scythe hung slack in his hand.

In accordance with both their wishes, Lily and George's wedding was a very quiet affair. Lily's mother and brother were to come, but only two of her oldest friends. The others were scattered too far away. George invited the local farmers, old Mr Anderson and Miss Hollow, and various villagers he had known all his life.

They were married on a hot day soon after the harvest had been gathered. In the church, where George's parents were buried, stooks of corn, bunched in the old-fashioned way before combine harvesters changed their shape, were propped up on the altar. The only flowers were poppies. Lily had organised them, in dozens of jam jars and vases, on every available ledge — scarlet, pink, orange against whitewashed stone. On their short honeymoon in the Shetland Isles she confessed her choice of flowers had been a mistake. Unable to withstand the heat, their fragile petals had fallen to the ground, crumpled, making natural confetti on the stone floor. They should have had roses and daisies, Lily said.

As they walked across the northern treeless hills, wiry with heather, they enjoyed reliving moments of their wedding day, reminding each other of details that had alighted, then flown, at the time. George confessed that in his daze he had scarcely noticed the flowers. His entire concentration, he said, had been on his wife, and the promises he made to her.

Part Two

CHAPTER
NINE

"George," said Lily, one evening in June, "*look*. Please look."

George looked. He saw the transformation she had made in the four years they had been married and stood in silent wonder. Preoccupied with developing the farm, he remembered he had given Lily permission to do what she liked within reason, but had been only half-conscious of diggers and rotavators and vans bearing dozens of plants and young trees. Now, walking behind her through the orchard that long ago had mouldered into a tangle of dead and dying trees, he observed new cherry, apple and plum. In the orderly grass that had replaced muddled undergrowth he saw that buttercups were rampant again, as they had been in his childhood.

George followed Lily into the garden. There, in what he remembered were previously dark corners, irises flared against the first pale roses. On the south side of the house wistaria that had languished for years had responded to Lily's severe pruning: now its sweet-smelling mauve pods turned to shift in the slightest breeze, sashayed against the grey stone walls. The lawn was mown, box hedges trimmed, brick paths weeded.

Yes, he had seen Lily mowing, trimming and weeding from time to time. He had been aware of gradual change. But no, he had not really *looked* as she now required him to do.

"Astonishing," he said. They sat on the bench beneath the sitting room window. Before them the garden stretched as far as a beautifully laid hawthorn hedge (Ben, of late, had become a keen and skilled hedger). Beyond that, fields rose up the hill where a flock of sheep were grazing.

"A garden's never finished, of course," said Lily. "But I think the major part of the work's complete — the clearing, the structure. But there's plenty still to be done. You should see my planting list for this autumn." She paused. "I'm glad I've got you to take it all in at last," she added. An almost imperceptible accusation tightened her comment.

"Oh, I've been *aware* . . . of course I've been aware." George put a hand on her knee. "I've been so totally taken up with the farm. But that's no excuse. I should have told you a thousand times how much I love all you've done to this place. Absolute wonders, really."

He glanced at her profile, then returned his eyes to the horizon, the edge of his land.

"I suppose, too, when a man has just jogged along for almost thirty years, neither unhappy nor consciously happy, and then his life, his entire being is changed by the arrival of a wife . . . Well, what happens? It's hard to register anything outside the small perfect world in which he finds himself. I mean, these days, building up the farm is my prime concern and pleasure simply because you exist. Do you see that? I'd always thought that love and work must be intertwined, and now I know that they are. As I finish doling out silage to the ewes, or the day's ploughing, I think: now back to Lily, my wife. You busying about in the kitchen, reading your books, whatever. A dozen times a day I'm tempted to return to the house to see you."

Lily gave the slightest nod of her head. George took his hand from her knee, put it round her shoulder. They both looked up at the sky, the veiled quartz-pink that precedes the sinking of the sun at the end of a fine day. There was no cloud, but a paling of the colour behind distant high land. A crow flew across the garden, wings blinking like thick black lashes. Its shadow ran with ghostly speed over the lawn.

"That's how it is," said George, feeling the weight of Lily's head on his shoulder. "How it goes on being, thank God. There's never a moment of the day when I'm not looking forward to you. Heavens, such declarations from a man not much good at saying things. How about that?"

"I love you," said Lily. "But I sometimes wonder . . ."

In the thrashing of his own astonishment at all he had just confessed, he was vaguely conscious that it was not the moment to enquire what Lily sometimes wondered. Besides, George had not finished explaining the reasons for his lack of appreciation. He wanted Lily to be absolutely sure of his regret at his failure to have told her a thousand times how much she had brought not only to him, but to this, the place he most loved.

"Does it ever occur to you," he asked, "that complete happiness can reduce, as well as expand? It can reduce your life to just the things you love, making the outer world irrelevant, or it can make the outer world feel more important, simply because of the strength of what you're feeling."

Lily nodded. George, looking down at her hair, so full of lights, felt she was only half concentrating on his words. Sleepy, she was, perhaps. She was up by six every morning. No wonder that at the end of a long day's manual labour in the garden she was sometimes tired.

"Shall I go on? For four years, I've been so completely . . . *marinated* in the happiness you've brought me —" he broke off to give a bashful laugh — "that I've been neglectful of the world beyond us."

"You have," said Lily, "a bit."

"So what I'm going to do is make amends. Let's call this a watershed evening. From now on I'm going to involve myself beyond our acres, make more effort in the community. With all my privileges I ought to take the chance to be of more positive help, somehow. God, Lily: when I think about it I can see I've been a bloody disgrace."

"Don't be so silly. You're going too far. You help a lot of people. Those who depend on you are never let down. You look after your land, and your animals, with rare passion —"

"I don't *look*," George interrupted, "in the way you would have me look. But I vow to change . . ." He gave a small laugh. This time, Lily joined him. She turned to kiss him on the cheek, then rose to go into the house.

"Supper in half an hour," she said.

"I'll be in. I'm just going to have another *look* at what you've done to the orchard . . ."

The longest day of the year was still two weeks away: dusk among Lily's new trees still held that summer lightness that never deepens into the sable dusks of autumn, but promises a night sky, thinned by the moon, that later merges confusingly with dawn. George, making his way through the trees (so carefully planted, he now saw — with a rhythm in their spacing, as his father would have said) felt strong with resolution. Happiness upon happiness. Layers of contentment that, now he reflected on them, were hard to believe.

He came to the fence that divided the orchard from Rising Meadow, a small field whose furthest boundary began to ascend the hill. Some of the Friesians were grazing here: fine specimens from the herd that had doubled since he had taken over the farm. Prodge, with his extraordinary eye for a prize cow, had helped choose most of them. The neighbouring herds were now almost equal in excellence, though George left competing in agricultural shows to Prodge. Prizes held no interest for him: they meant much to his old friend.

The wide silence was chipped by the cows pulling at the grass: a sound so familiar to George that sometimes, striding across a field full of cattle, he did not hear it — as on occasions a soft wind, or the rustle of trees, goes unheard. He remembered that as a boy of thirteen or fourteen he had tried secretly to find an adjective to describe the sound of a cow grazing, but had failed. He had come to the conclusion that there was no word in our language that could convey various sounds: music, or animals grazing in a field. One of the cows raised its head and stared at him, its jaws moving. Then, apparently uninterested in the sight of its reflective owner, it returned to eating. After four years of working closely with his animals, George felt no better able to guess what, if anything, went through their minds. He remained intrigued.

His own mind turned now to events beyond his life on the farm with Lily — things that had affected others. Cocooned in his own sense of tranquil — smug, perhaps — well-being, they had scarcely touched him. He had shown sympathy, of course, concern. But there was no lurching of the heart, none of the sickening worry that accosts a man when his *own* world is threatened.

He remembered, for instance, the evening he had found Lily in tears: the post office, she said, had finally given up the battle and was to close. The post office was the only shop in the nearest village two miles from the farm. For generations it had been run by the Head family: Jenny Head had taken over when her sister Betty, Saul's wife, had died, and had continued to run it with the same dedication as Betty before her. She had done everything she could to make it an agreeable meeting place. She had persuaded local women who were good bakers to sell their bread and cakes from her newly painted shelves: fruit and flowers from people's gardens were also willingly sold. She had added magazines to the range of newspapers, and postcards, that could never be called brash or vulgar, of local places for the tourists. The small shop, once the front room of a beamed cottage, smelt of peppermint and twine and beeswax polish. It was a place made for lingering, gossip, running into friends and neighbours. There was an air of permanence about it: its regular opening times part of the beat of the village. Should it vanish, God forbid, there would be a sense of irreparable loss. The pub, with its different atmosphere and function, was no substitute. No one ever imagined the post office would one day have to go.

But a few years ago a supermarket had been built on the outskirts of the market town five miles away. There was already a supermarket twenty miles away, but that had had little impact on the community: few people had the time, or could afford the petrol, for a forty-mile journey to buy their food. Jenny Head hoped the new supermarket would have as little appeal for the locals. At first, it seemed this was the case: they scoffed at the desecration of yet more green land and swore to ignore it. But eventually one or two tried it "out of curiosity" and inevitably they found they could save money on basic things. By comparison with the village shop it was very cheap, and the choice impressive. Others followed.

Within a year of the place opening Jenny Head knew she was fighting a losing battle. Her elderly customers still came in for their meagre needs, and the better-off, with an air of guilt, still bought their stamps, but Jenny could not compete with supermarket prices. As custom declined, a cheerlessness pervaded her small shop despite the sympathy and understanding she received from many of those who had nevertheless deserted her in favour of the supermarket. They would have liked her to stay for "sentimental reasons", they said. Sentimental reasons were no good for Jenny Head: she had to make a living. Pensioners begged her not to close down, for how would they manage to collect their money?

This was the question Lily tearfully put to George when she broke the news that the post office was definitely to shut. Then she had told him her idea of taking those without transport to the next nearest post office in the market town every week. George sometimes passed her on the road, station wagon full of old ladies and gentlemen. This weekly transport of pensioners furnished Lily with tales to tell George of their concerns for the future, the fears they bore with dignity, scarcely grumbling. George felt for them. He read stories in the press that claimed there was an upsurge in the closure of rural post offices all over the country. Concern wafted over him momentarily, as probably it did over many country-dwellers who resisted change for the worse, but who knew their feelings were of little interest to those in power. But George now guiltily recalled that his concern was not so great that he had tried to *do* anything to help: Lily was the one who had provided practical help.

Then it was learnt that Jenny and her disabled husband, much in debt, had decided to sell their cottage in which the post office had been housed for so long. The price the agents recommended, and acquired, shocked and surprised the villagers. It was understandable that Jenny should take all she could, but the price of the cottage was quite out of reach of young local couples looking for somewhere to live. The buyers were from Reading, owners of a large Mercedes. They spent a lot of money on refurbishment. No local was ever invited inside the place. There were reports of mirrored walls, but the owners of this tasteless glitter were rarely seen. Three or four weekends a year was the most they seemed to spend there: for the rest, the cottage was forlornly barred against intruders, its shutters closed, the life gone out of it.

Dismayed though he was by the demise of the post office and its sad transformation, George was not, again, disturbed enough to do anything about it. He remembered feeling a sense of helplessness, followed by ennui, and immersed himself further in the challenges of his own farm. He should have been writing some of his beadier letters to national newspapers, he thought now. He should have been protesting in the way he was best able — though he doubted this would have had any effect. The fact was that the rich were greedy, and sympathy for the decline of rural communities was not going to stop them from buying second homes.

George himself, at that time, was better off than he had ever been. The money from the family firm was well invested. The farm was thriving. Subsidies were modest compared with those of the grain farmers in the east, but they were generous. George decided to buy the small farm, whose land touched his, on the opposite side to the Prodgers. It had a dilapidated house surrounded by rotting farm buildings, but the potential was there, and the view. He remembered it in better days, and thought Lily would enjoy restoring the house while he supervised the outside.

But he was too late. The tenant farmer, a shy man with many problems, had not had his lease renewed and left the district with no farewells. The landlord, who had bought the property as an investment in the seventies, rightly judged this a good time to sell. A private deal was conducted with such secrecy that no one in the village knew about it. All was signed and sealed by the time George had made his decision. All he could do was join in the local horror when the new owner, a businessman from Cardiff, razed the spread of farm buildings to make a clock golf course and an ornamental pond. Plastic urns of geraniums (which had no hope of withstanding the wind from the moor, but he would learn) and an electronic gate earned the derision of everyone. But at least on the only occasion the businessman went to church he put a fifty-pound note in the plate.

Still leaning against the fence, all colour gone from the sky, the cattle now a single smudged shape huddled by the hedge, George realised that these things were all indications that had been amassing for several years. Statistics give no clue of the plight of individuals, but these were signs that were beginning to cause a shift in British country life, and there was reason for both sadness and alarm. The thing about change, George reflected, is that it's so easy to assess in retrospect, and so easy to anticipate. It's when the process is actually taking place that it's harder to be certain of what's happening. This, at least, was his excuse for not having looked more carefully, seen, appreciated, acted. It was with a sense of profound self-reproach that he turned at last to go back to the house. He pondered whether he should tell all this to Lily, but decided against it. The best antidote to regret, in his estimation, was privately to work out remedial action.

"Where've you been?" Lily asked.

As always she had laid supper with care. There were folded napkins and a jug of peonies on the table. She had taken trouble with the food, grilling fish in the way George liked and making a salad of lettuces and herbs from the garden. These suppers had come to seem like a prize at the end of each day: George could never quite accustom himself to such spoiling, and floundered about what he could do in return. Lily had so often said she required no help indoors that he had given up trying.

"I was thinking . . ." said George, in a sudden quandary about which of his thoughts to reveal, "I was thinking, among other things, about various reports I've been reading: the gradual erosion of wildlife, plant life, rural life . . . the general slaughter, as it were, of the country. It seems to be creeping up on us."

He paused. Lily looked at him.

"I realised —" But no. He did not want to elaborate on what he had realised. "As a matter of fact," he stumbled on, "I've heard both linnets and corn buntings quite recently, but I understand their numbers are dropping alarmingly. Skylarks, even nightingales . . ."

"Oh, there are signs," said Lily. "There are signs everywhere. By the end of the century the country will be one huge theme park, and farmers will be extinct."

"Nonsense. That's ridiculously pessimistic. There'll always be farms, farmers, crops, animals. The nation couldn't survive without them for a thousand reasons. Besides, farmers have been doing well with the subsidies. Look what Prodge has managed. Many of them are rich. There's no danger —"

"I just have a feeling." Lily shrugged. "The accumulation of signs — it frightens me."

George put his hand over hers. He never was able to understand how often she could read his mind. Sharply, Lily pulled her hand away, turned to look out of the window. It seemed to him that she had retreated a little. For all her care of him, her usual attention to the pleasures of the evening, she had distanced herself in a way George couldn't quite comprehend. Or perhaps, he thought, he was misreading everything, and her coolness was merely a reflection of his own melancholy this evening.

"A leaf," George said, surprising himself by his own cheerfully enquiring voice.

"What?"

"Do you remember when we first met you described yourself as a leaf blown about, or something?"

"I do, I think."

"It occurs to me you're not . . . blowing about so much, are you?"

There was a dying fall in Lily's eyes which passed so quickly, before she gathered together a smile, that George could not be sure it had existed. She shrugged.

"Well: I don't believe custom stales if custom is good enough, which of course it is. But we all stop blowing about quite so frenziedly after a while, don't we?"

"But you're still just as happy?"

Lily nodded. "I think I am. Why?"

"I sometimes wonder."

"And you?"

"Oh, me. I'm less airborne than you. Boots firmly stuck in the ground. A very straightforward fellow, your husband, as you may have noticed." He gave the kind of twinkling smile which she used to say was the most beguiling smile of any man she had ever met. Then he switched to his perfect imitation of a German farmer he knew. The German farmer had provided many an anecdote. Apparently she didn't mind how many times the stories were repeated: she always laughed. Tonight, he could see she tried to respond — she gave a small puff of laughter that was hollow at its centre. To keep impending silence at bay, he switched with a certain desperation to his equally good French farmer giving a lecture on the art of castrating a boar — a story he had not told since their honeymoon. Again Lily laughed a little, but the old warmth that used to emanate from his funny stories eluded them both this evening.

When they had finished eating, Lily took her customary place in the armchair by the unlit fire. They rarely sat in the study these days. Lily picked up her book on Vermeer. George skimmed through the pages of *Farmers Weekly* but could not concentrate. He flicked the magazine on to his knee, which did not disturb Lily's concentration. Then, while he contemplated his wife, he fell to wondering again.

In the first two years of their marriage, George recalled, Lily had been like an excited child. She kept declaring her happiness, but such daily pleasure, as is the nature of acute happiness, made her restless. It was hard to know, she explained, where to put such intense feeling. She skittered about from project to project: once the house was newly painted, and the curtains in place, she started to catalogue old David Elkin's vast collection of books. One moment she would be halfway up the library steps reorganising a shelf of leatherbound tomes: the next she was scattering pellets for the sheep. She walked the dogs several miles a day, she rode twice a week with Nell. Her energy seemed uncontainable. It fizzed about her, almost visible, infectious. George only had to be in her presence for a moment to be dazzled.

Her love of the farm and their acres of land was as keen as her love for George. She was thrilled by the acquisition of a larger herd, more sheep, further fields. She joined George's disappointment when the experiment with pigs failed, and no more were bought. She sympathised when the next-door farm was sold before George could buy it. As for her own work, its significance seemed to have diminished with the novelty of being a farmer's wife. She still wrote a few articles for minor art magazines: she was occasionally called upon to assess some West Country collection of watercolours for an auction house, or to review an exhibition. But she came to refuse work if it took her from home. She hated being away even for a night, she told George. She seemed to have no desire to see old friends in London or Norfolk. George, and the small world of the farm, was all she wanted.

George remembered that a year after their wedding the thought had come to him — he remembered exactly the moment: he was shoving a bull calf up the ramp of the trailer — that perhaps what Lily wanted, needed, was a child. He had put this to her, excited by the idea. But no, she said: she wanted to keep to their previous agreement — no children for five years so that they could have a period of married life to themselves. He had understood, and said no more about it.

He remembered, too, one fine summer day when, eating his lunch in silent haste, he had suddenly paused and asked if there was anything she would like. Surprised by the question, Lily assumed a look of mock seriousness.

"I think I'm almost perfectly provided for," she said, "but I could do with a deckchair."

"A deckchair?"

"I have this fantasy, sometimes: at the end of an afternoon's gardening I'd like to sit under the apple tree with my book. But there's nothing to sit on."

"A very modest fantasy," said George, getting up to leave, his moment of acute consideration over. "We used to have plenty of deckchairs. All rotted and thrown out, I suppose. I'll see what I can do."

Although several weeks went by and no deckchairs appeared, Lily did not mention the matter again.

George had more pressing matters to deal with than garden furniture. But she did observe that more frequently than usual he disappeared in the car, sometimes for two or three hours at a time, leaving Saul and Ben to manage without him. He never said where he had been.

"Where do you keep going?" Lily asked at last, "not on market day? A mistress on the moor? It's so unlike you to abandon your share of the work."

George smiled. "Skiving for a good cause," he said. "You might be surprised to hear this, but I'm *looking*."

A few days later he hitched the trailer to the jeep and returned with a large, covered object. He told Lily to stay in the house till he called. She saw Saul and Ben, faces tight with conspiracy, hurry to help him unload.

In the evening George suggested they should make their way to the apple tree. There, positioned precisely so that from its seat was a view of both the house and the fields beyond, was an old rattan swinging garden seat for two. Both its awning and its cushions were faded blue stripes, so pale they were no more than ghost stripes. Lily, enchanted, flung herself down on one end, pushed off with her foot and set it moving. George sat beside her.

"I really looked," he said. "That's why it's taken so long. Catalogues, auctions, antique shops. I was about to despair when an old girl in Somerset answered my plea in one of the local papers. Seemed she'd lived in India at the time of the Raj. Brought back tons of her stuff when she came home in the forties. It was made out there. Like it? You could always have new cushions."

"Never," said Lily. "It's perfect. Thank you for taking so much trouble to find the perfect thing."

On summer evenings, they often swung together on the Raj seat after supper till it was dark. At other times, when George was busy, Lily would swing alone, back and forth, while George, in his study working on the papers, would move a little from side to side in his father's old office chair — both, in their separate ways, lulled by the rhythm.

Now, as he sat at the kitchen table, eyes on the silent figure of his wife, George could feel the emptiness in his hand where she had snatched her own away from him at supper. The echoes of that emptiness still ran along his fingers, chilling, like snow. Lily's movement had been swift and firm, a matter of a moment, and possibly for practical purposes — she had then lifted a jug of water. But George thought not. It had been an almost imperceptible rejection, but firm of purpose. Of that he was certain.

In the second two years of their marriage the acute happiness that Lily had at first flaunted with such fervour, appeared very slightly to be on the wane. There were days when she laughed a little less, was briefly irritated by a domestic problem, declared an unusual tiredness and slept for an hour in the afternoon. On occasion, when George came into the kitchen in the evening and, as always, drew her to him, her response was dulled: she would kiss him quickly and push him away as if their contact was of no consequence and she wanted to be getting on with something else. Sometimes, when he was explaining a farming matter to her or describing childhood experiences with Prodge and Nell, she would turn her head away, the customary light of interest gone from her eyes. Even in bed, from time to time, her eagerness seemed subdued. These small changes now made pinpricks in George's heart, but he made no mention of them. His belief was not to ask questions if there was any risk of unearthing things that might unsettle their life. Besides, he reckoned, most of Lily's cool gestures were probably not caused by anything *he* had done (surely his uxoriousness was almost faultless) but the result of the general fluctuations of mood that beset most women.

At some point — it must have been winter: he remembered he was scraping mud from his boots — it occurred to him to ask Lily again if there was anything she would like. Once more, she was puzzled.

"No, why?" she said.

"Anything to ease the winter months, to entertain you apart from books and music, the long evenings?"

"I suppose a colour television would be an asset," she answered, having thought for a while. "I'd like occasionally to watch the news and the odd play. Our set only provides pictures of fog."

"Good idea." George cursed himself for not having thought of this before.

Some days later he came in with a small but modern television and a video. He also brought home a hand-made reed basket which some weeks before Lily had admired in the farmers' market, filled with videos

216

of the sort of films that were never shown outside London.

"*And*," he said, "here's a catalogue with a huge list of French and Italian films I know you like, so you can send off for them whenever you want."

Lily picked up a card that George had stuck among the videos. *I hereunto declare*, he had written, *that, whenever possible, Farmer Elkin will join his wife viewing films at least once a week. The whole idea comes with all my love.* Lily laughed, hugged him.

"If I asked for a puppy you'd bring back an elephant," she said. "Your imaginings always go further than mine. I love your surprises."

George had continued to surprise Lily from time to time: not through expensive purchases, but with unexpected treats or presents that had taken him a long time to plan. Her reactions reminded him of his mother's delight when his father would come home with a hideous old teapot, or a threadbare Eastern carpet that had taken his fancy. He reckoned surprising must be in his genes, but he was better at it than his father, and Lily's pleasure was always genuine. His mother's had been no more than a convincing act. All the same, George remained concerned that there was nothing he could do to recapture the old constancy of Lily's apparent contentedness. She seemed to have slipped down a few notches in the scale of happiness and George was loath to enquire why.

Trouble was, he supposed, he was so busy with the farm and the ever-increasing paperwork that he was not the ideal husband. But he had not been too worried:

after all, the exuberant heights of a honeymoon were bound not to last. For a while their own rapture had far exceeded any expectations. It was hardly surprising their life had settled down, now, into the duller hum of daily life, with all the external forces that daily rasp. For the majority of time there was so little reason to fear all was not well with Lily that George's occasional suspicions were eradicated. In the last three months, since she had turned her attentions to the garden, a project so wholly engaging that nothing had diverted her, she had been shimmering with energy, plans, laughter. Keeping him awake far into the night.

So it was all the more a shock, her small withdrawal tonight. George's conscience, already battered by his reflections in the orchard, was in no state to accommodate more regrets. And yet there they were, pressing upon him: perhaps he should ask what was assailing her, what was the reason for the dimming of her joy. But even as he tried to persuade himself, he could hear her scoffing laugh, her insistence that he was imagining things. Occasionally, she would say, she had every right to be out of sorts, and she was fine, happy as ever. That was it: her voice in his head spoke strongly. She *was* fine, Lily. His concerns were surely unfounded. Any form of change was too appalling to contemplate. Tides in the affairs of married couples constantly shifted: he knew that, and could accept it. What he could not conceive of was any change in the depth of their love, or the extraordinary joy of their life on the farm.

218

Late, Lily put down her book. She smiled, held out a hand, but George thought he saw an emptiness behind her eyes that alarmed him. He saw that she was heavy with sadness that she did not want questioned.

"I'd like to come to the market with you in the morning," she said, "see the bull calves go."

George was aware that he looked surprised. He could not believe that calves were uppermost in her mind. But then how wrong we are, over and over again, in guessing the thoughts of those nearest to us.

"Of course." George smiled. "Though you know what market day is — a lot of hanging about."

"I'd just like to be with you."

So it wasn't only the calves. George, encouraged, put out the lights. Arm in arm they made their way through the shallow darkness to the stairs. Not for a long time had George been so eager for a day to end, or so impatient for the morning.

CHAPTER
TEN

"Happiness is so difficult," said George at breakfast next morning. "Difficult to convey, difficult to contain, difficult to preserve, isn't it?" He'd been thinking about it for many hours of the night. But as he saw the expression of normal joy in Lily's eyes shrink to nothing, he realised he'd begun the day with a mistake. He should not have mentioned so delicate a subject at this time of the morning. New regret added to old.

"It is," said Lily, tightly. "What time are we leaving?"

"Soon as we've finished." His foolishness had probably spoilt the day.

They drove to the market in silence. Fierce summer rain fell from muddied skies. Clouds fretted this way and that, constantly changing direction, their course confused by cross-winds. When they arrived, Lily changed her mind about wanting to see the bull calves sold. She picked up her basket and said she was off to shop. George suggested they should meet at the Farmers' Rest for lunch. What was the matter with her? He felt queasy with alarm.

He went to find Saul, who had transported the calves earlier. As he made his way through the pens it seemed to him that the place was unusually lacking in cheer this morning. Maybe it was the rain, darkening battered jackets and dripping from sodden hats, that gave this impression. But no: farmers this dry summer would welcome a shower. Maybe it was his imagination. In his anxiety about Lily's strange mood George could not be sure of his judgement. But he was pretty certain the melancholy air was real. Men's faces were closed, their eyes hard with the kind of anxiety that has not yet turned to resignation. Greetings between them were curt, gruff. There was none of the usual banter. What was it all about?

George came to the pen where his own calves innocently awaited their future, their dark eyes more curious than anxious. A man was leaning on the rails. He appeared to be studying them, though his frown indicated that his mind was not entirely on the animals before him. It was Prodge.

"Fine lot: what d'you think?" asked George. In the noise of lowing cattle he could not be sure his question was heard. Prodge rose from his leaning position, faced George.

"Magnificent," he said.

Prodge, like so many others, was bleak of expression. Raindrops stuttered down the cracked wax of his jacket. Hatless, his blond hair was clamped darkly to his skull.

"What's the matter? What's wrong with everyone?" George asked.

"You mean you didn't seen the telly last night?"

"No."

"God Almighty. First pictures of a cow skittering all over the place, legs crumpling beneath it, falling." He shook his head. "Never seen anything like it. This BSE business is going to slaughter the lot of us, mark my words."

"Christ," said George. A picture of a mass cull of cattle, and the effect this would have on thousands of livelihoods, on the future of farming itself, notched through his mind. He felt the skin of his face tightening on the bones, and knew then that his expression was now identical to that of his comrades: fear and dread united them.

"You've heard?" At lunchtime Lily was waiting for George in the bar of the pub. She could tell at once from his face that he had. "We should have been watching the news."

"I daresay the pictures will be repeated a good many times," said George.

"What do we do?"

"Not much we can do." George sat down beside her. "Just pray."

"But it's inconceivable that after years and years of hard work whole herds of cattle could be wiped out, isn't it?"

"I hope to God it won't come to that." In his heart George thought that it probably would. He reflected how swiftly the difficulties of happiness, idly dwelt on just hours ago, were now replaced by misgivings of a quite different and more terrifying order. He also noted that Lily, despite her concern, was still cool, and mysteriously aloof. He was reminded of that first long-ago picnic, when neither of them meant anything to the other. Fear for their own future suddenly added to his fear for British farmers. He bowed his head, silent.

Three days later Prodge rang and asked George to come over as soon as possible. He would not say why.

George arrived just after the afternoon milking. The cows were in the yard waiting to go back to their pasture. Prodge, head on his arms, which were folded on the top rail, was studying them with such intense concentration that he did not hear George approach. George touched him on the shoulder. Prodge turned slowly. He was pale. He was fighting off a bad dream.

"So what's up?"

"Thanks for coming. I want you to look at Bessie." He pointed to a large cow near to them, one of the largest in the herd. George studied the animal as carefully as he could. She turned her great head towards the two men, perhaps aware of the acute observation. Her navy eyes, spiked with reflections from her pale lashes, regarded them patiently. She swished her tail: gave a slow, milky sigh. George smelt her breath, carried to him on the air of the sigh. Then she turned away, the jigsaw pattern of her black and white hide merging into the op-art confusion of the rest of the herd.

"What seems to be the trouble? She looks all right to me."

"I don't know. Can't put my finger on it. Just have a feeling."

"What are the signs?"

"Nothing very specific. She seemed a bit restless last night. Bit agitated."

"With this scare, it's easy to imagine signs when you're half expecting the worst."

"Perhaps that's it. But Bessie's a calm bugger. Dozy, even. My best milker. So — I don't know. Maybe it's all in my mind, like you say."

"I'm no judge, Prodge. You know much more about cows than me. As far as I can see, she's fine."

Nell appeared on the far side of the pen, opened the gate. The cows hustled out, eager to return to grass. Their huge udders now relieved of milk, there was a lightness of being among them as some of them broke into a few trotting steps. On their way in to be milked the general air was quite different: slow, heavy, sloomy. While George contemplated their general mood of post-milking gaiety, Prodge's eyes anxiously roved over every cow as they filed through the gate.

"I can't be sure," he said again, when the last one was gone. "But I've heard say there are some farmers see a few bad signs and quickly sell the animal. I don't want to be accused of anything like that. If one of my animals goes down, I want it slaughtered straight away."

"Of course. Just keep a close eye on them. Any more worries, call the vet."

"That I will," said Prodge. "Thanks for coming up. I better go and give Nell a hand." He paused for a moment. "Lily all right?"

"Lily's fine."

"That's good."

"Why?"

"I saw her and Nell on a hay bale the other day, jabbering sixteen to the dozen. Long faces, I thought. But then all this worry colours everything. Every day, there's this cloud."

George clenched his fist and tapped Prodge on the forearm — a gesture he had inherited from his father that was designed to comfort without words. But Prodge could not smile. He turned away to follow his cows.

Halfway up the hill, on his way back home, George stopped the car and got out. He leaned over a gate and looked down on the meadow where Prodge's cows were now grazing, spaces between them. Later, lying down to chew the cud, they would close ranks, move nearer to each other. The rhythm of their day, only briefly stirred by calving, made a discipline that all farmers had to abide by. For it suddenly to be snatched away would be unthinkable.

George could see the tiny figures of Prodge and Nell making their way back to the farm. Prodge had his arm round Nell's shoulder, a gesture so unusual it could only have been inspired by the worry they both felt. And Prodge's apprehension had affected George, though he tried to fight it, tried to tell himself there was nothing whatsoever the matter with Bessie. Thousands of farmers round the country must be going through the same thing — anxiously seeing signs that were not there. George looked from the cows to the landscape: Prodge's rented land, cultivated with such pride and skill by one so young. God forbid that his friend's lifework should be threatened. Renewing his efforts to shake off such morbid thoughts, he drove quickly home. There, he went straight to the field where his own cattle grazed. He began slowly to look over the entire hulk of each animal — though he knew Saul and Ben, with eyes far more expert than his own, had been doing this every day since the BSE scare began. As far as he could see, they were fine. His worry was for Prodge and, behind that, for Lily. Quiet, pale, strange Lily.

That evening, having told her of Prodge's fears, George was keen to leave the subject of cows. Instead, he turned to horses. Had she always, he asked Lily — a question he had been meaning to put to her for a long time — been such a keen rider? Lily shrugged. None of her old exuberance had returned, but he could see she was making an effort to be warm, friendly.

"No, not always. It's a case of having to make myself," she said. "I didn't want to be beaten." She was silent for a while, summing up in what vein to tell her story, George imagined. This was a habit of hers he had grown accustomed to.

"I had a nasty experience with a horse when I was a child," she said at last. "At home. Norfolk. I was walking along the marsh path to the staithe — hurrying along, actually, hoping to see some boy I'd met on the water the day before. I was twelve or thirteen, can't remember which."

She gave George a look, a half smile.

"There were always a few horses grazing on the marsh. They didn't take much notice of visitors, though sometimes they'd come up, want a pat, nuzzle you then

226

turn away, bored. Anyhow, this particular day there were three of them. I saw them far ahead of me, bashing their tails against the flies. It was terribly hot, overcast. Perhaps they were irritated by so many flies.

"They looked up at me with one accord — rather odd, that, I thought. Then they began to move towards me. I stood still for a minute, not in the slightest alarmed, but thought the best thing to do was to get off the path. Which I did. The first two horses, only yards away from me, suddenly veered back on to the marsh, bucking and squealing, which seemed to inspire the third one. That was a great black ugly animal, much larger than the others.

"I was now completely exposed to its view, and it began to gather speed with a kind of vicious intent. It covered the ground between us very quickly — I was still rooted to the spot beside the path, not knowing what to do, but some instinct told me not to run. It was slashing its head from side to side, nostrils flared like a charging warhorse, its great long yellow teeth bared, spittle flying from its mouth. I was sure it was going to kill me — do horses ever kill people? I don't know — but terror made me incapable of any decision. When it was about five yards from me, without thinking I should do this — I just did it — I threw myself to the ground, shut my eyes and screamed. Thank God, this seemed to work, confused the maddened horse. It swerved away from me, bucking, hooves thunderous in my ears. I could feel the air they cut whipping across my face. Then it was gone. Squealing off to its companions. It was the greatest moment of terror in my life so far."

Lily paused again, gave a small, self-deprecatory laugh. George filled her glass with wine.

"God knows how long I lay there shaking. Eventually I crawled on my stomach to the hedge. The horse was far away by now, grazing with the others as if nothing had happened. But I was too scared to stand up in case it turned and saw me and had another go. Silly, I know. But it had been a very . . . and then I began crawling to the staithe. Several hundred yards to go. I don't remember if I caught sight of the boy. I certainly didn't take my boat out, but ran home along the road. My father reported the vicious horse to its owner and it was taken away. Otherwise I might never have walked along that path again."

She paused once again, shrugged.

"So after that I decided I must make a big effort to go on liking horses, keep on riding — never a passion of mine, as with some children. But I'd always enjoyed it. I had to fight terrible nerves for a while, but I think I'm OK now. Though I still rather dread hot days, flies pestering, swishing tails . . ." She trailed off.

George took her hand. She didn't, as she used to, respond by weaving her fingers through his, or kneading his knuckles with her thumb. But she didn't withdraw it, either.

"What a terrifying experience," he said at last, conscious of the feebleness of his words. "But Nell tells me you're a really good rider — you've become much better, more confident, since you've been here. She mentioned you might even hunt this winter."

This startled Lily. She looked at George with apprehensive eyes.

"Did she say that? She's been trying to persuade me. But I've never definitely agreed. I'm not sure I'm brave enough. Though I'd love to try. Perhaps. Maybe, maybe . . ."

She shifted her chair so that she was close enough to George to lay her head on his shoulder.

"Oh, George," she said. He could feel the brief but strong shudder that went through her. Then she sighed, and he sensed a releasing of some long-harboured wistfulness, or melancholy. Or, perhaps, some profound unhappiness that she had chosen not to share with him. He gripped her, kissed the top of her head with kisses that smudged into each other. She allowed him to do this, but did not respond in kind.

Now it was his turn to be on a path facing some unknown beast that charged towards him, he thought. Frozen by fear, like Lily long ago, he had no idea what to do.

Ten days later there was a telephone call from Nell. Please come quickly, she said. Prodge had been right. The signs he had seen in Bessie were not his imagination.

Again Prodge and George stood looking at the huge cow. They leant on the rails of a small pen where she had been put away from the rest of the herd.

"Nothing I could be really sure about after you left," said Prodge. "Then last night she fell. I thought she'd just skidded on the muck. But no. She had quite a job to get up. Then she fell worse, legs splayed out like — well, like nothing I've ever seen. She managed to get up again, trembling all over, head jerking, frightened. I knew, then. Not much doubt, I thought."

"Christ, Prodge. You called the vet?"

"He's on his way."

They stood in silence contemplating Bessie. Her great head was lowered, her eyes flickered. Her left shoulder, fretted with an intricate pattern of black and white, trembled. The skin puckered like water in a pond stirred by a breeze. Then suddenly the trembling raced from shoulder to body, hide moving over ribs that had not been visible on George's last visit. Bessie lifted one foreleg, as if intent on moving, then thought better of it. As she returned her hoof to the ground the entire leg began to shudder.

"You know what this means?" Prodge's hand — great muddy fingers — half covered his mouth, making it difficult for George to hear him. "You know what this bloody means, George? Simon'll call some MAFF vet. She'll be slaughtered by this evening. They'll cut her head off, send the brain for analysis. Look: that great fine head chopped up. Makes you sick. Then what? I'll get something from the government one day. Oh yes: I'll get a cheque eventually. Money in return for Bessie. Some compensation."

George, hearing the break in his friend's voice, did not turn to look at him, but continued to regard the frightened animal. He remembered Prodge's excitement when, some years ago, Bessie, in her prime, had won first prize at a large agricultural show. She had produced God knows how many high-quality calves. She was Prodge's finest milker. And now, after another half-day terrified and confused by her own juddering limbs, she was to be beheaded in order to extract the neat tunnelled ball of her brain. This would be sliced by someone in a white laboratory coat, peered at through a microscope, analysed, discussed by those who had no picture of her life on Prodge's farm. George felt cold.

"And after that," Prodge went on, "will come the real tumble. The reckoning. No more exporting beef calves. French won't exactly be wanting them for their veal any longer, will they? We've been getting good prices, no one can say we haven't. But now they'll be useless, worthless. I've heard a farmer further west took a gun to his own bull calves. Can't blame him. It's curtains for a lot of us. Beginning of the end."

Before George could gather any words of comfort they heard footsteps behind them. It was Simon, their local vet for the past decade. He wore a stiff blue overall that looked as if it had been through a rigorous laundering process. His mouth was a downward curve that almost touched his jaw. Bessie, seeing the stranger, uneasily raised her head and gave a great bellow. Its anguish thundered through the stillness. The three men looked on, appalled, at her lashing mauve tongue, black nostrils running with slime. Then the sound was cut off as Bessie clamped shut her mouth and let her head fall again. A moment later came answering cries from her companions in a nearby field.

"Morning, Simon." Prodge nodded at the vet, folded his arms. His whole face slid about as he fought for control. "I'll leave it to you," he said. Then he walked away quickly without looking back.

George stayed at the Prodgers' farm for several hours. He and Nell sat indoors drinking cups of tea, hardly speaking. George took it upon himself to ring the Ministry about procedures while they awaited the official vet. Prodge was out on the farm somewhere, avoiding both Bessie's pen and the arrival of the unknown vet. Nell said it would be best to leave him. He'd work it off, somehow, she said, slashing at saplings in the north hedge, mixing feed, whatever.

When there was nothing left for him to do, George walked to his car in the yard. Nell came with him. He felt reluctant to leave her, but she said it was time she went and helped Prodge.

"He's not usually down for long," she said, "though this is a blow on a different scale. Much worse for him than for me, really. I mean, he's the genius behind the cows. I'm just the labourer. He's put his entire being into working up this herd: they're his life. If they're wiped out . . . it's hard to imagine the consequences."

She made a sudden, unpremeditated move towards George: put her arms round his neck, laid her head on his shoulder much as Lily had done so recently. It was the first time George had been this close to her since his marriage — their physical contact had been reduced to social kissing, their hugs of old abandoned. It felt

232

odd. Her hair smelt of hay, animal, chicken feed, vegetables — smells he was as used to as Lily's flower scent but certainly not unpleasant. Her arms, unlike Lily's, were heavy. George felt awkward, embarrassed. Then quickly he chided himself for such selfish sensations. Nell needed his comfort.

George put his arms round her, increasing his clasp. For a moment he laid his head on top of hers, surprised to find her wiry-looking curls were as soft as Lily's. In response, she clutched more tightly at his shoulders. He could feel the hard beating of her heart, and the strength of her distress.

Their union lasted only for a second or two, then Nell pulled back. She looked up at George, mouth open as if to speak — or wanting to be kissed? — he could not be certain which. But she backed away further, leant against the car.

"Christ," she said. "I'm sorry, crying on your shoulder. I'm all over the place."

"You're not crying," said George. "You never cry."

"True." Nell managed a smile. "But I nearly am. Goodness knows what this'll do to Prodge."

"He's strong. He'll . . . Anything, anything at all I can do?"

"Not really. Thanks for being here." She looked down, then up at him again. "Lily all right?"

"I think so."

"Good."

"Why?"

"I don't know." Nell shrugged. "I had the impression she's been a bit — I don't know. Not her usual self."

"Has she said anything?"

Nell shook her head.

"I must be off," said George, getting into the car. "I'll come over tomorrow. Let me know if you need us before then."

As he drove away he could see the figure of Nell in the driving mirror, watching him, legs planted apart, unmoving, all expression gone from her face. It was impossible to put aside the memory of the intensity of her clinging to him just now — a mixture of unhappiness and . . . fear, wasn't it? George could not be sure. During his marriage to Lily she had shown nothing but friendship, kindness, to them both. She had never appeared to be jealous of his marital status. But today, with her defences down due to the tragedy of a doomed cow, he had sensed feelings of vulnerability, wordless yearning.

Lily's car was not in the yard: it was the day she took three old people from the village to collect their pensions. Often she had tea with one of them on their return, and did not get home till just before supper. George hurried to the cowshed, anxious to break the news of the Prodgers' cow to Ben.

The parlour was thick with the warm sickly smell of newly drawn milk. There were the familiar sounds: the muted clank of machinery, the music of milk pulsing from udder to tube. Ben was bent over one cow, releasing its udders from the rubber teats that had finished their job. When he stood, hands full of what looked — from a distance — like a mechanical octopus, his face brimmed with satisfaction. Day after day, George had noticed, young Ben seemed to gain pleasure from the completion of a farm job, whatever its nature.

Ben, keen to hurry on to the next cow, scarcely acknowledged his employer. George went nearer. To make himself heard he had to speak more loudly than he wanted.

"One of Prodge's cows," he said. "BSE. Gone down with . . ."

Ben blinked very fast. He put a hand on the backside of the cow nearest to him. A pale sheen flared through the weatherbeaten bronze of his face.

"Shit," he said at last. George nodded. Ben looked up and down the parlour. "We're all right here, touch wood. No signs. I check every morning and night. Sometimes I go out in the field dinner time —"

"I know you do," said George. "Thanks." Then he left to walk back to the house.

Lily still had not returned. Passing through the kitchen George noticed that the table was already laid for supper, linen napkins folded on side plates, a jug of tulips — Lily's standards never failed. He decided, unusually, to have a bath before eating — to clear himself of some of the day, renew his strength and calm before breaking the horrible news.

He spent a long time in the bath, sorting through a vision of eyes he would never forget: Bessie's, frightened in her lowered head; Prodge's, miserable, full of foreboding; Nell's, impossible hope and irreparable hurt in equal measure; Ben's, the pupils huge with shock and sympathy. How would Lily's be? Full of tears, perhaps. Unlike Nell, she sometimes cried on behalf of others.

George stirred himself at last. He put on a clean shirt, hurried downstairs. He needed a drink. He needed to embrace his wife, watch her busying from table to stove, chopping, stirring, as she did every evening.

But the kitchen was still empty. George went to the dresser, poured himself a whisky. He was both anxious and impatient. It was unlike Lily to be so late. Where was she? Why hadn't she rung? As he moved past the table again to the chair by the fire, he noticed a letter propped up against the roses, half hidden. *George*, it said, in her writing on the envelope.

George picked it up. He held it warily, as if it were poisoned, or contagious. For the second or third time that day his heart began to pound. He sat down, finished his drink in two gulps. Then he tore open the envelope and opened the wodge of pages. He began to read.

Darling George,

I've gone. At the time of writing this I don't know where I'm going, but wherever it turns out to be I'll be all right. I promise you that. So whatever else you have to deal with, because of my flight, you can at least always be sure that I'm safe, provided for. No cause whatever to worry about my well-being . . .

How can I ever begin to explain? I tried on so many occasions. I thought it was only fair to make some attempt to let you know what was going on. But each time I determined to take the plunge, I failed. I was convinced you wouldn't understand, or would try to make me change my mind or wait patiently till this odd, frightening phase (if it is a phase) is over. How many times did I sit opposite you at the kitchen table, yearning to begin, to tell you . . . and was never able to bring myself to do it? On each occasion silence engulfed me. I couldn't do it. I dreaded too much your reaction, your face, your hurt. But it wasn't just that. I could never find the words. And I can't now, really.

In brief, the happiness just ran out. For me, that is. I'm not sure about you. I've observed you closely and seen that perhaps the edge has dulled a little, but you still seem to love me as always, find daily pleasure in our lives. This running out of happiness is absolutely not about anything you've ever done: you must believe that. I promise you it's the truth. Were that the case — had you done something dreadful — I would have forgiven you because I love you so much, and would have gone on from there. The running out of happiness is both more frightening than that and more mysterious. Simply, it's this: I don't feel anything any more — about you, about us, about the farm, the animals, the garden I planted, the Prodgers, the friends I made in the village . . . nothing. To feel absolutely nothing, darling George, when I've spent my entire life feeling so much, is absolutely terrifying. I don't know what to do.

Perhaps, I thought, it's an illness. I dreaded the idea of consulting a doctor and nothing in the world would get me to a psychiatrist or a therapist. Perhaps it's a sort of metaphysical melancholy that swoops upon a chosen few then, capriciously, recedes again. One just has to wait, I thought. But I've been waiting almost two years, and the mist hasn't risen one jot, and I'm desperate.

It would be mean not to describe how and when, as far as I know, it happened. But before that, let me remind you of what went before. If you remember, I was the happiest creature alive. *Everything* contributed to keeping my irrepressible spirits high. I only had to see a bright early sky, or swallows gathering, or a bowl of peonies, or you with shaving soap silly on your cheek, and happiness tore through me. On reflection, perhaps too much, too long. Perhaps I was too high all the time — wanting others to share the high, wanting them to *look*, to see as I saw. (I think I must vainly have thought that *seeing* was my only talent. How wrong I was! I can see nothing, now.) That's why I kept urging you, and others, to do so. I wanted you all to share in the extraordinary joy, in finding, that looking brings.

Anyhow: that terrible day. I was riding with Nell, whom I've grown to love. Although we never talked about what has led up to this, I think she had some inkling. I think, if you try to explain to her, she will understand. We were riding along High Ridge, looking down into the valley, and it had just stopped raining. Light April rain. The sun came out. We both looked for a rainbow. Unsurprisingly, we found one. You know me: very Wordsworthian on such occasions — heart leaping up and all that. But my heart didn't leap up: it didn't stir. The rainbow didn't touch me. Nor did the thought of being home within the hour, reading a chapter of my book before you came in for supper. I was stone within: stone, stone, stone. I remember Nell said I had suddenly gone very pale. Was I all right? she asked. Of course I assured her I was.

For me it was the most weird and horrible evening, though I don't think you noticed anything was amiss. I assumed I was coming down with some strange virus, and would be all right in the morning, or in a few days. But that was not the case. The stone stayed within me. Intellectually I could see with absolute clarity, still, all the myriad things that used to make my heart race with wild joy — but all I could now feel was how they *didn't* any more. You, material things, landscape, anticipation of exciting future plans — nothing, nothing touched me any more. At times I thought I was going mad. At times I thought, well, this is the result of being so over-the-top happy for so long: my turn to be drained of any kind of sensation — including happiness. I was just a walking zombie: still am.

I tried all sorts of remedies. I returned to look at pictures that used to make me cry — Van Gogh's windblown cypresses. I returned to all the poetry I loved, I went for endless walks, as you know, hoping some wildflower or the song of a meadow pipit would stir something within me. But nothing, nothing, nothing. I just looked, listened, read — and nothing. Then I thought that working really hard, physically, might help, and I began on the garden. And that's why you caught me sometimes lugging pitchforks of manure, or heaving bales of straw, "helping" Saul and Ben when there was no need. I thought physical exhaustion might induce sensation to trickle back. But it didn't. The terrifying stone within remains unmovable, and I hope you will understand, and forgive, if I try the last solution I believe is left to me: going away from all I know. I'm sure, at the very least, that I will feel homesick. Longing to be with you at home will course through my veins, and that could be the beginning of the melting of the stone.

You will think my decision is the most selfish, unkind and unreasonable act, and I don't blame you. You will blame yourself for not having observed the torment going on within me, though I did my best to disguise it. You will be rightly angry with me for not having at least tried to explain. You may never forgive me, never want me back. If you stop loving me — God forbid that that will ever happen — then that is a risk I must take. I ask only that you don't try to find me, or get in touch — let me do it my own strange way, which will be as hard for me as it is for you. I promise to keep you posted from time to time, and please try to understand. It will only be for a while, God willing.

My love to Nell and Prodge. My love to you, always.

Your wife, Lily.

George had to read many of the sentences several times to attempt to understand their meaning. The whole letter seemed to him to be a hopeless knitting together of thoughts which, in his shocked state, he could not begin to unravel. He let the pages fall to the ground when he had finished reading them over and over — so often that he knew them almost by heart — but still it all made no sense. He continued to sit in his chair, unaware of the passing of the hours, till dawn lighted the windows.

Then George got up and made himself a pot of strong coffee. Strangely, he felt physically buoyant. The adrenalin that comes from a sleepless night, provoking false energy for the first few hours of the new day, was upon him. Even his mind, battered by a night of remembrance, confusion and self-recrimination, was far from flayed: the incredulity he felt must be nature's protection for a while, he thought, just as a man gunned down does not immediately feel the agony of his wound. In a strange way, ironically, he knew now what Lily meant by numbness, the stone of unfeeling, though he knew that in his own case it would not last for long.

He returned to his chair with his coffee, picked up the scattered sheets of the letter and read it yet again. This time it made even less sense than before, but he had not the heart to keep trying to understand. Only one thing was clear in his mind: he would, for the love of her, do what Lily asked. He would not try to pursue her, find her. He would try to believe that she was safe, as she promised she would be. He would pray for patience. He would pray for her to return, restored, very soon. He would wait.

When the sun had risen George telephoned the Prodgers. Nell answered.

"Oh, George," she said at once. "It's over: she's gone."

"How did you know?"

"What do you mean, how did I know?" She sounded confused. "You were here. You saw . . . When you left the Ministry vet arrived. Instant verdict. And Prodge was right. They're going to cut off her head —"

"Oh, you mean *Bessie*." George drew himself back from some quite different place. Fragments of yesterday returned: Prodge, Bessie, BSE. "I'm sorry."

"What did you think I meant? You sound very odd, George."

"No. It's just that . . . Lily's gone too."

"Lily?"

"When I got back from you I found this long rambling letter. Can't make much sense of it."

"Christ. I had a feeling. I thought one day she just might —"

"What made you think that? What, what — ? Tell me, what, please —"

"George, stay where you are. I'm coming over. With you in five minutes."

"*Why?*" George said out loud as he put down the telephone. The sun was now so bright that he had to screw up his eyes as he looked out at Lily's garden. He remembered she had mentioned she was going to weed the border today. Perhaps that was still so. Perhaps he would come back at lunchtime and find her crouched over the weeds having thought better about leaving. It would be so unlike her to abandon her garden.

CHAPTER
ELEVEN

Five minutes later George heard a car draw up in the yard. In his state of shock he was not thinking clearly, but it did occur to him that Nell had come unusually fast for so notoriously slow a driver.

It was not Nell but a small white Ford. Beside it stood a thin man of uncertain age whose pallor suggested he spent much of his time in the car. He wore a cheap grey suit and the kind of so-called "fashion" shoes that would have earned Lily's deepest scorn. A man whose idea of the country was plainly a theme park twenty miles from London, there was no doubt that he found the Elkin farm, so far from civilisation, an alien place. He took a file from the car and unclipped a biro from his top pocket. This was also inhabited by a blazing yellow handkerchief folded into a lethal point. He looked up at the sky, frowned, opened the file and read. Or pretended to read. From his hidden view George guessed the visitor might be playing for time. Steadying himself before the journey across the treacheries of the yard to the house.

What right had this man, a born double-glazing salesman if ever there was one, to appear at this terrible moment? Irrational rage rose within George, almost

244

choking him. He moved outside the door. The visitor looked up from the notes he was studying and gave a stiff little wave. His hand was a solid piece of inhuman material, like the hand of an Action Man doll.

"Hi," he said, and looked down at the ground he would have to negotiate to reach his target. The yard, George was pleased to see, had not been scraped today. There were stretches of mud and slurry, not yet dried out by the sun, of menacing glitter. The cobbles looked slippery. There was a pile of horse shit from Nell's last visit which Lily must have intended for her roses. Looking at the stranger (*darling Lily, I'm looking*) George saw that through his eyes the yard was a plain of terrible hazards.

"Boots?" he said.

The man shrugged. He had not come equipped with boots. Boots were not required on his suburban patio. He had never been advised by the Ministry that boots were a necessity. The Prime Minister himself (very occasionally, very briefly and for public relations reasons only) visited farms without boots. No farmer was rude enough to suggest to *him* that a pair of boots would facilitate his way over to the cowshed. In fact rumour round the office said the PM never went within twenty yards of an actual cow, pig or sheep. And on a sunny day like this, in any case, you'd expect farm muck would have dried up. Any farmer worth his salt would have cleaned his yard, not caused all this hassle, all this dilemma when an official — only doing his duty, mind — came to call. The man hated the country, farms, animals, animal shit, the smell of dung and silage with his whole being — George could see all that, and smiled.

"I'm from the Ministry." The man looked down at his shoes again, reckoning they'd have to be sacrificed.

Something to do with TB registration? BSE? The reason for his visit held no interest for George. The very sight of the country-hating MAFF representative further enraged him almost to the point of incoherence. He heard himself bellowing.

"I don't care who the fuck you are — you can't just turn up unannounced and expect attention. My neighbour's cow has just been slaughtered, my wife has just left and I'd appreciate it if you'd get out of here as quickly as possible. Save your shoes!"

George watched the MAFF man's struggle with his conscience slink across his unmemorable features. But he was not one for a confrontation.

"Very well," he said. "Understood. Another time. Cheers." Speeded by relief, he got back into the car and drove away.

Ten minutes later Nell found George sitting at the kitchen table staring out of the window. For two or three minutes the appearance of the absurd man from the Ministry had deflected the pain of Lily's departure. Now here it was again: raw, tangible, activating the loathsome magic of making unrecognisable all that was familiar.

"I'll put the kettle on," said Nell.

"Don't ask me to try to explain Lily's reasons," said George, "because I can't. Maybe she's having some sort of breakdown. Maybe I should have seen it coming.

Did she say nothing to you that gave some clue as to what was on her mind?"

"Nothing." Nell sat down. "As I said yesterday afternoon, I had the impression she wasn't her usual self, recently. Vivacity gone. Nothing to worry about, I thought. Just a general sort of lowering of spirits, perhaps. Naturally I didn't ask her if anything was the matter. That wasn't our way, really. We talked about horses and farming things. She liked to learn about things that are second nature to me — harvesting, sowing, silage baling, everything. She said her grandmother had been a land girl not far from here in the war — a funny name, she had: Ag, or something. Anyhow, she'd loved her time working on the farm with two other girls, and told wonderful stories about what went on. Lily felt she'd missed out on country life, and now she was married to you she wanted to catch up. She seemed to feel very passionately about the erosion of the country, the plans for millions of new houses to be built in the south and so on, and she was obviously affected deeply by the landscape. Sometimes, on our rides, she'd pull up and say, 'Look, Nell.' I'd look, and see some stretch of land I've known and loved all my life. But I could see that for her the view wasn't just a good place for a postcard, it produced something spiritual, something elevating, like music does for some people. I suppose you could say that she's sentimental about the country in a way that those of us who've lived close to the land all our lives are not. I think she was aware of that herself — one of the reasons she was so

247

keen to learn the hard facts, see how farming works, experience at least some of the hardships."

Nell paused to smile.

"And then she used to love stories about our childhood, about what the three of us got up to. 'What was George like as a boy?' she was always asking. God knows if I gave an accurate picture. I think she has learnt far more about us than I ever did about her. She rarely talked about herself, except to say that she'd found it very hard to work out what exactly she'd like to do in the art world. But she also said that since your marriage, and coming here, she thought about it less and less. Being a farmer's wife was all she wanted, she said."

"It's beyond me," said George. "Maybe I'll wake up one morning and it'll all be clear. Why did she want to leave just because . . .? Surely the best place to be, when darkness strikes . . . I don't know, Nell. We never quarrelled. We were so happy, I thought. I feel completely —"

"Prodge is pretty low, too," Nell interrupted. "Not just Bessie. The whole future. Just as everything was going so well."

"I'm sorry. I haven't been . . . all this. I'll ring him."

"You know what he said last night? He said: d'you remember when our bull calves fetched £150 each? They're worth nothing, now. So his idea of buying the bike will have to go. He's been saving for years. We need those savings. It's the end of the good times for farming, he said. I pointed out to him that after the '67 outbreak of foot and mouth things got going again, did well, didn't they? Look at you, at us. We can't complain. But this time — this time it isn't *just* BSE that'll finish us. There's so much else that's been creeping up to the detriment of farmers and country life in general."

"I fear you're right," said George.

"Poor Prodge. He was so pleased, getting the jacket. He'll never get his bike now."

They smiled wanly at each other — two people in desperate want of something to smile at — and then Nell left, promising she would return as often as she was wanted.

But the days of real smiling were over. " 'As high as we have risen in delight, in our dejection do we sink as low.' That's the bugger of it," George said to himself. To fight his dejection, he worked harder than he ever had before, pushing himself to extremes of fatigue. He was forced to spend much longer hours at his desk, giving precious time, when he should have been helping on the farm, to studying reports written by bureaucrats who sledge-hammered language into near incomprehensible demands. A dozen times a day George was frustrated and enraged by their ungrammatical verbiage. Why was it not imperative for officials, whose job it was to compose instructions, to be compelled to take a course in concise and simple English? Maddened by the anguish they caused, when at last he could leave his desk George found the physical acts of heaving, scraping, weighing lambs, shovelling slurry, the never-ending job of feeding the animals went some way towards dulling the emptiness for as long as the job took. Then the sensation of burning ice within him would flare up again. Much of the time he felt faintly nauseous, had no appetite. He was conscious of losing weight.

What George most dreaded was being in the house alone. Before the arrival of Lily, before he loved her, he had enjoyed its emptiness. The pleasures of solitude increased. But when Lily had come into his life, she had transformed the house. She brought life to it, reminding him how it had been when he was a child — his mother had had the same talent for enlivening a place. Without her presence to fire them, its delights were as nothing. He was grateful only for its familiarity. To maintain that small comfort, George left everything exactly as Lily had arranged it. He left her papers on the desk, a forgotten hairbrush on the dressing-table. He did not remove the few clothes still hanging in the spare-room cupboard. When he had first opened the door, expecting to find nothing, the faded-rose smell of her — the scent that lived on the skin of her neck — swung out at him from three light dresses. He remembered their skirts dancing about as she hurried across the lawn, or the kitchen. Now they hung dead. Unnerved by their stillness, wondering whether to interpret them as a sign of intended return, George took up a bunch of flowered voile between his thumb and finger, felt it. It did not occur to him to move them.

His wish to keep everything precisely as Lily had left it was not just for his own benefit. Should she come back, he wanted her to find everything untouched. That would convey what her absence had meant — not that he wanted ever to burden her with guilt about his misery. Flowers on the kitchen table were the only change he could allow — or rather, no flowers. George was not a man who could contemplate plucking tulips or roses, plumping them into a jug to lean on the fan-leaves of alchemilla mollis. So once Lily's last jug of late tulips had died — their petals scrolled back, their remembrance of pink so faded it might never have been — the table remained without flowers. And fearful of resuming the pattern of life before marriage, George refused Dusty's offer to cook for him on a regular basis. After Lily's magically light food, he had no heart for Dusty's solid pies. He fended for himself, in the way that men alone often do. He would grill a pork or lamb chop, eat it with a baked potato (if he remembered to put one in the oven in time) and frozen peas whose brilliant green hurt his eyes. Picking at his food, he would eat his supper listening to the fat tick of the kitchen clock, willing the telephone to ring, willing the sound of Lily's car drawing up in the yard. But the silence persisted. Night after night it spread through the house, chased him upstairs, along the passage past the bad pictures that made Lily laugh and scoff — and into their aching bedroom. Physically as exhausted as he could ever remember, he would quickly fall into sleep shredded with nightmares, and awake unrestored.

The length of Lily's absence was imprecise in George's mind. He knew it was stretching on, but unless he sat down with his diary he could not be certain how many days and weeks she had been away. All he knew for sure was that summer was closing in. The silage had been baled: it was time now to cut the grass. George fastened the mower to the tractor and set off for the first of the hay fields.

It was a morning of clammy and oppressive heat. The sky was a flat colourless wash: the light it gave veiled the landscape, robbing shadows of their depth. George, jolted in the seat of the old Massey Fergusson tractor, was soon sweating heavily. As he drove back and forth, with the sweet smell of the grass and the chugging of the engine to drowse his head, he watched the arrival of a cloud that darkened as it spread. Soon the small coin of sun was obliterated. The air was gravid with the promise of rain, but no drops fell. The fretwork of trees against the sky, as if caught in freeze-frame, was absolutely still. There was an eeriness, more usually felt at dusk or nightfall, in the weight of the morning.

To George, in his state of misery and exhaustion, the cloud was an omen which added to the doom in his heart. This, he said to himself, was the cloud that was sweeping across British farming, and God knows if there would be any sun to follow it.

When he had finished the first field George stopped the tractor. He jumped down from the seat, shirt clinging to his body, legs damp and itching beneath his jeans. Feeling dizzy and unsteady, he began to walk back to the farmhouse. He had arranged to meet Prodge for a lunchtime drink in the Bell — a rare occurrence, but they had both agreed on the telephone the night before that they needed a short break from their farms. George was glad the arrangement had been for today, when he could not have borne his normal bread and cheese in the silent kitchen. And he could not cut another acre of hay: he would do the next field this afternoon.

Although he arrived early at the pub, Prodge was there before him — the mirror-image of himself, thought George: the wretched Prodge was sweating, tired, worried. His friend was suddenly no longer the young farmer — never carefree, exactly — no farmer could ever afford to be carefree — but full of hope, ambition, optimism. Here was an older-looking Prodge, shocked by the loss of his cow to BSE, fearful for the rest of his herd, alarmed by the financial implications as the disease gradually gripped the country.

George carried two tankards of beer over to the table in the pub's small back garden. He was grateful for the stinging cold of pewter in his hands. As he slumped down into the slatted wooden chair, it tottered, then recovered. Prodge nodded at him. Both men sipped their beer. George shut his eyes. The merciless buzz of flies worked against his brain like the drill of machinery. When he opened them, rather than look at Prodge again he let them follow the flies' spasmodic journeys through the thunderous air. He and Prodge were the only drinkers in the garden.

"How's things?" asked George, eventually.

"Not brilliant. I find myself going back to the cows every twenty minutes, looking for signs. Interrupts baling. I'm behind with the baling. Got to get a grip."

"Quite. I quit after just cutting Top Meadow this morning. Suddenly couldn't face any more. This bloody weather doesn't help." George swiped at a fly.

"And I've a great afternoon to look forward to — the bank. Got to ask for a top-up on the loan."

"Loan? I didn't know you had one."

"Nothing very much. But it's not going to last long, is it? This new situation. I've practically given away six bull calves."

"Nell said you'd saved a bit . . . for the bike."

"So I had." Prodge laughed. "That'll be gone in a trice. I'm telling you, George, it's all going to overwhelm us. Everything's gathering together to do us down. It's been building up — lots of signs. Now BSE's taken a hold, exports all gone to hell, everything — we'll be lucky if we survive. There's a hell of a lot round here — I know more of them than you do — fear they'll go under. And I daresay they're right. Farmers'll soon be a dying breed, a rare species."

He took a deep gulp of his beer.

"You've heard about Dave Goring?"

"No?"

"Dave's packing it in. These new rules for slaughterhouses — extra veterinary inspections, vets on tap all the time and all that — who can afford that in an outfit the size of Dave's? Course he could never manage that. So what now? We'll have to send stock God knows how many miles away to some bloody great abattoir where they don't give a fuck for animals except as meat. Doesn't occur to them it might be worth trying to make their last moments on earth easy as possible. What's more, they're bringing in foreign vets. I ask you: will a foreign vet know what a fluke looks like?" Prodge gave a grim laugh.

254

"And how are we going to afford to transport them, anyhow?" he went on. "Petrol prices rising again. My great uncle Matt — you remember, blacksmith in Adlesham for fifty years — he's just had to give up his old Morris Minor. Only used it to take my aunt Sal to the supermarket, now the village store's closed. But he says he can't afford the petrol any more. If it wasn't for a neighbour they'd be left with nothing but the weekly bus to get about. It makes you sick, what's happening." He was silent for a long time, then he said: "Nell reckons we should take guests in. That's what several are doing round here. *Diversifying*." He sniffed. "Apparently that's what the government advises. What the hell do they know about *diversifying* in a place like this? *Farming's* what this part of the country's made for. So there we are. I'd better talk to the bank about the possibility . . . I don't see what else —"

"No, no," said George. "Don't do that. It would add to all your work, put far too much on you and Nell."

"It would. But what's to do? You have to spend, of course, to set up in the B&B business. Can't just advertise a nice farmhouse. Oh no: tourist officials demand certain standards. *En suites*, waitresses in frilly aprons, I don't doubt — tourists want the works in their B&Bs. We'd have to paint the kitchen, stop the damp everywhere. Can't imagine it, but we've not decided yet. If the bank manager goes along with the idea . . ."

George ran his hands through his hair: thunderflies pricked at his scalp.

"Why don't I lend you the money?" he asked carefully. "No interest?"

Prodge shook his head.

George was feeling stronger. The beer had revived him. Prodge got up and took the empty tankards to the bar without asking. When he came back with them, refilled, George took his time. He had to go gently if he was to persuade Prodge of his plan.

"Look," he began, "you know I'm not a rich man by today's standards. I invested quite a bit of capital in the farm when I sold the firm, but I've also got a fair bit just sitting there. I'd like to put it to a good use. Far as I can see, there'd be no better way than helping a friend."

"No, George." Prodge shook his head again, moved. "Thanks all the same."

"Money's only important if you haven't got it: that's my way of seeing it. I've got enough for my own needs, some to spare. You've done wonders since you took over your farm, and rightly made a fair bit from your efforts. But as you say, the good times are coming to an end, if they're not already over. It's only sense for me to tide you over."

"I can see your argument," said Prodge, "but I couldn't find it in myself to agree. I don't think Nell could, either. We'll manage, somehow. She mentioned selling the horses —"

"She can't do that."

"Up against it, she can bring herself to do anything. Nell. And it's fair to say a B&B would be a bloody nuisance, having to tidy up and that. But it could bring in the necessary. Dave Goring's sister just registered with the Tourist Board, done her back room up like the Ritz. She's had a few to stay, quite enjoys it. But then she hasn't got a farm to run."

"You talk to the bank: let me know what they say. My offer's always on the table, should you change your mind. Any time."

"Thanks." A look of harrowed reluctance crossed Prodge's face. "And you?" he said after a while, jerking his thoughts from the grim alternatives that crowded his mind. "You, George? Any news from Lily?"

"None." George sighed.

"She'll be in touch."

"I doubt it."

"Perhaps you should contact her. Women often say what they don't mean, try to provoke you."

"Not Lily." George gave a wry smile. "She asked me not to try to get hold of her. If that's what she wants, that's what I must do. I'd never take the risk of going against her wishes."

"Huh! You're too much the gentleman, sometimes. That's what I think. If it was me, and a wife like Lily had just buggered off, no proper explanation, I'd be after her in a flash. Search the whole country till I found her."

"Wish I could be more like you, then. But I can't."

"I'll tell you something funny," said Prodge. He frowned. The humour of what he was about to reveal did not seem to have a happy effect on him. "Your Lily is something special. Fancy her rotten myself. In fact I told her that. One afternoon down by the river I ran into her and I told her. Course, all she did was laugh."

George looked at his friend enquiringly. He remembered the day. Both Lily and Prodge had briefly reported the meeting.

"Don't look so worried! I'm only joking. But I'm the first to see you've got yourself a good woman there. Terrific looker, kindest heart in the world, lively, serious, but funny, too: loving . . . the sort of woman, if I had an imagination, I would imagine . . . You're bloody lucky, there, George, and don't you forget it. Don't you let her slip through your fingers. She's at risk from Christ knows what dangers on her own. Men after her, that sort of thing. You mind my words. Do something before it's too late."

George nodded. This was probably the longest speech Prodge had ever made to him. He scratched his scalp again — damn flies.

For a few moments, deflected from his own problems by thinking of George's, Prodge had looked more cheerful. But now the earlier shadow recrossed his face.

"I must be off," he said. "Bank manager awaits, prepared to hand over thousands."

"Well, don't forget my offer."

Prodge nodded. George knew the matter was unlikely to be mentioned again.

By mid-afternoon a breeze had come from the south, dissipating the cloud and lightening the air. George, on his tractor, no longer uncomfortably hot, looked about the rise and fall of his own fields and woods — neat, ordered, productive — and felt something near to contentment. Grief, like happiness, is hard to sustain in its deepest form without a break. While he was conscious that in an hour or so, back in the empty kitchen, the misery would return, for a while this time on the tractor, this sense of achievement at cutting a field of hay, gave relief.

When he had finished his task, he walked up to the parlour. Milking over, Saul had taken the cows back to the pasture. Ben, having meticulously scraped the gutters and hosed them down, was sweeping away the water. The sweet, warm, furry smell of milk and cow shit that had become a part of his life struck George as he entered the building. Recently there had been a letter in the local paper from a man from Birmingham who had bought a farm not two miles from here, not to farm, naturally, but for the occasional weekend's sunbathing on a hastily installed terrace which he referred to as his patio.

While sunbathing on our patio, he wrote, *the revolting smell from a nearby cowshed assaults our noses. You can't walk down the lane without running into mud and cowpats, and a neighbour's cockerel wakes us at dawn every morning. Is it any wonder that the divide between urban and rural communities is ever-increasing? Those of us who appreciate the niceties of life fail to see the joys of so-called real country life. I for one am reselling my farm as soon as possible.*

There were several acerbic letters, the following week, from locals speeding him on his way. George smiled at the thought.

Ben paused in his sweeping, looked up at his boss. Since Lily's departure both he and his father, in their efforts to offer sympathy without sentiment, had become grim-faced in George's presence.

"Finished the hay," said George.

"I was planning on that, when I'm through here. Dad said you'd got more than enough on your shoulders."

"Thanks," said George. "But I enjoyed it. All well?" He meant: any signs of BSE?

"Touch wood." Ben patted his head, then resumed sweeping.

George stood looking at the young farmhand, wondering about him. He was an exceptionally strong youth, all muscle and bone: a man of few words and occasional bad jokes. Few of his contemporaries, George appreciated, could work with Ben's continual energy and zest. Few would want to. A farmer's life had little appeal to the young these days: relentless hard work, little time off, decreasing financial rewards. It was only for those with a passion for animals and the land — and that was something inherited in families, not a subject you learnt at school. Ben had few friends, went out with them rarely. Those he did see were now so far removed in a different life, working in mechanics or computers, earning a decent salary, that they had little left in common with Ben. On one occasion, Saul had admitted, his son had been pitied, scoffed at, by a few of his contemporaries who had once been friends.

What would happen to him? George wondered. When Saul retired — though George could not imagine him ever wanting to retire — would Ben want to continue working here? Or would he want to join a more mainstream way of life with all its more obvious rewards? Ben had given no hint of ever wanting to leave, but the greater world must surely hold its temptations. Should he go, George knew it would be impossible to find an equal replacement. He resolved one day soon to talk to the lad, see if there was anything he could do to make his life here more appealing.

George returned to the house. The kitchen was warm, stuffy, but clean and tidy — Dusty still attended to domestic matters three days a week. In fact, thought George, as the clock greeted him with its incessant, menacing tick, should Lily walk through the door at this very minute, she would be pleased.

As he had been out at lunchtime, he had not seen the post, which arrived at midday. The bundle of letters and magazines had been piled on the table by Dusty. George sighed. He could see he would have to spend a long evening dealing with it all. Best to do it straight away, was his theory. If you left it a few days it became unmanageable.

He began to sort through the gloomy mass of official envelopes, dreading the moment he must turn to the milk quota forms. A postcard fell from between two envelopes — a photograph of a Norfolk windmill. Scarcely daring to hope, he turned it over.

Oh, George, there are great PRAIRIES here, he read. *So many hedges gone, combine harvesters the size of houses racing over the corn, scarcely a human being in sight. Dehumanised farming personified. I thought how shocked you'd be. It's so sad. Yes, I came home. Horses still on the marsh. My boat leaking. Am off to Norwich to teach for a bit, H of A. Don't worry — if you were worrying — about our joint account. I promise not to touch it. I can manage perfectly OK on the rent from my flat. I expect you're busy with the harvest. Please keep my roses watered. Love to Nell and Prodge and you, L.*

George sat down. The card shook in his hands. He read it again. In his ungrounded state the words were flung about, confusing: he had to go over them several times to still them. They left him mystified. What was she doing, sending this jaunty little message after weeks of silence? Was it just a signal of reassurance that she was all right? Or did it mean there was some melting of the inner stone, and soon she would be back? *Water the roses . . .* That could mean she wanted to see them well cared for on her return before the last petal had fallen — which would be any day now. George's heart beat faster.

He spent the evening attaching meanings to phrases innocent of meaning, but the process gave him comfort. It renewed his hope, filled him with new expectation. That she was all right was the most important thing. That she even mentioned money was very odd — surely she must know she was welcome to every penny he owned? That she mentioned the horses signified she remembered conversations . . . Oh God, what was she up to, Lily?

George struggled to decide whether to do as she bade him, and not attempt to contact her, or whether — as every instinct now urged him — to try to persuade her to return. He was convinced he could assure her that whatever she felt — or didn't feel — home was the best place for her to be. He knew he could not fully understand her mysterious trauma, but he knew also that it would be best if she tried to solve it with his help.

George opened the desk drawer where there was a pile of postcards of some of her favourite paintings he had collected from time to time. He chose Van Gogh's chair: solid, calm, the magic of familiarity its only message. He picked up his pen and rejected the elaborate phrases that swarmed into his mind (he sometimes felt he was cursed for ever with a sonorous, legal style of writing). Constraint, he told himself. So: *Darling Lily,* he began, *we're keeping the roses watered. The Norwich plan sounds good. All well here. You're much missed. Please come home soon. I love you, G.*

After long contemplation of this brief missive he realised that, for all its stringency, it might well frighten her off. In her present state, the merest gesture could be counterproductive. George put the card back in the drawer. He might change his mind, he thought. But, more likely, he would never post it.

It was late by now, but he continued to sit at his desk thinking about his wife, and the loss of her. At least this Norfolk card showed that her husband and her home had not been entirely obliterated from her mind. For that, he was grateful. He could feel a rising of his natural optimism. Eventually he propped up the card on the dresser, only to take it down a moment later. He read it once more, put it in his shirt pocket. Then he took it out again to study its words one last time. By now he knew its message, so simple and yet so incomprehensible, by heart.

CHAPTER
TWELVE

A few days after the arrival of Lily's card George returned to the hay fields to decide if the time had come for baling. The hay had been turned several times and scattered about to dry. They had been lucky with the weather. The threatened rain on the day of mowing had not come. There had been constant sun, but not insufferable heat. A light breeze, there was, as well, which exploded Lily's roses but nicely dried the hay.

George walked back and forth across Top Meadow. He listened for the noise beneath his feet — there was a special note that came from scattered hay when it was fully dried. Every now and then he stooped to pick up a clump, felt its crispness. He would smell it, for the pleasure, before dropping it back on the ground. To George, freshly dried hay smelt of dusk. It took him back to haymaking in his childhood — they had machines then, yes, but also men raking till sundown, and his mother bringing strawberries and home-made lemonade. They would picnic sitting on the warm ground that tickled his bare legs. Unlike straw stubble, it did not prick uncomfortably.

This year's hay, he decided, had reached the perfect moment. He had learnt how to judge its readiness from

Saul in the last few summers. He had learnt so much from Saul, but this year there was no need for him to invite his opinion. George knew he was right. It was time to go over the field with the turner, marshalling the scattered hay back into rows, and then to call for the contractor with the baling machine.

This certainty in his own judgement gave George a feeling of quiet contentment. As he made his way back to the gate, a clump of crisp hay still in his hand, he was conscious of an ebbing of his misery. The void without Lily was still there, of course, but the physical pain seemed to be subsiding. In its place, he thought, he felt a kind of molten patience. He was in no doubt that his wife would return one day. It was inconceivable that she would do otherwise. Her card, he judged, was evidence of that. She would not be so cruel as to send him a signal, oblique though it was, if she had no intention of coming back. So he would wait for that day without fretting. From somewhere, strength to do that had filled him. He would put every mite of his energy into work on the farm: he would somehow help Nell and Prodge, and the waiting would go by — sometimes he'd be angry, sometimes impatient, perhaps. But it would not last for ever.

For all his new patience, strength and calm, George could not help dreading autumn. It was the time of year he loved most: berries turning scarlet on the rowan trees, Lily making blackberry jam. He loved the particular colour of autumn skies that arched over the land. Drained of their summer clarity, they dimmed into the milky blue of Burmese sapphires. Last year, bashfully, he had pointed this out to Lily. You're *looking*, George, she had said. I see just what you mean, she had said, because it so happened my mother had a Burmese star-sapphire ring. But I don't suppose many people would know what you're talking about. She had laughed, as if at his progress, as if she appreciated his hopeless attempt at poetical expression. Autumn: it was the time of year, those soft, steep steps up to Christmas, when his father used to begin bringing in the logs: the kitchen curtains would be drawn soon after tea, and early frosts clenched the ground each morning. Without Lily such joys would be dulled, though never quite gone. And with any luck there would be only one lost autumn.

In Lily's absence Nell came over most days. She would never stay long, but always brought an offer of help. If George was mucking out the calf shed, Nell would take up a second pitchfork and join him. If he was indoors at his desk, she would make him a cup of tea. When she was gone he would notice that the collection of cups, and his lunch plate, had disappeared from the draining board: dried, put away. Sometimes she would bring him a box of bantams' eggs, or a bottle of her home-made elderflower wine. At Christmas she knitted him a very large jumper made from her own spun and dyed wools.

At Christmas, as he thought she would, Lily sent George a card: Leonardo's *Madonna of the Rocks*. No message there. Apart from the printed "Best Wishes for Christmas and the New Year" (any message there?), Lily scrawled her brief news: *Teaching a History of Art course in Norwich. All fine. Love.* Other cards were thrown out after Twelfth Night: not Lily's. George left it on the dresser.

He was grateful to Nell for her visits. She was undemanding, didn't talk much. When she did have something to say it was bad news of a general kind which she delivered in staccato sentences.

"Hedge sparrows disappearing by the thousand now, George. Did you know that?"

"I did."

"God knows how many farmers are packing it in. Don't blame them." They were sorting bags of newly delivered feed. Nell slashed a bag so fiercely with her knife that dozens of pellets spilt on to the ground. "Soon there won't be a butterfly in the land: bloody pesticides. Let alone a village pub. Did you know something like a hundred and fifty country pubs a year are closing? And I read that a third of rural villages are now without a shop. As for village schools . . . How are people living in the country going to survive, George? It's dying."

It was on this occasion, a winter's afternoon in the shed, that George realised that beyond her usual concern about farming and the country in general, Nell was beginning to suffer an anguish about her own situation that she had previously disguised. George saw that she was near to tears.

"And there's another thing. These passports for every calf we have to apply for . . . We've got nearly a hundred cows. How the hell am I going to find the time to fill them all in? Prodge is useless with paperwork." She

268

bent down to retrieve some of the spilt pellets. There was something about her act that made it seem of huge significance — as if picking up pellets was of no less importance than any other farm job, but George knew that really she just needed to move her body and hands in order to hide a moment of despair.

"Sometimes I feel exhausted as it is. *Me*, George. Have you ever heard me complain of being tired before? I'd like to see a MAFF man on an icy morning drive the tractor through the cowshed delivering half a ton of silage for breakfast. I'd like to see him up at five every morning to milk, never a lie-in. It's always been bloody hard work, but possible. Now, with all the extra official paper business put on us, it's only possible at huge cost. So many people are cracking up, physically, mentally. Nothing's simple any more. There's no time to admire a new calf, to feel a sense of achievement in a fine row of cabbages or a field full of healthy lambs. There's so much extra to do now, most of the joy's being drained out of farming. The government just think they can send us a mass of new paperwork and we'll deal with it. Well, we will, of course. We have to. But have they any idea what they're putting on to us in terms of man hours? Working twelve or fourteen hours a day on the farm, then coming in for two or three hours' paperwork? Sometimes I feel if there's one more page of questions to answer, one more cow to milk or TB test to arrange or sheep to dip, I'll —" She stopped, brushed away a tear with a muddy fist.

"Nell, Nell," said George. "Look, I've far fewer cows than you. I can find time to help."

"Nonsense. You've got more than enough to do yourself."

By now her nose was red and several strands of blonde curls stuck to the mud on her cheek. George thought she looked much as she did when she was fourteen, except that worry was now alive in her small, kind eyes.

Once again this was an occasion to chide himself. He had not looked behind Nell's usual cheerful demeanour, had not guessed the extent of the worry BSE at their farm had caused. Full of self-reproach, he put an arm round her shoulder. "Shall we go in? It's getting cold."

"No. I must leave in a minute. Time to get the cows into the parlour, help Prodge. He does more than his fair share."

As if unaware of his arm, Nell sat down heavily on the hay bale behind her. George lowered himself beside her. An hour from now the shed would be crowded with animals, the warm fug of their breath and the various notes of their bleating. For the moment there was a husky silence and the faintly sour, sorrel smell of silage Ben had lugged down for the evening feed. George and Nell sat looking through the shed's huge doors to the fields, shrivelled beneath their thin winter grass.

George was aware of the comfort Nell found in their proximity. In her misery, all she desired was to sit on a hay bale beside him for a few moments, this bleak afternoon, before returning home.

"I can't moan to Prodge," she said at last. "He's in such low spirits himself. I spend all my time trying to cheer him up. What he's worried about, apart from the drop in income, is that Will Rogers, our landlord, seeing the way things are going, will want to sell up. There are a good few round here've sold their farms for a handsome price, and who can blame them? Debts mounting up, you can quite understand why these incomers with their millions are a temptation. You can quite understand why a wretched farmer might not think first about local property being out of reach of local people these days. She sniffed. "Makes you sick."

"I shouldn't think Will Rogers will want to sell," said George. "He comes from a very old farming family. Been his land for generations." He put a hand over Nell's. It was cold and dead. His touch sparked no reaction in her beyond a small, grateful smile.

"Let's hope, she said, "because that would be the last straw." Then she turned to him. "There is one thing you could do for me," she said.

"What's that? I'll do anything I can."

"Come for a ride with me."

George paused. He had expected to be able instantly to agree to any request. This one surprised him into hesitation.

"I'm not much of a rider. I could try."

Nell snatched her hand away. She laughed, punched George on the arm. "Nonsense! You may not be that keen, but you're perfectly competent."

"Of course I'll come. But why do you suddenly want me to? You've never asked before."

Nell shrugged, stood up. "Just a whim, really. I've missed my rides with Lily. You can ride the grey mare, like she always did. Quiet as a lamb."

George caught the lightness of her new mood.

"Very well. So when's this to be?"

"Tomorrow afternoon? What we might do is box them over to Dunkery Beacon — I haven't ridden over there for years. We can't be away that long, but Prodge said he'll hold the fort."

"You mean, you've already told him your plan?"

"I told him I was going to ask you. He said that in the very unlikely event of your agreeing, he'd be happy to do the milk by himself. Then he laughed. It was the first time he'd laughed for some days."

They rode side by side over the empty moorland that swirled up the sides of Dunkery Beacon. The high peak was half obliterated by a thin fog, its earth the colour of a bruise. To both of them it was familiar territory. There had been outings as children: hide and seek among the thick jungle of bracken, patches of it taller than they were. George remembered hiding in caverns of intense green, marvelling at the tightly curled fists at the end of each leaf. He remembered the three of them paddling in the stream at the bottom of the valley in their underpants, then racing away from the grown-ups — running up the steep narrow lanes that had turned into cool tunnels of oak tree shadow.

It was a place few ever came to, unless they were in search of solitude, for there were no attractions beyond the views and the sound of water. On one occasion they joined friends who owned a farm on high land for haymaking. It was then, aged nine and ten, that George, Prodge and Nell drank their first cider and sat slumped in the field as the sun went down, staring at the distant sea too tipsy to speak. They had to be helped to the car, and Prodge was sick on the way home. Often they saw deer: antlers on a fine, alert head cruising through the depths of bracken like some masted ship expecting danger. They had been taught not to move or speak, when sighting a deer. They were good at keeping absolutely still as they watched the animal's progress to a secret destination. When it was no longer visible Prodge would burst into giggles — nothing funny, he said. Just to relieve the tension, Nell always explained to George in her solemn, grown-up way. Often they climbed to the top of Dunkery Beacon and made private wishes. George, trying through the mist to see the place where he had screwed up his eyes and cast so many youthful aspirations to the skies, couldn't remember a single one of his own wishes. But he did remember that Prodge's wish (a secret he could never keep) was always for a bicycle.

The moor in winter was a more threatening place than it had been in those always summer days of youth. Its emptiness was full of surprises. They rode through a band of fog to come to a clearing of extraordinary brightness, though no sun. For a moment there was a half view of sloping land hemmed by skeletal fans of winter trees, then it was gone again. George was enjoying the ride more than he had expected. The grey mare was quiet but responsive. Her ears were constantly pricked. Occasionally she blew trumpet sounds through her nostrils and tossed her head. George could understand why Lily had become so constant a riding companion to Nell. It occurred to him that when she came back he would ride with them sometimes. They might even buy their own horses.

"You've not been hunting yet," he said.

"No." Nell reined in her mare so as to be level with George. "And I shan't be going again. Hunting days over."

"What on earth do you mean? I thought you loved it."

"I do. You know I do. And I'd like to keep on, not let those bloody animal rights bastards feel they are winning — or the MPs who want to take another slash at those of us to whom the hunt's an essential part of our lives. But I have to tell you something, George. I have to confess. This is my last ride. That's why I wanted you to come. I'm not sure I could have managed on my own —"

"I can't believe you —"

"— It's no good. We can't possibly afford the horses any more. You can imagine what they cost — winter oats, new saddlery, hunt subscription. I can't afford the petrol any longer to box them over to meets too far away to ride to. And as for shoeing, did you know the nearest blacksmith is now fourteen miles away? I haven't the time to ride there, and there's the petrol again. It's not that my horses are anything very special, as you can see. But any horses cost a bit to keep in condition, and all the hunting farmers are grumbling."

"But Nell —"

"So it's decided. Horses and all their stuff being sold next week. Box, if I can find some idiot to take such a run-down old thing, soon as possible. That should keep us going for a few weeks. Prodge was all against it, tried to persuade me to keep them. But things aren't improving. Interest on the bank loan —"

"Listen," said George, "you probably won't believe this, but not five minutes ago I was just thinking to myself how much I was enjoying riding again, and how when Lily comes back we ought to buy our own horses. Wouldn't the obvious solution be for me to buy your horses, but you carry on looking after them, riding them, as always, just as if they were still your own? In return for your looking after them, we'd share all costs . . ."

They had arrived in another patch clear of fog. Nell pulled up, turned to George with a tight, fierce face. She was affronted. Somehow George had put his suggestion wrongly. He cursed himself.

"No," she said. "Thanks for the thought, but I couldn't bear that. Besides, Lily's not here. Lily's gone." The sharpness in her voice was almost a taunt. "If only you'd stop being so bloody stupid and proud and get in touch with her, you could tell her about the horses. She'd want to know."

She jerked her mare's head round and set off at a trot. In a moment she was lost in another gathering of fog. George could not find her for some time. He rode alone in a troubled state, trying desperately to think what he could do to save Nell's horses. But even if there was a way that avoided making her feel patronised, George doubted he could ever change her mind. Nell was known for her stubbornness, a characteristic that was usually more useful than it was a hindrance. In this case it precluded her from the ongoing pleasure of her horses — though, of course, George's plan would partially erode that pleasure anyway. Borrowing animals that you had once owned . . . he could see that would not be the same.

At the top of the moor George saw Nell some yards away. She kicked her mare into a trot so that she would quickly be at his side. As he watched her rising and falling, an apologetic smile on her face, the sadness of the ride dissolved in the sudden thought of how appealing she looked on a horse, scatty hair bouncing under her cap, taut body, her whole demeanour one of intense liveliness and energy. He had often thought how good she looked, riding. But it occurred to him that never had he actually ridden out with her since they were children. Now, not only did she look *good*, but from his own saddle, his level vantage point, she looked curiously attractive. What might have come of his deep friendship with Nell, he wondered, if Lily had never appeared in his life? And if Lily never returned — well, a man can only bear so much celibacy, so much aloneness . . . It would be easy enough for him and Nell to slip into another mode, wouldn't it? They knew each other so well. There would be no surprises.

She was by his side now, trying to flatten her horse's mane with her whip.

"Sorry, and thanks," she said.

276

They rode back without speaking to where George had parked the trailer. When the horses were boxed, Nell moved a few paces from George, tapping at her knee with her whip.

"Anyhow, none of it really matters," she said, "because if this fox-hunting bill goes through none of us will be hunting any more. A great part of British life for centuries gone for ever. Hard to believe."

Driving back she seemed to shake off her melancholy and asked George if he was going to join the Countryside Alliance march in London.

"I'd like to," said George, "but someone's got to do the animals. I'm going to insist Saul and Ben go. They could do with a day out. I've volunteered to help organise transport and so on from the village, but I won't be able to go."

"Same with me. I'm determined it should be Prodge. They can all go together. Do him good to get away from the farm for more than an hour or so. He's in a right gloom, these days, I can tell you. To march along with thousands of others as passionate in their concern about what's happening might cheer him up."

"It might," said George. "Let's hope it does."

A couple of summers earlier, Prodge and Nell had been sitting outside at the Elkins' farm after Sunday lunch looking at photographs taken on a short holiday George and Lily had spent in Wales. A few of these photographs had fallen off the table. Prodge had picked them up. Crouched half under the tablecloth, unseen, he had managed to slip a print of Lily, alone on a mountainside, into his pocket. No one had noticed. He had no idea why he had done this: it was not a premeditated action. The small theft caused him guilt only for a moment or two. It was not a good photograph. There were plenty of others, better. Had he asked for it he was sure it would have been handed over willingly. But he knew he would not have been able to request it in the joking manner that would have looked innocent, so it remained unmentioned in his pocket.

This photograph was the only manifestation of Prodge's secret. He liked to carry it with him, always. So with each new shirt it was put in the pocket. If the shirt was too thin to disguise a photograph, he would transfer it to his wallet, which he kept in his trouser pocket. His surreptitious ploys, he knew, were dangerous: Nell, the avid laundrywoman, was inclined to swoop upon a shirt left on his floor in seconds. She seemed to enjoy the peculiar challenge of getting dirty clothes into the machine in record time, so it was essential that Prodge always remembered, as he abandoned a two-day shirt, to take out the photograph and hide it until it was time to lodge it in the next one. God knows what would happen if one day he forgot and Nell found it. There would be some difficult explaining to do. He knew he wouldn't be up to that — her sharp questions and sarcastic assumptions. Thus a small part of his life was lived in fear of discovery. In some odd way that he failed to understand, he rather enjoyed the danger he had created for himself.

By now, the photograph was battered and limp. Lily's face was covered in creases. The blue of her skirt seemed to have run into the green of the mountainside. The lights in her hair had gone: it was nothing but a dull smudge. But Prodge took out the photograph more often now — now the worry of things was weighing on him so heavily. At odd times of day, in the shed or out in a field, when Nell was safely distant, he would slip the snapshot from his pocket, cradle it in his hand, gaze upon the object of his desire — except he knew it was not mere desire, certainly nothing as crude as lust — though perhaps it had been that in the beginning. No, it was love he felt for her. Hopeless, useless love. "Lucky bugger, George," he would say out loud, and wonder for the thousandth time why his friend was so hopeless about retrieving his wife. Surely if he made the right move, even though that would be going against her wishes, she would return home. Surely it was worth trying — though of course Prodge still had no idea of her reasons for leaving. George had never told anyone those.

On the night before the Countryside March, Prodge went up to bed early. He was to rise at four in the morning. A bus from the village, one of the many buses leaving from the West Country, was to depart at four-thirty. He took a thick flannel shirt from the drawer, undid the button-down pocket. Before sliding the photograph into its new place he studied it for a while. It seemed to be talking to him. Scared by this feeling, Prodge sat on the bed and continued to stare at it. What was going on? Was he mad? His limbs had felt heavy as boulders, sometimes, of late. His head often spun, so that for moments on end nothing made sense.

Nell had to ask him questions several times. Was he ill? And what exactly was Lily saying? He sat without moving for some while, but could not make out any actual words. It was more a feeling of assurance that was coming from the photograph, a feeling — and he hardly dared say this to himself — that he was going to see her again. Possibly before she came home. Possibly before George. Possibly . . . tomorrow.

Prodge put the photograph into the pocket and buttoned it up against Nell's beady eyes. Then he got into bed. He doubted he would have much sleep.

George, too, was anxious to have an early night. He had arranged to pick up Ben and Saul and one or two others near by and drive them to the meeting place in the village. But as tomorrow would be a busy day on the farm, with no help, he knew there would not be a moment to attend to the rising pile of papers, so he decided to put in a couple of hours before going to bed.

Halfway through this tedious task he came upon a postcard of Norwich cathedral. He hadn't opened his post for two days or even looked through the piles, so this latest card from Lily had lain undiscovered. Heart beating faster, as it always did when he saw her handwriting, he turned it over. Another of her brief messages: *Wonderful about the Countryside March, isn't it, so many going to be there — I imagine you'll be among them. Love L.*

George tossed the card on to the desk to join the brown envelopes and sheaves of forms. Lily's message could only mean one thing, of that he was absolutely sure. She was going to be at the march. In view of her deep feelings about the country and hunting it was inconceivable that she would not join the protest. Yes: she would be there and he would not. He was going to be *here*, trying to get through a hundred jobs alone.

He closed his eyes and struggled for calm. To be rational, even if he had been going, the chances of seeing her among several hundred thousand was minimal, so there was no point grieving too hard. And it was far too late to make alternative arrangements for someone to look after the animals. Everyone in the locality wanted to be in London. No one for miles would be available to take over another man's job on this most vital of days. George told himself to stop imagining what might have been, and went to bed — far later than he had intended. But not to sleep. Instead, in his mind he wrote her a reply. *Darling Lily, I won't be there. So glad you're going. Please come home soon. I carry on, but it's scarcely a life without you. Love and miss you so much.* He would choose a card for his message in the morning — Serusier's Solitude, perhaps, and delete the self-pitying phrase. Then he would probably put it in the drawer and, like the last one, never post it.

It had been decided that marching through the city, Prodge, Saul and Ben would keep close to the other farmers from their bus. In the vast crowd it would have been easy to lose companions, so they were to form a small body, and Prodge was to carry their banner. The banner had caused some argument. Peter Friel, a middle-aged farmer over the hill from Prodge, wanted it to say "Will the PM bury our dead stock?" The others had suggested that, should it be seen on television, the question would make no sense to the average viewer. It would be a wasted message.

"Bloody well should make sense," Friel had snorted. "What the anti-hunting brigade should realise is how many thousands of vital jobs would be lost if there was no hunting — most importantly, carting off our dead animals for next to nothing to the kennels." He had banged down his mug of beer, his face plumped to an alarming shade of purple — a man both outraged and desperate. As nobody else had come up with a banner slogan that they felt about with equal passion, it was finally agreed that his should be adopted, although it was probably over the heads of the ignorant urban public.

In the bus on the journey to London Peter Friel took a seat beside Prodge. It was too early in the morning even for him to aim his usual blast of fury towards the government. His complexion had quietened, his eyes were bewildered. As he ate his bacon sandwich he talked in erratic sentences that Prodge could only just hear.

"Take yesterday," he said. "I've a dead sheep. I ring the kennels. The flesh van arrives in under two hours. I pay them a fiver. No problems. Hounds get fed. They give us a bloody marvellous service, always have. Always will, if they're allowed to, both to farmers who hunt, and farmers who don't. What those dunder-head anti-hunting politicians who want to ban hunting haven't worked out, mincing round Westminster, is that if this service goes, what do we do? To call the knackerman, if you can find one, it'll cost you seventy, even eighty quid. Which one of us these days can afford that? May be the price of lunch for two in Islington, but a bloody fortune to today's farmer. So what's the alternative?"

Grease from the bacon fat ran down Peter Friel's chin. He was hating this bus-breakfast. With a handkerchief he had some difficulty prising from his trouser pocket he dabbed ineffectively at his face.

"Alternative, Prodge, is we bury our own stock. Ha! Imagine that! Pollute the water system, create major health problems. How's the Minister of Ag. going to like that? How's the PM going to explain that?" He paused, heaved, chuckled. "Well, I tell you what, I have this plan. If the day comes foxhunting really is abolished, and God forbid that day should ever come, next time I have a dead cow I'm going to bring it up to London. No matter what it costs, I'm going to get it to London, dump it on the front steps of Downing Street. You'd help me, I daresay. I could count on others. Prime Minister, I'd say, you tell me what to do. You tell thousands of us how to dispose of our dead animals with no kennels to carry out the service. We haven't got £700 a year for the knackerman — we haven't got £700 a year for ourselves. So we bury them and cause havoc? Pollution? You tell me." Friel gave another melancholy laugh. "Anyhow," he said, "that's my dream." Then, very suddenly, he fell asleep.

283

Prodge looked at the man beside him. He had been a friend of his own father, but rather than abandon farming life for the easy option of Spain, he had kept at it. More than thirty-five years, Prodge reckoned. Friel had seen good times, some bad — but nothing like this. Prodge wondered if he would survive. He wondered if he himself would survive — but at least he had youth on his side. On the occasions he managed a good night's sleep, his energy was restored. Friel looked as if his energy was wearing down. Prodge sympathised with him, agreed with every word he said — and feared for him. Unless things improved there was a high chance Peter Friel would be one of the thousands of farmers forced to give up. And then what? Debts hanging over him, farming the only life he knew, what would he do to support his family? Only recently he had said to Prodge he was considering signing on for a course in plumbing — a three-year course, earning nothing while he studied. Friel was in his mid-fifties. Was that the reward for a life of ceaseless hard work producing fine meat and crops? After a while Prodge, too, fell asleep. He dreamt there was a dead cow at the back of the bus which they were to deliver to Downing Street.

He had been to London once before, as a child, and remembered only the enormity of Buckingham Palace. But it was not the sights they passed that interested him today: it was the hundreds of faces. An alien looking down from Mars could have told they were country folk marching: there was a uniform weatherbeaten sheen on their cheeks; anxiety and anger were shared equally among their eyes. Their clothes, too, were of the

284

uniform market-day kind — waxed jackets dulled with wear and rain, ancient frayed tweed jackets with leather patches at the elbows. Some of the older men wore flat caps, greasy round the edges, so closely moulded to their wearers' heads it was hard to imagine those heads without them. There were middle-aged women with bright faces and head scarves — the backbone of England, Prodge remembered they were sometimes called: the thousands of women in rural areas who could be relied on for help for dozens of different causes. The women the press liked to scorn, they were. Edgy voices, they had, yes: but they were good women and wouldn't have missed this show of dignified protest for anything.

Among the muted colours of the vast crowds, hunt servants and masters stood out in their pink coats, boots polished to mirror brightness, whips curled round their stems. They had a witty line in banners, and were the target of the Animal Rights members who in their cowardly balaclavas jeered at the marchers. Prodge was not surprised to see many of the crowd were old, well into retirement. Farmers all their lives, the least they could do was to show support, make their feelings known about the disaster that was now rural life. Coming from the generation who had believed in Sunday best, they had taken out their smart Sunday suits, their wife-pressed shirts and quiet wool ties. Several of them, hobbling, leant on shepherds' crooks.

Prodge remembered Lily had once told him that her grandmother had been a land girl in the West Country, and there had been an extraordinary feeling of closeness to people from different lives and backgrounds fighting for the same cause. Well, thought Prodge, there was something like that today. A great many of us fighting for our rights, joining together in the brilliantly organised and decorous protest which the government, if they had any heart at all, would surely find moving. Several times his own eyes filled with tears.

As they marched past giant buildings and shops filled with bright, unobtainable, unwanted things (Prodge saw a single ugly dress that was the pre-BSE price of two bull calves), a world light years from his normal morning of muck and mud and green fields, his head constantly swivelled in search. His conviction that Lily would be here, somewhere, was still strong within him. Occasionally he touched his shirt pocket and felt the photograph.

They'd not been walking for an hour when he thought he saw her some way behind. The long tail of the marchers was curving round into Trafalgar Square: she was a fair way from him, too far to be certain. But he was certain.

Lily, the figure he knew was Lily, was talking to a woman beside her. He caught a momentary sight of her profile. There was a scarf round her neck whose blue he thought he recognised. But it was the bouncing hair that convinced him. Surely, no one else but Lily . . . When he looked harder, wondering how to leave his group and make a dash for her, she was gone. For the next part of the march he walked half backwards, looking, looking. Peter Friel turned him round with a gentle push on the arm. "All of us are in a spin today," he said.

On the rest of the march through London Prodge reran the fragmentary image of her, the sighting that lasted for under a second, trying to determine whether he had been right, or whether his fevered imagination had merely supplied him with a taunting doubt.

By the end of the day Prodge was weary (a very different matter, marching through London streets, from tramping over fields) but still alert for another sighting of Lily. In the crowds jostling to get into the parked buses that were to return all over the country, he saw the blue scarf again. Lily? Surely Lily. Back view: she was being pushed towards a coach parked some yards away. Prodge touched Peter's arm.

"Back in a moment," he said.

With the kind of maddened urgency to which there are no barriers, Prodge thrashed his way through the dense mass of tired farmers. Somehow, he reached her. She was just a step away from the coach by now — from East Anglia, Prodge noted. He stretched out, tugged at the long tail of her scarf. She turned. Lily.

"Prodge?" Amazed, she was. Scared eyes.

"Lily —"

"Is George —?"

"No."

The crowd was moving her nearer to the steps. Prodge clung to the scarf.

"Lily: please come home. You've no idea how much George wants you back."

287

She turned, smiled at him. Someone was pushing her up the steps.

"I can't, Prodge. Wish I could explain." She was pushed through the door, gone.

Prodge, like a man in shock, stood looking up at the grey glass of the coach windows watching her dim figure move almost to the back. She took a seat by the window, looked for him, waved. Then she blew him a kiss, mouthed something he could not understand. Did she remember the river afternoon? The kitchen afternoon, when he had made his clumsy confession and hopelessly lied to her about his love dissolving? Had she believed him? Probably. In those early days Lily thought only of George.

Prodge put two fingers to his mouth to blow a returning kiss. He'd done his best, got nowhere, could not return home with news that would cheer George's heart. As the coach started up and began to roll forwards, he realised he could not move his poised fingers, which stemmed tears from running down his cheek, so Lily never received his return kiss, too heavy to fly. Desolate, he allowed himself to be buffeted by the crowd back to his coach. The West Country crowd, impatient to be off, joshed him for keeping them waiting. He didn't care. He cared for nothing but Lily. On the journey back he decided that, as he had failed to acquire any hopeful news for George, the kindest thing would be not to mention that he had seen her. Lily! Prodge slept. Dreamt of her.

★　★　★

For both George and Nell the day was a long one. Feeding the cows who were still in their winter quarters, milking, scraping and washing down the parlours, feeding the sheep and calves besides myriad other jobs was a struggle single-handed. Both were exhausted by the evening. Both, in their separate houses, sat watching the march on the nine o'clock news. When it was over Nell telephoned George. She was waiting up for Prodge, she said, who was due back shortly.

"I've bad news for him," she said, "but it'll wait till morning. He needs a good night's sleep." She paused. "There's another down with BSE, I reckon — Bracken. I had my suspicions yesterday but I managed to keep Prodge away from her. I was sure he wouldn't go to London if he knew."

"Oh, Nell . . ."

"She fell in the yard this morning, had a hard time getting up. I rang the vet at once, but of course he was at the march. So, first thing tomorrow morning she'll have to go off. Oldest cow in the herd, Bracken. I remember the night she was born. Prodge helped deliver her. He'll be devastated. I don't know how to tell him." Her voice broke.

"It's so unfair. Your prize herd. It should have been one of my cows. I'm fond of them, but they don't mean as much to me as your herd does to Prodge."

"No. But it's random, where it strikes, isn't it? You hear of cases all over the country. They've all eaten the same vile foodstuff, as we now know, but it only strikes at some. So odd."

"Shall I come over?"

From the long pause that followed his question, George knew that Nell tussled in her mind whether to accept his offer.

"No," she said at last. "Thanks all the same. Soon as Prodge is home we'll have a bowl of soup and go to bed."

"Right. I'll be over tomorrow. Why don't I ring the Ministry for you first thing? Tell him to get a vet to you as soon as possible? You'll have enough on your hands."

"That would be kind," said Nell.

Before he slept he thought of her. He was tired out but wakeful, dreading the morning. He knew her childhood bedroom was unchanged — sparse, narrow, chipped. Shelves filled with books about ponies, stuffed toys on the bed. Nell slept with a toy cat, she once told George, that he had given her on her eighth birthday (bought and wrapped up by his mother). In many ways she was still childlike. Unexposed to the world beyond the farm, her naivety if, sometimes, astonishing was not surprising.

George felt the confusion many people experience when regarding someone they have known all their lives. Proximity blurs the changes over the years, then suddenly a new figure emerges — surprising, almost shocking. Here, suddenly, was Nell, as she had been for several years, grown-up, capable, original: the eager-to-please, fearless child now an adult of formidable energy and good sense. The sweetness of her nature had never changed, but intriguing contradictions, so plain in her childhood, had developed within her: she was both the demure spinner of home-dyed wool, and the lover of coarse jokes. She was both touching in her friendliness, and yet capable of harshness. At variance with the modern world, whose ways held no appeal for her, she was a young woman whose goodness was not properly rewarded — not that she herself would ever think in terms of reward for charity.

And I love her, thought George, sensing the ache in his heart that always came when he reflected on the diverse parts of Nell's character. Her innocently exposed feelings, her blushes, the small frowns that flew across a face devoid of artifice, touched his heart. Many times he had wanted to put a protective arm round her. But it would be hard ever to think of her as anything but *Nell*, always *there*, the sister he had never had. Even if Lily never returned, it would be hard to reroute such ingrained sentiments, George thought, sleep nudging him at last. But not impossible . . .

CHAPTER
THIRTEEN

Over the next two years forty-seven thousand farmers in England and Wales gave up the work that had been their life. Those who remained struggled to survive on the lowest incomes, down by seventy per cent, for three generations. Many of them were forced to exist on two thousand pounds a year.

The devastation to farming life caused by BSE and the other gathering ills of the country united the small, mixed farmers in sympathy. (The farmers rich from East Anglian grain, although affected by the fall in subsidies and the rising pound, continued to thrive in their big-business way.) From the West Country, Cumbria and Wales came stories of extraordinary help among neighbouring farmers, all equal in their despair. Some, no prospect of hope left, gave up not just their business, but their lives. The number of suicides among farmers became shocking.

But united in their anger and anxiety though they were, every farmer's prime concern was to fight for the survival of his own family, animals and land. George, thanks to his wisely invested capital, was still able to pay Saul and Ben and keep up with all the costs required by the farm. This lack of financial worry, while most of those in his part of the country were suffering, caused him daily guilt. Surreptitiously he delivered anonymous sums of cash to several neighbouring farmers and paid off the feed bill of a supplier who had threatened to stop delivering to an old, widowed tenant farmer. As Prodge had discovered when he had tried to increase his overdraft, only tenant farmers lucky enough to have a sympathetic bank manager could get a decent loan, for security came only from owning land and buildings. A tenant farmer's only asset was his stock. With the outbreak of BSE this became almost valueless. In the event, George bought six of Prodge's milk cows — which he did not want or need — on the grounds that he'd like to add prize cattle to his herd, and feared his friend was not convinced by his story. Prodge was evidently desperate enough to want to believe him, but he still would not consider an interest-free loan or any other help that George offered.

Seven of Prodge's cows had gone down with BSE. With the slaughter of each one his spirits sank further. He made no attempt, as Nell did, to assume an optimistic face. His days passed in a robotic trance — feeding, milking, ploughing as always, but scarcely speaking. The young, cheerful, dynamic man, so full of plans for an ever more successful farm and a powerful motorbike, had been replaced by one grown prematurely old: grey-skinned, jaw muscles constantly moving, eyes dragged down with fatigue. George, anxious about his friend, now went over to his farm every day.

One October afternoon the men stood side by side looking at a pen of bull calves to be sold at the market the following day.

"Funny to think a gallon of bloody petrol costs more than you get for one of these." Prodge's taut hands were clawed to the top bar of the railing. "Can't afford to drive them to market, anyway," he added. "Can't afford to drive bloody anywhere. Day'll come I'll have to shoot them myself. There's others doing that." The chalky bones of his knuckles agitated beneath the weathered skin. George remembered Prodge's quality of stillness. He would stand for ages leaning against the side of a shed, or a gate, expounding his plans, fine body making no movement, eyes lit in anticipation. These days, there were always restive parts of him. Turbulent bone and muscle rippling the skin betrayed the despair within.

"So happens," said George, "I've plenty of room in my lorry tomorrow. I'll pick them up for you."

There was a long silence in which Prodge wavered.

"Thanks," he said eventually.

On another occasion George ran into Prodge on the hill road that ran towards the "farm" now owned by the Cardiff businessman. George pulled up and asked Prodge if he wanted a lift.

"I can walk a mile," was the terse reply.

"Where're you headed?"

Prodge looked away, over the hills.

"If you must know, a bit of moonlighting. Squire Cardiff wants his privet trimmed. Heard I was good at hedging." He grimaced. "That's what we're reduced to

— municipal gardeners. But got to do something if we're not to starve."

Prodge was half turned from George, who saw the bone wings of shoulder blades pointing through his jacket. In the last six months Prodge must have lost over a stone.

"You can go another day if you want," said George. "But today you're coming down to the pub with me for a bit of lunch. I was on my way there anyway. Come on. Get in."

Prodge was still turned away from George. He did not move for a long time, kept his silence. Then he got into the Land Rover. George saw that he was near to cracking, dared not speak. They drove with no word to the village.

There was a sharp autumn wind that day, even in the valley. In the Bell the wood fire warmed the few farmers who had gathered for a single pint and a plate of pork crackling: few of them could afford a proper lunch these days. George chose a table near the window, then went to the bar for two pints of beer. He saw Prodge give an involuntary shiver as the fire's heat reached him. He saw his friend tip back his head, shut his eyes for a moment, then spread his hands on the table to still their shaking. George felt his innards clench with worry. Prodge's state was profoundly disturbing.

At the bar, waiting for the drinks, George found himself next to Simon, the vet, who gave a small nod in the direction of Prodge. By now Prodge had opened his eyes and was looking blankly out of the window.

"We've been asked," he said quietly to George, "to keep a lookout, on our rounds, for cases potentially disturbing . . ." He paused, scratched his cheek. "I've been up to Prodge and Nell's several times recently. Have to say I'm concerned about your friend. Think we should keep a close eye. Nell says his moods come and go, and it's hardly unreasonable any farmer should feel the world is against him right now. But I have to say I'm worried. I'm wondering whether I should report —"

"No," said George. "I'm just as worried. I go up every day. If Nell or I see any further deterioration, we'll take action at once. Of course. But to send some counsellor up to 'talk things through' — I tell you, he'd shoot them on the spot along with the bull calves he's now threatening to shoot himself."

The vet gave a grim smile. "Let's keep in touch," he said.

George ordered two large steaks, baked potatoes, peas and carrots. The speed and eagerness with which Prodge ate suggested that this was not normal hunger after a hard morning's physical labour, but a deeper hunger that had built up over several months. George watched silently. By the time Prodge had finished two helpings of bread-and-butter pudding, colour had spread across his cheeks. The rigidity of his thin body had relaxed.

"That was good," he said, lighting a cigarette. (There had been much celebration at his giving up some years ago. His firm resolution had been broken after Bessie died.) He coughed. George said nothing. "Nell does her best," Prodge went on. "We feed mostly off stuff in the garden. Not much left in the freezer. I needed that steak. Thanks."

He drew deeply on his cigarette, watched the slow spin of smoke into the warm air muggy with the smell of food and burning cherry boughs. The weather outside was in more cheerful mood, too. In a bright blue sky there was a crowd of very curly clouds, sharp-edged as cauliflowers. They nudged each other, but their edges did not blur. Prodge leant back in his chair.

"Shit, George," he said, "the whole thing's a bloody disaster. Sometimes I feel it's all going to be OK, we might get back to normal. One day BSE'll be over, exports'll start up again, back to a decent living. Some days I believe that and I'm fine. Other times, I don't know. I wake up thinking there's no point in anything, not in a bloody thing. All my working life on the farm, and what for? This. No money, no future, the endless misery of seeing my cows go through agonies before they're slaughtered. I'd give it all up for two pins. I keep thinking that. Then on good days I tell myself not to be a bloody fool." He paused. "Bad days, I find it hard to move my legs, they're so heavy. Whole body seems heavy, won't respond. I carry on with the work, but mechanically. Something seems wrong in my mind: it won't turn over properly. I told all this to Nell the other day. She said she wasn't surprised and I ought to go to the doctor. Not bloody likely, I said. He's putting a lot of them round here on anti-depressants. I've scarcely taken a pill in my life, have I? So when it gets really bad

I walk up over the hill, look down at the fields I've been ploughing and sowing all these years, think to myself how lucky I am to have had the opportunity to live here . . . can't really imagine anything else. That cheers me up for a bit. That makes me think I'll not give up. Not for anything. But then I see a letter from the bank saying no more credit, and Nell confesses we're behind with the rent, and the black comes down again. If it wasn't for you and Nell, honestly, George, I don't know . . ."

George nodded.

"Nell's unbelievable," Prodge went on after a while. "No matter what, she manages to smile. And she's nothing much to smile about. With village shops for miles round now closed down there's nowhere left to sell her few jumpers. Anyway she's lost the heart to go on with them. It's just work, work, work for her: hasn't bought herself a new piece of clothing in three years. Hasn't even replaced her split boots, mud coming in. Us going anywhere for a drink, a film — those days are over. The petrol.

"We have a dream sometimes, Nell 'n me," Prodge continued. "A few days off. Nowhere very fancy. Just somewhere we can get a few good nights' sleep and three meals a day and drink. No worries for a few days. That'd restore us like nothing else. Nell says, believe me, it'll happen one day. We'll have a holiday. There are others worse off than us, she says. Barry Fenton, over Dulverton way, he's just sold off his herd for next to nothing and signed up for a course in plumbing, like old Peter Friel was planning to do. So for three years he'll not be earning a penny, and at the end of it he'll be stuck in a job he hates in order to keep his family. Barry Fenton," Prodge added, "is fifty-three. Third generation farm. Known nothing but farming all his life. His son, who should have inherited, flatly refused to have anything to do with the place. He's gone off to earn a fortune in some computer firm in Bristol. 'I'm buggered if I'm going to go through what you've gone through, Dad,' he said to Barry. And I suppose you can't blame him."

Their talk turned to the disaster of the high pound, the strangle-hold of Brussels, the hatred among farmers of EU directives — subjects that all over the country others were dismally mulling over to no effect. In the warmth of their agreement, and no longer hungry, Prodge found his spirits rising. The hour after lunch, by the pub fire, flew by: suddenly it was milking time and Nell was coping on her own. Guilt-ridden, but stronger, he rose hurriedly to go. George drove him home. He enquired about the gardening job. By now, Prodge was able to smile.

"Only from time to time," he said. "All helps. In fact he's not a bad chap. Doesn't know the difference between a robin and a crow, but loves his clock golf course. All he wants me to do is trim his prissy hedge, or water his hanging geraniums, or stick in annuals by the front door — doesn't pay by the hour, just slips me twenty quid no matter if I've only been there an hour. So I suppose he knows what farmers are going through. There's a lot of talk against these incomers. Well, of course they're ridiculous when they begin complaining about mud on the road: they get their view of the country from pictures in glossy magazines. But I'm not all against them. Some of them provide a bit of casual labour, contribute a bit to the community. I could never support the second-home syndrome when there are locals unable to buy houses, but they're not all bad, the townies. At least they've the money to save some of the rotten old buildings. Can't say I've anything against Squire Cardiff himself. We just don't see eye to eye when it comes to what's a garden. Nell refuses even to go and look. Says the sight of his suburban marigolds would make her sick." Prodge laughed. "She's a snob, Nell, sometimes. An outright snob."

They found her coming out of the house. The cows were all in, she said: she was about to begin milking. Prodge apologised for being late. Nell gave him one of her most exuberant smiles. She saw the colour in her brother's cheeks and guessed he had been in the pub with George. God knows he deserved an hour or two off, a mite of pleasure. If George had managed to cheer Prodge, then she was cheered too.

George noticed that Nell's baggy dungarees could not disguise her loss of weight. Like Prodge, an ashy paleness showed beneath the copper of her cheeks like the traces of an old picture beneath the surface colour. But she still walked jauntily, was bright-eyed. She still gave the appearance that all was manageable. In her support of her brother she was, George thought, infinitely strong. His admiration and love for her, as it so often did now, reverberated through him.

For the last year Nell had taken to visiting George far less frequently, and he missed her. But he understood. Since the advent of BSE, and the introduction of a passport for each cow, paperwork had doubled for all owners of cattle, and she had no help with that. Juggling their small income was her responsibility: the worry of the rent, which she tried to keep from Prodge, and dealing in general with their financial straits. On top of that she helped as always on the farm, grew her few vegetables, cooked and kept house. This, George had observed lately, was the area to which she attached least importance. The place was muddier, dustier, colder, more chaotic than it had ever been, revealing more than anything the state she was fighting. Her horses — her one indulgence and endless pleasure — had long been sold, and she had little time or energy to walk the land over which she used to ride. The frequent flashes of light and laughter had mostly gone from her, too. Her priorities now were to survive the farming crisis and to carry on as best she could, supporting her brother, into some easier future she could not precisely imagine.

By now, George had almost given up any hope of Lily returning, and wondered if Nell knew this. They never talked about her these days. They never speculated about what she might do. George had once thought that her absence would be no longer than a year. But almost three years had passed. During that time she had, as she promised, kept in touch. Postcards arrived erratically: sometimes three in a month, then nothing for six weeks. Their object, George grimly

301

understood, was to assure him she was safe and well, but they didn't convey the sort of information he craved. Usually she only wrote a line or two and — infuriatingly, George began to find — it mostly concerned some exhibition she had been to: a sharp observation about Utrillo or Van Gogh or Rembrandt's drawings, or "the piercing green of Matisse, like the grass in Top Meadow". Often George would write a card back — a few lines to convey the loss and sadness he felt, hoping to assuage it. But this it did not do, and he had quite a stack of these replies by now: messages she would never receive.

But after a year's teaching in Norwich Lily evidently flew about in an unplanned way. Cards came from Perpignan, Mexico, New York, Perugia. They were piled up, these cards, on a shelf in the kitchen, telling George nothing. Several times he had thought of burning the lot of them, then resisted. When hope drained from him — as increasingly it did — the number of missives was of some comfort: and to think she had not had a single word from him. Sometimes he wondered if, as Prodge and Nell advised, he should disobey her wishes and try to find her. But over the years he had abandoned this idea each time, believing she would not want him to, and fearing that if he did he might endanger the faint chance that was still left.

In the house, so many signs of Lily were still there: her arrangement of things, the tablecloths she had bought, her straw hats on hooks in the hall, her boots, the books by her side of the bed. Every time he came into the kitchen George felt the absence of her. He

302

longed for her. He thought of her, he dreamt of her, and always he puzzled over whether it was something he had done that caused her the crisis of no-feeling that was so traumatising she had to leave him. Of late he had felt himself a little stronger — able to cope with the problems of his neighbours and Nell and Prodge, able to keep up with the paperwork and the endless physical labour on the farm. But he still felt dull, empty, unfired, and was resigned to the fact that this heaviness of being might remain with him for ever unless Lily returned. "I'm a half-man," he said once to Nell, back in the days when they still sometimes mentioned her. Like Prodge, though for different reasons, he lived and worked mechanically.

In the autumn of 1999 there was a second Farmers' March, this time to Bournemouth where the Labour Party Conference was being held. It was decided that George should go, taking Ben. He suggested to Nell that she should come too, but, increasingly concerned about Prodge's silent, fragile state, she did not want to leave him even for a day.

The gathering of farmers was smaller and quieter than the Countryside March the year before in London. There was an air of deadly serious intent: the farmers, bursting with their grievances, wanted to make their voices heard. In this the marchers were frustrated: not a single delegate or minister was prepared to come out and listen to them, talk to them. While inside the conference hall, as George heard on his radio, the Chancellor of the Exchequer was boasting to his audience that Labour was going to reward the hardest working of the population, outside stood hundreds of despairing farmers quietly protesting at their sixty-hour weeks on zero incomes — the direct result of the government's inability to handle agriculture, or to understand the problems.

George had never seen Ben, by nature a quiet and shy young lad, so enraged. After hanging about for the whole morning to no avail — aware that the press were waiting for an outburst from a farmer whose patience finally snapped — at lunchtime they saw delegates slink out of the building to avoid the protestors' eyes. Ben slipped from George's side. George saw him approach an unsympathetic looking woman who cast a brief sneer at the patient crowd. George moved nearer. Ben's fists were clenched, threatening. But his natural shyness took over.

"Please," he said, "what are you going to do to help us? We're not being unreasonable."

The woman turned on him, brittle in her navy suit.

"You lot," she snapped, waving a hand at the farmers, "should realise you only represent a very small and very insignificant percentage of the workforce. Farmers are like any other business. They must learn to stand on their own two feet."

She was off, back to the safety of the other delegates, united in the smugness of their opinions about farmers. Ben turned pale, as if he had been attacked.

"Christ," he said. "She's sick." He resumed his place beside George. He was patted on the back: hero of the moment for having spoken up. And later he was further cheered by the friendliness and sympathy of some of the policemen who lined the route. In the late afternoon, police and farmers joined in barbecues organised by local companies.

"There are people on our side," George said in the coach on the way home. "Who's paid for our transport, the buses? People who believe in us. Who are those people waving, cheering us on? People who believe in us. It's the government who don't give a toss for farming — aren't interested, don't understand, urban almost to a man. A few years ago none of us could have imagined all this, could we? The stranglehold. But look: look at all those urging us on. New Labour's got a fight on its hands."

"What I don't understand," said Ben, very slowly, for he never spoke very fast, "is how that old bitch can say we're an insignificant part of the workforce. I mean, we drive for four hours through all this well-farmed country — how did it get to be like that? Has anyone in power ever given a thought as to exactly what it takes to keep the land in good order? Bet you anything you like scarcely a person in MAFF has sat on a tractor, lifted a bale of silage, buried a dead sheep. I don't understand what's going through their minds: perhaps they think we're just going to go away, stop being a nuisance. I don't understand their lack of sympathy, their blindness, their sheer bloody stupidity. They must know we've a good case, that's why they wouldn't speak to us. Didn't want to be confronted . . . shit, what a day."

George, achingly depressed by the disappointing outcome of the event, looked in wonder at the young lad who had worked for him unstintingly hard for ten years: Ben had never thought of anything but a farming life. He had little hope of ever having a farm of his own, but that did not worry him. To work with the animals and tend the land with the same skill as his father was all he wanted. Now, his face was crimson. Never before had he made such a speech, delivered such an attack on the powers beyond his reach. George could see he was moved, shaken, dismayed. His own feeling of gloom increased: today had confirmed the fact that farmers had long recognised — that there was no future for the young in this business. He handed Ben his small flask of whisky. Ben opened it, sniffed.

"Never touched this stuff before," he said, "but, yeah, I'll give it a go. Could do with something. Thanks." He took a couple of swigs, then fell asleep. George let his eyes trail over the passing fields, sheep and cows. The insignificant land, he thought. Green and pleasant, but *insignificant* in the opinion of the government.

By the time they got back to the farm it was dark. Instead of going to the cottage, Ben asked George if he could come in for a moment. In the kitchen they sat at the empty table, the dolorous tick of the clock fending off the silence between them. George suggested a drink. Ben said he'd like a beer this time. He sat with his hands spread out on the table — enormous they were, George observed, out of all proportion to the rest of the lad's narrow, sinewy body. So many pictures of those hands, with their rimed nails, came to George's mind: stroking a sick cow, wrenching a piece of stubborn machinery, grasping a bale of hay, patting his sheepdog Wench. Now they shook very slightly, losing the battle to relax. When George put down two opened bottles and glasses, they clenched up into fists taut not with the readiness for a fight, but trying for control. Ben looked down at them as if they were nothing to do with him, no part of him.

"I have to say something to you," he said at last.

He lifted one of his hands as if with a conscious effort and tugged at the knot of his tie. It was a woven thing, deep red, scrawny as Ben himself. The only other occasion on which George had ever seen Ben in the tie was at his and Lily's wedding. The thought that he had put it on — most probably at his father's suggestion — to protest to people who cared not a damn about his livelihood touched George deeply.

"It's something that's been boiling up in my mind," Ben went on at last, "and today has finally put it all into place for me. Maybe if I hadn't come with you, maybe if you'd taken Nell, or Dad, I wouldn't have come to this decision. But I'm going to have to go."

"Go?"

"Leave. Leave farming. Animals, land, all the stuff I've always liked. Put it out of my mind, do something else."

"I see," said George, and waited.

"There's thousands have come to the same decision, aren't there? At first I thought they were bloody pathetic. Now I understand why. Farming's not what it was. Maybe never will be again. I know I'm one of the lucky ones, employed by you, security. You're good and

307

generous, too — don't get me wrong. Working here's been bloody marvellous. But it's the whole . . . thing that's finally got me down. There's not a boy I was at school with whose Dad's a farmer is following on. They're all up and off making good money somewhere in the towns. My friend Tom — you remember him? — I hardly ever see him now. But I ran into him the other day. Told me he was making two hundred pounds a week, decent hours, in the motorbike business. Another mate's in some computer business doing nicely, and Mr Friel's son — I heard he'd gone into the supermarket, some kind of under-manager, bonuses and everything. They thought I was off my head, sticking at farm work eighteen hours a day all weathers. They thought I was bloody pathetic. It's only going to get worse, they said: get out while you can. So I began to think. I have to say, the thoughts kept on coming back to me. That they're right, I mean."

"I understand," said George. This stream of consciousness from a man of so few words — he found himself too moved even to try to express the sympathy he felt.

"I mean . . . look at it like this. I'm only twenty-five, Mr Elkin. What's going to happen to me if I stay? Will I ever get a life? The powers that be don't give a bugger about us. Farmers used to be respected, valued. I get the feeling we've become a very low priority now, and one day all they'll want us for is to keep the fields looking nice for tourists. I don't want any part of that. Give me a yard of muck to deal with and I'm happy. But what I'm saying is, I don't want to end up like my

308

dad, Mr Elkin. Works like a dog, old before his time, nothing but worry these days — and what when he retires? Doesn't own an acre of land, nothing."

"Of course I'll see Saul —"

"I know you will. You're the best employer for a hundred miles. Dad and I know that. But for me, I want independence. I'd like my own smallholding, thirty cows. I'd like to go away for a few years, make some money, come back and get on with the dream."

"Doubt you'd be able to live on thirty cows."

"That's what my granddad did, Mum's side. Very happy."

"Times have changed."

"I realise that. But with the money I'd made in . . . well, I'm not a bad electrician, for instance. I could do a course. Could make my fortune." He gave a rueful smile. "Because I'd want to come back. I mean, I want to die a farmer, not fade away above some bloody fish and chip shop in a city."

George shifted in his chair. A weariness went through his bones.

"I sympathise," he said quietly, "completely. I do. And you must go, you must try. If I can do anything to help you get a footing in the outer world . . . I mean, I have a friend who runs an electrical company, for instance."

"I'd appreciate that. And I realise of course that I'd be leaving you in the . . . letting you down. You and Dad'd be hard put to cope with everything here. You'd need someone to replace —"

"Don't worry about that. There's no shortage of men needing work. Alan Brooks — you know, Alan the haulier — I heard only yesterday he's had to lay off two men. There's a good chance he'll have to pack it in altogether, he said. Petrol prices, local slaughter-house closed, can't make ends meet —"

"But if it's all right with you," interrupted Ben, "I won't be off just yet awhile. I'll have to look around, take my bearings. I'll not leave you in the lurch."

"Thanks." George nodded. "Does Saul know of your decision?"

"Not yet. I didn't want to say anything till it was definite. It was only definite a few hours ago, coming back in the bus, thinking about the way we'd been treated. I'll tell Dad in the morning."

The two men stood up.

"It'll work out all right," said George. "I'm sure. The thing about a big shift in life is that it's easier to cope with once the decision's been firmly taken."

A look of doubt crossed Ben's troubled young face. He touched his tie again, still swung his jaw from side to side.

"Well thanks, Mr Elkin. Sorry to have kept you so late."

They shook hands. Last time they had done this it was Ben's twenty-first birthday, when in a short speech at a gathering in the pub he had shyly declared that nothing could ever beat farming.

The following day George noticed that Saul, whose cheek often twitched when he was particularly tired or anxious, kept touching his face as if to quell the constant spasm of his skin. He said nothing, but he made a point of helping George move the sheep from Top Meadow to a field in the valley. When they had finished they leant on the gate, as they often did, just looking at the flock. The ewes were bunched together at first. Then, as indeterminately as clouds, they moved away from each other, chose their patch of grass for a spell of independence before huddling together again for the night.

Saul screwed up his eyes against a hard orange sun low in the sky: it cast a chip of gold into each of his pupils. His was a face of battered handsomeness. Sometimes George thought it hadn't changed since, as a child, he had first known Saul. But looking at him this evening he realised, with reluctance, that anxiety, fatigue and relentless hard work had had their cruel effects.

"Sorry about the lad," said Saul eventually. "Suppose you can't blame him."

"Course not. I'm sorry too. But his decision's understandable."

"He'll not be off yet awhile, he says. Last thing he wants is to let you down. Could be he'll change his mind."

"Could be."

"The do yesterday seemed to have churned him up."

"Hostile lot, they were. Didn't give a damn. Wouldn't listen, wouldn't speak. Ben was a hero. Went up to this old bat —"

"So I heard." Saul moved his jaw back and forth in the manner of his son the night before. "Course, he

311

won't like the sort of job he's got in mind. Farming's in his blood — six generations of us have worked the land. His mother'll be turning in her grave. I'll grant you he'll be back. If he goes, that is."

"Perhaps," said George.

Saul's wife had died when Ben was four. Saul had brought the child up, with no help, in the cottage. Ben's departure, for his father, would mean a loss George could understand all too well.

They went on watching the sheep, bunches of grey against the dusk. By now the sun had disappeared leaving a single tinsel thread of gold strung across the acreage of grey, and it was turning cold.

CHAPTER
FOURTEEN

As a trained lawyer, George had always considered himself reasonably able when it came to paperwork, but as ever more near-incomprehensible booklets of instruction thundered through the door, even he despaired. His simple conclusion was that the Ministry of Agriculture had become more attached to the importance of bureaucracy than to the real life of farmers — rearing animals, tending the land, producing. The price of receiving subsidies — frustration, anger, precious time — was for many too high. It was being faced with the ludicrous amount of paperwork, even more than the rock-bottom prices for their animals, that was for many the last straw.

"How many times have I tried getting through to the help line?" Peter Friel asked George. Friel fought against his age by making a gallant effort to keep up with the new practices. "And when at last there's an answer it's a recorded voice telling you things that don't concern you. You can never speak to anyone in charge. I've given up. Most of us have given up."

Those who bothered to read the plethora of information sent out by MAFF were given to understand that within a few years all subsidies were to be paid through the internet, thus they would be paid several months earlier. This so-called "good news" implied that farmers would now have to buy computers to "ease" their lives. The help previously given by a sympathetic MAFF official in a regional office would be no more. Not only would farmers earning scarcely more than the price of a computer be expected to buy a terrifyingly complicated machine, they would then have to put aside working time to learn how to use the thing. When George told Saul this, the old man laughed a greater laugh than he had for a long time.

"You can see it, can't you? Us who's good at sheep and cows and crops and that, us men with big hands to deal with tractors and heavy jobs, trying to get our fingers round to understanding all that fiddle-faddle with office machinery."

On a grim November afternoon George sat at his desk before the huge pile of unattended papers. He wondered why it was that civil servants were inherently masochistic. Why did they enjoy increasing the hardships of EU red tape by translating the directives from Brussels in a form far more complicated than the original? And why were their rules so long-winded? A British form to apply for a CAP subsidy was twenty-two pages, though the same form in Ireland was only two. Why had none of these rule-writers ever learnt the art of précis? Was it beyond them, in their Whitehall offices, to imagine the life of the overworked, exhausted, despairing farmer who received them?

George's reflections broke off to read for the twentieth time the latest postcard from Lily. It came from Bournemouth. *Here for a few days*, she had written. She never said who with. Was her random flitting from place to place always alone? *A publisher seems interested in my idea of writing a book about How to Face a Picture. Love, love L.* — Bournemouth! They'd been there once, stayed with some old aunt. Perhaps that's where she was, safely, innocently, with the aunt, not that far away. George wondered whether if he left now and drove round the streets near the aunt's house — he could remember, roughly, where it was — he might run into her. He looked at the papers before him, and decided, as always when the foolishness of trying to find her seized him, that it was a bad idea.

But he would, as had become his odd habit, reply — pathetically, as he saw it, to record his anguish. For once, he decided against a card of a painting she loved and chose instead a sepia photograph of the farm that had been taken when his parents first bought it: a ramshackle place, so changed now — by Lily. That might jolt her, he thought. Remind her. *So pleased a publisher seems interested*, he wrote. *Darling Lily, please come home now. I want you, I miss you, I love you. G.* He flung the card into the drawer with the others. He was impatient with himself. The act of writing unseen words no longer brought relief. He couldn't think why he carried on with the hopeless ritual.

He picked up the three heavy booklets sent to aid filling in IACS forms. So turgid was their style, so soul-deadening their attempt at creative explanation, that he gave up after a few pages. He would try to struggle on without them, he thought: might even scribble a few suggestions in the margins. The grim job ahead required him to declare what he intended to grow on every field on his land, and precisely where the planting would be. On other forms he had to explain what subsidies he was applying for. What he dreaded — what all small farmers dreaded — was the possible failure of a crop. Should this happen and resowing become necessary, so were more forms. George picked up his pen, then put it down again. A pain had begun to bite at the back of his neck, rising through his skull. He opened, then quickly shut, a file of milk quota forms. He screwed up a form about The Assured Combinable Crop Scheme, and banged his fist on a pile of cow passports, knowing they were not up to date. They fell to the floor, scattering. He had no energy to pick them up. Instead he started dully to read about the Country Stewardship Scheme he had recently joined. The bonus was that they had paid to replace some of his old trees and for the renovation of hedges Ben had not had time to attend to. But was the subsidy worth the brain-numbing job of deciphering the complicated rules? And if all this paperwork was finally dementing him, what must it be like for those older, less educated, and less used to officialdom? George pictured some of the neighbouring farmers — Peter Friel, whose eyes were failing, Jack Lamont, who had had to lay off his helper. He pictured these and other men in their various kitchens, cold, tired, fed up, helpless. In better times, at the end of a long day of hard physical labour, they could be sure of an hour or so of peace in an armchair before bed. Now they were forever haunted by the nagging spectre of bloody *forms*. And the only time to deal with them, for most farmers, was at night, when energy was sapped from their tired bodies, and spirits were at their lowest.

George sat back, uncertain what to do. He wanted desperately to give up, go and heat the soup that Dusty had left on the stove. But the work hanging over him chafed his conscience. The weight of the empty room lapped over him. He had not bothered to light the fire, and it was cold. He wanted Lily to be here. He wanted her brightness, the warmth that emanated from her always, always . . .

There was a tap on the door. Wrenching himself from his reverie, George half expected her to walk in. Instead, it was Saul. He held his cap in his hands and wore the expression of acute indignation that preceded the bad news he frequently felt it was his duty to impart.

Saul always wore his father's old flat cap for outdoor work. By now it was a strange object held together by a glue of sweat and the dried-out rain of a thousand showers. The definite browns and greens of its youthful tweed had merged like the waters of a trout stream, only faintly indicating the bold patterns they had once made. Saul was often chided by both George and Ben about the state of his cap, but he was adamant. He would not replace it until the day it crumbled to dust in his hands, he said. It was his prop, as important to him as his crook, his father's old penknife and the silk handkerchief, sewn by his late wife, that he wore on Sundays to church.

Saul rarely came into the farmhouse. Lily had never been able to persuade him and Ben into the kitchen for tea breaks. They liked to go back to their cottage. But when he did, he always gently removed his cap and held on to it for comfort, for strength, or for whatever was needed on the particular occasion. This afternoon it was for the outrageous news of a visit from a man with his measuring tape. The man, George knew, was only doing his job — measuring the fields for which he had claimed subsidies. It was an unenviable job, to ensure no farmer was cheating. To the dutiful men from the Ministry who had to face the hostility of farmers while trying to carry out their work, such tasks can have held little appeal. George could imagine the scorn in Saul's eyes, in his bearing, as he led the measuring man to the fields.

"Him in his thin shoes came over this morning," he said. "I forgot to tell you, milking time." He laughed — a bass note that was more of a snort than a response to a humorous thought. "It was all plain sailing till he got to Top Meadow. Seemed to think everything you'd put in for was in order. Then — as I said to Ben, you can't really believe this — he spotted the water trough in the corner by the gate. He was on to it like light." Saul paused, enjoying the imminent climax of his story. "Tape measure attacking it. A lot of rechecking. Shook his head to tell me he was on to something big. Anyways: seems you got it wrong, there, Mr Elkin. You should've subtracted four feet by two feet in your total calculations as to the size of the field. Only of course Mr Thin Shoes spoke in centimetres. And what was he going to do, I asked? Take it off, of course, he said. Deny you a few pence, or whatever. He got out his calculator. Funny thing was, he was so overexcited, in my opinion, about finding this one little matter you'd overlooked that he dropped the calculator in the trough." A real smile cracked Saul's face. "So I stood there looking on while he tried to decide what to do. Getting it back, I could see, was beyond him. He couldn't go through with rolling up a sleeve, plunging his arm into the icy water — not in front of me, he couldn't, anyhows. Too humiliating. He couldn't ask me to help and I wasn't going to offer. In the end he said he'd leave it. Have to report it, of course. He said he'd most likely be in trouble. I thought, if that's your only trouble . . ."

His story over, Saul gave a sneeze that turned into a laugh. There were not many funny moments in the farming business these days, he said, but this was one of them. George laughed, too. He had always admired Saul's fierceness when it came to the protection of his employer or his land, and his somewhat unconventional methods of support. George offered him a cup of tea, but Saul declined. He said he wanted to take his dogs for a walk before it was dark.

"Old Thin Shoes was going on up to the Prodgers after us," he added. "Nell was in a bit of a spin about that. She said she could never get measurements quite right. She was dreading trouble. I don't know how she manages, that girl. And what with Prodge himself in no great shape these days."

"I'll go on up there when I've had a go at this lot," said George, his eyes travelling over the menacing piles of papers. "No: on second thoughts I'll go now."

His business over, Saul preceded George out of the kitchen door, settling the fragile cap on his head at the very moment they stepped outside to meet the dank November air.

George decided to walk up to the Prodgers. He felt in need of air, of stretching his limbs. A thick winter dusk was beginning to muffle the farm buildings, the fields and the distant rising land. Leafless trees were still scribbled precisely against the sky, but they would be blurred within moments. There was a sweet-sour smell of silage, and of fallen leaves marinated in mud and rain. George felt for the torch in his pocket and set off.

These days he approached Nell and Prodge's farm with a feeling of dread. Prodge was increasingly depressed though there were moments when he seemed cheerful and almost optimistic about the future. But these moments, which encouraged George and Nell to believe he was improving, were short-lived. He could be laughing at supper one evening, drinking toasts to the downfall of "bloody Brussels and all it had done to British farmers", and the next morning resume his rigid, silent demeanour. Sometimes, Nell reported to George, she would find him at the kitchen table, head buried in his arms. When she managed to prise him into a sitting position she would see he had been weeping.

To banish images of his wretched friend for the mile he had to walk, George thought instead of Saul, and of his debt to him. He was what George's mother used to call "a rural saint". Her belief was that there were thousands of such people spread across the country (fewer of them in cities, was her other belief) — people who would never be rich, nor had any great desire to be so, but who worked hard and willingly all their lives for what they believed in. The backbone of small communities, they were, always there to help each other out in a crisis. Their only complaints concerned policies made by people who had no knowledge of how the land worked, and their only rewards were the good harvests and fine animals it was their life to produce. Saul was the most reliable, skilled and able man George knew: the Elkin farm had been for almost three decades in great part dependent upon him. It was hard to imagine the place without him, although — as George had been reminded by the man's weary face this evening — Saul was getting on, and one day he would be forced, reluctantly, to retire. The particular hardship for him, when this day came, would be that he could not pass on the job of farm manager to Ben, for by then Ben would have long gone into the electrical industry. George knew what his son's decision meant to Saul, though he was not the kind of man who would have indulged his feelings to his employer or anyone else. Having briefly expressed his sorrow the other day, George knew it would never be mentioned again.

Saul had his funny ways, of course. His loathing of chickens meant that after Mrs Elkin died — she looked after a fluctuating number of free-range birds — he had given his ultimatum: either the Rhode Islands had to go, or he'd have to give in his notice. George had been puzzled by the vehemence of this announcement, made not long after his mother's funeral at a time when Mr Elkin had gone away for a few days. George had observed Saul's fast-blinking, frantic eyes as he made it, and realised he suffered from some phobia. Saul evidently despised himself for this weakness, but was helpless to fight it. When Mr Elkin returned he suggested the birds were taken to the market, and Saul had hurried off with a brief word of thanks.

One of his favoured pastimes was to give various authorities the benefit of his opinion by letter. Since the anti-hunting bill had threatened, every Sunday afternoon, after milking, Saul would change back into his Sunday best to write another letter to the Prime Minister. Each week he would provide another reason why, should the sport be abandoned, the effects would be catastrophic for farmers. Holding the not unreasonable belief that those in power were incapable of taking in many rational arguments at once, the weekly letter provided only one — "so that a store of reasons can be built up", he explained, "but studied one at a time." Despite the sense of this idea, Saul never received an acknowledgement from Downing Street. He himself had little time in which to hunt, but the few hours he managed each season either on his brother's old cob, or on foot, were to him more pleasurable than a month's holiday. (Not that he had any experience of a month's holiday: he abhorred the whole concept of going away. The furthest he had been from home was as a lad of twelve on a daytrip to Weymouth which had put him off such excursions for ever.)

Saul, who had farming relations in both Wales and the north, was the one on the farm who kept most closely in touch with the grim news that increasingly spread throughout the country. Every morning he listened to *Farming Today*, which he considered was no longer of any real service to farmers, and copiously read half a dozen weekly papers and magazines concerning rural life. It was Saul who would come to George, cap in hand in deference to the news he was about to convey, and apprise him of some new outrage. In his opinion, even a man of intellect, like George, could only take on board small particles of gloom at a time. So, like the Prime Minister, George was treated to small shavings of information. There was the occasion — on seeing the flutter of a common blue in a hayfield about to be cut — when he whipped off his cap and turned to George with saddened face. Seventy per cent of British butterflies were now extinct, he said. On an August evening, even more sadly, he announced that for the third year running there were far fewer swallows and swifts gathering on the telegraph wires. The birds had given up in many parts of Britain, he said. With so many rivers being dredged — though praise be to God that had not happened here — there was no mud for their nests. They might never come back. How many people, he had asked George, would find that a shame — no, more than a shame, a tragedy?

As Saul returned his cap to his bowed head, George had agreed it was a tragedy, as indeed was so much of what was happening to rural life and work today. The greatest tragedy of all, he thought, opening the gate into the Prodgers' yard, was the cost to the human heart: the despair, the fear, and, in so many cases, the end.

There were no lights on in the farmhouse. George made his way to the shed. The sky was by now a dense indigo, but it was still not quite dark. He had no need of his torch.

At the entrance to the shed he stood peering into the gloom, listening. A single sheep in a pen moved restlessly, bleating to its absent friends. The smell of dung was sour, rank, not unpleasant. George moved away, on up the path hedged with obsolete and rusting machinery, to the small barn. This was where the sheep had been housed in winter before Prodge had built the large shed. He had never had the time, energy or money to restore it. Its roof had partially caved in. Many of its beams were rotten. Its floor was perilously uneven. These days it was used for parking the tractors and storing a miscellany of farm implements. Only Prodge knew where to find anything in the iron jungle that grew ever more unruly in this rotting building.

George thought it unlikely Prodge would be there, but it was worth glancing in on his way to the cowshed. He stood with one hand on a mudguard of the old Fordson tractor. The place was empty. Prodge was not there.

He was about to leave when he heard the faint hoot of a barn owl in the rafters. Saul would be pleased, he thought. Not all birds are extinct. I must tell Saul . . . He reached for his torch, swung the small tunnel of light across the solemn army of machinery up into the roof. No sign of the owl, though it hooted again, its voice less distinct. The torch's beam speared down to a cross-rafter about ten feet high. From it hung some old bits of harness left from generations ago when Suffolk Punches still pulled the plough. Fascinated by the occasional patterns of blackened brass that punctuated the leather and the hugeness and heaviness of the tackle the horses had had to carry, George slowed the beam, edging it along the remnants of different farming days. The narrow light came to the end of the rafter and stopped on a hanging body.

For a second, in sickening disbelief, George left the beam where it had landed on Prodge's shoulder — he recognised the old shirt that he had been wearing for days. He swallowed back the sour bile that rose in his throat. He forced himself to tilt up the torch till the beam reached the back of his head, which was tipped so far forward that the only visible feature was a single, strange-looking ear. Then the light swooped downwards on to the hips of Prodge's grimiest jeans. In that moment, the whole of George's life with Prodge and Nell spun before him, the thousands of small events so blindingly refracted that he had to shut his eyes against them. The stillness of the corpse told him that it was too late to save him. He had failed his friend: his friend was dead.

George had no idea how much time passed till he reopened his eyes. Time was meaningless. He knew that his hand, shaking violently, still clutched the torch. He was not conscious of moving it, but saw that the beam had stuttered down the terrible legs to the feet.

Except that there were no feet. Instead, twists of straw hung from the bottoms of the trousers. On the ground beneath them lay two old socks.

November the fifth. This forgotten fact burned slowly through George's being. The hanging corpse was not Prodge, but a guy to be burnt on the village bonfire. Every year, Prodge made the guy and lit the fire. The realisation, gradually cancelling out George's discovery of death, buffeted his whole body with uncontrollable shaking. He backed into a pile of sacks stuffed with straw, let himself fall on to them. The owl hooted. The torch went out. George wept.

It couldn't have been more than a few moments since he had entered the barn, but time still played havoc in his head as relief, guilt and amorphous emotions he could not name spurred tears and more tears. Moments contracted and expanded, confusing and exhausting, until suddenly his weeping was interrupted by the sound of a car swishing through mud. He wiped his eyes, listened. A car door banged.

He heard Nell shouting his name. He let her shout several times, not trusting his voice, before he answered. Then she was beside him, out of breath. She carried a torch whose powerful beam, swirling about the barn, by chance missed George's face.

"We've been down in the village finishing the bonfire. I'm just back for the bags of straw and the guy. What're you doing in here?"

"Came over on a whim. I'd forgotten it was Guy Fawkes night."

"Well, come on down with me. You can help me with the sacks. I'll take the guy."

Had she suggested George do this, he knew he would have hesitated. Reality had not yet completely obliterated the nightmare. It was pushing through, slowly, but George's heart still pounded. Nell moved to the hanging guy, now lighted by her strong torch, and flung it over her shoulder. George caught a brief glimpse of its painted eyes, loathsome grin and pink plastic ears. A flash came to him of a distant childhood game involving false ears and noses fixed on with elastic. Prodge must have found the ears in some attic box of rubbish. He'd employed them to terrifying effect, thought George, calmer now that the shock was subsiding. He picked up a couple of bags of straw, pillows that had supported his moments of agony. They deserved to be burnt with the guy. He followed Nell to the car.

"I persuaded Prodge to go to the doctor yesterday," she said. "He seemed to think the trouble was nothing to do with contamination from sheep dip. He said that before organophosphates were licensed, lots of farmers were badly affected with mysterious ailments — Prodge had become convinced he'd been poisoned somehow. But when he said of course we'd been vaccinating our sheep against scab for a good many years, the doctor assured him there was nothing to worry about these days. You're suffering from understandable depression due to lack of sleep and the general worry of farming today, the doctor said. Prodge was so relieved he even agreed to take some pills, just for a while."

"Good. Thank God for that."

"So there's hope he'll get back to his normal self. As much as anyone can . . . present conditions." She stuffed the flopping guy into the back seat of George's car. "But guess what? There's less good news as well. Letter from our landlord this morning — not exactly a surprise. I'd been waiting for it. He said he'd sold his other two farms where the tenants had been having trouble with the rent, and he'd left us as long as he could because we'd always been good tenants. But now it was our turn. He's obviously sold the other two well, to townspeople who've had no interest in farming, just want a weekend place."

"Oh Christ," said George. "I'm —"

"— but he was as nice as could be about it all, I'll say that. He said he was giving us a year's notice, and had no intention of harrying us about the rent. I wouldn't like to tell you how behind we are. Then he said his advice was to get out of farming before it's too late. He seemed to think things are going to get worse, not better. Get out of farming, George! Imagine. What would we do? We can't give up."

"How did Prodge take the news?"

Nell gave an attempt at a laugh, and then sighed. "I haven't told him yet. Didn't want to spoil this evening for him. He always loves the bonfire. I'll tell him in the morning."

"So there's a year," mused George. "A year in which to find a solution. That must be possible. Whatever happens, we will."

"Actually," said Nell, "I don't believe there is one. This time next year we'll be out: animals sold, no property beyond our clothes, books and a few bits of tatty old furniture. I'm not going to think about it."

"Well I am."

"That's kind of you. But I can't say I've any hope. I rang the landlord, tried to persuade him to change his mind. He said it wasn't our fault, of course, the rent business. He quite understood, but he had to make a living, too. Huh! How much capital has he got, sale of two farms? I reminded him he'd be the owner of Prodge's shed. I reminded him what that shed added up to, in terms of love and effort . . . Got nowhere, of course. He just said that's life."

George put a hand over hers. They had arrived at the village, parked. Nell turned to him as she switched off the engine.

"Don't know what I'd do without you," she said in a small voice before snatching away her hand.

"Nor me without you."

"Please think of something."

"I will."

On the village green, they found Prodge waiting impatiently for the guy, which he was to hoist to the top of the huge pile of wood and old tyres. Apart from half a dozen children who followed him everywhere, eager for a pat on the head or some word of command, the crowd who had come to join the festivities was small. Few farmers had either the time or the energy to turn out on a cold winter's evening: they had their paperwork to struggle over after supper. Guy Fawkes night held too few attractions to lure them from their deadly work. Precious hours of sleep could not be missed for a bonfire.

But some of the old village women were there, shawls wrapped over their coats. The rural saints of Mrs Elkin's estimation, always eager to help, had brought thermoses of tea and coffee and hot sausage rolls still in their baking tins. There were no women of George's age. To the few left who still lived in the village but commuted to work in the local city, like the farmers and their wives, village celebrations could no longer be a priority.

The guy was secured in place. Prodge lit the bonfire. It caught immediately. Strong flames leapt up through its guts. They could hear the sounds of twigs shrieking and old boughs creaking as they were touched by the heat. A great sail of smoke swayed above the fire, paled by a moon that came and went between clouds. The guy himself was devoured within moments. His flopping head with its horrible grin and staring painted eyes was felled by a single flame: only the plastic ears survived a moment longer. George could laugh at himself now: how on earth could he ever have thought . . .? But the impression, and the fright it had given him, left him uneasy. It was a warning he must heed. More than ever he was determined to help Prodge in some acceptable way.

Thirty years ago, he reflected — or even ten years ago — there would have been a couple of hundred gathered on the green for this ceremony. It would have been an occasion no one wanted to miss. Now, there were how many? Twenty-five, perhaps? George looked round at their faces, solemn, transfixed by the slight element of danger as people are in the presence of a strong fire. Some stepped back a little, feeling its great heat. Nell and Prodge stood side by side. Prodge's old clothes were loose on him now, and in the firelight his exhausted face was little more than a moulding of bones covered with sheer flesh. Nell was hunched, hands in pockets, eyes narrowed. In the fire she was perhaps seeing the conflagration of their future, and thinking how best to put the latest grim news to her brother in the morning.

Suddenly Nell roused herself from whatever her dream and moved a little closer to the fire. A small boy, stick in hand, darted forward. In a second Nell had grabbed the child and picked him up. In her arms he was happy, waved the stick. She whispered something in his ear and made him laugh. The delight of the picture they made, young woman and child bound by the firelight, surprised George. He thought what a natural mother Nell would be, and could not help wondering if he himself would ever be a father.

George saw Prodge glance over to where his sister stood, still talking to the child. Quickly, like a man not wanting to be caught, he fumbled beneath his jacket, pulled something from his shirt pocket. As far as George could see it was a small piece of paper. But then, caught by the firelight for an infinitesimal moment, it glinted, which made George think it was a photograph. He saw Prodge screw it up without looking at it and throw it into the flames. This done, Prodge stepped back again, with a look of something like relief — though George could not be sure from this distance that's what it was — and turned his attention to the small children surrounding him. Their hero, he seemed to be: they would do anything he asked. He gestured to them to stand back while he approached the bonfire, jabbed at it with his pitchfork. But most of its life was over. Flames, snake-slow now, had given up leaping. They meandered among what was left of the wood, then died in a bed of ash. People began to move away.

What Prodge could be, George thought, was a very good father. He wondered if he had ever loved a woman, or if he had only ever known the feckless young girls he met at the pub, bent on taking rather than giving, and not the least interested in what motivated the rare man they had lighted on. One day, George hoped, Prodge would meet someone like Lily, who would become his wife and not run away.

Home in his cold, empty house, George poured himself a glass of neat whisky. He turned on some music: Brendel playing Mozart piano concertos. Since Lily's departure he had hardly ever listened in the way that he used to with her. As the yearning rills of notes reflected his own mood of bitter-sweetness, he wondered why he had denied himself this comfort for so long.

Restless, he wandered up and down sipping at his drink, then moved into the passage outside and went to the dining room, never once used since Lily's departure. Slowly, he made his way all over the house, listening to his own footsteps, switching lights on and off as he entered and left rooms not visited for a long time. In his bedroom the piled-up books on the table on Lily's side of the bed were in the very order she had left them. *Wolf Solent* had a marker halfway through. Perhaps one day she would remember to come back and finish it. There was a leatherbound volume of Keats's poems, inscribed by her father on her fourteenth birthday, and a collection of Hazlitt's essays. Lily had never been much of a one for modern fiction. George replaced the books in their order and went over to the dressing-table.

There, reluctance fighting a curiosity he'd never given into until now, he opened the middle drawer. It was empty but for an open box of powder and a swansdown puff, its drooping satin bow a small flare against the dull powder. George remembered the many times he had seen his mother, at this very table, pluck an identical puff from a box and dab it on her cheeks. Tiny specks of the stuff would fleck the glass top of the table. In the drawer, a dusting of powder now covered the paper lining. Memories merged: the scent of old roses, wife and mother. Quickly George shut the drawer. Opening it, he had known, was a foolish thing to do.

He sat on the bed for a while, wanting Lily. He picked up the photograph of her, taken on their wedding day, that lived on his bedside table. He wanted to tell her about his experience with the hanging guy: she was the only person in the world he could tell. He wanted her here, now, with him. Back where they used to be.

Still restless, George went downstairs again. It occurred to him that he had been in and out of five bedrooms apart from his, and three rooms downstairs that were never used. This had always been one of the larger longhouses built locally: far too big — ridiculously big — for a man alone. The only rooms he occupied were kitchen and study, bedroom and bathroom. Even when Lily was here, rooms remained unused. It was absurd, when his friends were about to be homeless. Perhaps, at last, there was something he really could do for Prodge and Nell, to which they might have no objection. For the moment, he began to feel the rising excitement of an idea beginning to emerge. The better to contemplate, he poured himself another large whisky, and settled at last in his chair by the unlit fire.

CHAPTER
FIFTEEN

The journey from an idea to a decision is often a long and difficult one, as George found after the night of the bonfire. He was forced to the conclusion that, except in matters concerning the farm, he was a procrastinator. In this case the procrastination was entirely due to the doubts that rose every time he tried to imagine a new life in which he shared the house with Prodge and Nell. The difficulty of putting this idea to them and persuading them of its benefits also caused him many hours of worry.

But even as he delayed announcing his suggestion (where would be best to do it? Their house? His?) George did not feel there was any great urgency to present his plan. He knew Prodge and Nell intended to spend their last year in the place that had always been their home, and did not spend much time thinking beyond that. He also knew that in some vague, unspoken way, they looked to him for a solution, which they expected him to produce when the time to depart was imminent. He hoped that the subject might come up naturally. When asked for his advice about what they should do, George would be ready with his strategy.

The only part over which he agonised concerned Nell. He tried to imagine her actually running the house. She would be efficient, of course. The place would be sort of orderly, she would provide good basic food, she would be able to return to her weaving and dyeing (George saw this in one of the unused south-facing rooms). On a whim, he tried to imagine her in his bed. If they could both shift from mere affection to the higher reaches of love, that would no doubt be perfectly possible, for he did love her, and would hope that the depth of his affection might produce adequate desire, if not passion. But he liked to think he would not actually have to face this possibility — unless in, say, five years' time Lily still had not returned and he was forced to believe she never would. It would be good to have more of the house occupied again. What he knew would be forever missing was the unique magic that was Lily's: the way her presence radiated the place, and she was able to conjure excitement from the ordinary. Still fiercely in love with his absent wife he had so patiently been waiting for, he was unwilling to replace the elements only she could provide with Nell's kind, loving, but lesser presence. He realised it was his increasing despair at Lily's absence that had spurred these alternative thoughts.

For the time being, George reckoned, Nell and Prodge seemed to be in better spirits, determined to make the best of their last year at the farm. There had been no more outbreaks of BSE among their cattle and Prodge's bouts of depression were on the wane. He had stopped taking the pills and put on a little weight. Nell, in contrast, seemed too thin, her heavy bones clearly outlined under trousers and thick jerseys. They rarely mentioned their money worries, or how they were going to deal with the now large debt hanging over them. The only time George ever heard them complain was on behalf of farmers in general, and the increasing disaster of British country life.

The proposed Countryside March for the spring of 2001 added to the pre-Christmas workload for all of them, but happily. They formed part of a group who met to plan their local contribution to the grand finale. It was going to be, they all felt, an occasion — massive, dignified, quietly passionate — that the government would not be able to ignore. It might even shake them into a reassessment of country matters. The meetings in the village hall, chaired by George, were impressive in their numbers. No matter how exhausted at the end of the day, every farmer within a twenty-mile radius would turn up ready with proposals for all manner of help. There was an extraordinary feeling of unity at those meetings — the warmth of mutual concern and belief, the sudden charge inspired by the feeling that the massive protest really could have some effect. Nell said she found herself much moved by the crowd of such skilled country men and women fighting for the same cause.

After one of the meetings, George drove Nell and Prodge, Saul and Ben to the pub for a drink. It was Nell's birthday. The landlord's wife, at George's request, had baked one of her excellent cakes.

The five of them sat at a table by the fire, drinking beer and wine, talking with a kind of understated excitement about the march. It was the event which they all looked forward to — the very thought of it stimulated hope. Then the cake was brought in, the candles lit. Nell was delighted. She pushed back her great bush of curly hair behind her ears in preparation for blowing them out. George had given her a pair of small opal earrings which she wore now. As they swung from her ears, the candle flames lighted the iridescent stones, firing them with miniature colours. She took a deep breath, blew. Not a candle escaped. Everyone laughed. Nell, looking through the small spirals of smoke they left behind, joined in the laughter.

"I've always been able to do that," she said. "That's my one boast. May I go on being capable for a good many years."

She smiled at George, suddenly pink-cheeked: he had not seen her so happy for some time. He wondered if in her instinctive way she had some idea about the thoughts that he had been grappling with, but he did not let himself dwell on this for more than a moment. Instead, he drank faster, and more, than was his custom. Soon the saloon bar was an agreeable blur: firelight, gleam of pewter tankards and polished wood, mess of chocolate cake on plates, and the faces — briefly free of concern — of the four people, beyond Lily, he most cared about.

At some time in the evening he heard Ben turn to Prodge and ask what his plans were. Prodge, after several beers, did not seem put out by the question.

"No plans yet. Nothing definite. Bit of time to go till we have to make up our minds. But I'm thinking I'd like to go and work for an organic farmer," he said.

"That's something we haven't discussed." Nell said this lightly, but turned to him, puzzled.

"No. But I've been thinking about it. It would be a challenge. A new thing to learn about. Aren't I right, George?"

"You are. It's something I've been contemplating myself." In his slightly inebriated state, it occurred to him that if he offered Prodge the possibility of turning the farm . . .

"You'll never get rich like that," said Saul.

"That's not my aim. Now I've not been able to get the bike, all I want is to cover my costs and do something about getting the land back to natural farming. The old method of rotating crops, putting a field down to clover one year, whatever. I'd like to learn all about that. I'd like to try it — have the chance to try it. It's what I believe in."

"There's nothing wrong with our way," said Saul. "It isn't as if we spray chemicals indiscriminately. We judge our soil very carefully, give it no more fertiliser than it needs. Well, you do the same. I'm not against the organic system, but it's a hard struggle, I'll tell you that."

"My belief," said Nell, "is that in twenty years' time most of the farmers left — if there are any — will have gone over to organic. It's what people want more and more. They've come to be wary of pesticides. They want to be able to trust their food —"

"Rubbish," interrupted Ben. He held up his hand, emboldened by several pints of beer. "There's too many farmers too impatient for profit to go organic: won't want to wait a long time for their money. But whatever happens it won't bother me so much any more." He glanced at George. "There's a chance of a job later this year in Cardiff. Some electrical place. Small industrial firm. I have to take a course. If I pass well enough, there's a chance —"

"Son, let's not talk about this now," said Saul, and his face tightened.

"Lovely drink," said Prodge, "though it's done nothing to take my mind off the price of soya rations, gone up thirty pounds a week. What'm I going to do about that? I think I'll walk home. Want to clear my head."

George drove Nell home. When they arrived at the farmyard she seemed in no hurry to get out. George sat with his hands on the steering wheel. His head still spun a little.

"Thanks for organising all that," said Nell. "It was a good evening."

George turned to look at her. Her head was tipped back against the headrest, her eyes shut. Most of her face was in darkness, but the strong moon shining through the windscreen softened and blanched her hair.

"Do you remember that time we were children, you kissed me?" she said.

"I do," said George. "Two occasions, in fact."

"It suddenly came back to me." She opened her eyes. "But then I've probably had a bit too much to drink. God knows what the morning milk will be like."

They both smiled.

"So I'd better get some sleep. So'd you. Thanks again." She leant towards George, cheek upraised. George kissed it. He let his mouth slur towards her mouth, which she kept tightly shut. They remained quite still, in this awkward position, for a matter of seconds. Then George could feel her whole body tighten. She gave a small whimper before pushing him away with both hands, suddenly fierce. "No point doing things for old times' sake," she said, and turned her head away.

"Nothing to do with old times' sake," George said.

A silvery night sky, its moon unhampered by a single cloud, flared through the windscreen. George looked at Nell's profile, every half-inch deeply familiar: the unplucked, arched brows, the sweet mouth, normally upturned but now cast down. She had made some attempt, on her birthday night, with her clothes: a flowered shirt replaced the usual jumper. Several top buttons were undone — whether by design, George could not guess. He could see the outline of a rounded breast. He had not touched a woman, or thought of touching one, since Lily left, but now, suddenly shot with uncomfortable desire, he longed to stretch out and cup Nell's breast in his hand.

She turned to him, scrunching up her eyes, willing herself to smile.

"It's funny, isn't it, how everyone's always thought of us as brother and sister."

"Well, we are almost, aren't we?"

"Suppose so." She put a hand on George's thigh. "Though would I do that if I were your sister?"

"Probably not."

She took it away again, leaving sparks flying through the skin of George's leg.

"Kissing me was almost incestuous," she said.

"Not really. We didn't really kiss."

"No. But it was nice."

George nodded. "You're a very remarkable girl, Nell —"

"Don't give me all that tosh —"

"— and you deserve an equally remarkable man."

"So likely I'm going to find one here." Nell laughed her scoffing laugh. She put a hand on the door but did not move. The fragment of an old song his mother used to play came to George's mind. *Moonlight becomes you* . . . "Why are you smiling?" Nell asked.

"I was just thinking how pretty you looked."

Nell hustled her shoulders far back against the seat. "Almost anybody can look OK by moonlight," she snapped. "Very unlike you to resort to that sort of line. But if you think you're going to ease your way into a seduction, after all these years, by paying some incredibly unoriginal compliment, you can think again." Her voice was harsh, her hostility shocking. "Don't think I don't know what's on your mind. Years of forced celibacy can screw up a man's judgement, lower his standards. You've been very restrained till now, I grant you that. And I feel for you: no wife, no sex. Must be bloody frustrating. But no reason to turn to the girl next door for a bit of relief —"

"Nell!" George had never seen her like this. "What are you saying? I've never even thought in those terms. I love you. I've always loved you. You must know that."

"Oh yes: *that* sort of love."

"I'd never want you just for . . . Surely you can't think that?"

Nell turned grimly to look at him. One cheek, caught by the moon, was a bleached triangle half hidden in dizzy white curls. "Don't tell me," she said, "it hasn't ever crossed your mind."

"What?"

"That one day, if Lily doesn't come back, then maybe Nell, good old Nell, friend for ever, might do."

There was silence. George shifted his back against the door, acutely uncomfortable.

"I've never thought that," he said. "Of course I haven't. Though I suppose I've sometimes wondered, if I hadn't met and married Lily . . . Perhaps you and I might've — ? Who knows?"

"Never," said Nell, so quietly that George only just caught the venom of the word.

A single, precise tear appeared at the edge of her moonlit eye. It tipped over, ran fast as a pearl escaping from a broken string down her cheek. She swiped at it impatiently. "I'm sorry if I've trespassed, ventured where we've never been before. But I just wanted to make sure you know where I stand in your calculations.

Lily's been away so long. It's only natural you might get to thinking . . . But no. I'm not available."

"Nell, you must believe —"

"There's Prodge coming up the road." Suddenly she was herself again. "I must go." She smiled. "Now you know the score I can see nothing whatsoever against kissing you goodnight." Her moment of darkness disappeared as quickly as it had come. She thrust herself towards George. Hard and fast she kissed him on the lips, this time opening her mouth. He could taste wine. "There. Just to say thank you for the earrings and the cake and everything. Last ever kiss. Put it down to the drink."

She was gone, slamming the door behind her, running not towards the house, but to Prodge, who was by now coming through the gate.

George drove home shaken, puzzled, sad. Was it arrogant to suppose that Nell's fierce rejection had conveyed how much she really wanted him? That she could not bear the thought of ever being taken up as second-best? George suspected — and he appreciated he was not always enlightened when it came to conundrums concerning women — that her outburst contradicted much of what she was feeling. Certainly her "final kiss", though brief, had been far from sisterly. And her instinctive knowledge of his occasional thoughts both astonished and troubled him. He could only hope that he had convinced her that she had misunderstood him.

Put it down to the drink, Nell said. Well, he would do that. All the same, the once smooth path ahead was now muddied. What, now, might she feel about the idea of sharing the house? Despite her protestations he was almost sure that, should he invite her, she would be willing to take Lily's place if the marriage finally dissolved. But was that what *he* wanted? When embroiled in a complicated situation, it's hard to envisage any kind of clarity beyond it. He knew in his heart his love for Nell would never be the kind that stirred wild feeling. Any kind of permanency with her would be calm, untroubled, but lacking in that profundity of love that guards against the rub of daily life. But that moment of lust that had assaulted him not ten minutes ago — what was that all about? He hoped Nell had not observed his briefly stirred state, for the very thought filled him with shame. It must have been the wine. Even now his head was still a little afloat. He was in no state to work things out satisfactorily, and still bruised by Nell's intense dismissal, for all that she could not have meant it. The fact was — oh, God knows what the fact was, he said to himself, striding across the yard. He hadn't any idea how it would all turn out. And of course things never resolved themselves: *he'd* have to take some kind of action. Present dilemmas were causing too much unease.

Home, in his own kitchen, among that morning's post he found a new card from Lily.

Wyoming, this time. God knows what I'm doing in America. I came out to see the Getty Museum but didn't much like LA. Stayed with an old schoolfriend near Cody. We rode up the mountains in a western saddle — very dramatic, beautiful, fantastic wild flowers, but not the same as riding with Nell at home. Love as always, L.

George read the card several times before he put it down. It was the longest message Lily had ever sent since her departure. And surely it contained a slight change of tone — a very slight indication that her peripatetic life was beginning to pall? Missing her rides with Nell meant her thoughts, at least, were sometimes here. Maybe the stone within her was beginning to melt. Perhaps she was beginning to feel again: loss, homesickness, melancholy. Or was he reading too much into it? He tried to make himself believe this was the case, but at the end of this strange evening, his old tired hope came winging back. His love for Lily was as strong as it had always been. Until she declared she *never* intended to return, thus releasing him from hope, there was nothing he could do but keep his silence and continue to wait. For once, he did not write a reply that would never be sent. For once, he felt so optimistic there was no need.

Ben's plan to take a course in Cardiff did not come to anything, but he took days off for interviews, leaving George and Saul with an extra workload. George dreaded the day Ben finally gave in his notice and the even longer hours that would mean for the two of them. The thought of employing a new third party did not appeal, and in all probability would not be possible. The days of eager farmhands were long gone.

346

So busy was George on the farm by day that most evenings he had to work late in his study. He could not remember being so tired for a long time, but he was nevertheless undaunted. He had a strange, half-formed feeling that some sort of conclusion was on its way. That last postcard . . . When Lily still did not appear, as November slugged on through fog and rain, he shifted his hopes to December. Christmas, perhaps.

By now, Prodge's health had recovered, although his old lightness of heart had still not returned in its entirety. George's world was tightly bound to his own farm. He ceased to visit the Prodgers every day: they saw each other just two or three times a week. George sensed that they, too, were wholly concentrating on their own lives. Time was running out for them, and they did not want to miss a moment of it. This time next year their farm would be the property of someone else.

George went only occasionally to the village, for Countryside March meetings, and bought his provisions on market day, so there was no need for journeys to the city. Saul, as always, was the one to keep him in touch with news of the outer world, which he had not had time to read about in the papers or listen to on the radio. On one occasion, when in the milking parlour on a murky afternoon, Saul had whipped off his cap to alert George to one of his gloomy pronouncements. Surprisingly, instead, it was a rare bit of good news. It seemed there was some cause for a little local triumph: an application to build fifty-one thousand new houses in the south in the next twelve years had been turned

347

down: now the final number was to be a mere forty-four thousand eight hundred. This inspired one of Saul's rare smiles.

On another occasion he reported that the government was to increase rural bus services by fifty per cent. "Though I'll believe that when I next see a bus in the village," he said. "There's people marooned there. Since Mrs Elkin left, they've been without regular lifts to collect their pensions. Some of them have been desperate. Mrs Field had a heart attack last week, only sixty-seven. The doctor said it was the stress of living in a dying place, and in my opinion he wasn't far wrong."

Lily did not appear for Christmas but she did send a card. She was in Bournemouth again, and again she wrote at greater length than usual.

I've taken the small flat attached to my aunt's house and intend to start my book. It's very quiet here in winter, some might say dull, but I like it. I walk by the sea. I'm getting a little tired, I think, of the constant wandering about, and need to pause for a while, wait quietly for the old pump to get going again. Have a happy Christmas, darling George, love L.

Have a happy Christmas, too, darling Lily, George wrote on the last of the sepia cards of the farm. I'm getting a little tired of waiting but send you all my love.

Whatever she meant by this oblique message, George did not dwell on it for too long, for it came to him, blindingly, that all this living in the darkness, not knowing, might be coming to an end. As soon as he had a few free days he would be off to find her — at last. If he succeeded, and she still refused to return home — well, there was nothing to lose. It would be his turn, then, to make the decisions and to get on with his life. The sadness of his failure would always be there, but at least he would be released from the exhausting business of hoping, hoping, which he felt was beginning to corrode his soul.

He was glad she was back in England, relieved she was not far away. Lily would always be on his mind, in his heart: his longing for her would not fade. But from now on he would try to diminish her place in his life, concentrate harder on those with whom he was daily bound — his animals, his farm, his oldest friends. His preoccupations for the moment, he told himself sternly, were the march, Nell and Prodge's departure and his plan for them. The right time to put this to them still had not come: early spring, lambing over, could be it, he thought.

The next morning George stopped off at the field in the valley called Elm Field, though the trees had been cut down years ago at the time of the fatal elm disease. It was New Year's Eve and a mild morning for December.

There was still early dew on the grass and on the cobwebs that spun in the hedgerows. George leant on the gate — a gate made by a carpenter in the village

349

who had often worked for his father and other neighbouring farmers. George remembered the old man measuring wood, sawing it up in the small barn. He remembered the bright, musty smell of wood shavings as they fell to the ground, and the way they curled round his fingers when he picked them up. He must have been about four at the time, he thought, and wondered why the gate-making remained such a vivid childhood memory. And now here was that very gate, several decades on, weathered, but good as ever: a magnificent thing produced by a carpenter of great skill, plainly a man who knew and loved his wood. It was hard not to compare it with the machine-made gates of today, and to feel nostalgia for the days when every village was inhabited by various craftsmen.

George's body and arms felt heavy, stiff. He had been heaving old bits of fence the day before, against Saul's advice. It was a luxury he occasionally allowed himself, to lean on a gate and contemplate the land. He was in no hurry: Ben was doing the morning milk. So he went on leaning on the gate, and let his eyes meander over the sheep. What a fine flock, at last, they were, he thought. He and Saul had taken great pains over their breeding, and were expecting a good crop of lambs early next year. He looked forward to the lambing: despite his efforts to avoid sentimentality, it was always hard not to be moved by an event of such copious birth. He had become skilled in helping with the births — often two or three happened simultaneously, taxing his judgement and speed. And he could never quite relinquish the feeling of wonder and satisfaction each time a new lamb arrived alive and in good health.

By now George easily recognised many of his ewes. He could spot small differences in long black noses, the topaz eyes of the Poll Dorsets, the difference in the bulk of curly fringe overhanging the Exmoor Horns' eyes. He knew the ones who caused trouble every time they were herded into the shed: the ringleaders and the followers. He was frequently aware of their indignation, their boredom, but mostly of their satisfaction.

One of two of the older ewes raised their heads from their grazing, turned to give him a look. The tops of their thick winter coats were specked with dew, putting George in mind of shaggy old dowagers who had overdone the diamonds. Their legs were silvered from the wet grass, to add to the illusion of a flock of sparkling creatures. Last year, several of them had suffered the agonies of scab: their wool hung from raw, rubbed skin in filthy globules, there was panic in their eyes as the irritation drove them nearly mad. Luckily, all but one had recovered. Now they were a good and healthy flock: not so long ago they would have fetched rewarding prices at market.

George wondered this morning, as he often did, at the link between man and beast, most especially when the beast is simply part of a flock or herd, whose fate it is to be slaughtered and eaten if its owner is to make a living. Each animal's life at the farm was short in human terms, and each animal's fate was the same. And yet, while it existed, living out its regular days that gave (as old Mr Elkin would have said) rhythm to life, it held an importance in its owner's heart that numbers could never quite extinguish. Whenever an animal died, or was taken off to the abattoir, there was a moment of — not sadness, exactly, but a pinpoint of regret. Farmers resisted the charm of calves and lambs, for it was no use becoming attached to creatures who would soon cast off their youthful appeal, and whose days were numbered. None the less, there was a secret feeling of achievement — certainly for George — to have bred high-quality animals. It was perhaps this reward, more than the sight of crops gathered safely in, that kept many farmers going despite all the odds against them. A rum old business indeed, thought George: and for the thousandth time he was glad he had made farming his life. He would not want any other.

February, George decided, would be a good time to go in search of Lily. She had been gone for almost six years. He made arrangements to be away for a couple of days. Nell and Prodge congratulated him on his plan. At last, they said. George looked forward to his quest, but also dreaded failing. He packed a small bag.

But on the morning of his departure, Peter Friel rang George, who had overslept, at six in the morning. He had heard on the news of the outbreak of foot and mouth disease in the North.

"God knows what this'll mean," he said. "I remember '67, so many farmers wiped out. Let's hope the Ministry will be on to it straight away. Do something effective to stop it *at once*. Vaccinate," he added. "Mass vaccination, now."

There was no possibility, for George, of leaving. His priority was to protect his farm and animals. The day was spent with Saul and Ben organising safeguards. They laid disinfected straw at both gates of the farm, and put out footbaths for swabbing boots.

From that day, whenever George came into his house he found the telephone ringing. The network of news and rumour spread round the country. No matter how late a man had been working, how exhausted, he stayed up to watch the ten o'clock news, and was listening to the radio again at dawn. While the solidarity of the farmers, in their dread of the disease reaching them, and their fear for their future if it did, bound them in the utmost concern, the impression given by the government was that foot and mouth was nothing more than a little local difficulty that could soon be dealt with. The swift spread of the disease quickly put paid to this idea.

George, in common with thousands of others, looked at the maps of Britain published in the newspapers every day, saw the gradual accumulation of black dots that indicated new outbreaks. Within twelve days the first outbreak in Devon was confirmed. It was heading west: they were in its path. George ran to the shed where dozens of in-lamb ewes were already gathered to shelter from the weather until they gave birth. Saul was there, tight-faced. He took off his cap when George appeared.

353

"I've heard," he said. "May the Lord spare us, all's I can say. Ben's looking at the cows."

He was staring at a pen of ewes, his eyes carefully scouring each one. George was beside him. He thought back to that morning so recently when he had stood, in all innocence, studying his flock, his eyes admiring. Now he knew they were fearful as Saul's as he looked over heads, mouths, feet, searching for signs.

"Think of those poor buggers it's already hit," said Saul. "One minute owners of three hundred sheep — the next, nothing. Nothing. I remember the last time. Whole lot never recovered. Never got back to farming." He blinked. "Think we're clean today, but I'll be looking them over morning and night."

"Right," said George. "If —"

"I'm not going to think about that, Mr Elkin," said Saul, and wandered away, cap replaced.

Back in the house George found Nell and Prodge in the kitchen. They had stopped by on their way to the village. George made them coffee. They sat round the table, listening to the clock's impervious tick, each one heavy with his own imaginings.

"Trying to find more disinfectant," said Prodge. "It ran out everywhere almost at once. The Farmers' Co-operative says they'll ring as soon as it's delivered. But seems the manufacturers've been caught out. Meantime, what do we do?"

"I can let you have a couple of cans," said George.

"Thanks." Prodge, sat in his usual chair, leant back, spread his legs wide and closed his eyes. A man, thought George, in whom exhaustion was beginning to tell, and hope was beginning to wane. He gave the faintest smile, opened his eyes.

"Could be a premature end for Nell and me," he said. "I was banking on a bit of cash when we sold the stock before leaving. Still, if the worst comes to the worst, I suppose there'll be compensation."

"Don't tempt fate," said Nell. "Maybe it'll be scotched before it gets out of hand. Maybe we'll be lucky."

"No hope," said Prodge. "Massive culling isn't the answer, I'm telling you. Not unless it's done immediately. And that isn't happening, is it? They're dithering. They should be vaccinating *now*."

"Did you see the pictures on the news last night?" Nell asked George. "The pyres? Hard to believe." It had taken the crisis to convert Nell to television. George nodded.

"Of course, none of this is very helpful to a government about to go to the country," he said. "Daresay that'll come into their calculations. And what about the march?"

"There's already talk of that being cancelled," said Prodge. "Well, it'd have to be. That'll be a relief for the ministers." He paused. "And you not being able to get away to find Lily. That's the bugger of it."

"Plan only postponed, not scotched," said George.

"Good," said Nell.

There was a weariness in their brief exchanges: their anxious eyes revealing their dread of what might come. After half an hour Prodge and Nell rose to collect the disinfectant from George's store.

355

When they had gone, George settled himself down to the vast pile of papers on his desk. For the last few days he had felt too agitated to attend to it and had abandoned it every time he tried. Now, he looked through the pile that had arrived this morning and plucked out a postmark — a picture of a land girl holding a lamb. A Norfolk postmark. So she was home again.

Darling George, he read, *I'm saying prayers for you and all farmers. Love as always, L.*

George did not add the card to his collection on the dresser, nor did he write her an unpostable reply. He was weary of her postcards, of her cryptic little messages. Never had he so wanted Lily to be here, and there she was still flitting about, no nearer to coming home. And now, due to his own foolish procrastination, an unforeseen disaster had destroyed his chance of retrieving her. He had no wish to read any more meanings into any more messages. When this foot and mouth epidemic was over — and according to MAFF there was every chance it would be stamped out pretty soon — he was going to resolve things once and for all. Find her, bring her back. Or give up. Make decisions that would change his bleak emotional life: what, exactly, they would be, he was not sure, and for the moment he had no time to think. But changes there would be.

Eight days after the first case was confirmed at an Essex abattoir, the Prime Minister announced the situation was "grave". George doubted whether anyone not living on a farm could begin to understand the anguish that now pervaded both Cumbria and the West Country, while farmers elsewhere predicted it would reach them eventually. The long-planned march for Liberty and Livelihood which would have been the biggest protest to date, so brilliantly plotted for months, was cancelled. So were hotel bookings by tourists. Meat prices rose, festivals and race meetings were cancelled, movement of stock was forbidden.

For George, as for thousands of farmers, each day went by in dread lest they became the next doomed farm. By 11 March the NFU admitted the disease was "out of control geographically", and half a million healthy sheep and lambs awaited slaughter. Daily there were terrible statistics concerning financial hardship and emotional despair: livelihoods wiped out at a stroke, officialdom in chaos, the future a black hole. Saul was constantly holding his cap to his chest as he relayed the latest ghastly news to George and Ben.

The nearest confirmed case to the Elkin farm was still fifteen miles away. But as no one knew precisely how the disease travelled, this gave no feeling of comfort or safety. The lambing season began well: a high proportion of fine healthy lambs. As always the three men worked their long shifts and felt the bone-hard fatigue that is part of lambing time. Their work was increased by the daily examination of both sheep and cattle. Each evening, no signs reported, George felt a tenuous relief but would allow himself little optimism. Each evening he and Prodge or Nell would telephone: to date, their farm was clear, too.

357

On 14 March, having done a shift until 3a.m. in the lambing pen, George did not come down for breakfast until eight. He turned on the news, as he always did nowadays, to hear the background to the terrible headlines that Saul recited every day. This morning the news was that the NFU had joined opponents to the May election, and the Prince of Wales had donated £500,000 to help farmers. Perhaps, George thought, this would convey to the government that sympathy and understanding were elements lacking in this crisis.

As George finished his cereal Saul came through the kitchen door without knocking. This was the first time George could ever remember Saul failing in his own code of behaviour. He held his cap in both hands. His face was the colour of an old mushroom. His mouth moved silently, then the words came with a rush.

"It's the old ewe we thought was about to birth yesterday afternoon," he said. "She was fine last evening, I know she was. But this morning." He stopped, clutched harder at his cap. George stood up.

"Yes?"

"I know it's hard to spot on a sheep, but I know my ewes. I found a small sore on her mouth."

"Shit. Any others?"

"I'm just going round them now. None to date."

"You go back and carry on inspecting. I'll ring Simon, get on to MAFF straight away."

George caught their local vet on his mobile travelling to another farm a few miles away. He was able to stop off at the Elkin farm, quickly confirm his belief that the sheep was infected. George then took some time to get through to the Ministry and report the case. A harassed sounding voice promised an official vet would be sent round as soon as possible. Finally George rang Prodge and broke the news. Prodge could find no words for a moment or two, then apologised for the inadequacy of his sympathy.

"Your lot gone, then it's us gone too," he said.

"Not necessarily. It seems the whole thing is so erratic. You might be lucky."

"This policy of contiguous slaughter: we might not get infected, but we're in the three-mile radius, so we'll have to be culled. Though there seem to be no hard rules about culling at the moment — no one knows what's going on. But if we're for the chop, that's it. Premature exit from the farming world, as I reckoned the other day."

"Again, nothing's very firm, Prodge. The road between us might mean you're spared."

"But our fields meet on Higher Ridge."

"So they do. We can only hope."

"Not much point," said Prodge, dully. "It's the end for thousands of us. At least it'll mean Nell and I don't have to hang around for the rest of the year, things getting worse every day. But Jesus, I'm sorry, George. It's bloody awful. I don't know what to say."

"My turn," said George. "You get BSE. I get foot and mouth."

George walked over to the sheep shed. As usual he was greeted by the cacophonous music of his flock. Many of them were lying down, their lambs beside them. Those, George fleetingly thought, looked less indignant than usual. Their almond eyes were peaceful, relieved.

Ben was in a corner pen helping a ewe deliver a large lamb. George went over to him.

"Bit of trouble here," he said. His overall was covered in blood. He tugged hard at the forelegs in his hands, and a black lamb, misty in its caul, slipped on to the bed of straw. There was the sudden sweet-sour smell of birth. Threads of steam, like the smoke from dying candles, rose in the air from the lamb's body. All these things were so familiar to George that he could not imagine a life denied this annual experience.

"It'll be OK," said Ben. "Near thing, though." He wiped his bloody hands — soon, now, to spend their days among bloodless tools and wires — on a rag. He stood. "She's the one." He gave her a pat. "Poor lass. As for the lamb, what'll it have? Two, three days of life on this earth? Bloody hell, Mr Elkin." He scraped a forearm across his eyes. "Tell you one thing, though. I'd rather the lamb was shot out of the womb. What's been getting me is the thought of all those unborn . . . Who knows how long it takes them to die inside their dead mothers? I can't get my head round that thought."

"Me neither," said George. "And we've still a good many to give birth. It's . . . well."

He left the shed, walked back to the house. A farmer two miles away rang in commiseration — news among neighbouring farmers travelled with astonishing speed. He also told George of the pyre being built nearby. "Lorries everywhere. You can't get down the lanes. A lot of people confined to their houses, holing themselves up, leaving boxes at their gates for groceries to be delivered. It's like the war, George. It's a bloody nightmare."

When he looked back later, George had no clear picture of how he spent that day: lambs birthing, the telephone constantly ringing, the exhausting examination of every animal, the tricks of the imagination, the slurry of grim thought to be put aside while trying to get through the work. The two days of waiting were spared the tension of hope, for there was no hope. It was quite apparent that the Elkin farm was doomed: it was just a matter of waiting for confirmation.

The three men worked harder than they had ever worked in their lives. But the normal exhaustion of lambing, on top of everything else, was made manageable by a strange sense of abnormal energy. Perhaps, thought George, it's because all three of us know it's the last few days of working together for what could be a very long time.

The results came, as the official vet — a confused Spaniard — predicted, forty-eight hours after his visit. In this they were lucky. So chaotic was the ministerial organisation when the disease first broke that many farms were left for days waiting for their animals to be killed. Arrangements were made for the slaughter to take place. George went down to the cowshed to tell Saul and Ben. Before he could do so, Ben broke news of his own.

"I was coming to find you," he said. "Orchid's in a bad way. Drooling. Horrible blistered tongue. You were right." He swallowed. "An' I always fancied the cows more 'n the sheep, didn't I?"

"I'm afraid I've had the confirmation," said George, quietly. "As we thought. No surprise. The ewes. Now the cows . . ." He stopped for a moment to firm his voice. "That's it, for us, I daresay. I suppose we're lucky they're coming to do their job so soon."

Saul swallowed, turned, hurried out. His son's eyes followed him.

"It's not so bad for you and me," he said at last. "I'm still young, there's plenty for me in another world. You — well, like, you're an employer. I don't want to be cheeky, but I daresay you'll survive. It's Dad I worry about. His whole life farming. In his late fifties. What can he do? He knows nothing but farming."

"Don't worry," said George. "I'll take care of your father, I promise you. We might be going under, but only for a while. Look at this lot, Ben: good cows. You and Saul did a wonderful job, building up this herd. Now I must go and ring the vet about Orchid. Though what's the point? She'll be shot anyway, day after tomorrow. Thursday, they'll all be gone." He patted Ben on the shoulder, quickly left.

Back in the kitchen he forced himself to eat eggs and bacon, needing energy for the night ahead. It would be his — their — penultimate night in the sheep shed, helping the birth of lambs destined to live for scarcely two days. The only thing that gave George the strength to make his way to the shed, scan his flock, engrave their bleating on his memory, was that these appalling facts were unbelievable.

362

CHAPTER
SIXTEEN

Slaughter day: a morning brightened by invisible sun. George, with both Ben and Saul, had been in the shed all night attending to two difficult births. One of the ewes had died — thank God it was that way, said Saul. There were two fine lambs who would taste fresh air, warm milk and the protection of their mother for a few hours, then be gone. When the three men were not engaged with a ewe, they stood without speaking, looking over the sheep, trying to hold back the morning.

At 5 a.m. Ben went off to bring in the cows. George collected a fresh flask of strong coffee for himself and Saul. He felt light-headed. But also he felt in control of the acute fatigue which was creeping up behind him. He had the power to postpone it, for once the killing was over, he could sleep for days. There would be nothing to do.

He and Saul sat side by side on a bale of hay in the shed drinking their coffee. Saul kept rubbing at the back of his neck with a cupped hand. His lips quivered as he put the plastic mug to his mouth.

"I heard this good joke on the wireless," he said. "The Prime Minister was up on his back legs saying something about the supermarkets having an arm-lock on farmers. But what made me laugh —" his mouth turned down, denying laughter — "was the bit where he said he could imagine the pain *us guys* were going through. How about that? By my reckoning that's the first time in history us farmers have been called guys. If he thinks he can win us over like that . . ." He paused, affronted on behalf of all farmers. "Better go and help Ben."

"Ben can manage. You stay here."

"I'd like to stay with the sheep. But Ben's that upset about Orchid. She's drooling. You don't like to see a cow drooling. Suffering."

Time went by in a jumble of stops and starts. One moment it giddied out of control, an hour passing in a second. Then a few minutes dragged mercifully, as if reluctant to bring the end of an era. The ewes, who had been sleepy, muted, during the night, began to stir. They stood up, bleating in their usual indignant way.

"Better feed them." George did not say *for the last time*.

"Innocent buggers," said Saul, well knowing what his employer meant.

Soon after eight there was the sound of several vehicles driving into the yard. George went out to meet them. The day was now oddly bright for March: sky churned up with cloud like a rough sea. He saw the men coming at him — men from Mars, men from outer space in identical white overalls, boots creamily laced with disinfectant they had hosed over themselves at the gate. Tired, clamped faces. They carried face masks and gloves. One of them held a plastic lunch box. George saw him swivel round, looking for somewhere to put it. *Lunch*, thought George. A lunch break in the killing. God Almighty.

The man in charge shook George's hand. There was apology in his grasp, and yet he and his band had come to take over the farm, finish it.

"The latrines, sir," he said. "Would it be all right to put them up over there? I'm from the Health and Safety Executive." He waved vaguely in some direction. George nodded. This campaign was the stuff of madness.

The men followed George to the shed. One of them explained to him how they would go about their job. George kept nodding, but could not bring himself really to listen. He summoned a curtain across his inner ear, a device that had often served him well in boring lessons at school, so that he could make no sense of the words.

Saul was waiting for them at the shed, sitting staring at the animals. When George and the men in white appeared, he stood up. The leader shook his hand. There was a certain sympathy exuded by the whole overalled team for which George, even in his desolate state, registered admiration. They must have become used to the horror of snatching people's livelihoods by now: they felt for them, their concern was to carry out their loathsome job causing as little pain as possible. But they were busy, overworked men under great pressure. There was no time to confirm their sympathy by procrastination. They had to get on with the job.

The lambs were to be segregated from their mothers. Saul had set aside the small barn for them at the far side of the yard. George, Saul and the aliens carried the lambs away. The ewes bleated in outrage, their anguish thick in the air. They tossed their heads, turned in circles. A few of them, who had lambed in the night, stood without moving, paralysed by loss. That their last living moments should be so agonised seemed to George the final outrage.

Back at the shed he stood by Saul to watch the beginning of the slaughter. Ben appeared. He made no attempt to hide the tears guttering down his face. Saul gave his son a brief glance. Then he tipped up his own chin, dry-eyed, like an old soldier on parade, and stared blankly at the men with their .32 revolvers.

They did their job with skill and efficiency, these men, not all of them vets, whose work during this crisis must have been the least desirable of their lives. While one man would control a ewe's body, another would steady her head between his gloved hands. Some of the sheep skittered in alarm, or annoyance: others looked in grateful anticipation towards their killer, perhaps expecting an extra feed.

Then, the silent shot between those hopeful eyes. Then, the slump and fall of the body, some heavy with an unborn lamb. There was a dignity about each tumble to the ground: shocking as a landslide, awesome as a waterfall. When the first ewe was slain Saul removed his cap and bowed his head.

"Can't fucking take any more of this," whispered Ben to George. "Cows next." He turned and left.

George left soon after him. He saw no point in watching the killing of every sheep, and knew he might be needed when it came to the lambs.

He went up to the house, sat at his desk in the swivel chair that had been in his father's office. He was immensely glad the old man had not lived to see this. Although there was nothing to say, he wanted to speak to Prodge. He picked up the telephone. With his free hand he fingered a pile of unopened envelopes collected from the gate — communications from MAFF that he had not the heart to deal with. They didn't matter. Tomorrow he would have all the time in the world.

"Prodge? They're here. They're at it. Dead efficient at their job, I'll say that."

"Bloody hell." Prodge paused. His voice cracked. "I don't know what to say."

"It's rough."

"It's the end."

"No. It isn't. Not for you. Not for us. But we'll talk about that when the slaughter's over."

"Have you asked when they're going to be taken away? You don't want dead animals lying around for days."

"I'll do that. A pyre's being built up on High Ridge."

"We're just waiting to hear when the killers are coming to us. *If* they are."

"Let me know. And love to Nell."

George sat for a while, swivelling the chair. His eyes were on the photograph of Lily on their wedding day: another life, that. Then he stood, stretching, still feeling that he was in charge of the impending fatigue. He reckoned he could put it off till tonight. He felt a slight giddiness from lack of food, made himself a piece of toast and honey and wondered what to do. A walk, he decided. *Solvitur ambulando* was something he had always believed in. The healing power of nature was his chosen medicine. For him it worked.

He made his way down to the valley, walked beside the river for a while. It moved as fast as the clouds reflected in its waters, lapping at the quietness. Then he went into the oak wood, where many of the trees had been planted by his grandfather. George himself had done a certain amount of planting on his land, but now, with the animals gone, that was something on which he would be able to concentrate. To leave a heritage of woods, fine trees, would make up a little for no children. In the country at large, thousands of acres of woodland had been razed over the last fifty years, taking with it incalculable wildlife. The thought of planting, replenishing, deflected a little from the ghastly business of the day at the farm. But only for a short while. George hurried back to the shed.

There he found Saul in exactly the same position as he had left him, hands crossed over his cap, head bowed. The vets had almost completed their job. George watched as the last few sheep were despatched and fell on to the vast lumpen wool carpet made of their companions. Then there was no more bleating.

The vet in charge came over. He expressed brief satisfaction that the job had been accomplished with such haste.

"I think we can take care of the lambs," was how he put the next part of his plan, "before we break for lunch. Cows this afternoon." As if to release George and the rigid Saul from their misery, he went on to explain how foolproof was the slaughter of cattle. "We shoot them with a captive-bolt pistol, then they're pithed with a special rod through their brain to make quite sure they're dead. We do a good job."

"I suppose you could say that's good," muttered Saul, struggling up from the weed of his own thoughts. "I suppose we should be glad of that."

The lambs, the cows. George wandered about his farmyard, no clear aim in mind, thoughts unstill, face unsmiling. The place had been taken over — the official vehicles, the block of latrines, the vets whose pristine white of the early morning was now blood-spattered and stained. They had rendered the ewe shed silent. Now they would cut off the squeal of the lambs. Then they were to finish their job with the greater slaughter of the Friesians.

Ben was not there to see the slaughter of the cows he loved. Had he asked, George would have reported that they died more importantly, somehow, than the sheep. Briefly they lurched before they fell, with curved neck and head uneasily turned, alert for a last second to the bellows of their companions, still alive. Fallen, there was still a magnificence about them, each one with its singular markings of black and white, its piebald nostrils shining. Only the udders, slumped to one side, were uniform in their veined swelling, their last balloon of milk denied its last draining. George had never been as fond of his cows as of his sheep, but he felt a sort of pride in the way they had met their death. They had co-operated with their slaughterers, making it easy for the men trained in this loathsome job.

By the end of the afternoon ninety-two cows, some three hundred sheep and forty-two lambs had been slaughtered. The chief vet removed his protective glove to shake George's hand again. He said he had no idea when the stock would be collected. As soon as possible, he said. But it wasn't up to him.

The vehicles drove away, the temporary lavatories were removed, Saul and Ben went to their cottage. It would be the first time for God knows how many years that they would have the chance to sit down together indoors at this time of day. George imagined them barely speaking in their grief, sipping at untimely cups of tea.

An immeasurable silence had fallen over the farm. George longed for a breeze, the ruffle of branches, but the air was still. The quiet gushed everywhere, unbreakable. George walked about for a while, avoiding the shed, the barn of the dead lambs, the cattle yard. He looked across the empty fields — four hundred acres of well-tended land with no animals to graze it, now. Only the barley fields left to work. He thought how fortunate he had been for so long, and knew he was not going to be one of those who would be beaten. He, with Prodge and Nell and Saul, would start again.

It was nearly seven, dusk thickening, by the time he crossed the empty yard to go back into the kitchen. Too tired to eat, the sickness in his stomach making the whole idea obnoxious, he went straight up to bed. Now he could allow himself to give in to exhaustion. Within moments he was asleep.

The next morning George woke at his usual early hour. He felt the drugged heaviness that comes from one good night after many bad ones. He lay, not wanting to get up, but unable to go back to sleep. After a while — he could not judge how long — he remembered there was no need to get up. No cows to milk, no sheep to feed. Apart from the piles of stuff to be dealt with on his desk, he had nothing to do. Here he was, a farmer like many others by now, *with nothing to do.*

George leapt out of bed, dressed quickly and went downstairs. A smell of frying came from the kitchen. Dusty was at the stove shaking sausages and bacon in a pan.

"Thought you could do with a good breakfast this morning," she said. "Suppose I shouldn't have come, what with the regulations. But now there are no . . . I practically bathed in disinfectant at the gate. Don't think I'm a liability." She was very pale.

"Thanks, Dusty. I'm ravenous."

"I hear Ben and Saul have taken it deep. Ben was crying into the night, Saul said." She put a plate of fried things in front of George. She had cut triangles of toast, made from her homemade bread, and stood them in a rack. Such unusual niceties conveyed the depth of her sympathy. George had not had such a breakfast in a long time, and despite the carnage outside he was hungry. He ate gratefully. During lambing Dusty did not come in early, never knowing when George would be there. This rare breakfast was the best comfort she could have provided.

"I shouldn't go out there if I were you, Mr George," she went on. "The yard, the shed and that. I caught a glimpse, though I didn't mean to, on my way in. Talk about a battlefield. I hope they're coming to take them away today. They'll begin to smell quick enough."

"I'll ring MAFF again in a moment. You have to hang on for hours. It's almost impossible to get through. Thanks for all this, Dusty. Wonderful."

When eventually he did get through to the local office George was given the answer he had expected: they could give no definite time as to when the carcasses would be removed. They were short-staffed. There was a backlog to get through. They'd do their best. Already there were hundreds of carcasses waiting to be burnt, George must understand. It wasn't easy, organising a crisis. Often there were conflicting instructions from Whitehall, no one knew quite where they were. The harassed man George spoke to tried to sound sympathetic and apologised for being unable to give some kind of assurance. The local MAFF representatives, men who lived in the country and knew first-hand what the farmers were going through, were always a great deal easier to deal with than the men in London.

George put on his jacket. "No good news there," he said to Dusty.

"Really, you don't want to go out."

"I can't stay cooped up in the house all day, can I? There are things to be seen to. I must go and talk to Ben and Saul. In a way, it's worse than yesterday. I feel I must face it."

"I suppose so."

George went out of the kitchen door into the yard. Today it was cold. There was a flawless, almost blue sky. It was a familiar morning of early spring but, because of the uncanny silence, it was unlike any other. The usual background sounds of animal cries, tractor engine, slurry scraping, men's footsteps, were not there. Not a bird sang. Ben's expert whistling after he'd finished the morning milk was no longer a shaft of music lurking behind a wall or building. Indeed, there was no sign of either Saul or Ben. George considered shouting, but decided against it. In their own time they would appear to oversee the next part of the grim business.

George walked slowly down to the milking parlour. It was immaculately clean as always, gutters sluiced down, troughs cleaned. At some point yesterday, George realised, while waiting for the cows to be slaughtered, Ben must have made himself do all this — mechanically, perhaps — the job he had done every day of the week for a good many years of his youth. Just because there were no more cows, it would not have occurred to him not to clean the milking parlour. He was a rare lad: he'd have made a wonderful farmer. We'll miss him: we'll miss him so much, thought George.

He stood holding on to one of the rails that divided the stalls, trying to accustom himself to the silence of the parlour. No humming suck of milking machines, clank of chain, splurge of shit, deep lowing. Only the old, ripe smell of milk was still slung about the place. How soon would that fade? George took a deep breath. He wanted to remember it.

His good fortune, in the quick slaughter of his animals after they were declared infected, did not continue. It was now his turn to join the many others suffering from the total chaos caused by official strategy.

He had no idea how many hours he spent trying to telephone those in charge in the next five days, how many dozens of vague estimates he received as to *when* the animals would be collected. "It's not in our power to say," he was told, over and over again. Hour after hour he sat in his study, windows closed, for the stench of rotting flesh began to make vile the air. Most exasperating of all was the apparent inability of those he spoke to to understand that there was any urgency to arrange for the removal of several hundred putrifying animals. But then urban civil servants in offices of clean air perhaps couldn't be expected to imagine the horror hundreds of miles away. Most of them wouldn't know a ewe from a ram. It was incomprehensible to George and his neighbours that there were dozens of local experts — hunts' kennel men and vets — offering their services, but their offers were ignored. At this time, too, the armed forces, with their impressive skills at organising large operations, were not called upon. The government insisted in continuing in its own way. Frequently the men they employed to do the killing made a grotesque hash of it, causing further suffering. There were stories of inexperienced marksmen chasing calves round fields, finishing them off with blows on the head. It was no wonder farmers, locked into the same desperate state as George, felt that ministers were uncaring as well as incompetent. Did they not realise that further disease was being spread by unburied corpses?

"It's inhuman, it's obscene," roared George one evening on the telephone to Prodge. "I've been shut in for five days, no answers, kept in the dark. What the hell's going on? All these announcements about everything being under control. God Almighty. It's chaos. And lonely and exhausting," he added. "Ben came up one afternoon with a scarf over his nose to ask what's happening. The stench is making Saul ill."

Prodge himself was in a state of fearful anticipation, wondering when he would hear if his animals were to be victims of contiguous culling. Though the two friends spoke every day, they were unable to offer any comfort to each other.

On the afternoon of the sixth day the telephone rang. The animals would be collected on Thursday morning.

"That's another three days," George shouted. "Don't you realise we're surrounded by *stinking, rotting* animals?" He slammed down the receiver, shaking. All morning George sat at his desk, yet another mug of cold tea not drunk beside him, trying to picture not only his own future but the future of British farming in general. Thousands of farmers had been driven to bankruptcy by the overzealous adoption of EU red tape, collapsing world prices, the huge fall in the price they could get for milk and meat. They'd been assailed by BSE, swine fever, bovine TB. This final tragedy of foot and mouth was probably the last straw. The view looked so grim that George feared that if he did not force himself to move he would weep, crumble, crack up in some undignified way. He knew what he had to do: he must assess the state of devastation of his farm.

He wound a thick wool scarf round the bottom of his face and over his nose. He went out. Walked in dread towards the yard of dead cows.

His herd of slain Friesians was now nothing more than an undulating black and white landscape on the ground. Already some of their bellies were swollen, their legs stiff and at odd angles. They lay awkwardly, some with tipped-back heads and mildew-coloured eyes. Others were open-mouthed, purple swollen tongues bursting from black caverns. George forced his eyes over every animal. He recognised each one — some singular detail, a scrap of its character still there, in death, he thought. Or maybe that was being fanciful. But Daisy, for instance, prettiest of the herd with her near-white hide and one black ear — she had a look about her he remembered on so many occasions coming in from the pasture. Skittish, she was, Daisy. She would give a small buck to show she wasn't merely one of the crowd. Now stiff and swollen, death seemed not to have deprived her of her flirtatious look. — I'm going mad, thought George, suddenly pulling himself up. I'm suffering hallucinations. His eyes rested on Bustle, whose birth he remembered — a huge calf who stood up almost at once, and later became the best milker of the herd.

George left the yard. He walked back up to the house avoiding the barn where the mound of dead lambs was piled. A small silver car was parked in the farmyard. Some official, he presumed. He was almost used to officials coming and going as if the place was theirs. He had no inclination to discuss compensation, removal of carcasses, anything. He did not in truth know what he wanted to do, or where he wanted to go, but he knew he could not face a conversation with anyone. He made his way to the shed, moved very slowly through the great doors to look upon the next plain of slaughter, his sheep.

There was, as always, a husky light in the shed. This made it easier to look upon the wool rug that stretched before him. The individual shapes of death were less precise than in the cows' yard. He saw the odd horn, an open eye gleaming like a slug, a raised hoof. But his dead sheep were no more than an animal porridge, his favourites among them indiscernible. Thank God, he thought.

George lifted his eyes from the mush of sheepskin to the far side of the shed, where bales of straw and hay were stacked to the roof. A figure in a blue coat was leaning on the wooden barrier of one of the pens. Oh no, he thought: this is the cruellest hallucination of them all.

The figure, a woman, who was looking at him — who had perhaps been looking at him since he came in — began to move towards him. But after a yard or so, she stopped. George put a hand to his thumping heart, transfixed. They stood regarding each other like strangers. But in their unknowingness of each other they were also conscious of what already existed between them. Lily recognised this at the same moment as George. She gave a little spurt of speed, her feet silenced by the straw on the ground. Then she was close to him, hands clenched by her sides.

"I've come too late," she said.

"No."

"When did they do it?"

"Days ago."

"Oh, George."

"Not good."

"Prodge and Nell?"

"Waiting their turn."

"George, George, George."

She bent her head forward so that it touched George's heart. He looked down on it. Even in this light her hair still sparkled. Perhaps it really was her. George put his hand on her shoulder.

"I'd like us to go away from here, straight away, just for a few hours," he said, quietly. "But I'm afraid that's not possible."

"No."

"Let's go in. You've seen enough."

Leaving the shed, his hand still on her shoulder, George leant a little on his wife. He walked like a man rescued from the sea, aware of firm land beneath his feet again. Dazed, stunned, his legs shaking, the familiar bones of Lily's shoulder beneath his hand and the flower scent of her, unfaded, gave some assurance that all this was really happening.

On the way, they ran into Saul, cap in hands — its almost permanent place of late. The trauma of the last week had aged him with dreadful speed: his stubbled skin was the chipped blue of a dead starling, his eyes had moved further back into deep hollows. He showed no surprise at seeing Lily, but put his hand to his head to raise his cap. It was only when he realised it was not there that confusion increased the trembling in his hands.

"Welcome back, Mrs Elkin."

"Saul . . ." They shook hands.

"Not the best time."

Lily shook her head.

"Ben's taken it bad. It was the cows that finished him. Awake all night he was. Said he didn't dare sleep for fear of nightmares."

"I'll be down to see him," said George. "Tell him I'll be down."

In the kitchen they stood one each side of the table. Lily spread her hands on its battered wooden surface as if for confirmation. Then she sat in her usual chair.

"I don't know what we do, with all that outside," said George.

"There's time," said Lily, looking at her hands. "We just tread water for a while." Her desire to *look*, to scour the room she had transformed with such sympathy and spirit, seemed to have left her in the difficulty of the moment. Her eyes did not explore. Perhaps they would later.

The telephone rang. George moved to answer it. He listened for a moment. Then he spoke quietly.

"Oh God, I'm sorry Prodge. Bloody hell. Who's going to escape round here? We'll speak this evening." He put the receiver down and turned to Lily. "Their turn tomorrow, apparently. Prize herd of healthy animals. Years of work to be blasted in a moment." He returned to the table and sat opposite his wife, looking on her with the dazed regard of one who cannot be sure that what he is seeing is real. "Their farm is being sold: they've got to get out anyway. It's so unfair, what's happened to Prodge and Nell, after their years of work. But I've been thinking hard about how to help. I do have an idea that might work."

"I wonder," said Lily, "if it could possibly be the same idea as mine?"

"Perhaps," said George, with a shrug — not a gesture lacking in care, but one of supreme exhaustion. This was not the moment to discuss practicalities for Prodge and Nell. They sat in silence for a long time.

"You realise we're prisoners here, for the time being?" George asked at last.

"I know," said Lily. "I knew it was breaking the rules to come. But I had to. I was scrupulous about disinfecting at the gate, and there was no one to stop me."

380

"You're staying a while, are you?" George's voice sounded to him like a distant echo, empty as the hoot of a far-off train.

"If that's all right with you."

"That's all right with me." George longed to put a hand over one of hers, but resisted. "In fact, it'd be difficult for you to get away, now, unless you want to break more rules." He made no attempt to lend humour to his observation. All the same, Lily smiled.

Once again, time jerked, stopped, started. George spent much of it trying, and failing, to get through to the authorities to persuade them to come before Thursday. Lily sat beside him. At some point in the evening he carried her suitcases upstairs, obeying her request to take them to the spare room where she had first stayed. After a supper of tinned soup, scarcely touched by either of them, George went to the cottage to spend an hour with Ben, whose eyes were shrunk from weeping, and listened to his repeated words of incomprehension: his cows, his cows *gone*. At nine, Prodge rang.

"Bloody hell, George," he said, his voice shaking. "You were lucky with your killers. We got a right bunch of incompetent cold bloods here, shooting an animal several times without killing it. One dunderhead left Jessy thrashing about, half dead — said she'd die in a minute or two. I took a gun to her myself. I couldn't bear it." He paused. "George, I shot sixteen of my own cows. I can't say any more. Here, speak to Nell."

Nell, too, was in a devastated state.

"What finished me," she sobbed, "was the bantams. Even worse than seeing the calves go. My bantams, my hens, George. They said *everything* had to go. Can you believe it? Prodge and I are just sitting here, nothing to do, stranded on an island in a sea of slaughtered healthy animals. It's a nightmare. Not a single good thing left."

"Just one good thing," George said. "I only tell you at this ghastly time because it might cheer you up. Lily's back."

"*Lily?*" Nell stopped sobbing. "Let me speak to her."

The two friends were engaged on the telephone for a long time. George went into the study. He sat in his father's office chair, gently swinging from side to side as if moved by a languorous tide. His mind was frozen by the events of the past few days and the spectre of the carnage outside. There was no space in his heart, for the moment, to reflect on the implications of Lily's return.

In the two long days they spent marooned in the house, Lily kept her quiet distance. If she made any changes, George did not notice them, but he did see her looking out of various windows at the garden where most of her hard work had fallen into disrepair. They did not talk of themselves, of the lost years, or of the future. The clearing of the farm and the dead animals was their only concern.

By now the smell of them was terrible. Lily closed all windows against the stink of rotting flesh. But it was pervasive, sickening. It slunk into the house like a snake and resisted all efforts to extinguish it. Everywhere, it was — in hair, in clothes. George, putting his hand to his face, smelt it on his flesh. And outside, by now, it was far worse. An invisible mould, the stench clung to the buildings, the cobbled yard, the stone walls: it was rampant in the air.

George, holding a handkerchief to his nose, forced himself to do a final round of his animals. He was shocked by the speed of their deterioration. No longer singular sheep and cows, each one had become merely a part of the pile of putrid flesh contorted into obscene, swollen shapes. Effluent ran from them. A pale sun lighted the liquid mess. George felt the rise and fall of bile in his throat. It had been necessary to do this inspection in order to persuade MAFF of the speed needed to rid his farm of this vile matter. It was the most horrific morning, he later told Lily, of his life.

On the Wednesday evening he was assured by the local MAFF representative (apologetic, sympathetic, but evidently helpless) that collection of the stock would definitely be the next morning: the pyre was ready for burning hundreds of animals in the locality. As he talked on the telephone, George saw through the window that Ben was pushing a wheelbarrow, stacked with sandbags, towards the cowshed. George opened the window, shouted at him not to bother: it wasn't worth it. The men were coming in the morning, he said.

"I want to soak up some of the mess," Ben shouted back. "There's not many sacks but it's the least I can do for my bloody cows." Purposefully he moved on, a young man shed of all his tears, strong in his determination to carry out a final, useless job on the farm he had loved all his life.

From a distance, early next morning, George, Saul and Ben watched their bloated animals scraped ignominiously from the ground into open lorries. The huge diggers employed to carry out this task were driven by skilled men, but there were still errors of judgement. A stiffened cow would fall from the jaws of the machine, recalcitrant in death, and have to be prodded this way and that by the great steel teeth until she was secured again and dumped in the truck. The sheep and lambs, by now no more than wool soup flecked with heads, were ladled up more easily — all distinguishing features, thank God, thought, George, now disappeared.

By evening, they had gone, leaving nothing but Ben's sodden sandbags to blot the emptiness. Fierce sprays of disinfectant to scour the place would come next, but first there was to be the burning. Saul and Ben came up to the house to say they were on their way to the pyre.

"Best we go 'n show our farewell," said Saul.

"I'll want to remember these last days," added Ben. "Every time I'm fiddling with some bastard of an electrical thing and I ask myself if I was right to give up farming."

They went on their way, walking far apart.

In the kitchen, George sat at the table trying to make up his mind whether to join them. Lily put a mug of tea in front of him. He felt her hand on his shoulder. At least, he was aware of her touch, but it caused no sensation within him. Until the final event was over, he continued to be a man — in common with so many thousands of others — too traumatised to feel anything at all. Feeling nothing, he reflected grimly, was the reason Lily had left.

"I'm going too," he said.

George walked across his fields. From a cloud of acrid black smoke flakes of ash were falling. They flew about like flocks of small silent birds, sometimes touching him. As he approached the pyre the noise of hungry flames grew louder.

Saul and Ben, along with Prodge and Nell and several others, were already there: a stiff little row of farmers who watched in incredulous silence as the machines tipped the carcasses into the giant fire. Behind its flames the sky was a clashing, ugly red which made the fields beyond the pyre into a stretching sore of land. Smoke — the vile, stinking smoke from roasting, rotted flesh — joined in confusion with the rose-edged clouds and, as if in final outrage, the legs of dead animals, like giant hatpins, pierced the whole bloody mess of sky and flames.

George felt Lily beside him. He shifted, to show he was glad. Then he turned to look at Prodge and Nell. Prodge's eyes, in his empty, exhausted face, were on Lily. Nell, her wild curls reddened by the fire, stared at the flames that were the end for her and Prodge. It was too soon for her to acknowledge Lily with more than a slight nod. Saul stood close to his son. The rigid Ben was committing the sight to memory, for when he was an electrician in a less cruel world.

Gradually darkness fell, but the men in charge kept feeding the fire. The savage scarlets and oranges of its flames, flaring across the sky, could have been taken for a wild sunset.

CHAPTER
SEVENTEEN

That night, within the house, George was able to feel the emptiness without. The shadow and stench of the slain animals now gone, he shut the kitchen windows against the smell of disinfectant and turned to contemplate his wife.

It occurred to him that externally she hadn't changed — neither thinner nor fatter, she was: nor older, nor less burning with life. But there was about her a new steadiness, a less frantic way of looking, a touching quietness in response to his own melancholy that he found profoundly moving. There was time, at last, to look on her with hope and wonder.

With Lily's return, Dusty had changed her mind about the regulations and had not been up to the house since the day of the slaughter. (She hadn't left, she assured George, she was just taking a break.) So Lily cooked a simple herb omelette and found a new candle to light their supper. George opened a bottle of her favourite wine.

They talked little of themselves. Drained by the events of the last two days, they acknowledged there was plenty of time for that: this was not the moment. Instead, they discovered that their ideas concerning help for Prodge and Nell were as one. In the joy of this discovery the evening rose on an invisible wave. They sat by the fire, when they had finished eating, for a long time, planning.

"We divide the house in two, making both ends completely independent," said George.

"And our end will still have four bedrooms," Lily pointed out with a sudden merriness. "Plenty of room for at least three children."

"Quite." George paused, envisaging this. "And Prodge and Nell become equal partners in the farm. With our compensation money, and Prodge's expertise, we can begin again as soon as all this business is over. Do things a bit differently, perhaps. Turn completely organic — it's more and more what consumers want. Buy some new horses for you and Nell. It shouldn't take Prodge too long to pay off his overdraft. I don't suppose he'd mind if I guaranteed it for him."

"But the thing is, will they ever accept this? Or will they want a new life somewhere quite different — to give up farming like their parents?" Lily asked.

"I wouldn't have thought so. But oddly, although I've known them for so long, it's impossible to guess what their reaction will be. Cautious, I would guess. We can only hope."

They finished the wine. George damped down the fire.

"And you, my wife," he said. "You're back. You're back, aren't you? It'll take me some time to believe that."

388

"I'm back. Yes, I'm back." Lily stood, stretching. Then she blew out the candle, displaying a sense of disbelief in her own words. "Thank you for not pursuing me. Thank you for your forgiveness, your understanding —"

"I'm not sure I ever really understood, or ever will," broke in George. "A thousand times I nearly came after you. Prodge and Nell constantly urged me to do so. But I believed you really didn't want that, and that if I tried I might scupper my chances. It was hard, but anything's possible when you love someone, and the most important thing is to do what that person wants." George gestured towards the farmyard. He felt not drunk, but agreeably unsoldered from his base, which enabled him to make this small declaration. "I like to think this ending must be the right time for our own new beginning," he went on after a pause to see how Lily was reacting. "Don't you?"

Lily, in her old familiar way, moved to him and leant her head in the place beneath his shoulder so that he could kiss her hair.

"I do."

George held her silently, imagining the night ahead, the empty farm outside, and the feeling of strangeness of married life regained now Lily was back, soon to be lying by his side.

Prodge and Nell came over from their own empty farm, guilty at breaking the rules. They spent a long time disinfecting their boots at the gate. Both had the constrained, expectant look of those aware of news that might not be welcome, thought George — though he could have been imagining this.

Lily and Nell hugged each other in the same restrained fashion as do mourners at a funeral: sympathy and understanding made plain in controlled, silent gestures. They had gathered, the four of them, in the study — the meeting place for so many different kinds of conferences over the years. George remembered a less solemn occasion of his youth when they had come to discuss the future of an ailing guinea pig.

Prodge made for his favourite end of the sofa and deprived George of his opening (carefully composed during the night) with an announcement of his own.

"Mum and Dad must be feeling bad," he began, "on their Spanish terraces reading about British farmers — just like they did during BSE." He gave a grim smile. "Only this time they've done something about it. They've sent a cheque that will deal with about a quarter of the overdraft. Compensation should take care of most of the rest."

"That's good," said George. "That's a relief." In the following silence he chose his words carefully. He wanted to put his plan in a way that would show it was essential for all their futures, rather than a benevolent gesture on the part of a reasonably well-off friend. "Any ideas, have you, yet, what, when —?"

"We'll be off pretty soon," said Prodge. "They're taking away the animals tomorrow. Thank God we won't have the wait you've had. Nothing to hang on for, now. The place is loathsome. MAFF asked us if we'd like to do our own disinfecting — ten pounds an

390

hour. We said yes. Give us something to do. So soon it'll be ready for the landlord to sell as a nice little second home with carriage lamps and hanging geraniums —"

"No need to go on," Nell interrupted.

"Lily and I, it so happened, quite independently came up with exactly the same idea about a possible solution." George was still playing for time.

"We thought that might be the case," said Nell. "We thought you might have something in mind for us, though God knows what. Come on. Don't keep us in suspense any longer."

In the most delicate terms George put to them the plan of dividing the house and becoming equal partners in the farm. Encouraged by the approval in Lily's eyes at his progress, he fluently sketched possibilities, reasons, details, in a way which he hoped they would find difficult to refuse. The initial huffiness in Prodge's expression, he could see, was slowly ebbing. The slight nodding of his head indicated that he saw good sense and reason in George's suggestions. What George could not have guessed was the relief his friend felt as he anticipated living at such close quarters to Lily. All that was fine, now. Untroubling. The curious storm she had caused him had ended the night he had burnt her photograph. He was now free of his irrational fantasy — besides, she looked older, graver, no longer a figure so mysteriously desirable. (Perhaps it had been the kindness of the light, and the confidence that sprang from the leather jacket, that afternoon by the river.) Now she held no power to disturb him. He knew he could be in a room alone with her and the will to touch her would no longer be there. So he was safe, he would always be safe in her company now. Had this not been the case, he would not have been able to agree to George's generous plan.

"Sounds good," he said, when all possibilities had been laid before him. "I go for all that, I do. Marvellous ideas. I could never see myself in another part of the country, anywhere else but here. This land's in my boots, always has been. And it'd be good to put the neglected end of your house to rights — long overdue. So I don't know about Nell, we haven't had much time to discuss the future, but I'm on for it, myself. It'd be a future to get to grips with, wouldn't it, Nell?" Nell, pale, made no movement of agreement. Prodge looked back at George. "We'd never be able to start again without you, and I daresay our experience could be useful, choosing a new herd and so on. We suspected you might have something up your sleeve, but never guessed it was this. Thanks."

"You must understand we'd be equally unable to start again without you," said George, the relief of Prodge's acceptance surging through him. "And I think we'd make a good team, the four of us and Saul. Think: a year from now we could be up and running again."

"We could," said Prodge, "God help us." He turned again to his sister. Her silence dulled the edge of happy anticipation among the other three, making them all uneasy. Nell was looking out of the window, as if scarcely listening to all that was being said. Her eyes followed a moving cloud.

392

"Yes," she said at last. "You could. It's the most wonderful idea, George. Typically generous of you." She moved her look from him to Lily, her severe expression only partially masking the depth of sadness she felt. "But I'm afraid I can't be part of the package. I can't begin to tell you how much I appreciate the invitation, but I can't accept it. I won't be coming here. Prodge can manage fine, with you two to look after him." Her eyes now met George's: strong, firm. Inwardly he quailed, hating her public message. "I'll be off to New Zealand. We've a distant cousin there who breeds horses. Always something I've wanted to do, as you know."

"*New Zealand?*" shouted Prodge, appalled.

"I've been in touch with Isabel. We've been communicating for some time — long before this last crisis." Nell spoke lightly now. "We've great plans, great hopes. I shall like New Zealand — new country, new life. Something like England used to be," she added.

"You never mentioned a word of this to me." Prodge stood up, hurt, betrayed, shocked. "Why didn't you say anything? You dark horse, you."

"Some things are best kept to yourself until the right moment," answered Nell, a little harsh in her sudden detachment. "Had things been different, I might not have needed to go to New Zealand. No, don't try to dissuade me." She turned to George. "My mind's made up. It's what I want to do. I'll have time to concentrate on horses at last. I'll be very happy." She stood up, wearing the look of brave defiance George knew so well. She looked round, her silent message igniting each one of them.

"Well, obviously, Nell 'n me'll have to talk a lot more about all this," Prodge said, unnerved. "Could be I'll persuade her —" Nell gave him a scathing glance — "could be I won't. And we can talk a lot more about your idea, the ins and outs, can't we? I mean I'd like to leave our farm soon as possible, myself."

"Of course," said George.

Prodge and George gripped each other's forearms, nodded: no one knew what further to say. Lily went to kiss Nell, then drew back. Nell had retreated to a place of her own. They could see she wanted no contact to endanger her facade. "'Bye," was all she said, and followed Prodge out of the door.

"I can see it wouldn't have been possible for her," said Lily, later, "feeling as she feels — as she's always felt."

"I thought, being Nell, knowing the impossibility . . . she'd get over it."

"*Get over it?*" Lily was more ruffled than George had ever seen her. "But she's been in love with you for ever. I knew that the moment I met her."

"Why didn't you tell me?"

Lily gave an incredulous laugh. "I thought you knew. I thought you didn't want to talk about it any more than Nell wanted to talk about you."

"God preserve us from our sensitivities! I only had the faintest intimations. Only very recently did I realise just what . . ." He shrugged. "But I thought it best not to mention what I guessed was the truth. I thought it

394

would be even harder for her. She wouldn't have wanted my pity or empty consolation. There was nothing I could do."

"I suppose not. I hate the idea of her leaving."

"So do I." He sighed. "But there was never anything I could have done, was there?" By now George was roving the kitchen, miserable. "It's arrogant to think I've been the cause of so much despair in her life, but I suppose that's the truth of it, and I've never wanted to face it. Of course there were signs. I never wanted to acknowledge them. I tried to ignore them. And now nothing'll change her mind. She's a stubborn old thing. She'll go, certainly. But I hope she knows it wasn't unrequited love she felt: it was requited, but not in the way she wanted. Not in a way that was much good to her. Oh God, poor Nell. She'll make a go of it, of course. She's always successful if she puts her mind to something. But I'll miss her. We'll miss her, won't we?"

Lily nodded. She set about small domestic acts in the hope that George would find consolation in her sympathy, and comfort in her busy presence.

In the weeks that followed, the Elkins and the Prodgers watched the playing out of the disease and its tragic results from their empty farms — new outbreaks every day, horror stories of incompetent killing, thousands of healthy animals awaiting slaughter, thousands of rotting carcasses awaiting burial, and some, already buried, dug up again to be buried a second time. Compared with many other farmers, the four of them realised their luck: they were neither bankrupt, jobless nor homeless.

Starting again would be a long and difficult process, but possible. For so many, foot and mouth disease was the final disaster at the end of a decade of hardship.

For Ben, there was nothing left to do. He wanted to leave the empty fields and sheds as soon as possible, he said. He didn't want the memory of them now to blot out how they used to be before the animals were killed. On the day it was announced that the General Election was to be postponed, he left to begin his apprenticeship with a firm of electrical engineers, scoffing at the idea that one more month would see the end of the disease. Saul, who had passed scarcely a day without his son since he was born, wandered the fields like a man confused, dazed. He bashed the hedges with his stick, called his dogs to heel if they wandered more than a few yards from him. Then he set to oiling machinery, checking much earlier than he would have done in a normal year that the tractors were in good shape for the harvest.

Prodge and George spoke endlessly on the telephone. It was decided that Prodge, master-builder of the great shed, was the one to renovate the far end of the house that was to be his. With Nell there was little exchange. She used regulations about not visiting her excuse for not coming over, and rang only twice, the second time to say her flight was booked. Finally, afraid she might feel incapable of saying goodbye, George went over to find her. He came upon her among dozens of packing cases, for she was sorting Prodge's stuff as well as her own. She was pulling at straps and lifting heavy boxes as if weight was nothing to her, but her sharp shoulder blades were visible beneath the fuzz of her jersey. The farmhouse as George had always known it had disappeared in the upheaval. Furniture moved, pictures taken down, carpets rolled up — its sad state, previously half hidden in the general chaos, was now painfully revealed.

"I'm so busy, George," Nell said, scarcely looking up.

"I can see that. But I've come to say goodbye. Thought you might just slip away."

Nell said nothing, continued wrapping a photograph in newspaper.

"You could always change your mind, come back if things didn't work out," George went on, floundering.

"Things'll be fine. I won't be coming back. I'll have the horses, won't I?"

"You'll have the horses. Maybe —"

"If you want to know, this foot and mouth disaster has made the decision easier for me. I always knew that if . . . Lily came back, that would be the time for me to go. God knows I wanted her to, for you. But it wouldn't have been possible, years and years more of . . . it wouldn't have been possible for me. And I can't stay forever the farmer's sister."

"No."

"Prodge might get married one day, want me out. And as you and Lily have relieved me of the one stumbling block to my leaving — Prodge's well-being — there's nothing left to keep me, is there?" She met George's eye. "I mean, that old myth: you and me like brother and sister. For years it's been rubbish as far as

I was concerned. I wish it had been so — would've been much easier. But you must have known that."

She gave a shaky laugh.

"And I would never have done for you, George, except in the way we've always known. And *that's* always been pretty good, hasn't it? We've been so lucky: our shared passions in our farms, our jokes and teasing and understanding. And then, goodness, we've been able to comfort each other in our time, too, haven't we?" Her voice lightened. "But you need more than all that. Perhaps I do. You need a woman with knowledge and ideas and information that you can call on when you come in from the farm, to transport you to another place. I haven't got that range — no, don't deny it. It's the truth. You need someone who can put magic into things, like Lily. I'm more the practical kind. I don't really believe in magic. And then — well, there's nothing I could show you that you don't already know."

"Nonsense. You've taught me thousands of things."

Nell looked George sternly in the eye. "What you should remember is that you and I were granted something rather rare between men and women — near-perfect friendship. The sort that lasts, survives anything. I suppose we've been slightly drawn to each other physically, too — I hate that word *attracted* —" Nell turned up her nose, smiling — "but never so much as to make complications. *Think* how lucky we've been." She laughed convincingly.

"I suppose we have," said George. He sighed. "They're so confusing, all the permutations of love. But you know I've always loved you. I hope you've always known —"

"Oh yes. I've known and been grateful for that kind of love." She paused, gathered herself. "You've been my life, here, George. Our life. Take good care of Prodge for me. Please look after him well."

"Of course."

"And don't think I don't realise what a gift from heaven your idea is: you and Prodge equal partners, new house, staying on the land he knows and loves . . . a new prize herd one day. I shall miss seeing that, miss seeing what the three of you and Saul achieve." She tipped up her chin, tried to revive her smile. "But I'll be fine. I'll manage. I'm not too old for a new life, but if I hung around much longer I would be. I'm quite excited in a way, honestly."

"Nell." George held out his arms. In this moment of parting, the jumble of sensations and messages burning to be imparted, but too complex to be expressed, made words impossible. Nell suddenly dropped the bundle of paper and pranced towards him — a high, jaunty step he had never seen before.

Despite huge sadness of the moment George could still register how this false gaiety ill suited her, but what courage it came from. She kissed him briefly on the cheek, then backed away into the rubbish again.

"Don't let Lily go this time," she said. "Give her my love. Say I'll write. Now please, George, I've so much to do."

"I'm on my way."

"My bantams," she said. "I never knew how much I'd miss them. Funny, isn't it? Anyway: thanks for coming over."

George's eyes slurred with tears that did not fall as he hurried from the house. He could not help wondering whether Nell, alone again, would allow herself tears, too, or whether she would keep her own weeping for the other side of the world.

The Elkin farm, like the Prodgers' and thousands of others, was now a ghost farm: the buildings were empty of everything but the smell of disinfectant. Every corner that could harbour the disease had been scoured by men in protective clothing with high-powered jet machines. George read that the average age for the British farmer was now fifty-six. Indeed, on the days when there was a reason to go to market, he had noticed the acute shortage of young men and wondered with some trepidation how he and Prodge would fare. Farm incomes were the lowest for sixty years: when, and how, would things improve? The future looked arid, but nothing would deter him from starting again. It was announced that the suicide rate among farmers was now higher than in any other business in the land — and the Prime Minister declared there was no crisis in the countryside.

Nell left for New Zealand with two smallish suitcases and her spinning wheel. (Prodge had insisted she take the fare from their parents' cheque, and enough to see her through a month or so.) The same day he moved in with George and Lily and began work on what was to be his end of the house. It became alive with the noise of hammering and sawing, filling the silence left by the animals. Prodge worked with great speed and vigour: absorbed in the job, he ceased to talk about his old herd. But in the evenings, when the three of them sat down to supper together (Prodge promised to return the hospitality as soon as his new kitchen was finished), talk was now of Friesians and a new mixed flock of sheep.

On a warm spring day, 192,000 animals awaiting slaughter, George and Lily took their postponed break from the farm. They drove to the north coast. George knew of a walk through an oak wood that led to a small, unfrequented cove.

They sat on the pebbled shore, a warm sun on their backs, watching the waves lumber in as slowly as fat old seals. Once landed, quickly they fanned their foam on the pebbles, then receded, leaving nothing more than a skeletal trace of their brief lives to be washed away completely by the next wave. The rhythm again, thought George. Further out to sea the occasional wave broke prematurely, its crest making a white feather to dance for a moment on the water, then was gone.

"I like this place," Lily said. She wore a blue scarf, bluer than the sea. They drank apple juice. There was an echo of their first picnic on the river bank, but not a pure comparison: time, events, a million sensations divided then from now.

It was the only occasion, that time by the sea, that they spoke of what had happened. It was as if neither of them had liked to unsettle their renewed happiness at

401

the farm by dwelling on all that was past: neither believed in sterile analysis of matters of the heart, but both observed in the other the need to leap from the last stepping stone to the final bank of reassurance.

"The feeling of no feeling," said George, with a small sardonic smile to ease the way, "has it gone now, do you think?"

"I think it has." Lily played with a collection of silvery pebbles, running them through her fingers. "I don't think I can ever explain what happened, because I'm not sure myself. But I know that I never stopped loving you. I just couldn't feel that love, couldn't feel anything. It was terrifying."

"And now?"

"Now? It's been such a long, despairing process. But I think — I really do believe — it's roaring back now. By that I mean roaring gently, if you can understand the oxymoron. — I wonder if you ever guessed how fed up I became with all my restless roving, waiting? Sometimes I thought, this is it: I'm fine, I'll go home. Then I knew I was deluding myself. I'd look at Van Gogh's chair, or a copper beech in May — you know, that strange transparency of the leaves before the colour quite reaches them — and I still felt nothing, nothing. So I knew I had to carry on waiting." She paused. "The first awful, welcome, lurch here —" she touched her ribs — "was when I heard about foot and mouth. Ironic, really, something so appalling jolting me back into sensation. All I could think of was you and Nell and Prodge, and all the farmers waiting to know if they were doomed, and tears came into my eyes. I knew I couldn't bear for you to go through it all alone. I had to be there with you. It was time to come home. No more thoughts, no more procrastinating, I just got into my car and drove. And here I am. So pleased . . ."

She tipped the pebbles into George's hand.

"And now?" he asked again.

"And now? Well, as it should be. I mean, given that you in all your love and generosity have taken me back with not a word of reproof, and have made no demands for an explanation. So — from this time forth, as it were. Promises. Beginning again. Wiser. For my part, hoping to do better, be a better wife. Not so much urging you to look, but looking myself at all the good things you are." She laughed.

"But I loved your lessons in observation," said George. "All that time you were away I tried to practise, and I think I sometimes saw. In so many things — except for Nell, and that was because I didn't want to face the truth — you relieved me of my blindness. You showed me how to abandon preconceptions, see what was really there. What more can any one creature do for another?"

Lily took the pebbles back again. The small clinking they made in her hand was the only sound against the brush of the waves.

They stayed there till the tide turned, mid-afternoon. On the way home each of them was aware of the pervading light of resolution in the other. They both sensed that some discovery had been made without resorting to the danger of excavation. At home, they found Saul sandpapering the rust from the mudguard of a tractor, and Prodge lifting a beautifully made frame into the window of his new kitchen.

By May, it was estimated that if the slaughtered animals were laid in a line they would stretch 1,908 miles — from London to the Sahara. By now the army had been called in to help. Soldiers were reported to be unhappy at instructions to finish off half-dead animals by bashing them over the head with lorry spanners, or drowning them in a river. Prodge painted his front door black and white.

In June, following the election, MAFF became DEFRA, to no apparent advantage, and in the Queen's speech there was no mention of the crisis in the country. Decisions to deal with the crisis continued to be taken by scientists with computers but no veterinary experience.

Nell wrote from New Zealand to say she was happily installed with her cousin and horses. Prodge moved into his end of the farmhouse, still not quite finished but wonderfully transformed. Lily helped him choose colours and made curtains. Unmoved by her presence, he was now able to enjoy her help and friendship, and seemed deeply content with the whole arrangement.

At the beginning of August many footpaths were reopened, giving a signal that the worst was over. By the third week in August 3,750,000 animals had been slaughtered. 20,000 awaited slaughter, 9,000 were piled up waiting to be burnt. Birds were seen on the corpses. There were fears that the inefficient disposal of the dead animals would cause further contamination. It was announced by the new DEFRA minister, a woman not known for her love or knowledge of the country, that there were to be three separate inquiries into the disaster. Farmers, enraged by what they considered the mishandling of the whole catastrophe, accused the government of a cover-up. But they understood why there was not to be a general inquiry: as Prodge said, who would come worst out of that? The government hinted that some farmers were perpetuating the disease for their own good. While they conveyed some sympathy for those in the country tourist trade, rural disasters were plainly not the stuff of natural ministerial concern. The Prime Minister's brief attempt at "taking charge" had made no perceptible difference. The feeling was that his government remained impervious to the farmers' distress, and had no real idea how to overcome the ongoing catastrophe.

After so much rain the previous autumn and winter, it was a poor harvest. With no animals to look after, George and Saul had been left with more free time on their hands, despite cutting silage and hay, than they could ever remember. But they made good use of it, repairing machinery, and the roof of the small barn where the lambs had been slaughtered. They checked fencing and hedges, replaced a gate that had been damaged by lorries carrying animals to the pyre. There was much to do to prepare for the day new stock would arrive.

One evening, George, Lily and Prodge sat in the garden sensing intimations of the grim summer's ending. There was that gentle sharpness in the air that precedes September, when the sun sinks faster than it does in high summer. In the sheds the hay was piled to the roof. The silage was baled.

George went indoors to get more beer for Prodge and himself and a cup of tea for Lily. She felt sick, morning and evening, and tired. In that respect she was one of the unlucky ones, the nausea lasting so long. When he returned he found Saul had joined them. Since Ben's departure Saul was more inclined to drop in occasionally, though he would never accept anything to eat or drink. He held his cap to his chest.

"Plovers," he said. "On the wane, along with all the others. But it's the song thrush I miss most."

George, in no mood to be dispirited on such an evening, countered with a cheering fact. The otter was coming back, he told them. He'd read that since it was now illegal to dump toxic waste in the water, the otter was seen to be returning. Saul acknowledged this with a small bow, then his attention was caught by a single late swallow swerving across the sky. His eyes followed the tiny arrowhead-body until it was out of sight, and talk turned once more to the prospect of a fine herd of Friesians. The sun, low in the west, trailed a net of gold, unsullied by the recent killer flames. It grew cooler, but the four of them sat talking of sheep and cows until it was dark.

By mid-September 3,864,000 animals had been slaughtered.

His work on the house finished, Prodge had started improvements on the sheep shed. He spent most of his time there, determined it would all be in good order for the new animals. He was in high spirits, Prodge: he was enjoying his spell of carpentry, and he'd met a girl, he told Lily, with nice eyes. Not as nice as *hers*, he added, but he had hopes that she might not be a disappointment when he got to know her better. Confiding in Lily about such matters, with Nell gone, was one of the many benefits of his new life. He was able to laugh at himself, now, when he thought back to that silly passion of a summer afternoon, which had lingered because he had needed something beyond farming to sustain his heart. Lucky he came to his senses, bonfire night, he often thought, or being friends with Lily, as he was now, would not have been possible.

In mid-September, too, the British outbreak of foot and mouth disease was officially declared the worst the world had ever seen.

George ordered new trees. He thought of Nell.

The experts continued to argue about the pros and cons of vaccination. DEFRA's progress in country matters was slow. George read somewhere that a farmer telephoned requesting permission to move his bull. A DEFRA official rang back to ask what sex it was. Occasionally, there was cause to smile.

In that same month, when people's concern was for the troubles of the greater world, it was announced that all forty million sheep — the entire British flock — would be culled should they become infected with BSE.

"Preparing the public for the grand finale of farming in this country," said George.

"How the hell's the land going to be kept in order, no animals to graze it?" said Prodge. "I suppose we'll all be asked to be park keepers. Whole countryside one bloody great theme park." This had long been his fear. He sighed. "Daresay there's one thing Nell and I can be grateful for — we decided against *diversifying*, going in for all the hassle of B&B. Look at the poor sods who tried. No tourists, no customers, just huge debts."

The vision of a sheepless land was shortlived, for just two weeks later it was learnt (in a late-night report) that there had been a muddle. Four years of testing ovine brains for BSE were worthless, for the mush so scrupulously studied had turned out to be bovine. Cause for another weary smile.

George and Prodge recognised, along with thousands of traditional farmers, that the outlook for the future was bleak. Profits for many were down to £2,500 a year. Those who could not move their stock, because of regulations, were running out of food and losing hundreds of pounds a week. It would be a hard winter.

But it was the warmest October on record. In the evenings, George, Lily and Prodge were still able to sit outside, for the summery air stayed with them till dusk. There was time to ponder on the troubled state of the land: it was odd to have so much time. An independent report concluded that if there had been *instant* culling at the outbreak of foot and mouth, 1.6 million animals and £800 million of public money would have been saved. The handling of the whole affair had been "lamentable". Hardly news to farmers.

408

A few days later it was announced that in any future outbreak of the disease it would be unlawful to appeal against culling. In ministerial opinion, some farmers had helped to spread the disease by activating their rights to appeal against the slaughter of their animals. Nothing inspired optimism, as George said. But he, Prodge, Lily and Saul were not deterred. They continued with their plans for resuscitating the farm. At the end of the month they were to buy their new stock.

Often they spoke of Nell.

By now, George noticed that Lily arched her back slightly whenever she sat down, as women do when pregnancy becomes uncomfortable. He looked forward to their child being born at Christmas, and to the birth of new lambs in the spring.

Also available in ISIS Large Print:

Sun Child

Angela Huth

Sun Child *is an exceptional book about a child's world*

"Huth's talent is entirely original." **The Times**

"Children begin by loving their parents. After a time they judge them. Rarely, if ever, do they forgive them."

Emily has not yet reached the age of judgement. For her, normality consists of contentment and magic and there is no possibility of change in the seeming happiness of her parents — Fen, beautiful and mercurial, and Idle, a hardworking and gentle man. She loves them both dearly and her image of them is together — indivisible, laughing, dancing, making every day scintillate with life. When change does come, Emily is a helpless spectator, confused by the puzzle of ill-fitting events.

ISBN 0-7531-7141-4 (hb)
ISBN 0-7531-7142-2 (pb)

Is There Anything You Want?

Margaret Forster

Mrs H. is generous and helpful to a fault, and lives alone with a secret that she tells no one. Her niece is a young doctor who can't take the strain, and who wants something different from life. Alongside them are the other walking wounded, getting on with their lives: Ida, once beautiful and now hiding her scars under layers of fat; tiny Dot who is stronger than she seems; Edwina, a mother who lives vicariously through others, even her wild daughter; Rachel, who finds almost too late what it's like to soar above the crowd; and not to mention the men in their lives.

This is a novel about what it means to live in the shadow of disease and with its scars, looking back over one's shoulder while trying to go forward. You can trip up or, if you're careful, you might make it . . .

ISBN 0-7531-7391-3 **(hb)**
ISBN 0-7531-7392-1 **(pb)**

Undercurrents

Tamara McKinley

In 1894 the SS *Arcadia* sets sail from Liverpool. On board are Eva Hamilton and her husband Frederick, a newly married couple setting off for a new life. Only, a few miles from the western shores of Australia the *Arcadia* is hit by an unexpected storm . . .

Years later, Olivia Hamilton makes the same journey. Still dealing with her mother's death and her experiences of war torn London, she has returned to her homeland to discover the truth behind the secret cache of documents among her late mother's effects.

Olivia had grown up in the secure knowledge that her mother loved her. This had more than compensated for her older sister's dislike. Olivia believes that the documents could tell her why, but she needs Irene's help. But the years have not mellowed her sister's hatred. And while Olivia is determined to pursue her quest, like Eva Hamilton all those years before, she has no idea where this journey will take her . . .

ISBN 0-7531-7281-X (hb)
ISBN 0-7531-7282-8 (pb)

As Far As You Can Go

Lesley Glaister

Writing of human behaviour at its most edgy and unnerving, this is Lesley Glaister at the top of her form

"Glaister's novels always appear to be as effortless for her to write as they are for us to read." **The Times**

"Great opportunity for the right applicants: Western Australia. Housekeeper/companions required. Would suit young couple. Remote, rural location. Cooking, cleaning, gardening and caring duties. Applicants must be self-sufficient and resourceful."

Cassie is at a turning point. She wants a child and a bigger commitment from Graham, her artist boyfriend. A year away with him, in the wilds of Australia, could be just the answer. The enigmatic Larry Drake and his strange wife Mara live in Woolagong, an immense farm at the edge of the desert. It is a place of bleak, breathtaking landscape, a world far away from civilization and London. But its remoteness can make Woolagong a dangerous prison. And the more Graham and Cassie begin to uncover the dark secrets of their mysterious employers, the more trapped they feel.

ISBN 0-7531-7165-1 (hb)
ISBN 0-7531-7166-X (pb)